TABLE OF STO[

C000067367

GHOST STORIES

Edith Wharton

SUGAR SKULL PRESS
LOS ANGELES, CALIFORNIA

Copyright © 2015, Sugar Skull Press

Originally published in 1910

ISBN-13: 978-0692548356

ISBN-10: 0692548351

EMAIL: sugarskullpress@gmail.com

GHOST STORIES

THE BOLTED DOOR

I

Hubert Granice, pacing the length of his pleasant lamp-lit library, paused to compare his watch with the clock on the chimneypiece.

Three minutes to eight.

In exactly three minutes Mr. Peter Ascham, of the eminent legal firm of Ascham and Pettilow, would have his punctual hand on the doorbell of the flat. It was a comfort to reflect that Ascham was so punctual—the suspense was beginning to make his host nervous. And the sound of the doorbell would be the beginning of the end—after that there'd be no going back, by God—no going back!

Granice resumed his pacing. Each time he reached the end of the room opposite the door he caught his reflection in the Florentine mirror above the fine old walnut *credence* he had picked up at Dijon—saw himself spare, quick-moving, carefully brushed and dressed, but furrowed, gray about the temples, with a stoop which he corrected by a spasmodic straightening of the shoulders whenever a glass confronted him: a tired middle-aged man, baffled, beaten, worn out.

As he summed himself up thus for the third or fourth time the door opened and he turned with a thrill of relief to greet his guest. But it was only the manservant who entered, advancing silently over the mossy surface of the old Turkey rug.

"Mr. Ascham telephones, sir, to say he's unexpectedly detained and can't be here till eight-thirty."

Granice made a curt gesture of annoyance. It was becoming harder and harder for him to control these reflexes. He turned on his heel, tossing to the servant over his shoulder: "Very good. Put off dinner."

Down his spine he felt the man's injured stare. Mr. Granice had always been so mild-spoken to his people—no doubt the odd change in his manner had already been noticed and discussed below stairs. And very likely they suspected the cause.

He stood drumming on the writing table till he heard the servant go out; then he threw himself into a chair, propping his elbows on the table and resting his chin on his locked hands.

Another half hour alone with it!

He wondered irritably what could have detained his guest. Some professional matter, no doubt—the punctilious lawyer would have allowed nothing less to interfere with a dinner engagement, more especially since Granice, in his note, had said: "I shall want a little business chat afterward."

But what professional matter could have come up at that unprofessional hour? Perhaps some other soul in misery had called on the lawyer; and, after all, Granice's note had given no hint of his own need! No doubt Ascham thought he merely wanted to make another change in his will. Since he had come into his little property, ten years earlier, Granice had been perpetually tinkering with his will.

Suddenly another thought pulled him up, sending a flush to his sallow temples. He remembered a word he had tossed to the lawyer some six weeks earlier, at the Century Club. "Yes—my play's as good as taken. I shall be calling on you soon to go over the contract. Those theatrical chaps are so slippery—I won't trust anybody but you to tie the knot for me!" That, of course, was what Ascham would think he was wanted for. Granice, at the idea, broke into an audible laugh—a queer stage laugh, like the cackle of a baffled villain in a melodrama. The absurdity, the unnaturalness of the sound abashed him, and he compressed his lips angrily. Would he take to soliloquy next?

He lowered his arms and pulled open the upper drawer of the writing table. In the right-hand corner lay a thick manuscript, bound in paper folders, and tied with a string beneath which a letter had been slipped. Next to the manuscript was a small revolver. Granice stared a moment at these oddly associated objects; then he took the letter from under the string and slowly began to open it. He had known he should do so from the moment his hand touched the drawer. Whenever his eye fell on that letter some relentless force compelled him to reread it.

8

It was dated about four weeks back, under the letterhead of "The Diversity Theatre."

My Dear Mr. Granice:

I have given the matter my best consideration for the last month, and it's no use—the play won't do. I have talked it over with Miss Melrose—and you know there isn't a gamer artist on our stage—and I regret to tell you she feels just as I do about it. It isn't the poetry that scares her—or me either. We both want to do all we can to help along the poetic drama—we believe the public's ready for it, and we're willing to take a big financial risk in order to be the first to give them what they want. *But we don't believe they could be made to want this.* The fact is, there isn't enough drama in your play to the allowance of poetry—the thing drags all through. You've got a big idea, but it's not out of swaddling clothes.

If this was your first play I'd say: *Try again.* But it has been just the same with all the others you've shown me. And you remember the result of 'The Lee Shore,' where you carried all the expenses of production yourself, and we couldn't fill the theatre for a week. Yet 'The Lee Shore' was a modern problem play—much easier to swing than blank verse. It isn't as if you hadn't tried all kinds—

Granice folded the letter and put it carefully back into the envelope. Why on earth was he rereading it, when he knew every phrase in it by heart, when for a month past he had seen it, night after night, stand out in letters of flame against the darkness of his sleepless lids?

"*It has been just the same with all the others you've shown me.*"

That was the way they dismissed ten years of passionate unremitting work!

"*You remember the result of 'The Lee Shore'*"

Good God—as if he were likely to forget it! He relived it all now in a drowning flash: the persistent rejection of the play, his

9

sudden resolve to put it on at his own cost, to spend ten thousand dollars of his inheritance on testing his chance of success—the fever of preparation, the dry-mouthed agony of the "first night," the flat fall, the stupid press, his secret rush to Europe to escape the condolence of his friends!

"It isn't as if you hadn't tried all kinds."

No—he had tried all kinds: comedy, tragedy, prose and verse, the light curtain-raiser, the short sharp drama, the bourgeois-realistic and the lyrical-romantic—finally deciding that he would no longer "prostitute his talent" to win popularity, but would impose on the public his own theory of art in the form of five acts of blank verse. Yes, he had offered them everything—and always with the same result.

Ten years of it—ten years of dogged work and unrelieved failure. The ten years from forty to fifty—the best ten years of his life! And if one counted the years before, the silent years of dreams, assimilation, preparation—then call it half a man's lifetime: half a man's lifetime thrown away!

And what was he to do with the remaining half? Well, he had settled that, thank God! He turned and glanced anxiously at the clock. Ten minutes past eight—only ten minutes had been consumed in that stormy rush through his whole past! And he must wait another twenty minutes for Ascham. It was one of the worst symptoms of his case that, in proportion as he had grown to shrink from human company, he dreaded more and more to be alone...But why the devil was he waiting for Ascham? Why didn't he cut the knot himself? Since he was so unutterably sick of the whole business, why did he have to call in an outsider to rid him of this nightmare of living?

He opened the drawer again and laid his hand on the revolver. It was a small slim ivory toy—just the instrument for a tired sufferer to give himself a "hypodermic" with. Granice raised it slowly in one hand, while with the other he felt under the thin hair at the back of his head, between the ear and the nape. He knew just where to place the muzzle: he had once got a young surgeon to show him. And as he found the spot, and

10

lifted the revolver to it, the inevitable phenomenon occurred. The hand that held the weapon began to shake, the tremor communicated itself to his arm, his heart gave a wild leap which sent up a wave of deadly nausea to his throat, he smelt the powder, he sickened at the crash of the bullet through his skull, and a sweat of fear broke out over his forehead and ran down his quivering face...

He laid away the revolver with an oath and, pulling out a cologne-scented handkerchief, passed it tremulously over his brow and temples. It was no use—he knew he could never do it in that way. His attempts at self-destruction were as futile as his snatches at fame! He couldn't make himself a real life, and he couldn't get rid of the life he had. And that was why he had sent for Ascham to help him...

The lawyer, over the Camembert and Burgundy, began to excuse himself for his delay.

"I didn't like to say anything while your man was about—but the fact is, I was sent for on a rather unusual matter—"

"Oh, it's all right," said Granice cheerfully. He was beginning to feel the usual reaction that food and company produced. It was not any recovered pleasure in life that he felt, but only a deeper withdrawal into himself. It was easier to go on automatically with the social gestures than to uncover to any human eye the abyss within him.

"My dear fellow, it's sacrilege to keep a dinner waiting—especially the production of an artist like yours." Mr. Ascham sipped his Burgundy luxuriously. "But the fact is, Mrs. Ashgrove sent for me."

Granice raised his head with a quick movement of surprise. For a moment he was shaken out of his self-absorption.

"*Mrs. Ashgrove?*"

Ascham smiled. "I thought you'd be interested; I know your passion for *causes celebres*. And this promises to be one. Of course it's out of our line entirely—we never touch criminal cases. But she wanted to consult me as a friend. Ashgrove was a distant connection of my wife's. And, by Jove, it *is* a queer

11

case!" The servant re-entered, and Ascham snapped his lips shut.

Would the gentlemen have their coffee in the dining room?

"No—serve it in the library," said Granice, rising. He led the way back to the curtained confidential room. He was really curious to hear what Ascham had to tell him.

While the coffee and cigars were being served he fidgeted about the library, glancing at his letters—the usual meaningless notes and bills—and picking up the evening paper. As he unfolded it a headline caught his eye.

ROSE MELROSE WANTS TO PLAY POETRY.
"THINKS SHE HAS FOUND HER POET.

He read on with a thumping heart—found the name of a young author he had barely heard of, saw the title of a play, a "poetic drama," dance before his eyes, and dropped the paper, sick, disgusted. It was true, then—she *was* "game"—it was not the manner but the matter she mistrusted!

Granice turned to the servant, who seemed to be purposely lingering. "I shan't need you this evening, Flint. I'll lock up myself."

He fancied the man's acquiescence implied surprise. What was going on, Flint seemed to wonder, that Mr. Granice should want him out of the way? Probably he would find a pretext for coming back to see. Granice suddenly felt himself enveloped in a network of espionage.

As the door closed he threw himself into an armchair and leaned forward to take a light from Ascham's cigar.

"Tell me about Mrs. Ashgrove," he said, seeming to himself to speak stiffly, as if his lips were cracked.

"Mrs. Ashgrove? Well, there's not much to *tell*."

"And you couldn't if there were?" Granice smiled.

"Probably not. As a matter of fact, she wanted my advice about her choice of counsel. There was nothing especially confidential in our talk."

"And what's your impression, now you've seen her?"

"My impression is, very distinctly, *that nothing will ever be known*."

12

"Ah—?" Granice murmured, puffing at his cigar.

"I'm more and more convinced that whoever poisoned Ashgrove knew his business, and will consequently never be found out. That's a capital cigar you've given me."

"You like it? I get them over from Cuba." Granice examined his own reflectively. "Then you believe in the theory that the clever criminals never *are* caught?"

"Of course I do. Look about you—look back for the last dozen years—none of the big murder problems are ever solved." The lawyer ruminated behind his blue cloud. "Why, take the instance in your own family: I'd forgotten I had an illustration at hand! Take old Joseph Lenman's murder—do you suppose that will ever be explained?"

As the words dropped from Ascham's lips his host looked slowly about the library, and every object in it stared back at him with a stale unescapable familiarity. How sick he was of looking at that room! It was as dull as the face of a wife one has wearied of. He cleared his throat slowly; then he turned his head to the lawyer and said: "I could explain the Lenman murder myself."

Ascham's eye kindled: he shared Granice's interest in criminal cases.

"By Jove! You've had a theory all this time? It's odd you never mentioned it. Go ahead and tell me. There are certain features in the Lenman case not unlike this Ashgrove affair, and your idea may be a help."

Granice paused and his eye reverted instinctively to the table drawer in which the revolver and the manuscript lay side by side. What if he were to try another appeal to Rose Melrose? Then he looked at the notes and bills on the table, and the horror of taking up again the lifeless routine of life—of performing the same automatic gestures another day—displaced his fleeting vision.

"I haven't a theory. I *know* who murdered Joseph Lenman."

Ascham settled himself comfortably in his chair, prepared for enjoyment.

"You *know?* Well, who did?" he laughed.

"I did," said Granice, rising.

He stood before Ascham, and the lawyer lay back staring up at him. Then he broke into another laugh.

"Why, this is glorious! You murdered him, did you? To inherit his money, I suppose? Better and better! Go on, my boy! Unbosom yourself! Tell me all about it! Confession is good for the soul."

Granice waited till the lawyer had shaken the last peal of laughter from his throat; then he repeated doggedly: "I murdered him."

The two men looked at each other for a long moment, and this time Ascham did not laugh.

"Granice!"

"I murdered him—to get his money, as you say."

There was another pause, and Granice, with a vague underlying sense of amusement, saw his guest's look change from pleasantry to apprehension.

"What's the joke, my dear fellow? I fail to see."

"It's not a joke. It's the truth. I murdered him." He had spoken painfully at first, as if there were a knot in his throat; but each time he repeated the words he found they were easier to say.

Ascham laid down his extinct cigar.

"What's the matter? Aren't you well? What on earth are you driving at?"

"I'm perfectly well. But I murdered my cousin, Joseph Lenman, and I want it known that I murdered him."

"You want it known?"

"Yes. That's why I sent for you. I'm sick of living, and when I try to kill myself I funk it." He spoke quite naturally now, as if the knot in his throat had been untied.

"Good Lord—good Lord," the lawyer gasped.

"But I suppose," Granice continued, "there's no doubt this would be murder in the first degree? I'm sure of the chair if I own up?"

Ascham drew a long breath; then he said slowly: "Sit down, Granice. Let's talk."

II

Granice told his story simply, connectedly.

He began by a quick survey of his early years—the years of drudgery and privation. His father, a charming man who could never say "no," had so signally failed to say it on certain essential occasions that when he died he left an illegitimate family and a mortgaged estate. His lawful kin found themselves hanging over a gulf of debt, and young Granice, to support his mother and sister, had to leave Harvard and bury himself at eighteen in a broker's office. He loathed his work, and he was always poor, always worried and in ill health. A few years later his mother died, but his sister, an ineffectual neurasthenic, remained on his hands. His own health gave out, and he had to go away for six months, and work harder than ever when he came back. He had no knack for business, no head for figures, no dimmest insight into the mysteries of commerce. He wanted to travel and write—those were his inmost longings. And as the years dragged on, and he neared middle age without making any more money, or acquiring any firmer health, a sick despair possessed him. He tried writing, but he always came home from the office so tired that his brain could not work. For half the year he did not reach his dim uptown flat till after dark, and could only "brush up" for dinner, and afterward lie on the lounge with his pipe, while his sister droned through the evening paper. Sometimes he spent an evening at the theatre; or he dined out, or, more rarely, strayed off with an acquaintance or two in quest of what is known as "pleasure." And in summer, when he and Kate went to the seaside for a month, he dozed through the days in utter weariness. Once he fell in love with a charming girl—but what had he to offer her, in God's name? She seemed to like him, and in common decency he had to drop out of the running. Apparently no one replaced him, for she never married, but grew stoutish, grayish, philanthropic—yet how sweet she had been when he had first kissed her! One more wasted life, he reflected...

15

But the stage had always been his master passion. He would have sold his soul for the time and freedom to write plays! It was *in him*—he could not remember when it had not been his deepest-seated instinct. As the years passed it became a morbid, a relentless obsession—yet with every year the material conditions were more and more against it. He felt himself growing middle-aged, and he watched the reflection of the process in his sister's wasted face. At eighteen she had been pretty, and as full of enthusiasm as he. Now she was sour, trivial, insignificant—she had missed her chance of life. And she had no resources, poor creature, was fashioned simply for the primitive functions she had been denied the chance to fulfill! It exasperated him to think of it—and to reflect that even now a little travel, a little health, a little money, might transform her, make her young and desirable...The chief fruit of his experience was that there is no such fixed state as age or youth—there is only health as against sickness, wealth as against poverty; and age or youth as the outcome of the lot one draws.

At this point in his narrative Granice stood up, and went to lean against the mantelpiece, looking down at Ascham, who had not moved from his seat, or changed his attitude of rigid fascinated attention.

"Then came the summer when we went to Wrenfield to be near old Lenman—my mother's cousin, as you know. Some of the family always mounted guard over him—generally a niece or so. But that year they were all scattered, and one of the nieces offered to lend us her cottage if we'd relieve her of duty for two months. It was a nuisance for me, of course, for Wrenfield is two hours from town; but my mother, who was a slave to family observances, had always been good to the old man, so it was natural we should be called on—and there was the saving of rent and the good air for Kate. So we went.

"You never knew Joseph Lenman? Well, picture to yourself an amoeba or some primitive organism of that sort, under a Titan's microscope. He was large, undifferentiated, inert—since I could remember him he had done nothing but take his

16

temperature and read the *Churchman*. Oh, and cultivate melons—that was his hobby. Not vulgar, out-of-door melons—his were grown under glass. He had miles of it at Wrenfield—his big kitchen garden was surrounded by blinking battalions of greenhouses. And in nearly all of them melons were grown—early melons and late, French, English, domestic—dwarf melons and monsters: every shape, color and variety. They were petted and nursed like children—a staff of trained attendants waited on them. I'm not sure they didn't have a doctor to take their temperature—at any rate the place was full of thermometers. And they didn't sprawl on the ground like ordinary melons; they were trained against the glass like nectarines, and each melon hung in a net that sustained its weight and left it free on all sides to the sun and air...

"It used to strike me sometimes that old Lenman was just like one of his own melons—the pale-fleshed English kind. His life, apathetic and motionless, hung in a net of gold, in an equable warm ventilated atmosphere, high above sordid earthly worries. The cardinal rule of his existence was not to let himself be 'worried.' I remember his advising me to try it myself, one day when I spoke to him about Kate's bad health, and her need of a change. 'I never let myself worry,' he said complacently. 'It's the worst thing for the liver—and you look to me as if you had a liver. Take my advice and be cheerful. You'll make yourself happier and others too.' And all he had to do was to write a cheque, and send the poor girl off for a holiday!

"The hardest part of it was that the money half-belonged to us already. The old skinflint only had it for life, in trust for us and the others. But his life was a good deal sounder than mine or Kate's—and one could picture him taking extra care of it for the joke of keeping us waiting. I always felt that the sight of our hungry eyes was a tonic to him.

"Well, I tried to see if I couldn't reach him through his vanity. I flattered him, feigned a passionate interest in his melons. And he was taken in, and used to discourse on them by the hour. On fine days he was driven to the greenhouses in his pony chair, and waddled through them, prodding and leering at the fruit, like a fat Turk in his seraglio. When he bragged to me of the expense of growing them I was reminded of a hideous old Lothario bragging of what his pleasures cost. And the resemblance was completed by the fact that he couldn't eat as much as a mouthful of his melons—had lived for years on buttermilk and toast. 'But, after all, it's my only hobby—why shouldn't I indulge it?' he said sentimentally. As if I'd ever been able to indulge any of mine! On the keep of those melons Kate and I could have lived like gods...

"One day toward the end of the summer, when Kate was too unwell to drag herself up to the big house, she asked me to go and spend the afternoon with cousin Joseph. It was a lovely soft September afternoon—a day to lie under a Roman stone-pine, with one's eyes on the sky, and let the cosmic harmonies rush through one. Perhaps the vision was suggested by the fact that, as I entered cousin Joseph's hideous black walnut library, I passed one of the under-gardeners, a handsome full-throated Italian, who dashed out in such a hurry that he nearly knocked me down. I remember thinking it queer that the fellow, whom I had often seen about the melon-houses, did not bow to me, or even seem to see me.

"Cousin Joseph sat in his usual seat, behind the darkened windows, his fat hands folded on his protuberant waistcoat, the last number of the *Churchman* at his elbow, and near it, on a huge dish, a fat melon—the fattest melon I'd ever seen. As I looked at it I pictured the ecstasy of contemplation from which I must have roused him, and congratulated myself on finding him in such a mood, since I had made up my mind to ask him a favour. Then I noticed that his face, instead of looking as calm as an eggshell, was distorted and whimpering—and without stopping to greet me he pointed passionately to the melon.

"'Look at it, look at it—did you ever see such a beauty? Such firmness—roundness—such delicious smoothness to the touch?' It was as if he had said 'she' instead of 'it,' and when he put out his senile hand and touched the melon I positively had to look the other way.

"Then he told me what had happened. The Italian under-gardener, who had been specially recommended for the melon-houses—though it was against my cousin's principles to employ a Papist—had been assigned to the care of the monster: for it had revealed itself, early in its existence, as destined to become a monster, to surpass its plumpest, pulpiest sisters, carry off prizes at agricultural shows, and be photographed and celebrated in every gardening paper in the land. The Italian had done well—seemed to have a sense of responsibility. And that very morning he had been ordered to pick the melon, which was to be shown next day at the county fair, and to bring it in for Mr. Lenman to gaze on its blonde virginity. But in picking it, what had the damned scoundrelly Jesuit done but drop it—drop it crash on the sharp spout of a watering pot, so that it received a deep gash in its firm pale rotundity, and was henceforth but a bruised, ruined, fallen melon?

"The old man's rage was fearful in its impotence—he shook, spluttered and strangled with it. He had just had the Italian up and had sacked him on the spot, without wages or character—had threatened to have him arrested if he was ever caught prowling about Wrenfield. 'By God, and I'll do it—I'll write to Washington—I'll have the pauper scoundrel deported! I'll show him what money can do!' As likely as not there was some murderous Black-hand business under it—it would be found that the fellow was a member of a 'gang.' Those Italians would murder you for a quarter. He meant to have the police look into it...And then he grew frightened at his own excitement. 'But I must calm myself,' he said. He took his temperature, rang for his drops, and turned to the *Churchman*. He had been reading an article on Nestorianism when the melon was brought in. He asked me to go on with it, and I read to him for an hour, in the dim close room, with a fat fly buzzing stealthily about the fallen melon.

"All the while one phrase of the old man's buzzed in my brain like the fly about the melon. *'I'll show him what money can do!'* Good heaven! If *I* could but show the old man! If I could make him see his power of giving happiness as a new outlet for his monstrous egotism! I tried to tell him something about my situation and Kate's—spoke of my ill health, my unsuccessful drudgery, my longing to write, to make myself a name—I stammered out an entreaty for a loan. 'I can guarantee to repay you, sir—I've a half-written play as security...'

"I shall never forget his glassy stare. His face had grown as smooth as an eggshell again—his eyes peered over his fat cheeks like sentinels over a slippery rampart.

"'A halfwritten play—a play of *yours* as security?' He looked at me almost fearfully, as if detecting the first symptoms of insanity. 'Do you understand anything of business?' he enquired mildly. I laughed and answered: 'No, not much.'

"He leaned back with closed lids. 'All this excitement has been too much for me,' he said. 'If you'll excuse me, I'll prepare for my nap.' And I stumbled out of the room, blindly, like the Italian."

Granice moved away from the mantelpiece, and walked across to the tray set out with decanters and soda water. He poured himself a tall glass of soda water, emptied it, and glanced at Ascham's dead cigar.

"Better light another," he suggested.

The lawyer shook his head, and Granice went on with his tale. He told of his mounting obsession—how the murderous impulse had waked in him on the instant of his cousin's refusal, and he had muttered to himself: "By God, if you won't, I'll make you." He spoke more tranquilly as the narrative proceeded, as though his rage had died down once the resolve to act on it was taken. He applied his whole mind to the question of how the old man was to be "disposed of." Suddenly he remembered the outcry: "Those Italians will murder you for a quarter!" But no definite project presented itself: he simply waited for an inspiration.

Granice and his sister moved to town a day or two after the incident of the melon. But the cousins, who had returned, kept them informed of the old man's condition. One day, about three weeks later, Granice, on getting home, found Kate excited over a report from Wrenfield. The Italian had been there again—had somehow slipped into the house, made his way up to the library, and "used threatening language." The housekeeper found cousin Joseph gasping, the whites of his eyes showing "something awful." The doctor was sent for, and the attack warded off; and the police had ordered the Italian from the neighbourhood.

But cousin Joseph, thereafter, languished, had "nerves," and lost his taste for toast and buttermilk. The doctor called in a colleague, and the consultation amused and excited the old man—he became once more an important figure. The medical men reassured the family—too completely!—and to the patient they recommended a more varied diet: advised him to take whatever "tempted him." And so one day, tremulously, prayerfully, he decided on a tiny bit of melon. It was brought up with ceremony, and consumed in the presence of the housekeeper and a hovering cousin; and twenty minutes later he was dead...

"But you remember the circumstances," Granice went on; "how suspicion turned at once on the Italian? In spite of the hint the police had given him he had been seen hanging about the house since 'the scene.' It was said that he had tender relations with the kitchen maid, and the rest seemed easy to explain. But when they looked round to ask him for the explanation he was gone—gone clean out of sight. He had been 'warned' to leave Wrenfield, and he had taken the warning so to heart that no one ever laid eyes on him again."

Granice paused. He had dropped into a chair opposite the lawyer's, and he sat for a moment, his head thrown back, looking about the familiar room. Everything in it had grown grimacing and alien, and each strange insistent object seemed craning forward from its place to hear him.

"It was I who put the stuff in the melon," he said. "And I don't want you to think I'm sorry for it. This isn't 'remorse,' understand. I'm glad the old skinflint is dead—I'm glad the others have their money. But mine's no use to me any more. My sister married miserably, and died. And I've never had what I wanted."

Ascham continued to stare; then he said: "What on earth was your object, then?"

"Why, to *get* what I wanted—what I fancied was in reach! I wanted change, rest, *life*, for both of us—wanted, above all, for myself, the chance to write! I traveled, got back my health, and came home to tie myself up to my work. And I've slaved at it steadily for ten years without reward—without the most distant hope of success! Nobody will look at my stuff. And now I'm fifty, and I'm beaten, and I know it." His chin dropped forward on his breast. "I want to chuck the whole business," he ended.

III

It was after midnight when Ascham left.

His hand on Granice's shoulder, as he turned to go—"District Attorney be hanged; see a doctor, see a doctor!" he had cried; and so, with an exaggerated laugh, had pulled on his coat and departed.

Granice turned back into the library. It had never occurred to him that Ascham would not believe his story. For three hours he had explained, elucidated, patiently and painfully gone over every detail—but without once breaking down the iron incredulity of the lawyer's eye.

At first Ascham had feigned to be convinced—but that, as Granice now perceived, was simply to get him to expose himself, to entrap him into contradictions. And when the attempt failed, when Granice triumphantly met and refuted each disconcerting question, the lawyer dropped the mask suddenly, and said with a good-humored laugh: "By Jove, Granice you'll write a successful play yet. The way you've worked this all out is a marvel."

Granice swung about furiously—that last sneer about the play inflamed him. Was all the world in a conspiracy to deride his failure?

"I did it, I did it," he muttered sullenly, his rage spending itself against the impenetrable surface of the other's mockery; and Ascham answered with a smile: "Ever read any of those books on hallucination? I've got a fairly good medico-legal library. I could send you one or two if you like..."

Left alone, Granice cowered down in the chair before his writing table. He understood that Ascham thought him off his head.

"Good God—what if they all think me crazy?"

The horror of it broke out over him in a cold sweat—he sat there and shook, his eyes hidden in his icy hands. But gradually, as he began to rehearse his story for the thousandth time, he saw again how incontrovertible it was, and felt sure that any criminal lawyer would believe him.

"That's the trouble—Ascham's not a criminal lawyer. And then he's a friend. What a fool I was to talk to a friend! Even if he did believe me, he'd never let me see it—his instinct would be to cover the whole thing up...But in that case—if he *did* believe me—he might think it a kindness to get me shut up in an asylum..." Granice began to tremble again. "Good heaven! If he should bring in an expert—one of those damned alienists! Ascham and Pettilow can do anything—their word always goes. If Ascham drops a hint that I'd better be shut up, I'll be in a straitjacket by tomorrow! And he'd do it from the kindest motives—be quite right to do it if he thinks I'm a murderer!"

The vision froze him to his chair. He pressed his fists to his bursting temples and tried to think. For the first time he hoped that Ascham had not believed his story.

"But he did—he did! I can see it now—I noticed what a queer eye he cocked at me. Good God, what shall I do—what shall I do?"

He started up and looked at the clock. Half-past one. What if Ascham should think the case urgent, rout out an alienist, and come back with him? Granice jumped to his feet, and his sudden gesture brushed the morning paper from the table. Mechanically he stooped to pick it up, and the movement started a new train of association.

He sat down again, and reached for the telephone book in the rack by his chair.

"Give me three-o-ten...yes."

The new idea in his mind had revived his flagging energy. He would act—act at once. It was only by thus planning ahead, committing himself to some unavoidable line of conduct, that he could pull himself through the meaningless days. Each time he reached a fresh decision it was like coming out of a foggy weltering sea into a calm harbour with lights. One of the queerest phases of his long agony was the intense relief produced by these momentary lulls.

"That the office of the *Investigator?* Yes? Give me Mr. Denver, please...Hallo, Denver...Yes, Hubert Granice...Just caught you? Going straight home? Can I come and see you...yes, now...have a talk? It's rather urgent...yes, might give you some first-rate 'copy.'...All right!" He hung up the receiver with a laugh. It had been a happy thought to call up the editor of the *Investigator*—Robert Denver was the very man he needed...

Granice put out the lights in the library—it was odd how the automatic gestures persisted!—went into the hall, put on his hat and overcoat, and let himself out of the flat. In the hall, a sleepy elevator boy blinked at him and then dropped his head on his folded arms. Granice passed out into the street. At the corner of Fifth Avenue he hailed a crawling cab, and called out an uptown address. The long thoroughfare stretched before him, dim and deserted, like an ancient avenue of tombs. But from Denver's house a friendly beam fell on the pavement; and as Granice sprang from his cab the editor's electric turned the corner.

The two men grasped hands, and Denver, feeling for his latchkey, ushered Granice into the brightly lit hall.

"Disturb me? Not a bit. You might have, at ten tomorrow morning...but this is my liveliest hour...you know my habits of old."

Granice had known Robert Denver for fifteen years—watched his rise through all the stages of journalism to the

24

Olympian pinnacle of the *Investigator's* editorial office. In the thickset man with grizzling hair there were few traces left of the hungry-eyed young reporter who, on his way home in the small hours, used to "bob in" on Granice, while the latter sat grinding at his plays. Denver had to pass Granice's flat on the way to his own, and it became a habit, if he saw a light in the window, and Granice's shadow against the blind, to go in, smoke a pipe, and discuss the universe.

"Well—this is like old times—a good old habit reversed." The editor smote his visitor genially on the shoulder. "Reminds me of the nights when I used to rout you out...How's the play, by the way? There *is* a play, I suppose? It's as safe to ask you that as to say to some men: 'How's the baby?'"

Denver laughed good-naturedly, and Granice thought how thick and heavy he had grown. It was evident, even to Granice's tortured nerves, that the words had not been uttered in malice—and the fact gave him a new measure of his insignificance. Denver did not even know that he had been a failure! The fact hurt more than Ascham's irony.

"Come in—come in." The editor led the way into a small cheerful room, where there were cigars and decanters. He pushed an armchair toward his visitor, and dropped into another with a comfortable groan.

"Now, then—help yourself. And let's hear all about it."

He beamed at Granice over his pipe bowl, and the latter, lighting his cigar, said to himself: "Success makes men comfortable, but it makes them stupid."

Then he turned, and began: "Denver, I want to tell you—"

The clock ticked rhythmically on the mantelpiece. The room was gradually filled with drifting blue layers of smoke, and through them the editor's face came and went like the moon through a moving sky. Once the hour struck—then the rhythmical ticking began again. The atmosphere grew denser and heavier, and beads of perspiration began to roll from Granice's forehead.

"Do you mind if I open the window?"

"No. It *is* stuffy in here. Wait—I'll do it myself." Denver pushed down the upper sash, and returned to his chair. "Well—go on," he said, filling another pipe. His composure exasperated Granice.

"There's no use in my going on if you don't believe me."

The editor remained unmoved. "Who says I don't believe you? And how can I tell till you've finished?"

Granice went on, ashamed of his outburst. "It was simple enough, as you'll see. From the day the old man said to me, 'Those Italians would murder you for a quarter,' I dropped everything and just worked at my scheme. It struck me at once that I must find a way of getting to Wrenfield and back in a night—and that led to the idea of a motor. A motor—that never occurred to you? You wonder where I got the money, I suppose. Well, I had a thousand or so put by, and I nosed around till I found what I wanted—a secondhand racer. I knew how to drive a car, and I tried the thing and found it was all right. Times were bad, and I bought it for my price, and stored it away. Where? Why, in one of those no-questions-asked garages where they keep motors that are not for family use. I had a lively cousin who had put me up to that dodge, and I looked about till I found a queer hole where they took in my car like a baby in a foundling asylum...Then I practiced running to Wrenfield and back in a night. I knew the way pretty well, for I'd done it often with the same lively cousin—and in the small hours, too. The distance is over ninety miles, and on the third trial I did it under two hours. But my arms were so lame that I could hardly get dressed the next morning...

"Well, then came the report about the Italian's threats, and I saw I must act at once...I meant to break into the old man's room, shoot him, and get away again. It was a big risk, but I thought I could manage it. Then we heard that he was ill—that there'd been a consultation. Perhaps the fates were going to do it for me! Good Lord, if that could only be!"

Granice stopped and wiped his forehead: the open window did not seem to have cooled the room.

"Then came word that he was better; and the day after, when I came up from my office, I found Kate laughing over the news that he was to try a bit of melon. The housekeeper had just telephoned her—all Wrenfield was in a flutter. The doctor himself had picked out the melon, one of the little French ones that are hardly bigger than a large tomato—and the patient was to eat it at his breakfast the next morning.

"In a flash I saw my chance. It was a bare chance, no more. But I knew the ways of the house—I was sure the melon would be brought in over night and put in the pantry icebox. If there were only one melon in the icebox I could be fairly sure it was the one I wanted. Melons didn't lie around loose in that house—every one was known, numbered, catalogued. The old man was beset by the dread that the servants would eat them, and he took a hundred mean precautions to prevent it. Yes, I felt pretty sure of my melon...and poisoning was much safer than shooting. It would have been the devil and all to get into the old man's bedroom without his rousing the house; but I ought to be able to break into the pantry without much trouble.

"It was a cloudy night, too—everything served me. I dined quietly, and sat down at my desk. Kate had one of her usual headaches, and went to bed early. As soon as she was gone I slipped out. I had got together a sort of disguise—red beard and queer-looking ulster. I shoved them into a bag, and went round to the garage. There was no one there but a half-drunken machinist whom I'd never seen before. That served me, too. They were always changing machinists, and this new fellow didn't even bother to ask if the car belonged to me. It was a very easygoing place...

"Well, I jumped in, ran up Broadway, and let the car go as soon as I was out of Harlem. Dark as it was, I could trust myself to strike a sharp pace. In the shadow of a wood I stopped a second and got into the beard and ulster. Then away again—it was just eleven-thirty when I got to Wrenfield.

"I left the car in a dark lane behind the Lenman place, and slipped through the kitchen garden. The melon houses winked at me through the dark—I remember thinking that they knew what I wanted to know...By the stable a dog came out growling—but he nosed me out, jumped on me, and went back...The house was as dark as the grave. I knew everybody went to bed by ten. But there might be a prowling servant—the kitchen maid might have come down to let in her Italian. I had to risk that, of course. I crept around by the back door and hid in the shrubbery. Then I listened. It was all as silent as death. I crossed over to the house, pried open the pantry window and climbed in. I had a little electric lamp in my pocket, and shielding it with my cap I groped my way to the icebox, opened it—and there was the little French melon...only one.

"I stopped to listen—I was quite cool. Then I pulled out my bottle of stuff and my syringe, and gave each section of the melon a hypodermic. It was all done inside of three minutes—at ten minutes to twelve I was back in the car. I got out of the lane as quietly as I could, struck a back road that skirted the village, and let the car out as soon as I was beyond the last houses. I only stopped once on the way in, to drop the beard and ulster into a pond. I had a big stone ready to weight them with and they went down plump, like a dead body—and at two o'clock I was back at my desk."

Granice stopped speaking and looked across the smoke fumes at his listener; but Denver's face remained inscrutable.

At length he said: "Why did you want to tell me this?"

The question startled Granice. He was about to explain, as he had explained to Ascham; but suddenly it occurred to him that if his motive had not seemed convincing to the lawyer it would carry much less weight with Denver. Both were successful men, and success does not understand the subtle agony of failure. Granice cast about for another reason.

"Why, I—the thing haunts me...remorse, I suppose you'd call it..."

Denver struck the ashes from his empty pipe.

"Remorse? Bosh!" he said energetically.

Granice's heart sank. "You don't believe in—*remorse?*"

"Not an atom: in the man of action. The mere fact of your talking of remorse proves to me that you're not the man to have planned and put through such a job."

Granice groaned. "Well—I lied to you about remorse. I've never felt any."

Denver's lips tightened sceptically about his freshly filled pipe. "What was your motive, then? You must have had one."

"I'll tell you—" And Granice began again to rehearse the story of his failure, of his loathing for life. "Don't say you don't believe me this time...that this isn't a real reason!" he stammered out piteously as he ended.

Denver meditated. "No, I won't say that. I've seen too many queer things. There's always a reason for wanting to get out of life—the wonder is that we find so many for staying in!"

Granice's heart grew light. "Then you *do* believe me?" he faltered.

"Believe that you're sick of the job? Yes. And that you haven't the nerve to pull the trigger? Oh, yes—that's easy enough, too. But all that doesn't make you a murderer—though I don't say it proves you could never have been one."

"I *have* been one, Denver—I swear to you."

"Perhaps." He meditated. "Just tell me one or two things."

"Oh, go ahead. You won't stump me!" Granice heard himself say with a laugh.

"Well—how did you make all those trial trips without exciting your sister's curiosity? I knew your night habits pretty well at that time, remember. You were very seldom out late. Didn't the change in your ways surprise her?"

"No; because she was away at the time. She went to pay several visits in the country soon after we came back from Wrenfield, and was only in town for a night or two before—before I did the job."

"And that night she went to bed early with a headache?"

"Yes—blinding. She didn't know anything when she had that kind. And her room was at the back of the flat."

Denver again meditated. "And when you got back—she didn't hear you? You got in without her knowing it?"

"Yes. I went straight to my work—took it up at the word where I'd left off—*why, Denver, don't you remember?*" Granice suddenly, passionately interjected.

"Remember—?"

"Yes; how you found me—when you looked in that morning, between two and three...your usual hour?"

"Yes," the editor nodded.

Granice gave a short laugh. "In my old coat—with my pipe: looked as if I'd been working all night, didn't I? Well, I hadn't been in my chair ten minutes!"

Denver uncrossed his legs and then crossed them again. "I didn't know whether *you* remembered that."

"What?"

"My coming in that particular night—or morning."

Granice swung round in his chair. "Why, man alive! That's why I'm here now. Because it was you who spoke for me at the inquest, when they looked round to see what all the old man's heirs had been doing that night—you who testified to having dropped in and found me at my desk as usual...I thought *that* would appeal to your journalistic sense if nothing else would!"

Denver smiled. "Oh, my journalistic sense is still susceptible enough—and the idea's picturesque, I grant you: asking the man who proved your alibi to establish your guilt."

"That's it—that's it!" Granice's laugh had a ring of triumph.

"Well, but how about the other chap's testimony—I mean that young doctor: what was his name? Ned Ranney. Don't you remember my testifying that I'd met him at the elevated station, and told him I was on my way to smoke a pipe with you, and his saying: 'All right; you'll find him in. I passed the house two hours ago, and saw his shadow against the blind, as usual.' And the lady with the toothache in the flat across the way: she corroborated his statement, you remember."

"Yes; I remember."

"Well, then?"

"Simple enough. Before starting I rigged up a kind of mannequin with old coats and a cushion—something to cast a
30

shadow on the blind. All you fellows were used to seeing my shadow there in the small hours—I counted on that, and knew you'd take any vague outline as mine."

"Simple enough, as you say. But the woman with the toothache saw the shadow move—you remember she said she saw you sink forward, as if you'd fallen asleep."

"Yes; and she was right. It *did* move. I suppose some extra-heavy dray must have jolted by the flimsy building—at any rate, something gave my mannequin a jar, and when I came back he had sunk forward, half over the table."

There was a long silence between the two men. Granice, with a throbbing heart, watched Denver refill his pipe. The editor, at any rate, did not sneer and flout him. After all, journalism gave a deeper insight than the law into the fantastic possibilities of life, prepared one better to allow for the incalculableness of human impulses.

"Well?" Granice faltered out.

Denver stood up with a shrug. "Look here, man—what's wrong with you? Make a clean breast of it! Nerves gone to smash? I'd like to take you to see a chap I know—an ex-prizefighter—who's a wonder at pulling fellows in your state out of their hole—"

"Oh, oh—" Granice broke in. He stood up also, and the two men eyed each other. "You don't believe me, then?"

"This yarn—how can I? There wasn't a flaw in your alibi."

"But haven't I filled it full of them now?"

Denver shook his head. "I might think so if I hadn't happened to know that you *wanted* to. There's the hitch, don't you see?"

Granice groaned. "No, I didn't. You mean my wanting to be found guilty—?"

"Of course! If somebody else had accused you, the story might have been worth looking into. As it is, a child could have invented it. It doesn't do much credit to your ingenuity."

Granice turned sullenly toward the door. What was the use of arguing? But on the threshold a sudden impulse drew him

31

back. "Look here, Denver—I daresay you're right. But will you do just one thing to prove it? Put my statement in the *Investigator*, just as I've made it. Ridicule it as much as you like. Only give the other fellows a chance at it—men who don't know anything about me. Set them talking and looking about. I don't care a damn whether *you* believe me—what I want is to convince the Grand Jury! I oughtn't to have come to a man who knows me—your cursed incredulity is infectious. I don't put my case well, because I know in advance it's discredited, and I almost end by not believing it myself. That's why I can't convince *you*. It's a vicious circle." He laid a hand on Denver's arm. "Send a stenographer, and put my statement in the paper."

But Denver did not warm to the idea. "My dear fellow, you seem to forget that all the evidence was pretty thoroughly sifted at the time, every possible clue followed up. The public would have been ready enough then to believe that you murdered old Lenman—you or anybody else. All they wanted was a murderer—the most improbable would have served. But your alibi was too confoundedly complete. And nothing you've told me has shaken it." Denver laid his cool hand over the other's burning fingers. "Look here, old fellow, go home and work up a better case—then come in and submit it to the *Investigator*."

IV

The perspiration was rolling off Granice's forehead. Every few minutes he had to draw out his handkerchief and wipe the moisture from his haggard face.

For an hour and a half he had been talking steadily, putting his case to the District Attorney. Luckily he had a speaking acquaintance with Allonby, and had obtained, without much difficulty, a private audience on the very day after his talk with Robert Denver. In the interval between he had hurried home, got out of his evening clothes, and gone forth again at once into the dreary dawn. His fear of Ascham and the alienist made it impossible for him to remain in his rooms. And it seemed to him that the only way of averting that hideous peril was by establishing, in some sane impartial mind, the proof of

32

his guilt. Even if he had not been so incurably sick of life, the electric chair seemed now the only alternative to the strait-jacket.

As he paused to wipe his forehead he saw the District Attorney glance at his watch. The gesture was significant, and Granice lifted an appealing hand. "I don't expect you to believe me now—but can't you put me under arrest, and have the thing looked into?"

Allonby smiled faintly under his heavy grayish moustache. He had a ruddy face, full and jovial, in which his keen professional eyes seemed to keep watch over impulses not strictly professional.

"Well, I don't know that we need lock you up just yet. But of course I'm bound to look into your statement—"

Granice rose with an exquisite sense of relief. Surely Allonby wouldn't have said that if he hadn't believed him!

"That's all right. Then I needn't detain you. I can be found at any time at my apartment." He gave the address.

The District Attorney smiled again, more openly. "What do you say to leaving it for an hour or two this evening? I'm giving a little supper at Rector's—quiet, little affair, you understand: just Miss Melrose—I think you know her—and a friend or two; and if you'll join us..."

Granice stumbled out of the office without knowing what reply he had made.

He waited for four days—four days of concentrated horror. During the first twenty-four hours the fear of Ascham's alienist dogged him; and as that subsided, it was replaced by the exasperating sense that his avowal had made no impression on the District Attorney. Evidently, if he had been going to look into the case, Allonby would have been heard from before now...And that mocking invitation to supper showed clearly enough how little the story had impressed him!

Granice was overcome by the futility of any farther attempt to inculpate himself. He was chained to life—a "prisoner of consciousness." Where was it he had read the phrase? Well, he was learning what it meant. In the glaring night hours, when his brain seemed ablaze, he was visited by a sense of his fixed identity, of his irreducible, inexpugnable *selfness*, keener, more insidious, more unescapable, than any sensation he had ever known. He had not guessed that the mind was capable of such intricacies of self-realization, of penetrating so deep into its own dark windings. Often he woke from his brief snatches of sleep with the feeling that something material was clinging to him, was on his hands and face, and in his throat—and as his brain cleared he understood that it was the sense of his own loathed personality that stuck to him like some thick viscous substance.

Then, in the first morning hours, he would rise and look out of his window at the awakening activities of the street—at the street cleaners, the ash cart drivers, and the other dingy workers flitting hurriedly by through the sallow winter light. Oh, to be one of them—any of them—to take his chance in any of their skins! They were the toilers—the men whose lot was pitied— the victims wept over and ranted about by altruists and economists; and how gladly he would have taken up the load of any one of them, if only he might have shaken off his own! But, no—the iron circle of consciousness held them too: each one was handcuffed to his own hideous ego. Why wish to be any one man rather than another? The only absolute good was not to be...And Flint, coming in to draw his bath, would ask if he preferred his eggs scrambled or poached that morning?

On the fifth day he wrote a long urgent letter to Allonby; and for the succeeding two days he had the occupation of waiting for an answer. He hardly stirred from his rooms, in his fear of missing the letter by a moment; but would the District Attorney write, or send a representative: a policeman, a "secret agent," or some other mysterious emissary of the law?

On the third morning Flint, stepping softly—as if, confound it! his master were ill—entered the library where Granice sat behind an unread newspaper, and proferred a card on a tray.

34

Granice read the name—J. B. Hewson—and underneath, in pencil, "From the District Attorney's office." He started up with a thumping heart, and signed an assent to the servant.

Mr. Hewson was a slight sallow nondescript man of about fifty—the kind of man of whom one is sure to see a specimen in any crowd. "Just the type of the successful detective," Granice reflected as he shook hands with his visitor.

And it was in that character that Mr. Hewson briefly introduced himself. He had been sent by the District Attorney to have "a quiet talk" with Mr. Granice—to ask him to repeat the statement he had made about the Lenman murder.

His manner was so quiet, so reasonable and receptive, that Granice's self-confidence returned. Here was a sensible man—a man who knew his business—it would be easy enough to make *him* see through that ridiculous alibi! Granice offered Mr. Hewson a cigar, and lighting one himself—to prove his coolness—began again to tell his story.

He was conscious, as he proceeded, of telling it better than ever before. Practice helped, no doubt; and his listener's detached, impartial attitude helped still more. He could see that Hewson, at least, had not decided in advance to disbelieve him, and the sense of being trusted made him more lucid and more consecutive. Yes, this time his words would certainly carry conviction...

V

Despairingly, Granice gazed up and down the shabby street. Beside him stood a young man with bright prominent eyes, a smooth but not too smoothly shaven face, and an Irish smile. The young man's nimble glance followed Granice's.

"Sure of the number, are you?" he asked briskly.

"Oh, yes—it was 104."

"Well, then, the new building has swallowed it up—that's certain."

He tilted his head back and surveyed the half-finished front of a brick and limestone flathouse that reared its flimsy elegance above a row of tottering tenements and stables.

"Dead sure?" he repeated.

"Yes," said Granice, discouraged. "And even if I hadn't been, I know the garage was just opposite Leffler's over there." He pointed across the street to a tumbledown stable with a blotched sign on which the words "Livery and Boarding" were still faintly discernible.

The young man dashed across to the opposite pavement. "Well, that's something—may get a clue there. Leffler's— same name there, anyhow. You remember that name?"

"Yes—distinctly."

Granice had felt a return of confidence since he had enlisted the interest of the *Explorer's* "smartest" reporter. If there were moments when he hardly believed his own story, there were others when it seemed impossible that every one should not believe it; and young Peter McCarren, peering, listening, questioning, jotting down notes, inspired him with an exquisite sense of security. McCarren had fastened on the case at once, "like a leech," as he phrased it—jumped at it, thrilled to it, and settled down to "draw the last drop of fact from it, and had not let go till he had." No one else had treated Granice in that way—even Allonby's detective had not taken a single note. And though a week had elapsed since the visit of that authorized official, nothing had been heard from the District Attorney's office: Allonby had apparently dropped the matter again. But McCarren wasn't going to drop it—not he! He positively hung on Granice's footsteps. They had spent the greater part of the previous day together, and now they were off again, running down clues.

But at Leffler's they got none, after all. Leffler's was no longer a stable. It was condemned to demolition, and in the respite between sentence and execution it had become a vague place of storage, a hospital for broken-down carriages and carts, presided over by a blear-eyed old woman who knew nothing of Flood's garage across the way—did not even remember what had stood there before the new flat-house began to rise.

"Well—we may run Leffler down somewhere; I've seen harder jobs done," said McCarren, cheerfully noting down the name.

36

As they walked back toward Sixth Avenue he added, in a less sanguine tone: "I'd undertake now to put the thing through if you could only put me on the track of that cyanide."

Granice's heart sank. Yes—there was the weak spot; he had felt it from the first! But he still hoped to convince McCarren that his case was strong enough without it; and he urged the reporter to come back to his rooms and sum up the facts with him again.

"Sorry, Mr. Granice, but I'm due at the office now. Besides, it'd be no use till I get some fresh stuff to work on. Suppose I call you up tomorrow or next day?"

He plunged into a trolley and left Granice gazing desolately after him.

Two days later he reappeared at the apartment, a shade less jaunty in demeanor.

"Well, Mr. Granice, the stars in their courses are against you, as the bard says. Can't get a trace of Flood, or of Leffler either. And you say you bought the motor through Flood, and sold it through him, too?"

"Yes," said Granice wearily.

"Who bought it, do you know?"

Granice wrinkled his brows. "Why, Flood—yes, Flood himself. I sold it back to him three months later."

"Flood? The devil! And I've ransacked the town for Flood. That kind of business disappears as if the earth had swallowed it."

Granice, discouraged, kept silence.

"That brings us back to the poison," McCarren continued, his notebook out. "Just go over that again, will you?"

And Granice went over it again. It had all been so simple at the time—and he had been so clever in covering up his traces! As soon as he decided on poison he looked about for an acquaintance who manufactured chemicals; and there was Jim Dawes, a Harvard classmate, in the dyeing business—just the man. But at the last moment it occurred to him that suspicion might turn toward so obvious an opportunity, and he decided on a more tortuous course. Another friend, Carrick Venn, a student of medicine whom irremediable ill health had kept from the practice of his profession, amused his leisure with experiments in physics, for the exercise of which he had set up a simple laboratory. Granice had the habit of dropping in to smoke a cigar with him on Sunday afternoons, and the friends generally sat in Venn's workshop, at the back of the old family house in Stuyvesant Square. Off this workshop was the cupboard of supplies, with its row of deadly bottles. Carrick Venn was an original, a man of restless curious tastes, and his place, on a Sunday, was often full of visitors: a cheerful crowd of journalists, scribblers, painters, experimenters in divers forms of expression. Coming and going among so many, it was easy enough to pass unperceived; and one afternoon Granice, arriving before Venn had returned home, found himself alone in the workshop, and quickly slipping into the cupboard, transferred the drug to his pocket.

But that had happened ten years ago; and Venn, poor fellow, was long since dead of his dragging ailment. His old father was dead, too, the house in Stuyvesant Square had been turned into a boardinghouse, and the shifting life of New York had passed its rapid sponge over every trace of their obscure little history. Even the optimistic McCarren seemed to acknowledge the hopelessness of seeking for proof in that direction.

"And there's the third door slammed in our faces." He shut his notebook, and throwing back his head, rested his bright inquisitive eyes on Granice's furrowed face.

"Look here, Mr. Granice—you see the weak spot, don't you?"

The other made a despairing motion. "I see so many!"

"Yes: but the one that weakens all the others. Why the deuce do you want this thing known? Why do you want to put your head into the noose?"

Granice looked at him hopelessly, trying to take the measure of his quick light irreverent mind. No one so full of a cheerful animal life would believe in the craving for death as a sufficient motive; and Granice racked his brain for one more convincing. But suddenly he saw the reporter's face soften, and melt to a naive sentimentalism.

"Mr. Granice—has the memory of it always haunted you?"

Granice stared a moment, and then leapt at the opening. "That's it—the memory of it...always..."

McCarren nodded vehemently. "Dogged your steps, eh? Wouldn't let you sleep? The time came when you *had* to make a clean breast of it?"

"I had to. Can't you understand?"

The reporter struck his fist on the table. "God, sir! I don't suppose there's a human being with a drop of warm blood in him that can't picture the deadly horrors of remorse—"

The Celtic imagination was aflame, and Granice mutely thanked him for the word. What neither Ascham nor Denver would accept as a conceivable motive the Irish reporter seized on as the most adequate; and, as he said, once one could find a convincing motive, the difficulties of the case became so many incentives to effort.

"Remorse—*remorse*," he repeated, rolling the word under his tongue with an accent that was a clue to the psychology of the popular drama; and Granice, perversely, said to himself: "If I could only have struck that note I should have been running in six theatres at once."

He saw that from that moment McCarren's professional zeal would be fanned by emotional curiosity; and he profited by the fact to propose that they should dine together, and go on afterward to some music hall or theatre. It was becoming necessary to Granice to feel himself an object of preoccupation, to find himself in another mind. He took a kind of gray penumbral pleasure in riveting McCarren's attention on his case; and to feign the grimaces of moral anguish became a passionately engrossing game. He had not entered a theatre for months; but he sat out the meaningless performance in rigid tolerance, sustained by the sense of the reporter's observation.

Between the acts, McCarren amused him with anecdotes about the audience: he knew every one by sight, and could lift the curtain from every physiognomy. Granice listened indulgently. He had lost all interest in his kind, but he knew that he was himself the real centre of McCarren's attention, and that every word the latter spoke had an indirect bearing on his own problem.

"See that fellow over there—the little dried-up man in the third row, pulling his moustache? *His* memoirs would be worth publishing," McCarren said suddenly in the last *entr'acte*.

Granice, following his glance, recognized the detective from Allonby's office. For a moment he had the thrilling sense that he was being shadowed.

"Caesar, if *he* could talk—!" McCarren continued. "Know who he is, of course? Dr. John B. Stell, the biggest alienist in the country—"

Granice, with a start, bent again between the heads in front of him. "*That* man—the fourth from the aisle? You're mistaken. That's not Dr. Stell."

McCarren laughed. "Well, I guess I've been in court enough to know Stell when I see him. He testifies in nearly all the big cases where they plead insanity."

A cold shiver ran down Granice's spine, but he repeated obstinately: "That's not Dr. Stell."

"Not Stell? Why, man, I *know* him. Look—here he comes. If it isn't Stell, he won't speak to me."

The little dried-up man was moving slowly up the aisle. As he neared McCarren he made a slight gesture of recognition.

"How'do, Doctor Stell? Pretty slim show, ain't it?" the reporter cheerfully flung out at him. And Mr. J. B. Hewson, with a nod of amicable assent, passed on.

Granice sat benumbed. He knew he had not been mistaken— the man who had just passed was the same man whom Allonby had sent to see him: a physician disguised as a detective. Allonby, then, had thought him insane, like the others—had regarded his confession as the maundering of a maniac. The discovery froze Granice with horror—he seemed to see the madhouse gaping for him.

"Isn't there a man a good deal like him—a detective named J. B. Hewson?"

But he knew in advance what McCarren's answer would be. "Hewson? J. B. Hewson? Never heard of him. But that was J. B. Stell fast enough—I guess he can be trusted to know himself, and you saw he answered to his name."

VI

SOME days passed before Granice could obtain a word with the District Attorney: he began to think that Allonby avoided him.

But when they were face-to-face Allonby's jovial countenance showed no sign of embarrassment. He waved his visitor to a chair, and leaned across his desk with the encouraging smile of a consulting physician.

Granice broke out at once: "That detective you sent me the other day—"

Allonby raised a deprecating hand.

"—I know: it was Stell the alienist. Why did you do that, Allonby?"

The other's face did not lose its composure. "Because I looked up your story first—and there's nothing in it."

"Nothing in it?" Granice furiously interposed.

"Absolutely nothing. If there is, why the deuce don't you bring me proofs? I know you've been talking to Peter Ascham, and to Denver, and to that little ferret McCarren of the *Explorer*. Have any of them been able to make out a case for you? No. Well, what am I to do?"

Granice's lips began to tremble. "Why did you play me that trick?"

"About Stell? I had to, my dear fellow: it's part of my business. Stell *is* a detective, if you come to that—every doctor is."

The trembling of Granice's lips increased, communicating itself in a long quiver to his facial muscles. He forced a laugh through his dry throat. "Well—and what did he detect?"

"In you? Oh, he thinks it's overwork—overwork and too much smoking. If you look in on him some day at his office

41

he'll show you the record of hundreds of cases like yours, and advise you what treatment to follow. It's one of the commonest forms of hallucination. Have a cigar, all the same."

"But, Allonby, I killed that man!"

The District Attorney's large hand, outstretched on his desk, had an almost imperceptible gesture, and a moment later, as if an answer to the call of an electric bell, a clerk looked in from the outer office.

"Sorry, my dear fellow—lot of people waiting. Drop in on Stell some morning," Allonby said, shaking hands.

McCarren had to own himself beaten: there was absolutely no flaw in the alibi. And since his duty to his journal obviously forbade his wasting time on insoluble mysteries, he ceased to frequent Granice, who dropped back into a deeper isolation. For a day or two after his visit to Allonby he continued to live in dread of Dr. Stell. Why might not Allonby have deceived him as to the alienist's diagnosis? What if he were really being shadowed, not by a police agent but by a mad doctor? To have the truth out, he suddenly determined to call on Dr. Stell.

The physician received him kindly, and reverted without embarrassment to the conditions of their previous meeting. "We have to do that occasionally, Mr. Granice; it's one of our methods. And you had given Allonby a fright."

Granice was silent. He would have liked to reaffirm his guilt, to produce the fresh arguments that had occurred to him since his last talk with the physician; but he feared his eagerness might be taken for a symptom of derangement, and he affected to smile away Dr. Stell's allusion.

"You think, then, it's a case of brain fag—nothing more?"

"Nothing more. And I should advise you to knock off tobacco. You smoke a good deal, don't you?"

He developed his treatment, recommending massage, gymnastics, travel, or any form of diversion that did not—that in short—

Granice interrupted him impatiently. "Oh, I loathe all that—and I'm sick of traveling."

42

"H'm. Then some larger interest—politics, reform, philan-thropy? Something to take you out of yourself."

"Yes. I understand," said Granice wearily.

"Above all, don't lose heart. I see hundreds of cases like yours," the doctor added cheerfully from the threshold.

On the doorstep Granice stood still and laughed. Hundreds of cases like his—the case of a man who had committed a murder, who confessed his guilt, and whom no one would be-lieve! Why, there had never been a case like it in the world. What a good figure Stell would have made in a play: the great alienist who couldn't read a man's mind any better than that!

Granice saw huge comic opportunities in the type.

But as he walked away, his fears dispelled, the sense of list-lessness returned on him. For the first time since his avowal to Peter Ascham he found himself without an occupation, and un-derstood that he had been carried through the past weeks only by the necessity of constant action. Now his life had once more become a stagnant backwater, and as he stood on the street corner watching the tides of traffic sweep by, he asked himself despairingly how much longer he could endure to float about in the sluggish circle of his consciousness.

The thought of self-destruction recurred to him; but again his flesh recoiled. He yearned for death from other hands, but he could never take it from his own. And, aside from his insuper-able physical reluctance, another motive restrained him. He was possessed by the dogged desire to establish the truth of his story. He refused to be swept aside as an irresponsible dreamer—even if he had to kill himself in the end, he would not do so before proving to society that he had deserved death from it.

He began to write long letters to the papers; but after the first had been published and commented on, public curiosity was quelled by a brief statement from the District Attorney's office, and the rest of his communications remained unprinted. Ascham came to see him, and begged him to travel. Robert Denver dropped in, and tried to joke him out of his delusion; till Granice, mistrustful of their motives, began to dread the reappearance of Dr. Stell, and set a guard on his lips. But the words he kept back engendered others and still others in his brain. His inner self became a humming factory of arguments, and he spent long hours reciting and writing down elaborate statements of his crime, which he constantly retouched and developed. Then gradually his activity languished under the lack of an audience, the sense of being buried beneath deepening drifts of indifference. In a passion of resentment he swore that he would prove himself a murderer, even if he had to commit another crime to do it; and for a sleepless night or two the thought flamed red on his darkness. But daylight dispelled it. The determining impulse was lacking and he hated too promiscuously to choose his victim...So he was thrown back on the unavailing struggle to impose the truth of his story. As fast as one channel closed on him he tried to pierce another through the sliding sands of incredulity. But every issue seemed blocked, and the whole human race leagued together to cheat one man of the right to die.

Thus viewed, the situation became so monstrous that he lost his last shred of self-restraint in contemplating it. What if he were really the victim of some mocking experiment, the centre of a ring of holidaymakers jeering at a poor creature in its blind dashes against the solid walls of consciousness? But, no—men were not so uniformly cruel: there were flaws in the close surface of their indifference, cracks of weakness and pity here and there...

Granice began to think that his mistake lay in having appealed to persons more or less familiar with his past, and to whom the visible conformities of his life seemed a final disproof of its one fierce secret deviation. The general tendency was to take for the whole of life the slit seen between the blinders of habit: and in his walk down that narrow vista Granice cut a correct enough figure. To a vision free to follow his whole orbit his story would be more intelligible: it would be easier to convince a chance idler in the street than the trained intelligence hampered by a sense of his antecedents. This idea shot up in him with the tropic luxuriance of each new seed of

44

thought, and he began to walk the streets, and to frequent out-of-the-way chophouses and bars in his search for the impartial stranger to whom he should disclose himself.

At first every face looked encouragement; but at the crucial moment he always held back. So much was at stake, and it was so essential that his first choice should be decisive. He dreaded stupidity, timidity, intolerance. The imaginative eye, the furrowed brow, were what he sought. He must reveal himself only to a heart versed in the tortuous motions of the human will; and he began to hate the dull benevolence of the average face. Once or twice, obscurely, allusively, he made a beginning—once sitting down at a man's side in a basement chophouse, another day approaching a lounger on an east-side wharf. But in both cases the premonition of failure checked him on the brink of avowal. His dread of being taken for a man in the clutch of a fixed idea gave him an unnatural keenness in reading the expression of his interlocutors, and he had provided himself in advance with a series of verbal alternatives, trapdoors of evasion from the first dart of ridicule or suspicion.

He passed the greater part of the day in the streets, coming home at irregular hours, dreading the silence and orderliness of his apartment, and the critical scrutiny of Flint. His real life was spent in a world so remote from this familiar setting that he sometimes had the mysterious sense of a living metempsychosis, a furtive passage from one identity to another—yet the other as unescapably himself!

One humiliation he was spared: the desire to live never revived in him. Not for a moment was he tempted to a shabby pact with existing conditions. He wanted to die, wanted it with the fixed unwavering desire which alone attains its end. And still the end eluded him! It would not always, of course—he had full faith in the dark star of his destiny. And he could prove it best by repeating his story, persistently and indefatigably, pouring it into indifferent ears, hammering it into dull brains, till at last it kindled a spark, and some one of the careless millions paused, listened, believed...

It was a mild March day, and he had been loitering on the west-side docks, looking at faces. He was becoming an expert in physiognomies: his eagerness no longer made rash darts and awkward recoils. He knew now the face he needed, as clearly as if it had come to him in a vision; and not till he found it would he speak. As he walked eastward through the shabby reeking streets he had a premonition that he should find it that morning. Perhaps it was the promise of spring in the air—certainly he felt calmer than for many days...

He turned into Washington Square, struck across it obliquely, and walked up University Place. Its heterogeneous passers always allured him—they were less hurried than in Broadway, less enclosed and classified than in Fifth Avenue. He walked slowly, watching for his face.

At Union Square he felt a sudden relapse into discouragement, like a votary who has watched too long for a sign from the altar. Perhaps, after all, he should never find his face...The air was languid, and he felt tired. He walked between the bald grass plots and the twisted trees, making for an empty seat. Presently he passed a bench on which a girl sat alone, and something as definite as the twitch of a cord made him stop before her. He had never dreamed of telling his story to a girl, had hardly looked at the women's faces as they passed. His case was man's work: how could a woman help him? But this girl's face was extraordinary—quiet and wide as a clear evening sky. It suggested a hundred images of space, distance, mystery, like ships he had seen, as a boy, quietly berthed by a familiar wharf, but with the breath of far seas and strange harbours in their shrouds...Certainly this girl would understand. He went up to her quietly, lifting his hat, observing the forms—wishing her to see at once that he was "a gentleman."

"I am a stranger to you," he began, sitting down beside her, "but your face is so extremely intelligent that I feel...I feel it is the face I've waited for...looked for everywhere; and I want to tell you—"

The girl's eyes widened: she rose to her feet. She was escaping him!

46

In his dismay he ran a few steps after her, and caught her roughly by the arm.

"Here—wait—listen! Oh, don't scream, you fool!" he shouted out.

He felt a hand on his own arm; turned and confronted a policeman. Instantly he understood that he was being arrested, and something hard within him was loosened and ran to tears.

"Ah, you know—you *know* I'm guilty!"

He was conscious that a crowd was forming, and that the girl's frightened face had disappeared. But what did he care about her face? It was the policeman who had really understood him. He turned and followed, the crowd at his heels...

VII

In the charming place in which he found himself there were so many sympathetic faces that he felt more than ever convinced of the certainty of making himself heard.

It was a bad blow, at first, to find that he had not been arrested for murder; but Ascham, who had come to him at once, explained that he needed rest, and the time to "review" his statements; it appeared that reiteration had made them a little confused and contradictory. To this end he had willingly acquiesced in his removal to a large quiet establishment, with an open space and trees about it, where he had found a number of intelligent companions, some, like himself, engaged in preparing or reviewing statements of their cases, and others ready to lend an interested ear to his own recital.

For a time he was content to let himself go on the tranquil current of this existence; but although his auditors gave him for the most part an encouraging attention, which, in some, went the length of really brilliant and helpful suggestion, he gradually felt a recurrence of his old doubts. Either his hearers were not sincere, or else they had less power to aid him than they boasted. His interminable conferences resulted in nothing, and as the benefit of the long rest made itself felt, it produced an increased mental lucidity that rendered inaction more and more unbearable. At length he discovered that on certain days visitors from the outer world were admitted to his retreat; and he wrote out long and logically constructed relations of his crime, and furtively slipped them into the hands of these messengers of hope.

This occupation gave him a fresh lease of patience, and he now lived only to watch for the visitors' days, and scan the faces that swept by him like stars seen and lost in the rifts of a hurrying sky.

Mostly, these faces were strange and less intelligent than those of his companions. But they represented his last means of access to the world, a kind of subterranean channel on which he could set his "statements" afloat, like paper boats which the mysterious current might sweep out into the open seas of life.

One day, however, his attention was arrested by a familiar contour, a pair of bright prominent eyes, and a chin insufficiently shaved. He sprang up and stood in the path of Peter McCarren.

The journalist looked at him doubtfully, then held out his hand with a startled deprecating, "*Why—?*"

"You didn't know me? I'm so changed?" Granice faltered, feeling the rebound of the other's wonder.

"Why, no; but you're looking quieter—smoothed out," McCarren smiled.

"Yes: that's what I'm here for—to rest. And I've taken the opportunity to write out a clearer statement—"

Granice's hand shook so that he could hardly draw the folded paper from his pocket. As he did so he noticed that the reporter was accompanied by a tall man with grave compassionate eyes. It came to Granice in a wild thrill of conviction that this was the face he had waited for...

"Perhaps your friend—he *is* your friend?—would glance over it—or I could put the case in a few words if you have time?" Granice's voice shook like his hand. If this chance escaped him he felt that his last hope was gone. McCarren and the stranger looked at each other, and the former glanced at his watch.

"I'm sorry we can't stay and talk it over now, Mr. Granice; but my friend has an engagement, and we're rather pressed—"

Granice continued to proffer the paper. "I'm sorry—I think I could have explained. But you'll take this, at any rate?"

The stranger looked at him gently. "Certainly—I'll take it." He had his hand out. "Goodbye."

"Goodbye," Granice echoed.

He stood watching the two men move away from him through the long light hall; and as he watched them a tear ran down his face. But as soon as they were out of sight he turned and walked hastily toward his room, beginning to hope again, already planning a new statement.

Outside the building the two men stood still, and the journalist's companion looked up curiously at the long monotonous rows of barred windows.

"So that was Granice?"

"Yes—that was Granice, poor devil," said McCarren.

"Strange case! I suppose there's never been one just like it? He's still absolutely convinced that he committed that murder?"

"Absolutely. Yes."

The stranger reflected. "And there was no conceivable ground for the idea? No one could make out how it started? A quiet conventional sort of fellow like that—where do you suppose he got such a delusion? Did you ever get the least clue to it?"

McCarren stood still, his hands in his pockets, his head cocked up in contemplation of the barred windows. Then he turned his bright hard gaze on his companion.

"That was the queer part of it. I've never spoken of it—but I *did* get a clue."

"By Jove! That's interesting. What was it?"

McCarren formed his red lips into a whistle. "Why—that it wasn't a delusion."

He produced his effect—the other turned on him with a pallid stare.

"He murdered the man all right. I tumbled on the truth by the merest accident, when I'd pretty nearly chucked the whole job."

"He murdered him—murdered his cousin?"

"Sure as you live. Only don't split on me. It's about the queerest business I ever ran into...*Do about it?* Why, what was I to do? I couldn't hang the poor devil, could I? Lord, but I was glad when they collared him, and had him stowed away safe in there!"

The tall man listened with a grave face, grasping Granice's statement in his hand.

"Here—take this; it makes me sick," he said abruptly, thrusting the paper at the reporter; and the two men turned and walked in silence to the gates.

.

HIS FATHER'S SON

I

After his wife's death Mason Grew took the momentous step of selling out his business and moving from Wingfield, Connecticut, to Brooklyn.

For years he had secretly nursed the hope of such a change, but had never dared to suggest it to Mrs. Grew, a woman of immutable habits. Mr. Grew himself was attached to Wingfield, where he had grown up, prospered, and become what the local press described as "prominent." He was attached to his ugly brick house with sandstone trimmings and a cast-iron area railing neatly sanded to match; to the similar row of houses across the street, the "trolley" wires forming a kind of aerial pathway between, and the sprawling vista closed by the steeple of the church which he and his wife had always attended, and where their only child had been baptized.

It was hard to snap all these threads of association, visual and sentimental; yet still harder, now that he was alone, to live so far from his boy. Ronald Grew was practicing law in New York, and there was no more chance of returning to live at Wingfield than of a river's flowing inland from the sea. Therefore to be near him his father must move; and it was characteristic of Mr. Grew, and of the situation generally, that the translation, when it took place, was to Brooklyn, and not to New York.

"Why you bury yourself in that hole I can't think," had been Ronald's comment; and Mr. Grew simply replied that rents were lower in Brooklyn, and that he had heard of a house that would suit him. In reality he had said to himself—being the only recipient of his own confidences—that if he went to New York he might be on the boy's mind; whereas, if he lived in Brooklyn, Ronald would always have a good excuse for not popping over to see him every other day. The sociological isolation of Brooklyn, combined with its geographical nearness, presented in fact the precise conditions for Mr. Grew's case. He wanted to be near enough to New York to go there often, to

51

feel under his feet the same pavement that Ronald trod, to sit now and then in the same theatres, and find on his breakfast-table the journals that, with increasing frequency, inserted Ronald's name in the sacred bounds of the society column. It had always been a trial to Mr. Grew to have to wait twenty-four hours to read that "among those present was Mr. Ronald Grew." Now he had it with his coffee, and left it on the break-fast table to the perusal of a "hired girl" cosmopolitan enough to do it justice. In such ways Brooklyn attested the advantages of its propinquity to New York, while remaining, as regards Ronald's duty to his father, as remote and inaccessible as Wingfield.

It was not that Ronald shirked his filial obligations, but rather because of his heavy sense of them, that Mr. Grew so persistently sought to minimize and lighten them. It was he who insisted, to Ronald, on the immense difficulty of getting from New York to Brooklyn.

"Any way you look at it, it makes a big hole in the day; and there's not much use in the ragged rim left. You say you're din-ing out next Sunday? Then I forbid you to come over here for lunch. Do you understand me, sir? You disobey at the risk of your father's malediction! Where did you say you were dining? With the Waltham Bankshires again? Why, that's the second time in three weeks, ain't it? Big blowout, I suppose? Gold plate and orchids—opera singers in afterward? Well, you'd be in a nice box if there was a fog on the river, and you got hung up halfway over. That'd be a handsome return for the attention Mrs. Bankshire has shown you—singling out a whippersnapper like you twice in three weeks! (What's the daughter's name— Daisy?) No, *sir*—don't you come fooling round here next Sun-day, or I'll set the dogs on you. And you wouldn't find me in anyhow, come to think of it. I'm lunching out myself, as it happens—yes sir, *lunching out*. Is there anything especially comic in my lunching out? I don't often do it, you say? Well, that's no reason why I never should. Who with? Why, with— with old Dr. Bleaker: Dr. Eliphalet Bleaker. No, you wouldn't

52

know about him—he's only an old friend of your mother's and mine."

Gradually Ronald's insistence became less difficult to overcome. With his customary sweetness and tact (as Mr. Grew put it) he began to "take the hint," to give in to "the old gentleman's" growing desire for solitude.

"I'm set in my ways, Ronny, that's about the size of it; I like to go tick-ticking along like a clock. I always did. And when you come bouncing in I never feel sure there's enough for dinner—or that I haven't sent Maria out for the evening. And I don't want the neighbors to see me opening my own door to my son. That's the kind of cringing snob I am. Don't give me away, will you? I want 'em to think I keep four or five powdered flunkeys in the hall day and night—same as the lobby of one of those Fifth Avenue hotels. And if you pop over when you're not expected, how am I going to keep up the bluff?"

Ronald yielded after the proper amount of resistance—his intuitive sense, in every social transaction, of the proper amount of force to be expended, was one of the qualities his father most admired in him. Mr. Grew's perceptions in this line were probably more acute than his son suspected. The souls of short thickset men, with chubby features, mutton-chop whiskers, and pale eyes peering between folds of fat like almond kernels in half-split shells—souls thus encased do not reveal themselves to the casual scrutiny as delicate emotional instruments. But in spite of the dense disguise in which he walked Mr. Grew vibrated exquisitely in response to every imaginative appeal; and his son Ronald was perpetually stimulating and feeding his imagination.

Ronald in fact constituted his father's one escape from the impenetrable element of mediocrity that had always hemmed him in. To a man so enamored of beauty, and so little qualified to add to its sum total, it was a wonderful privilege to have bestowed on the world such a being. Ronald's resemblance to Mr. Grew's early conception of what he himself would have liked

53

to look might have put new life into the discredited theory of prenatal influences. At any rate, if the young man owed his beauty, his distinction and his winning manner to the dreams of one of his parents, it was certainly to those of Mr. Grew, who, while outwardly devoting his life to the manufacture and dissemination of Grew's Secure Suspender Buckle, moved in an enchanted inward world peopled with all the figures of romance. In this high company Mr. Grew cut as brilliant a figure as any of its noble phantoms; and to see his vision of himself suddenly projected on the outer world in the shape of a brilliant popular conquering son, seemed, in retrospect, to give to that image a belated objective reality. There were even moments when, forgetting his physiognomy, Mr. Grew said to himself that if he'd had "half a chance" he might have done as well as Ronald; but this only fortified his resolve that Ronald should do infinitely better.

Ronald's ability to do well almost equaled his gift of looking well. Mr. Grew constantly affirmed to himself that the boy was "not a genius"; but, barring this slight deficiency, he was almost everything that a parent could wish. Even at Harvard he had managed to be several desirable things at once—writing poetry in the college magazine, playing delightfully "by ear," acquitting himself honorably in his studies, and yet holding his own in the fashionable sporting set that formed, as it were, the gateway of the temple of Society. Mr. Grew's idealism did not preclude the frank desire that his son should pass through that gateway; but the wish was not prompted by material considerations. It was Mr. Grew's notion that, in the rough and hurrying current of a new civilization, the little pools of leisure and enjoyment must nurture delicate growths, material graces as well as moral refinements, likely to be uprooted and swept away by the rush of the main torrent. He based his theory on the fact that he had liked the few "society" people he had met—had found their manners simpler, their voices more agreeable, their views more consonant with his own, than those of the leading citizens of Wingfield. But then he had met very few.

Ronald's sympathies needed no urging in the same direction. He took naturally, dauntlessly, to all the high and exceptional things about which his father's imagination had so long sheepishly and ineffectually hovered—from the start he *was* what Mr. Grew had dreamed of being. And so precise, so detailed, was Mr. Grew's vision of his own imaginary career, that as Ronald grew up, and began to travel in a widening orbit, his father had an almost uncanny sense of the extent to which that career was enacting itself before him. At Harvard, Ronald had done exactly what the hypothetical Mason Grew would have done, had not his actual self, at the same age, been working his way up in old Slagden's button factory—the institution which was later to acquire fame, and even notoriety, as the birthplace of Grew's Secure Suspender Buckle. Afterward, at a period when the actual Grew had passed from the factory to the bookkeeper's desk, his invisible double had been reading law at Columbia—precisely again what Ronald did! But it was when the young man left the paths laid out for him by the parental hand, and cast himself boldly on the world, that his adventures began to bear the most astonishing resemblance to those of the unrealized Mason Grew. It was in New York that the scene of this hypothetical being's first exploits had always been laid; and it was in New York that Ronald was to achieve his first triumph. There was nothing small or timid about Mr. Grew's imagination; it had never stopped at anything between Wingfield and the metropolis. And the real Ronald had the same cosmic vision as his parent. He brushed aside with a contemptuous laugh his mother's tearful entreaty that he should stay at Wingfield and continue the dynasty of the Grew Suspender Buckle. Mr. Grew knew that in reality Ronald winced at the Buckle, loathed it, blushed for his connection with it. Yet it was the Buckle that had seen him through Groton, Harvard and the Law School, and had permitted him to enter the office of a distinguished corporation lawyer, instead of being enslaved to some sordid business with quick returns. The Buckle had been Ronald's fairy godmother—yet his father did not blame him for abhorring and disowning it. Mr. Grew himself often bitterly regretted having bestowed his own name on the instrument of his material success, though, at the time, his doing so had been the natural expression of his romanticism. When he invented the Buckle, and took out his patent, he and his wife both felt that to bestow their name on it was like naming a battleship or a peak of the Andes.

Mrs. Grew had never learned to know better; but Mr. Grew had discovered his error before Ronald was out of school. He read it first in a black eye of his boy's. Ronald's symmetry had been marred by the insolent fist of a fourth former whom he had chastised for alluding to his father as "Old Buckles;" and when Mr. Grew heard the epithet he understood in a flash that the Buckle was a thing to blush for. It was too late then to dissociate his name from it, or to efface from the hoardings of the entire continent the picture of two gentlemen, one contorting himself in the abject effort to repair a broken brace, while the careless ease of the other's attitude proclaimed his trust in the Secure Suspender Buckle. These records were indelible, but Ronald could at least be spared all direct connection with them; and from that day Mr. Grew resolved that the boy should not return to Wingfield.

"You'll see," he had said to Mrs. Grew, "he'll take right hold in New York. Ronald's got my knack for taking hold," he added, throwing out his chest.

"But the way you took hold was in business," objected Mrs. Grew, who was large and literal.

Mr. Grew's chest collapsed, and he became suddenly conscious of his comic face in its rim of sandy whiskers. "That's not the only way," he said, with a touch of wistfulness that escaped his wife's analysis.

"Well, of course you could have written beautifully," she rejoined with admiring eyes.

" *Written?* Me!" Mr. Grew became sardonic.

56

"Why, those letters—weren't *they* beautiful, I'd like to know?"

The couple exchanged a glance, innocently allusive and amused on the wife's part, and charged with a sudden tragic significance on the husband's.

"Well, I've got to be going along to the office now," he merely said, dragging himself out of his rocking chair.

This had happened while Ronald was still at school; and now Mrs. Grew slept in the Wingfield cemetery, under a life-size theological virtue of her own choosing, and Mr. Grew's prognostications as to Ronald's ability to "take right hold" in New York were being more and more brilliantly fulfilled.

II

Ronald obeyed his father's injunction not to come to luncheon on the day of the Bankshires' dinner; but in the middle of the following week Mr. Grew was surprised by a telegram from his son.

"Want to see you important matter. Expect me tomorrow afternoon."

Mr. Grew received the telegram after breakfast. To peruse it he had lifted his eye from a paragraph of the morning paper describing a fancy dress dinner that had taken place the night before at the Hamilton Gliddens' for the housewarming of their new Fifth Avenue palace.

"Among the couples who afterward danced in the Poets' Quadrille were Miss Daisy Bankshire, looking more than usually lovely as Laura, and Mr. Ronald Grew as the young Petrarch."

Petrarch and Laura! Well—if *anything* meant anything, Mr. Grew supposed he knew what that meant. For weeks past he had noticed how constantly the names of the young people appeared together in the society notes he so insatiably devoured. Even the soulless reporter was getting into the habit of coupling them in his lists. And this Laura and Petrarch business was almost an announcement...

Mr. Grew dropped the telegram, wiped his eyeglasses, and reread the paragraph. "Miss Daisy Bankshire...more than usually lovely..." Yes; she *was* lovely. He had often seen her photograph in the papers—seen her represented in every conceivable attitude of the mundane game: fondling her prize bulldog, taking a fence on her thoroughbred, dancing a *gavotte*, all patches and plumes, or fingering a guitar, all tulle and lilies; and once he had caught a glimpse of her at the theatre. Hearing that Ronald was going to a fashionable first night with the Bankshires, Mr. Grew had for once overcome his repugnance to following his son's movements, and had secured for himself, under the shadow of the balcony, a stall whence he could observe the Bankshire box without fear of detection. Ronald had never known of his father's presence at the play; and for three blessed hours Mr. Grew had watched his boy's handsome dark head bent above the dense fair hair and white averted shoulder that were all he could catch of Miss Bankshire's beauties.

He recalled the vision now; and with it came, as usual, its ghostly double: the vision of his young self bending above such a white shoulder and such shining hair. Needless to say that the real Mason Grew had never found himself in so enviable a situation. The late Mrs. Grew had no more resembled Miss Daisy Bankshire than he had looked like the happy victorious Ronald. And the mystery was that from their dull faces, their dull endearments, the miracle of Ronald should have sprung. It was almost—fantastically—as if the boy had been a changeling, child of a Latmian night, whom the divine companion of Mr. Grew's early reveries had secretly laid in the cradle of the Wingfield bedroom while Mr. And Mrs. Grew slept the deep sleep of conjugal indifference.

The young Mason Grew had not at first accepted this astral episode as the complete cancelling of his claims on romance. He too had grasped at the high-hung glory; and, with his fatal tendency to reach too far when he reached at all, had singled out the prettiest girl in Wingfield. When he recalled his stammered confession of love his face still tingled under her cool bright stare. The wonder of his audacity had struck her dumb; and when she recovered her voice it was to fling a taunt at him.

"Don't be too discouraged, you know—have you ever thought of trying Addie Wicks?"

All Wingfield would have understood the gibe: Addie Wicks was the dullest girl in town. And a year later he had married Addie Wicks...

He looked up from the perusal of Ronald's telegram with this memory in his mind. Now at last his dream was coming true! His boy would taste of the joys that had mocked his thwarted youth and his dull gray middle age. And it was fitting that they should be realized in Ronald's destiny. Ronald was made to take happiness boldly by the hand and lead it home like a bridegroom. He had the carriage, the confidence, the high faith in his fortune, that compel the willful stars. And, thanks to the Buckle, he would have the exceptional setting, the background of material elegance that became his conquering person. Since Mr. Grew had retired from business his investments had prospered, and he had been saving up his income for just such a contingency. His own wants were few: he had transferred the Wingfield furniture to Brooklyn, and his sitting room was a replica of that in which the long years of his married life had been spent. Even the florid carpet on which Ronald's tottering footsteps had been taken was carefully matched when it became too threadbare. And on the marble center table, with its chenille-fringed cover and bunch of dyed pampas grass, lay the illustrated Longfellow and the copy of Ingersoll's lectures that represented literature to Mr. Grew when he had led home his bride. In the light of Ronald's romance, Mr. Grew found himself reliving, with a strange tremor of mingled pain and tenderness, all the poor prosaic incidents of his own personal history. Curiously enough, with this new splendor on them they began to emit a small faint ray of their own. His wife's armchair, in its usual place by the fire, recalled her placid unperceiving presence, seated opposite to him during the long drowsy years; and he felt her kindness, her equanimity, where formerly he had only ached at her obtuseness. And from the chair he glanced up at the large discolored photograph on the wall above, with a brittle brown wreath suspended on a corner of the frame. The photograph represented a young man with a poetic necktie and untrammeled hair, leaning negligently against a Gothic chair back, a roll of music in his hand; and beneath was scrawled a bar of Chopin, with the words: " *Adieu, Adele.*"

The portrait was that of the great pianist, Fortune Dolbrowski; and its presence on the wall of Mr. Grew's sitting room commemorated the only exquisite hour of his life save that of Ronald's birth. It was some time before the latter memorable event, a few months only after Mr. Grew's marriage, that he had taken his wife to New York to hear the great Dolbrowski. Their evening had been magically beautiful, and even Addie, roused from her habitual inexpressiveness, had quivered into a momentary semblance of life. "I never—I never—" she gasped out helplessly when they had regained their hotel bedroom, and sat staring back entranced at the evening's evocations. Her large immovable face was pink and tremulous, and she sat with her hands on her knees, forgetting to roll up her bonnet strings and prepare her curl papers.

"I'd like to *write* him just how I felt—I wisht I knew how!" she burst out suddenly in a final effervescence of emotion.

Her husband lifted his head and looked at her.

"Would you? I feel that way too," he said with a sheepish laugh. And they continued to stare at each other shyly through a transfiguring mist of sound.

Mr. Grew recalled the scene as he gazed up at the pianist's faded photograph. "Well, I owe her that anyhow—poor Addie!" he said, with a smile at the inconsequences of fate. With Ronald's telegram in his hand he was in a mood to count his mercies.

III

"A clear twenty-five thousand a year: that's what you can tell 'em with my compliments," said Mr. Grew, glancing complacently across the center table at his boy's charming face.

It struck him that Ronald's gift for looking his part in life had never so romantically expressed itself. Other young men, at such a moment, would have been red, damp, tight about the

60

collar; but Ronald's cheek was only a shade paler, and the contrast made his dark eyes more expressive.

"A clear twenty-five thousand; yes, sir—that's what I always meant you to have."

Mr. Grew leaned back, his hands thrust carelessly in his pockets, as though to divert attention from the agitation of his features. He had often pictured himself rolling out that phrase to Ronald, and now that it was actually on his lips he could not control their tremor.

Ronald listened in silence, lifting a nervous hand to his slight dark moustache, as though he, too, wished to hide some involuntary betrayal of emotion. At first Mr. Grew took his silence for an expression of gratified surprise; but as it prolonged itself it became less easy to interpret.

"I—see here, my boy; did you expect more? Isn't it enough?" Mr. Grew cleared his throat. "Do *they* expect more?" he asked nervously. He was hardly able to face the pain of inflicting a disappointment on Ronald at the very moment when he had counted on putting the final touch to his felicity.

Ronald moved uneasily in his chair and his eyes wandered upward to the laurel-wreathed photograph of the pianist above his father's head.

" *Is* it that, Ronald? Speak out, my boy. We'll see, we'll look round—I'll manage somehow."

"No, no," the young man interrupted, abruptly raising his hand as though to silence his father.

Mr. Grew recovered his cheerfulness. "Well, what's the matter than, if *she's* willing?"

Ronald shifted his position again, and finally rose from his seat.

"Father—I—there's something I've got to tell you. I can't take your money."

Mr. Grew sat speechless a moment, staring blankly at his son; then he emitted a puzzled laugh. "My money? What are you talking about? What's this about my money? Why, it ain't *mine*, Ronny; it's all yours—every cent of it!" he cried.

The young man met his tender look with a gaze of tragic rejection.

"No, no, it's not mine—not even in the sense you mean. Not in any sense. Can't you understand my feeling so?"

"Feeling so? I don't know how you're feeling. I don't know what you're talking about. Are you too proud to touch any money you haven't earned? Is that what you're trying to tell me?"

"No. It's not that. You must know—"

Mr. Grew flushed to the rim of his bristling whiskers. "Know? Know *what?* Can't you speak?"

Ronald hesitated, and the two men faced each other for a long strained moment, during which Mr. Grew's congested countenance grew gradually pale again.

"What's the meaning of this? Is it because you've done something...something you're ashamed of...ashamed to tell me?" he suddenly gasped out; and walking around the table he laid his hand on his son's shoulder. "There's nothing you can't tell me, my boy."

"It's not that. Why do you make it so hard for me?" Ronald broke out with passion. "You must have known this was sure to happen sooner or later."

"Happen? What was sure to hap—?" Mr. Grew's question wavered on his lip and passed into a tremulous laugh. "Is it something *I've* done that you don't approve of? Is it—is it *the Buckle* you're ashamed of, Ronald Grew?"

Ronald laughed too, impatiently. "The Buckle? No, I'm not ashamed of the Buckle; not any more than you are," he returned with a sudden bright flush. "But I'm ashamed of all I owe to it— all I owe to you—when—when—" He broke off and took a few distracted steps across the room. "You might make this easier for me," he protested, turning back to his father.

"Make what easier? I know less and less what you're driving at," Mr. Grew groaned.

Ronald's walk had once more brought him beneath the photograph on the wall. He lifted his head for a moment and looked at it; then he looked again at Mr. Grew.

"Do you suppose I haven't always known?"

"Known—?"

"Even before you gave me those letters—after my mother's death—even before that, I suspected. I don't know how it began...perhaps from little things you let drop...you and she...and resemblances that I couldn't help seeing...in myself...How on earth could you suppose I shouldn't guess? I always thought you gave me the letters as a way of telling me—"

Mr. Grew rose slowly from his chair. "The letters? Dolbrowski's letters?"

Ronald nodded with white lips. "You must remember giving them to me the day after the funeral."

Mr. Grew nodded back. "Of course. I wanted you to have everything your mother valued."

"Well—how could I help knowing after that?"

"Knowing *what?*" Mr. Grew stood staring helplessly at his son. Suddenly his look caught at a clue that seemed to confront it with a deeper bewilderment. "You thought—you thought those letters...Dolbrowski's letters...you thought they meant..."

"Oh, it wasn't only the letters. There were so many other signs. My love of music—my—all my feelings about life...and art...And when you gave me the letters I thought you must mean me to know."

Mr. Grew had grown quiet. His lips were firm, and his small eyes looked out steadily from their creased lids.

"To know that you were Fortune Dolbrowski's son?"

Ronald made a mute sign of assent.

"I see. And what did you mean to do?"

"I meant to wait till I could earn my living, and then repay you...as far as I can ever repay you...But now that there's a chance of my marrying...and your generosity overwhelms me ...I'm obliged to speak."

"I see," said Mr. Grew again. He let himself down into his chair, looking steadily and not unkindly at the young man. "Sit down, Ronald. Let's talk."

Ronald made a protesting movement. "Is anything to be gained by it? You can't change me—change what I feel. The reading of those letters transformed my whole life—I was a boy till then: they made a man of me. From that moment I understood myself." He paused, and then looked up at Mr. Grew's face. "Don't imagine I don't appreciate your kindness—your extraordinary generosity. But I can't go through life in disguise. And I want you to know that I have not won Daisy under false pretences—"

Mr. Grew started up with the first expletive Ronald had ever heard on his lips.

"You damned young fool, you, you haven't *told* her—?"

Ronald raised his head quickly. "Oh, you don't know her, sir! She thinks no worse of me for knowing my secret. She is above and beyond all such conventional prejudices. She's *proud* of my parentage—" he straightened his slim young shoulders—"as I'm proud of it...yes, sir, proud of it..."

Mr. Grew sank back into his seat with a dry laugh. "Well, you ought to be. You come of good stock. And you're father's son, every inch of you!" He laughed again, as though the humor of the situation grew on him with its closer contemplation.

"Yes, I've always felt that," Ronald murmured, flushing.

"Your father's son, and no mistake." Mr. Grew leaned forward. "You're the son of as big a fool as yourself. And here he sits, Ronald Grew."

The young man's flush deepened to crimson; but Mr. Grew checked his reply with a decisive gesture. "Here he sits, with all your young nonsense still alive in him. Don't you see the likeness? If you don't, I'll tell you the story of those letters."

Ronald stared. "What do you mean? Don't they tell their own story?"

"I supposed they did when I gave them to you; but you've given it a twist that needs straightening out." Mr. Grew squared his elbows on the table, and looked at the young man across the gift books and the dyed pampas grass. "I wrote all the letters that Dolbrowski answered."

Ronald gave back his look in frowning perplexity. "You wrote them? I don't understand. His letters are all addressed to my mother."

"Yes. And he thought he was corresponding with her."

"But my mother—what did she think?"

Mr. Grew hesitated, puckering his thick lids. "Well, I guess she kinder thought it was a joke. Your mother didn't think about things much."

Ronald continued to bend a puzzled frown on the question. "I don't understand," he reiterated.

Mr. Grew cleared his throat with a nervous laugh. "Well, I don't know as you ever will—*quite*. But this is the way it came about. I had a toughish time of it when I was young. Oh, I don't mean so much the fight I had to put up to make my way—there was always plenty of fight in me. But inside of myself it was kinder lonesome. And the outside didn't attract callers." He laughed again, with an apologetic gesture toward his broad blinking face. "When I went round with the other young fellows I was always the forlorn hope—the one that had to eat the drumsticks and dance with the leftovers. As sure as there was a blighter at a picnic I had to swing her, and feed her, and drive her home. And all the time I was mad after all the things you've got—poetry and music and all the joy-forever business. So there were the pair of us—my face and my imagination—chained together, and fighting, and hating each other like poison.

"Then your mother came along and took pity on me. It sets up a gawky fellow to find a girl who ain't ashamed to be seen walking with him Sundays. And I was grateful to your mother, and we got along first-rate. Only I couldn't say things to her—and she couldn't answer. Well—one day, a few months after we were married, Dolbrowski came to New York, and the whole place went wild about him. I'd never heard any good music, but I'd always had an inkling of what it must be like, though I couldn't tell you to this day how I knew. Well, your mother read about him in the papers too, and she thought it'd be the swagger thing to go to New York and hear him play—so we went...I'll never forget that evening. Your mother wasn't easily stirred up—she never seemed to need to let off steam. But that night she seemed to understand the way I felt. And when we got back to the hotel she said suddenly: 'I'd like to tell him how I feel. I'd like to sit right down and write to him.'

"'Would you?' I said. 'So would I.'

"There was paper and pens there before us, and I pulled a sheet toward me, and began to write. 'Is this what you'd like to say to him?' I asked her when the letter was done. And she got pink and said: 'I don't understand it, but it's lovely.' And she copied it out and signed her name to it, and sent it."

Mr. Grew paused, and Ronald sat silent, with lowered eyes.

"That's how it began; and that's where I thought it would end. But it didn't, because Dolbrowski answered. His first letter was dated January 10, 1872. I guess you'll find I'm correct. Well, I went back to hear him again, and I wrote him after the performance, and he answered again. And after that we kept it up for six months. Your mother always copied the letters and signed them. She seemed to think it was a kinder joke, and she was proud of his answering my letters. But she never went back to New York to hear him, though I saved up enough to give her the treat again. She was too lazy, and she let me go without her. I heard him three times in New York; and in the spring he came to Wingfield and played once at the Academy. Your mother was sick and couldn't go; so I went alone. After the performance I meant to get one of the directors to take me in to see him; but when the time came, I just went back home and wrote to him instead. And the month after, before he went back to Europe, he sent your mother a last little note, and that picture hanging up there..."

Mr. Grew paused again, and both men lifted their eyes to the photograph.

"Is that all?" Ronald slowly asked.

"That's all—every bit of it," said Mr. Grew.

"And my mother—my mother never even spoke to Dolbrowski?"

"Never. She never even saw him but that once in New York at his concert."

The blood crept again to Ronald's face. "Are you sure of that, sir?" he asked in a trembling voice.

"Sure as I am that I'm sitting here. Why, she was too lazy to look at his letters after the first novelty wore off. She copied the answers just to humor me—but she always said she couldn't understand what we wrote."

"But how could you go on with such a correspondence? It's incredible!"

Mr. Grew looked at his son thoughtfully. "I suppose it is, to you. You've only had to put out your hand and get the things I was starving for—music, and good talk, and ideas. Those letters gave me all that. You've read them, and you know that Dolbrowski was not only a great musician but a great man. There was nothing beautiful he didn't see, nothing fine he didn't feel. For six months I breathed his air, and I've lived on it ever since. Do you begin to understand a little now?"

"Yes—a little. But why write in my mother's name? Why make it a sentimental correspondence?"

Mr. Grew reddened to his bald temples. "Why, I tell you it began that way, as a kinder joke. And when I saw that the first letter pleased and interested him, I was afraid to tell him—*I couldn't* tell him. Do you suppose he'd gone on writing if he'd ever seen me, Ronny?"

Ronald suddenly looked at him with new eyes. "But he must have thought your letters very beautiful—to go on as he did," he broke out.

"Well—I did my best," said Mr. Grew modestly.

Ronald pursued his idea. "Where *are* all your letters, I wonder? Weren't they returned to you at his death?"

Mr. Grew laughed. "Lord, no. I guess he had trunks and trunks full of better ones. I guess Queens and Empresses wrote to him."

"I should have liked to see your letters," the young man insisted.

"Well, they weren't bad," said Mr. Grew drily. "But I'll tell you one thing, Ronny," he added suddenly. Ronald raised his head with a quick glance, and Mr. Grew continued: "I'll tell you where the best of those letters is—it's in *you*. If it hadn't been for that one look at life I couldn't have made you what you are. Oh, I know you've done a good deal of your own making—but I've been there behind you all the time. And you'll never know the work I've spared you and the time I've saved you. Fortune Dolbrowski helped me do that. I never saw things in little again after I'd looked at 'em with him. And I tried to give you the big view from the stars...So that's what became of my letters."

Mr. Grew paused, and for a long time Ronald sat motionless, his elbows on the table, his face dropped on his hands.

Suddenly Mr. Grew's touch fell on his shoulder.

"Look at here, Ronald Grew—do you want me to tell you how you're feeling at this minute? Just a mite let down, after all, at the idea that you ain't the romantic figure you'd got to think yourself...Well, that's natural enough, too; but I'll tell you what it proves. It proves you're my son right enough, if any more proof was needed. For it's just the kind of fool nonsense I used to feel at your age—and if there's anybody here to laugh at it's myself, and not you. And you can laugh at me just as much as you like..."

THE DAUNT DIANA

I

"What's become of the Daunt Diana? You mean to say you never heard the sequel?"

Ringham Finney threw himself back into his chair with the smile of the collector who has a good thing to show. He knew he had a good listener, at any rate. I don't think much of Ringham's snuffboxes, but his anecdotes are usually worthwhile. He's a psychologist astray among *bibelots*, and the best bits he brings back from his raids on Christie's and the Hotel Drouot are the fragments of human nature he picks up on those historic battlefields. If his *flair* in enamel had been half as good we should have heard of the Finney collection by this time.

He really has—queer fatuous investigator!—an unusually sensitive touch for the human texture, and the specimens he gathers into his museum of heterogeneous memories have almost always some mark of the rare and chosen. I felt, therefore, that I was really to be congratulated on the fact that I didn't know what had become of the Daunt Diana, and on having before me a long evening in which to learn. I had just led my friend back, after an excellent dinner at Foyot's, to the shabby pleasant sitting room of my *rive-gauche* hotel; and I knew that, once I had settled him in a good armchair, and put a box of cigars at his elbow, I could trust him not to budge till I had the story.

II

You remember old Neave, of course? Little Humphrey Neave, I mean. We used to see him pottering about Rome years ago. He lived in two tiny rooms over a wine shop, on polenta and lentils, and prowled among the refuse of the Ripetta whenever he had a few *soldi* to spend. But you've been out of the collector's world for so long that you may not know what happened to him afterward...

He was always a queer chap, Neave; years older than you and me, of course—and even when I first knew him, in my raw Roman days, he gave me an extraordinary sense of age and experience. I don't think I've ever known any one who was at once so intelligent and so simple. It's the precise combination that results in romance; and poor little Neave was romantic.

He told me once how he'd come to Rome. He was *originaire* of Mystic, Connecticut—and he wanted to get as far away from it as possible. Rome seemed as far as anything on the same planet could be; and after he'd worried his way through Harvard—with shifts and shavings that you and I can't imagine—he contrived to get sent to Switzerland as tutor to a chap who'd failed in his examinations. With only the Alps between, he wasn't likely to turn back; and he got another fellow to take his pupil home, and struck out on foot for the seven hills.

I'm telling you these early details merely to give you a notion of the man's idealism. There was a cool persistency and a headlong courage in his dash for Rome that one wouldn't have guessed in the little pottering chap we used to know. Once on the spot, he got more tutoring, managed to make himself a name for coaxing balky youths to take their fences, and was finally able to take up the more congenial task of expounding "the antiquities" to cultured travelers. I call it more congenial—but how it must have seared his soul! Fancy unveiling the sacred scars of Time to ladies who murmur: "Was this *actually* the spot—?" while they absently feel for their hatpins! He used to say that nothing kept him at it but the exquisite thought of accumulating the *lire* for his collection. For the Neave collection, my dear fellow, began early, began almost with his Roman life, began in a series of little nameless odds and ends, broken trinkets, torn embroideries, the amputated extremities of maimed marbles: things that even the rag picker had pitched away when he sifted his haul. But they weren't nameless or meaningless to Neave; his strength lay in his instinct for identifying, putting together, seeing significant relations. He was a regular Cuvier of bric-a-brac. And during those early years, when he had time to brood over trifles and note imperceptible differences, he gradually sharpened his instinct, and made it into the delicate and redoubtable instrument it is. Before he had a thousand francs' worth of *anticaglie* to his name he began to be known as an expert, and the big dealers were glad to consult him. But we're getting no nearer the Daunt Diana...

Well, some fifteen years ago, in London, I ran across Neave at Christie's. He was the same little man we'd known, effaced, bleached, indistinct, like a poor "impression"—as unnoticeable as one of his own early finds, yet, like them, with a *quality*, if one had an eye for it. He told me he still lived in Rome, and had contrived, by fierce self-denial, to get a few decent bits together—"piecemeal, little by little, with fasting and prayer; and I mean the fasting literally!" he said.

He had run over to London for his annual "look-round"—I fancy one or another of the big collectors usually paid his journey—and when we met he was on his way to see the Daunt collection. You know old Daunt was a surly brute, and the things weren't easily seen; but he had heard Neave was in London, and had sent—yes, actually sent!—for him to come and give his opinion on a few bits, including the Diana. The little man bore himself discreetly, but you can imagine his pride. In his exultation he asked me to come with him—"Oh, I've the *grandes et petites entrees*, my dear fellow: I've made my conditions—" and so it happened that I saw the first meeting between Humphrey Neave and his fate.

For that collection *was* his fate: or, one may say, it was embodied in the Diana who was queen and goddess of the realm. Yes—I shall always be glad I was with Neave when he had his first look at the Diana. I see him now, blinking at her through his white lashes, and stroking his seedy wisp of a moustache to hide a twitch of the muscles. It was all very quiet, but it was the *coup de foudre*. I could see that by the way his hands trembled when he turned away and began to examine the other things. You remember Neave's hands—thin, sallow, dry, with long inquisitive fingers thrown out like antennae? Whatever they hold—bronze or lace, hard enamel or brittle glass—they have an air of conforming themselves to the texture of the thing, and sucking out of it, by every fingertip, the mysterious essence it has secreted. Well, that day, as he moved about among Daunt's treasures, the Diana followed him everywhere. He didn't look back at her—he gave himself to the business he was there for—but whatever he touched, he felt her. And on the threshold he turned and gave her his first free look—the kind of look that says: *"You're mine."*

It amused me at the time—the idea of little Neave making eyes at any of Daunt's belongings. He might as well have co-quetted with the Kohinoor. And the same idea seemed to strike him; for as we turned away from the big house in Belgravia he glanced up at it and said, with a bitterness I'd never heard in him: "Good Lord! To think of that lumpy fool having those things to handle! Did you notice his stupid stumps of fingers? I suppose he blunted them gouging nuggets out of the gold fields. And in exchange for the nuggets he gets all that in a year—only has to hold out his callous palm to have that great ripe sphere of beauty drop into it! That's my idea of heaven—to have a great collection drop into one's hand, as success, or love, or any of the big shining things, drop suddenly on some men. And I've had to worry along for nearly fifty years, saving and paring, and haggling and intriguing, to get here a bit and there a bit—and not one perfection in the lot! It's enough to poison a man's life."

The outbreak was so unlike Neave that I remember every word of it: remember, too, saying in answer: "But, look here, Neave, you wouldn't take Daunt's hands for yours, I imagine?"

He stared a moment and smiled. "Have all that, and grope my way through it like a blind cave fish? What a question! But the sense that it's always the blind fish that live in that kind of aquarium is what makes anarchists, sir!" He looked back from the corner of the square, where we had paused while he delivered himself of this remarkable metaphor. "God, I'd like to throw a bomb at that place, and be in at the looting!"

And with that, on the way home, he unpacked his grievance—pulled the bandage off the wound, and showed me the
ugly mark it had made on his little white soul.

It wasn't the struggling, stinting, self-denying that galled
him—it was the inadequacy of the result. It was, in short, the
old tragedy of the discrepancy between a man's wants and his
power to gratify them. Neave's taste was too exquisite for his
means—was like some strange, delicate, capricious animal,
that he cherished and pampered and couldn't satisfy.

"Don't you know those little glittering lizards that die if
they're not fed on some wonderful tropical fly? Well, my
taste's like that, with one important difference—if it doesn't
get its fly, it simply turns and feeds on me. Oh, it doesn't die,
my taste—worse luck! It gets larger and stronger and more fas-
tidious, and takes a bigger bite of me—that's all."

That was all. Year by year, day by day, he had made himself into this delicate register of perceptions and sensations—as
far above the ordinary human faculty of appreciation as some
scientific registering instrument is beyond the rough human
senses—only to find that the beauty which alone could satisfy
him was unattainable—that he was never to know the last deep
identification which only possession can give. He had trained
himself in short, to feel, in the rare great thing—such an utterance of beauty as the Daunt Diana, say—a hundred elements of
perfection, a hundred *reasons why*, imperceptible, inexplicable
even, to the average "artistic" sense; he had reached this point
by a long austere process of discrimination and rejection, the
renewed great refusals of the intelligence which perpetually
asks more, which will make no pact with its self of yesterday,
and is never to be beguiled from its purpose by the wiles of the
next-best-thing. Oh, it's a poignant case, but not a common
one; for the next-best-thing usually wins...

You see, the worst of Neave's state was the fact of his not
being a mere collector, even the collector raised to his highest
pitch of efficiency. The whole thing was blent in him with poetry—his imagination had romanticized the acquisitive instinct,

as the religious feeling of the Middle Ages turned passion into love. And yet his could never be the abstract enjoyment of the philosopher who says: "This or that object is really mine because I'm capable of appreciating it." Neave *wanted* what he appreciated—wanted it with his touch and his sight as well as with his imagination.

It was hardly a year afterward that, coming back from a long tour in India, I picked up a London paper and read the amazing headline: "Mr. Humphrey Neave buys the Daunt collection"...I rubbed my eyes and read again. Yes, it could only be our old friend Humphrey. "An American living in Rome...one of our most discerning collectors"; there was no mistaking the description. I clapped on my hat and bolted out to see the first dealer I could find; and there I had the incredible details. Neave had come into a fortune—two or three million dollars, amassed by an uncle who had a corset factory, and who had attained wealth as the creator of the Mystic Super-straight. (Corset factory sounds odd, by the way, doesn't it? One had fancied that the corset was a personal, a highly specialized garment, more or less shaped on the form it was to modify; but, after all, the Tanagras were all made from two or three moulds—and so, I suppose, are the ladies who wear the Mystic Super-straight.)

The uncle had a son, and Neave had never dreamed of seeing a penny of the money; but the son died suddenly, and the father followed, leaving a codicil that gave everything to our friend. Humphrey had to go out to "realize" on the corset factory; and his description of *that*...Well, he came back with his money in his pocket, and the day he landed old Daunt went to smash. It all fitted in like a Chinese puzzle. I believe Neave drove straight from Euston to Daunt House: at any rate, within two months the collection was his, and at a price that made the trade sit up. Trust old Daunt for that!

I was in Rome the following spring, and you'd better believe I looked him up. A big porter glared at me from the door of the Palazzo Neave: I had almost to produce my passport to get in. But that wasn't Neave's fault—the poor fellow was so beset by people clamouring to see his collection that he had to barricade himself, literally. When I had mounted the state *Scalone*, and come on him, at the end of half a dozen echoing saloons, in the farthest, smallest *reduit* of the vast suite, I received the same welcome that he used to give us in his little den over the wine shop.

"Well—so you've got her?" I said. For I'd caught sight of the Diana in passing, against the bluish blur of an old *verdure*—just the background for her poised loveliness. Only I rather wondered why she wasn't in the room where he sat.

He smiled. "Yes, I've got her," he returned, more calmly than I had expected.

"And all the rest of the loot?"

"Yes. I had to buy the lump."

"Had to? But you wanted to, didn't you? You used to say it was your idea of heaven—to stretch out your hand and have a great ripe sphere of beauty drop into it. I'm quoting your own words, by the way."

Neave blinked and stroked his seedy moustache. "Oh, yes. I remember the phrase. It's true—it *is* the last luxury." He paused, as if seeking a pretext for his lack of warmth. "The thing that bothered me was having to move. I couldn't cram all the stuff into my old quarters."

"Well, I should say not! This is rather a better setting."

He got up. "Come and take a look round. I want to show you two or three things—new attributions I've made. I'm doing the catalogue over."

The interest of showing me the things seemed to dispel the vague apathy I had felt in him. He grew keen again in detailing his redistribution of values, and above all in convicting old Daunt and his advisers of their repeated aberrations of judgment. "The miracle is that he should have got such things, knowing as little as he did what he was getting. And the egregious asses who bought for him were no better, were worse in fact, since they had all sorts of humbugging wrong reasons for admiring what old Daunt simply coveted because it belonged to some other rich man."

Never had Neave had so wondrous a field for the exercise of his perfected faculty; and I saw then how in the real, the great collector's appreciations the keenest scientific perception is suffused with imaginative sensibility, and how it's to the latter undefinable quality that in the last resort he trusts himself.

Nevertheless, I still felt the shadow of that hovering apathy, and he knew I felt it, and was always breaking off to give me reasons for it. For one thing, he wasn't used to his new quarters—hated their bigness and formality; then the requests to show his things drove him mad. "The women—oh, the women!" he wailed, and interrupted himself to describe a heavy-footed German Princess who had marched past his treasures as if she were inspecting a cavalry regiment, applying an unmodulated *Mugneeficent* to everything from the engraved gems to the Hercules torso.

"Not that she was half as bad as the other kind," he added, as if with a last effort at optimism. "The kind who discriminate and say: 'I'm not sure if it's Botticelli or Cellini I mean, but *one of that school*, at any rate.' And the worst of all are the ones who know—up to a certain point: have the schools, and the dates and the jargon pat, and yet wouldn't know a Phidias if it stood where they hadn't expected it."

He had all my sympathy, poor Neave; yet these were trials inseparable from the collector's lot, and not always without their secret compensations. Certainly they did not wholly explain my friend's attitude; and for a moment I wondered if it were due to some strange disillusionment as to the quality of his treasures. But no! the Daunt collection was almost above criticism; and as we passed from one object to another I saw there was no mistaking the genuineness of Neave's pride in his possessions. The ripe sphere of beauty was his, and he had found no flaw in it as yet...

A year later came the amazing announcement—the Daunt collection was for sale. At first we all supposed it was a case of weeding out (though how old Daunt would have raged at the thought of anybody's weeding *his* collection!) But no—the catalogue corrected that idea. Every stick and stone was to go under the hammer. The news ran like wildfire from Rome to Berlin, from Paris to London and New York. Was Neave ruined, then? Wrong again—the dealers nosed that out in no time. He was simply selling because he chose to sell; and in due time the things came up at Christie's.

But you may be sure the trade had found an answer to the riddle; and the answer was that, on close inspection, Neave had found the collection less impeccable than he had supposed. It was a preposterous answer—but then there was no other. Neave, by this time, was pretty generally recognized as having the subtlest *flair* of any collector in Europe, and if he didn't choose to keep the Daunt collection it could be only because he had reason to think he could do better.

In a flash this report had gone the rounds and the buyers were on their guard. I had run over to London to see the thing through, and it was the queerest sale I ever was at. Some of the things held their own, but a lot—and a few of the best among them—went for half their value. You see, they'd been locked up in old Daunt's house for nearly twenty years, and hardly shown to any one, so that the whole younger generation of dealers and collectors knew of them only by hearsay. Then you know the effect of suggestion in such cases. The undefinable sense we were speaking of is a ticklish instrument, easily thrown out of gear by a sudden fall of temperature; and the sharpest experts grow shy and self-distrustful when the cold current of depreciation touches them. The sale was a slaughter—and when I saw the Daunt Diana fall at the wink of a little third-rate *brocanteur* from Vienna I turned sick at the folly of my kind.

For my part, I had never believed that Neave had sold the collection because he'd "found it out"; and within a year my incredulity was justified. As soon as the things were put in circulation they were known for the marvels they are. There was hardly a poor bit in the lot; and my wonder grew at Neave's madness. All over Europe, dealers began to be fighting for the spoils; and all kinds of stuff were palmed off on the unsuspecting as fragments of the Daunt collection!

Meanwhile, what was Neave doing? For a long time I didn't hear, and chance kept me from returning to Rome. But one day, in Paris, I ran across a dealer who had captured for a song one of the best Florentine bronzes in the Daunt collection—a marvellous *plaquette* of Donatello's. I asked him what had become of it, and he said with a grin: "I sold it the other day," naming a price that staggered me.

"Ye gods! Who paid you that for it?"

His grin broadened, and he answered: "Neave."

" *Neave?* Humphrey Neave?"

"Didn't you know he was buying back his things?"

"Nonsense!"

"He is, though. Not in his own name—but he's doing it."

And he *was*, do you know—and at prices that would have made a sane man shudder! A few weeks later I ran across his tracks in London, where he was trying to get hold of a Penicaud enamel—another of his scattered treasures. Then I hunted him down at his hotel, and had it out with him.

"Look here, Neave, what are you up to?"

He wouldn't tell me at first: stared and laughed and denied. But I took him off to dine, and after dinner, while we smoked, I happened to mention casually that I had a pull over the man who had the Penicaud—and at that he broke down and confessed.

"Yes, I'm buying them back, Finney—it's true." He laughed nervously, twitching his moustache. And then he let me have the story.

"You know how I'd hungered and thirsted for the *real thing*—you quoted my own phrase to me once, about the 'ripe sphere of beauty.' So when I got my money, and Daunt lost his, almost at the same moment, I saw the hand of Providence in it. I knew that, even if I'd been younger, and had more time, I

78

could never hope, nowadays, to form such a collection as *that*. There was the ripe sphere, within reach; and I took it. But when I got it, and began to live with it, I found out my mistake. It was a *mariage de convenance*—there'd been no wooing, no winning. Each of my little old bits—the rubbish I chucked out to make room for Daunt's glories—had its own personal history, the drama of my relation to it, of the discovery, the struggle, the capture, the first divine moment of possession. There was a romantic secret between us. And then I had absorbed its beauties one by one, they had become a part of my imagination, they held me by a hundred threads of far-reaching association. And suddenly I had expected to create this kind of intense personal tie between myself and a roomful of new cold alien presences—things staring at me vacantly from the depths of unknown pasts! Can you fancy a more preposterous hope? Why, my other things, my *own* things, had wooed me as passionately as I wooed them: there was a certain little bronze, a little Venus Callipyge, who had drawn me, drawn me, drawn me, imploring me to rescue her from her unspeakable surroundings in a vulgar bric-a-brac shop at Biarritz, where she shrank out of sight among sham Sevres and Dutch silver, as one has seen certain women— rare, shy, exquisite—made almost invisible by the vulgar splendours surrounding them. Well! that little Venus, who was just a specious seventeenth century attempt at the 'antique,' but who had penetrated me with her pleading grace, touched me by the easily guessed story of her obscure, anonymous origin, was more to me imaginatively—yes! more than the cold bought beauty of the Daunt Diana..."

"The Daunt Diana!" I broke in. "Hold up, Neave—*the Daunt Diana?*"

He smiled contemptuously. "A professional beauty, my dear fellow—expected every head to be turned when she came into a room."

"Oh, Neave," I groaned.

"Yes, I know. You're thinking of what we felt that day we first saw her in London. Many a poor devil has sold his soul as

79

the result of such a first sight! Well, I sold *her* instead. Do you want the truth about her? *Elle etait bete a pleurer.*"

He laughed, and stood up with a little shrug of disenchantment.

"And so you're impenitent?" I paused. "And yet you're buying some of the things back?"

Neave laughed again, ironically. "I knew you'd find me out and call me to account. Well, yes: I'm buying back." He stood before me half sheepish, half defiant. "I'm buying back because there's nothing else as good in the market. And because I've a queer feeling that, this time, they'll be *mine*. But I'm ruining myself at the game!" he confessed.

It was true: Neave was ruining himself. And he's gone on ruining himself ever since, till now the job's nearly done. Bit by bit, year by year, he has gathered in his scattered treasures, at higher prices than the dealers ever dreamed of getting. There are fabulous details in the story of his quest. Now and then I ran across him, and was able to help him recover a fragment; and it was wonderful to see his delight in the moment of reunion. Finally, about two years ago, we met in Paris, and he told me he had got back all the important pieces except the Diana.

"The Diana? But you told me you didn't care for her."

"Didn't care?" He leaned across the restaurant table that divided us. "Well, no, in a sense I didn't. I wanted her to want me, you see; and she didn't then! Whereas now she's crying to me to come to her. You know where she is?" he broke off.

Yes, I knew: in the centre of Mrs. Willy P. Goldmark's yellow and gold drawing room, under a thousand-candle-power chandelier, with reflectors aimed at her from every point of the compass. I had seen her wincing and shivering there in her outraged nudity at one of the Goldmark "crushes."

"But you can't get her, Neave," I objected.

"No, I can't get her," he said.

Well, last month I was in Rome, for the first time in six or seven years, and of course I looked about for Neave. The Palazzo Neave was let to some rich Russians, and the splendid new porter didn't know where the proprietor lived. But I got on

80

his trail easily enough, and it led me to a strange old place in the Trastevere, an ancient crevassed black palace turned tenement house, and fluttering with pauper clotheslines. I found Neave under the leads, in two or three cold rooms that smelt of the *cuisine* of all his neighbours: a poor shrunken little figure, seedier and shabbier than ever, yet more alive than when we had made the tour of his collection in the Palazzo Neave.

The collection was around him again, not displayed in tall cabinets and on marble tables, but huddled on shelves, perched on chairs, crammed in corners, putting the gleam of bronze, the opalescence of old glass, the pale lustre of marble, into all the angles of his low dim rooms. There they were, the proud presences that had stared at him down the vistas of Daunt House, and shone in cold transplanted beauty under his own painted cornices: there they were, gathered in humble promiscuity about his bent shabby figure, like superb wild creatures tamed to become the familiars of some harmless old wizard.

As we went from bit to bit, as he lifted one piece after another, and held it to the light of his low windows, I saw in his hands the same tremor of sensation that I had noticed when he first examined the same objects at Daunt House. All his life was in his fingertips, and it seemed to communicate life to the exquisite things he touched. But you'll think me infected by his mysticism if I tell you they gained new beauty while he held them...

We went the rounds slowly and reverently; and then, when I supposed our inspection was over, and was turning to take my leave, he opened a door I had not noticed, and showed me into a slit of a room beyond. It was a mere monastic cell, scarcely large enough for his narrow iron bed and the chest which probably held his few clothes; but there, in a niche of the bare wall, facing the foot of the bed—there stood the Daunt Diana.

I gasped at the sight and turned to him; and he looked back at me without speaking.

"In the name of magic, Neave, how did you do it?"

He smiled as if from the depths of some secret rapture. "Call it magic, if you like; but I ruined myself doing it," he said.

I stared at him in silence, breathless with the madness and the wonder of it; and suddenly, red to the ears, he flung out his boyish confession. "I lied to you that day in London—the day I said I didn't care for her. I always cared—always worshipped—always wanted her. But she wasn't mine then, and I knew it, and she knew it...and now at last we understand each other." He looked at me shyly, and then glanced about the bare cold cell. "The setting isn't worthy of her, I know; she was meant for glories I can't give her; but beautiful things, my dear Finney, like beautiful spirits, live in houses not made with hands..."

His face shone with extraordinary sweetness as he spoke; and I saw he'd got hold of the secret we're all after. No, the setting isn't worthy of her, if you like. The rooms are as shabby and mean as those we used to see him in years ago over the wine shop. I'm not sure they're not shabbier and meaner. But she rules there at last, she shines and hovers there above him, and there at night, I doubt not, steals down from her cloud to give him the Latmian kiss.

THE DEBT

I

You remember—it's not so long ago—the talk there was about Dredge's "Arrival of the Fittest"? The talk has subsided, but the book of course remains: stands up, in fact, as the tallest thing of its kind since—well, I'd almost said since "The Origin of Species."

I'm not wrong, at any rate, in calling it the most important contribution yet made to the development of the Darwinian theory, or rather to the solution of the awkward problem about which that theory has had to make such a circuit. Dredge's hypothesis will be contested, may one day be disproved; but at least it has swept out of the way all previous conjectures, including of course Lanfear's magnificent attempt; and for our generation of scientific investigators it will serve as the first safe bridge across a murderous black whirlpool.

It's all very interesting—there are few things more stirring to the imagination than that sudden projection of the new hypothesis, light as a cobweb and strong as steel, across the intellectual abyss; but, for an idle observer of human motives, the other, the personal, side of Dredge's case is even more interesting and arresting.

Personal side? You didn't know there was one? Pictured him simply as a thinking machine, a highly specialized instrument of precision, the result of a long series of "adaptations," as his own jargon would put it? Well, I don't wonder—if you've met him. He does give the impression of being something out of his own laboratory: a delicate scientific instrument that reveals wonders to the initiated, and is absolutely useless in an ordinary hand.

In his youth it was just the other way. I knew him twenty years ago, as an awkward lout whom young Archie Lanfear had picked up at college, and brought home for a visit. I happened to be staying at the Lanfears' when the boys arrived, and I shall never forget Dredge's first appearance on the scene. You know the Lanfears always lived very simply. That summer they had gone to Buzzard's Bay, in order that Professor Lanfear might be near the Biological Station at Wood's Holl, and they were picnicking in a kind of sketchy bungalow without any attempt at elegance. But Galen Dredge couldn't have been more awestruck if he'd been suddenly plunged into a Fifth Avenue ballroom. He nearly knocked his shock head against the low doorway, and in dodging this peril trod heavily on Mabel Lanfear's foot, and became hopelessly entangled in her mother's draperies—though how he managed it I never knew, for Mrs. Lanfear's dowdy muslins ran to no excess of train.

When the Professor himself came in it was ten times worse, and I saw then that Dredge's emotion was a tribute to the great man's proximity. That made the boy interesting, and I began to watch. Archie, always enthusiastic but vague, had said: "Oh, he's a tremendous chap—you'll see—" but I hadn't expected to see quite so clearly. Lanfear's vision, of course, was sharper than mine; and the next morning he had carried Dredge off to the Biological Station. And that was the way it began.

Dredge is the son of a Baptist minister. He comes from East Lethe, New York State, and was working his way through college—waiting at White Mountain hotels in summer—when Archie Lanfear ran across him. There were eight children in the family, and the mother was an invalid. Dredge never had a penny from his father after he was fourteen; but his mother wanted him to be a scholar, and "kept at him," as he put it, in the hope of his going back to "teach school" at East Lethe. He developed slowly, as the scientific mind generally does, and was still adrift about himself and his tendencies when Archie took him down to Buzzard's Bay. But he had read Lanfear's "Utility and Variation," and had always been a patient and curious observer of nature. And his first meeting with Lanfear explained him to himself. It didn't, however, enable him to explain himself to others, and for a long time he remained, to all but Lanfear, an object of incredulity and conjecture.

84

"*Why* my husband wants him about—" poor Mrs. Lanfear, the kindest of women, privately lamented to her friends; for Dredge, at that time—they kept him all summer at the bungalow—had one of the most encumbering personalities you can imagine. He was as inexpressive as he is today, and yet oddly obtrusive: one of those uncomfortable presences whose silence is an interruption.

The poor Lanfears almost died of him that summer, and the pity of it was that he never suspected it, but continued to lavish on them a floundering devotion as uncomfortable as the endearments of a dripping dog—all out of gratitude for the Professor's kindness! He was full, in those days, of raw enthusiasms, which he forced on any one who would listen when his first shyness had worn off. You can't picture him spouting sentimental poetry, can you? Yet I've seen him petrify a whole group of Mrs. Lanfear's callers by suddenly discharging on them, in the strident drawl of Western New York, "Barbara Frietchie" or "The Queen of the May." His taste in literature was uniformly bad, but very definite, and far more assertive than his views on biological questions. In his scientific judgments he showed, even then, a remarkable temperance, a precocious openness to the opposite view; but in literature he was a furious propagandist, aggressive, disputatious, and extremely sensitive to adverse opinion.

Lanfear, of course, had been struck from the first by his gift of accurate observation, and by the fact that his eagerness to learn was offset by his reluctance to conclude. I remember Lanfear's telling me that he had never known a lad of Dredge's age who gave such promise of uniting an aptitude for general ideas with the plodding patience of the accumulator of facts. Of course when Lanfear talked like that of a young biologist his fate was sealed. There could be no question of Dredge's going back to "teach school" at East Lethe. He must take a course in biology at Columbia, spend his vacations at the Wood's Holl laboratory, and then, if possible, go to Germany for a year or two.

All this meant his virtual adoption by the Lanfears. Most of Lanfear's fortune went in helping young students to a start, and he devoted his heaviest subsidies to Dredge.

"Dredge will be my biggest dividend—you'll see!" he used to say, in the chrysalis days when poor Galen was known to the world of science only as a perpetual slouching presence in Mrs. Lanfear's drawing room. And Dredge, it must be said, took his obligations simply, with that kind of personal dignity, and quiet sense of his own worth, which in such cases saves the beneficiary from abjectness. He seemed to trust himself as fully as Lanfear trusted him.

The comic part of it was that his only idea of making what is known as "a return" was to devote himself to the Professor's family. When I hear pretty women lamenting that they can't coax Professor Dredge out of his laboratory I remember Mabel Lanfear's cry to me: "If Galen would only keep away!" When Mabel fell on the ice and broke her leg, Galen walked seven miles in a blizzard to get a surgeon; but if he did her this service one day in the year, he bored her by being in the way for the other three hundred and sixty-four. One would have imagined at that time that he thought his perpetual presence the greatest gift he could bestow; for, except on the occasion of his fetching the surgeon, I don't remember his taking any other way of expressing his gratitude.

In love with Mabel? Not a bit! But the queer thing was that he *did* have a passion in those days—a blind, hopeless passion for Mrs. Lanfear! Yes: I know what I'm saying. I mean Mrs. Lanfear, the Professor's wife, poor Mrs. Lanfear, with her tight hair and her loose figure, her blameless brow and earnest eyeglasses, and her perpetual attitude of mild misapprehension. I can see Dredge cowering, long and many-jointed, in a diminutive drawing room chair, one square-toed shoe coiled round an exposed ankle, his knees clasped in a knot of red knuckles, and his spectacles perpetually seeking Mrs. Lanfear's eyeglasses. I never knew if the poor lady was aware of the sentiment she inspired, but her children observed it, and it provoked them to

86

irreverent mirth. Galen was the predestined butt of Mabel and Archie; and secure in their mother's virtuous obtuseness, and in her worshipper's timidity, they allowed themselves a latitude of banter that sometimes turned their audience cold. Dredge meanwhile was going on obstinately with his work. Now and then he had queer fits of idleness, when he lapsed into a state of sulky inertia from which even Lanfear's admonitions could not rouse him. Once, just before an examination, he suddenly went off to the Maine woods for two weeks, came back, and failed to pass. I don't know if his benefactor ever lost hope; but at times his confidence must have been sorely strained. The queer part of it was that when Dredge emerged from these eclipses he seemed keener and more active than ever. His slowly growing intelligence probably needed its periodical pauses of assimilation; and Lanfear was marvellously patient.

At last Dredge finished his course and went to Germany; and when he came back he was a new man—was, in fact, the Dredge we all know. He seemed to have shed his blundering, encumbering personality, and come to life as a disembodied intelligence. His fidelity to the Lanfears was unchanged; but he showed it negatively, by his discretions and abstentions. I have an idea that Mabel was less disposed to deride him, might even have been induced to softer sentiments; but I doubt if Dredge even noticed the change. As for his ex-goddess, he seemed to regard her as a motherly household divinity, the guardian genius of the darning needle; but on Professor Lanfear he looked with a deepening reverence. If the rest of the family had diminished in his eyes, its head had grown even greater.

II

From that day Dredge's progress continued steadily. If not always perceptible to the untrained eye, in Lanfear's sight it never deviated, and the great man began to associate Dredge with his work, and to lean on him more and more. Lanfear's health was already failing, and in my confidential talks with him I saw how he counted on Galen Dredge to continue and amplify his doctrine. If he did not describe the young man as his predestined Huxley, it was because any such comparison between himself and his great predecessors would have been repugnant to his taste; but he evidently felt that it would be Dredge's role to reveal him to posterity. And the young man seemed at that time to take the same view of his calling. When he was not busy about Lanfear's work he was recording their conversations with the diligence of a biographer and the accuracy of a naturalist. Any attempt to question or minimize Lanfear's theories roused in his disciple the only flashes of wrath I have ever seen a scientific discussion provoke in him. In defending his master he became almost as intemperate as in the early period of his literary passions.

Such filial dedication must have been all the more precious to Lanfear because, about that time, it became evident that Archie would never carry on his father's work. He had begun brilliantly, you may remember, by a little paper on *Limulus Polyphemus* that attracted a good deal of notice when it appeared in the *Central Blatt*; but gradually his zoological ardour yielded to an absorbing passion for the violin, which was followed by a sudden plunge into physics. At present, after a sideglance at the drama, I understand he's devoting what is left of his father's money to archaeological explorations in Asia Minor.

"Archie's got a delightful little mind," Lanfear used to say to me, rather wistfully, "but it's just a highly polished surface held up to the show as it passes. Dredge's mind takes in only a bit at a time, but the bit stays, and other bits are joined to it, in a hard mosaic of fact, of which imagination weaves the pattern. I saw just how it would be years ago, when my boy used to take my meaning in a flash, and answer me with clever objections, while Galen disappeared into one of his fathomless silences, and then came to the surface like a dripping retriever, a long way beyond Archie's objections, and with an answer to them in his mouth."

It was about this time that the crowning satisfaction of Lanfear's career came to him: I mean, of course, John Weyman's gift to Columbia of the Lanfear Laboratory, and the founding, in connection with it, of a chair of Experimental Evolution. Weyman had always taken an interest in Lanfear's work, but no one had supposed that his interest would express itself so magnificently. The honour came to Lanfear at a time when he was fighting an accumulation of troubles: failing health, the money difficulties resulting from his irrepressible generosity, his disappointment about Archie's career, and perhaps also the persistent attacks of the new school of German zoologists.

"If I hadn't Galen I should feel the game was up," he said to me once, in a fit of half-real, half-mocking despondency. "But he'll do what I haven't time to do myself, and what my boy can't do for me."

That meant that he would answer the critics, and triumphantly affirm Lanfear's theory, which had been rudely shaken, but not displaced.

"A scientific hypothesis lasts till there's something else to put in its place. People who want to get across a river will use the old bridge till the new one's built. And I don't see any one who's particularly anxious, in this case, to take a contract for the new one," Lanfear ended; and I remember answering with a laugh: "Not while Horatius Dredge holds the other."

It was generally known that Lanfear had not long to live, and the Laboratory was hardly opened before the question of his successor in the chair of Experimental Evolution began to be a matter of public discussion. It was conceded that whoever followed him ought to be a man of achieved reputation, some one carrying, as the French say, a considerable "baggage." At the same time, even Lanfear's critics felt that he should be succeeded by a man who held his views and would continue his teaching. This was not in itself a difficulty, for German criticism had so far been mainly negative, and there were plenty of good men who, while they questioned the permanent validity of Lanfear's conclusions, were yet ready to accept them for their provisional usefulness. And then there was the added inducement of the Laboratory! The Columbia Professor of Experimental Evolution has at his disposal the most complete instrument of biological research that modern ingenuity has yet produced; and it's not only in theology or politics *que Paris vaut bien une messe!* There was no trouble about finding a candidate; but the whole thing turned on Lanfear's decision, since it was tacitly understood that, by Weyman's wish, he was to select his successor. And what a cry there was when he selected Galen Dredge!

Not in the scientific world, though. The specialists were beginning to know about Dredge. His remarkable paper on Sexual Dimorphism had been translated into several languages, and a furious polemic had broken out over it. When a young fellow can get the big men fighting over him his future is pretty well assured. But Dredge was only thirty-four, and some people seemed to feel that there was a kind of deflected nepotism in Lanfear's choice.

"If he could choose Dredge he might as well have chosen his own son," I've heard it said; and the irony was that Archie—will you believe it?—actually thought so himself! But Lanfear had Weyman behind him, and when the end came the Faculty at once appointed Galen Dredge to the chair of Experimental Evolution.

For the first two years things went quietly, along accustomed lines. Dredge simply continued the course that Lanfear's death had interrupted. He lectured well even then, with a persuasive simplicity surprising in the slow, inarticulate creature one knew him for. But haven't you noticed that certain personalities reveal themselves only in the more impersonal relations of life? It's as if they woke only to collective contacts, and the single consciousness were an unmeaning fragment to them.

If there was anything to criticize in that first part of the course, it was the avoidance of general ideas, of those brilliant rockets of conjecture that Lanfear's students were used to seeing him fling across the darkness. I remember once saying this to Archie, who, having recovered from his absurd disappointment had returned to his old allegiance to Dredge.

90

"Oh, that's Galen all over. He doesn't want to jump into the ring till he has a big swishing knockdown argument in his fist. He'll wait twenty years if he has to. That's his strength: he's never afraid to wait."

I thought this shrewd of Archie, as well as generous; and I saw the wisdom of Dredge's course. As Lanfear himself had said, his theory was safe enough till somebody found a more attractive one; and before that day Dredge would probably have accumulated sufficient proof to crystallize the fluid hypothesis.

III

The third winter I was off collecting in Central America, and didn't get back till Dredge's course had been going for a couple of months. The very day I turned up in town Archie Lanfear descended on me with a summons from his mother. I was wanted at once at a family council.

I found the Lanfear ladies in a state of incoherent distress, which Archie's own indignation hardly made more intelligible. But gradually I put together their fragmentary charges, and learned that Dredge's lectures were turning into an organized assault on his master's doctrine.

"It amounts to just this," Archie said, controlling his women with the masterful gesture of the weak man. "Galen has simply turned round and betrayed my father."

"Just for a handful of silver he left us," Mabel sobbed in parenthesis, while Mrs. Lanfear tearfully cited Hamlet.

Archie silenced them again. "The ugly part of it is that he must have had this up his sleeve for years. He must have known when he was asked to succeed my father what use he meant to make of his opportunity. What he's doing isn't the result of a hasty conclusion: it means years of work and preparation."

Archie broke off to explain himself. He had returned from Europe the week before, and had learned on arriving that Dredge's lectures were stirring the world of science as nothing had stirred it since Lanfear's "Utility and Variation." And the incredible outrage was that they owed their sensational effect to the fact of being an attempted refutation of Lanfear's great work.

I own that I was staggered: the case looked ugly, as Archie said. And there was a veil of reticence, of secrecy, about Dredge, that always kept his conduct in a half-light of uncertainty. Of some men one would have said offhand: "It's impossible!" But one couldn't affirm it of him.

Archie hadn't seen him as yet; and Mrs. Lanfear had sent for me because she wished me to be present at the interview between the two men. The Lanfear ladies had a touching belief in Archie's violence: they thought him as terrible as a natural force. My own idea was that if there were any broken bones they wouldn't be Dredge's; but I was too curious as to the outcome not to be glad to offer my services as moderator.

First, however, I wanted to hear one of the lectures; and I went the next afternoon. The hall was jammed, and I saw, as soon as Dredge appeared, what increased security and ease the interest of his public had given him. He had been clear the year before, now he was also eloquent. The lecture was a remarkable effort: you'll find the gist of it in Chapter VII of "The Arrival of the Fittest." Archie sat at my side in a white rage; he was too clever not to measure the extent of the disaster. And I was almost as indignant as he when we went to see Dredge the next day.

I saw at a glance that the latter suspected nothing; and it was characteristic of him that he began by questioning me about my finds, and only afterward turned to reproach Archie for having been back a week without notifying him.

"You know I'm up to my neck in this job. Why in the world didn't you hunt me up before this?"

The question was exasperating, and I could understand Archie's stammer of wrath.

"Hunt you up? Hunt you up? What the deuce are you made of, to ask me such a question instead of wondering why I'm here now?"

Dredge bent his slow calm scrutiny on his friend's quivering face; then he turned to me.

92

"What's the matter?" he said simply.

"The matter?" shrieked Archie, his clenched fist hovering excitedly above the desk by which he stood; but Dredge, with unwonted quickness, caught the fist as it descended.

"Careful—I've got a *Kallima* in that jar there." He pushed a chair forward, and added quietly: "Sit down."

Archie, ignoring the gesture, towered pale and avenging in his place; and Dredge, after a moment, took the chair himself.

"The matter?" Archie reiterated with rising passion. "Are you so lost to all sense of decency and honour that you can put that question in good faith? Don't you really *know* what's the matter?"

Dredge smiled slowly. "There are so few things one *really knows.*"

"Oh, damn your scientific hairsplitting! Don't you know you're insulting my father's memory?"

Dredge stared again, turning his spectacles thoughtfully from one of us to the other.

"Oh, that's it, is it? Then you'd better sit down. If you don't see at once it'll take some time to make you."

Archie burst into an ironic laugh.

"I rather think it will!" he conceded.

"Sit down, Archie," I said, setting the example; and he obeyed, with a gesture that made his consent a protest.

Dredge seemed to notice nothing beyond the fact that his visitors were seated. He reached for his pipe, and filled it with the care which the habit of delicate manipulations gave to all the motions of his long, knotty hands.

"It's about the lectures?" he said.

Archie's answer was a deep scornful breath.

"You've only been back a week, so you've only heard one, I suppose?"

"It was not necessary to hear even that one. You must know the talk they're making. If notoriety is what you're after—"

"Well, I'm not sorry to make a noise," said Dredge, putting a match to his pipe.

Archie bounded in his chair. "There's no easier way of doing it than to attack a man who can't answer you!"

Dredge raised a sobering hand. "Hold on. Perhaps you and I don't mean the same thing. Tell me first what's in your mind."

The request steadied Archie, who turned on Dredge a countenance really eloquent with filial indignation.

"It's an odd question for you to ask; it makes me wonder what's in yours. Not much thought of my father, at any rate, or you couldn't stand in his place and use the chance he's given you to push yourself at his expense."

Dredge received this in silence, puffing slowly at his pipe.

"Is that the way it strikes you?" he asked at length.

"God! It's the way it would strike most men."

He turned to me. "You too?"

"I can see how Archie feels," I said.

"That I'm attacking his father's memory to glorify myself?"

"Well, not precisely: I think what he really feels is that, if your convictions didn't permit you to continue his father's teaching, you might perhaps have done better to sever your connection with the Lanfear lectureship."

"Then you and he regard the Lanfear lectureship as having been founded to perpetuate a dogma, not to try and get at the truth?"

"Certainly not," Archie broke in. "But there's a question of taste, of delicacy, involved in the case that can't be decided on abstract principles. We know as well as you that my father meant the laboratory and the lectureship to serve the ends of science, at whatever cost to his own special convictions; what we feel—and you don't seem to—is that you're the last man to put them to that use; and I don't want to remind you why."

A slight redness rose through Dredge's sallow skin. "You needn't," he said. "It's because he pulled me out of my hole, woke me up, made me, shoved me off from the shore. Because he saved me ten or twenty years of muddled effort, and put me where I am at an age when my best working years are still ahead of me. Every one knows that's what your father did for me, but

94

I'm the only person who knows the time and trouble that it took."

It was well said, and I glanced quickly at Archie, who was never closed to generous emotions.

"Well, then—?" he said, flushing also.

"Well, then," Dredge continued, his voice deepening and losing its nasal edge, "I had to pay him back, didn't I?"

The sudden drop flung Archie back on his prepared attitude of irony. "It would be the natural inference—with most men."

"Just so. And I'm not so very different. I knew your father wanted a successor—some one who'd try and tie up the loose ends. And I took the lectureship with that object."

"And you're using it to tear the whole fabric to pieces!"

Dredge paused to relight his pipe. "Looks that way," he conceded. "This year anyhow."

" *This year*—?" Archie gasped at him.

"Yes. When I took up the job I saw it just as your father left it. Or rather, I didn't see any other way of going on with it. The change came gradually, as I worked."

"Gradually? So that you had time to look round you, to know where you were, to see you were fatally committed to undoing the work he had done?"

"Oh, yes—I had time," Dredge conceded.

"And yet you kept the chair and went on with the course?"

Dredge refilled his pipe, and then turned in his seat so that he looked squarely at Archie.

"What would your father have done in my place?" he asked.

"In your place—?"

"Yes: supposing he'd found out the things I've found out in the last year or two. You'll see what they are, and how much they count, if you'll run over the report of the lectures. If your father'd been alive he might have come across the same facts just as easily."

There was a silence that Archie at last broke by saying: "But he didn't, and you did. There's the difference."

"The difference? What difference? Would your father have suppressed the facts if he'd found them? It's *you* who insult his

95

memory by implying it! And if I'd brought them to him, would he have used his hold over me to get me to suppress them?"

"Certainly not. But can't you see it's his death that makes the difference? He's not here to defend his case."

Dredge laughed, but not unkindly. "My dear Archie, your father wasn't one of the kind who bother to defend their case. Men like him are the masters, not the servants, of their theories. They respect an idea only as long as it's of use to them; when it's usefulness ends they chuck it out. And that's what your father would have done."

Archie reddened. "Don't you assume a good deal in taking it for granted that he would have had to in this particular case?"

Dredge reflected. "Yes: I was going too far. Each of us can only answer for himself. But to my mind your father's theory is refuted."

"And you don't hesitate to be the man to do it?"

"Should I have been of any use if I had? And did your father ever ask anything of me but to be of as much use as I could?"

It was Archie's turn to reflect. "No. That was what he always wanted, of course."

"That's the way I've always felt. The first day he took me away from East Lethe I knew the debt I was piling up against him, and I never had any doubt as to how I'd pay it, or how he'd want it paid. He didn't pick me out and train me for any object but to carry on the light. Do you suppose he'd have wanted me to snuff it out because it happened to light up a fact he didn't fancy? I'm using *his* oil to feed my torch with: yes, but it isn't really his torch or mine, or his oil or mine: they belong to each of us till we drop and hand them on."

Archie turned a sobered glance on him. "I see your point. But if the job had to be done I don't see that you need have done it from his chair."

"There's where we differ. If I did it at all I had to do it in the best way, and with all the authority his backing gave me. If I owe your father anything, I owe him that. It would have made him sick to see the job badly done. And don't you see that the way to honour him, and show what he's done for science, was to spare no

96

advantage in my attack on him—that I'm proving the strength of his position by the desperateness of my assault?" Dredge paused and squared his lounging shoulders. "After all," he added, "he's not down yet, and if I leave him standing I guess it'll be some time before anybody else cares to tackle him."

There was a silence between the two men; then Dredge continued in a lighter tone: "There's one thing, though, that we're both in danger of forgetting: and that is how little, in the long run, it all counts either way." He smiled a little at Archie's outraged gesture. "The most we can any of us do—even by such a magnificent effort as your father's—is to turn the great marching army a hair's breadth nearer what seems to us the right direction; if one of us drops out, here and there, the loss of headway's hardly perceptible. And that's what I'm coming to now."

He rose from his seat, and walked across to the hearth; then, cautiously resting his shoulder blades against the mantel shelf jammed with miscellaneous specimens, he bent his musing spectacles on Archie.

"Your father would have understood why I've done, what I'm doing; but that's no reason why the rest of you should. And I rather think it's the rest of you who've suffered most from me. He always knew what I was *there for*, and that must have been some comfort even when I was most in the way; but I was just an ordinary nuisance to you and your mother and Mabel. You were all too kind to let me see it at the time, but I've seen it since, and it makes me feel that, after all, the settling of this matter lies with you. If it hurts you to have me go on with my examination of your father's theory, I'm ready to drop the lectures tomorrow, and trust to the Lanfear Laboratory to breed up a young chap who'll knock us both out in time. You've only got to say the word."

There was a pause while Dredge turned and laid his extinguished pipe carefully between a jar of embryo sea urchins and a colony of regenerating planarians.

Then Archie rose and held out his hand.

"No," he said simply; "go on."

FULL CIRCLE

I

Geoffrey Betton woke rather late—so late that the winter sunlight sliding across his warm red carpet struck his eyes as he turned on the pillow.

Strett, the valet, had been in, drawn the bath in the adjoining dressing room, placed the crystal and silver cigarette box at his side, put a match to the fire, and thrown open the windows to the bright morning air. It brought in, on the glitter of sun, all the shrill crisp morning noises—those piercing notes of the American thoroughfare that seem to take a sharper vibration from the clearness of the medium through which they pass.

Betton raised himself languidly. That was the voice of Fifth Avenue below his windows. He remembered that when he moved into his rooms eighteen months before, the sound had been like music to him: the complex orchestration to which the tune of his new life was set. Now it filled him with horror and weariness, since it had become the symbol of the hurry and noise of that new life. He had been far less hurried in the old days when he had to be up by seven, and down at the office sharp at nine. Now that he got up when he chose, and his life had no fixed framework of duties, the hours hunted him like a pack of bloodhounds.

He dropped back on his pillows with a groan. Yes—not a year ago there had been a positively sensuous joy in getting out of bed, feeling under his bare feet the softness of the sunlit carpet, and entering the shining tiled sanctuary where his great porcelain bath proffered its renovating flood. But then a year ago he could still call up the horror of the communal plunge at his earlier lodgings: the listening for other bathers, the dodging of shrouded ladies in "crimping" pins, the cold wait on the landing, the reluctant descent into a blotchy tin bath, and the effort to identify one's soap and nail brush among the promiscuous implements of ablution. That memory had faded now, and Betton saw only the dark hours to which his blue and white temple of refreshment formed a kind of glittering antechamber. For after his bath came his breakfast, and on the breakfast tray his letters. His letters!

He remembered—and *that* memory had not faded!—the thrill with which he had opened the first missive in a strange feminine hand: the letter beginning: "I wonder if you'll mind an unknown reader's telling you all that your book has been to her?"

Mind? Ye gods, he minded now! For more than a year after the publication of "Diadems and Faggots" the letters, the inane indiscriminate letters of condemnation, of criticism, of interrogation, had poured in on him by every post. Hundreds of unknown readers had told him with unsparing detail all that his book had been to them. And the wonder of it was, when all was said and done, that it had really been so little—that when their thick broth of praise was strained through the author's anxious vanity there remained to him so small a sediment of definite specific understanding! No—it was always the same thing, over and over and over again—the same vague gush of adjectives, the same incorrigible tendency to estimate his effort according to each writer's personal preferences, instead of regarding it as a work of art, a thing to be measured by objective standards!

He smiled to think how little, at first, he had felt the vanity of it all. He had found a savor even in the grosser evidences of popularity: the advertisements of his book, the daily shower of "clippings," the sense that, when he entered a restaurant or a theatre, people nudged each other and said "That's Betton." Yes, the publicity had been sweet to him—at first. He had been touched by the sympathy of his fellow men: had thought indulgently of the world, as a better place than the failures and the dyspeptics would acknowledge. And then his success began to submerge him: he gasped under the thickening shower of letters. His admirers were really unappeasable. And they wanted him to do such preposterous things—to give lectures, to head movements, to be tendered receptions, to speak at banquets, to address mothers, to plead for orphans, to go up in balloons, to lead the struggle for sterilized milk. They wanted his photograph for literary supplements, his autograph for charity bazaars, his name on committees, literary, educational, and social; above all, they wanted his opinion on everything: on Christianity, Buddhism, tight lacing, the drug habit, democratic government, female suffrage and love. Perhaps the chief benefit of this demand was his incidentally learning from it how few opinions he really had: the only one that remained with him was a rooted horror of all forms of correspondence. He had been unutterably thankful when the letters began to fall off.

"Diadems and Faggots" was now two years old, and the moment was at hand when its author might have counted on regaining the blessed shelter of oblivion—if only he had not written another book! For it was the worst part of his plight that his first success had goaded him to the perpetration of this particular folly—that one of the incentives (hideous thought!) to his new work had been the desire to extend and perpetuate his popularity. And this very week the book was to come out, and the letters, the cursed letters, would begin again!

Wistfully, almost plaintively, he contemplated the breakfast tray with which Strett presently appeared. It bore only two notes and the morning journals, but he knew that within the week it would groan under its epistolary burden. The very newspapers flung the fact at him as he opened them.

READY ON MONDAY.

GEOFFREY BETTON'S NEW NOVEL

ABUNDANCE.

BY THE AUTHOR OF DIADEMS AND FAGGOTS.

FIRST EDITION OF ONE HUNDRED AND FIFTY THOUSAND ALREADY SOLD OUT.

ORDER NOW.

A hundred and fifty thousand volumes! And an average of three readers to each! Half a million of people would be reading him within a week, and every one of them would write to him, and their friends and relations would write too. He laid down the paper with a shudder.

The two notes looked harmless enough, and the calligraphy of one was vaguely familiar. He opened the envelope and looked at the signature: *Duncan Vyse*. He had not seen the name in years—what on earth could Duncan Vyse have to say? He ran over the page and dropped it with a wondering exclamation, which the watchful Strett, re-entering, met by a tentative "Yes, sir?"

"Nothing. Yes—that is—" Betton picked up the note. "There's a gentleman, a Mr. Vyse, coming to see me at ten."

Strett glanced at the clock. "Yes, sir. You'll remember that ten was the hour you appointed for the secretaries to call, sir."

Betton nodded. "I'll see Mr. Vyse first. My clothes, please."

As he got into them, in the state of irritable hurry that had become almost chronic with him, he continued to think about Duncan Vyse. They had seen a lot of each other for the few years after both had left Harvard: the hard happy years when Betton had been grinding at his business and Vyse—poor devil!—trying to write. The novelist recalled his friend's attempts with a smile; then the memory of one small volume came back to him. It was a novel: "The Lifted Lamp." There was stuff in that, certainly. He remembered Vyse's tossing it down on his table with a gesture of despair when it came back from the last publisher. Betton, taking it up indifferently, had sat riveted till daylight. When he ended, the impression was so strong that he said to himself: "I'll tell Apthorn about it—I'll go and see him tomorrow." His own secret literary yearnings gave him a passionate desire to champion Vyse, to see him triumph over the ignorance and timidity of the publishers. Apthorn was the youngest of the guild, still capable of opinions and the courage of them, a personal friend of Betton's, and, as it happened, the man afterward to become known as the privileged publisher of "Diadems and Faggots." Unluckily the next day something unexpected turned up, and Betton forgot about Vyse and his manuscript. He continued to forget for a month, and then came a note from Vyse, who was ill, and wrote to ask what his friend had done. Betton did not like to say "I've done nothing," so he left the note unanswered, and vowed again: "I'll see Apthorn."

The following day he was called to the West on business, and was gone a month. When he came back, there was another note from Vyse, who was still ill, and desperately hard up. "I'll take anything for the book, if they'll advance me two hundred dollars." Betton, full of compunction, would gladly have advanced the sum himself; but he was hard up too, and could only swear inwardly: "I'll write to Apthorn." Then he glanced again at the manuscript, and reflected: "No—there are things in it that need explaining. I'd better see him."

Once he went so far as to telephone Apthorn, but the publisher was out. Then he finally and completely forgot.

One Sunday he went out of town, and on his return, rummaging among the papers on his desk, he missed "The Lifted Lamp," which had been gathering dust there for half a year. What the deuce could have become of it? Betton spent a feverish hour in vainly increasing the disorder of his documents, and then bethought himself of calling the maid servant, who first indignantly denied having touched anything ("I can see that's true from the dust," Betton scathingly interjected), and then mentioned with hauteur that a young lady had called in his absence and asked to be allowed to get a book.

"A lady? Did you let her come up?"

"She said somebody'd sent her."

Vyse, of course—Vyse had sent her for his manuscript! He was always mixed up with some woman, and it was just like him to send the girl of the moment to Betton's lodgings, with instructions to force the door in his absence. Vyse had never been remarkable for delicacy. Betton, furious, glanced over his table to see if any of his own effects were missing—one couldn't tell, with the company Vyse kept!—and then dismissed the matter from his mind, with a vague sense of magnanimity in doing so. He felt himself exonerated by Vyse's conduct.

The sense of magnanimity was still uppermost when the valet opened the door to announce "Mr. Vyse," and Betton, a moment later, crossed the threshold of his pleasant library.

His first thought was that the man facing him from the hearthrug was the very Duncan Vyse of old: small, starved, bleached-looking, with the same sidelong movements, the same queer air of anaemic truculence. Only he had grown shabbier, and bald.

Betton held out a hospitable hand.

"This is a good surprise! Glad you looked me up, my dear fellow."

Vyse's palm was damp and bony: he had always had a disagreeable hand.

"You got my note? You know what I've come for?" he said.

"About the secretaryship? (Sit down.) Is that really serious?"

Betton lowered himself luxuriously into one of his vast Maple armchairs. He had grown stouter in the last year, and the cushion behind him fitted comfortably into the crease of his nape. As he leaned back he caught sight of his image in the mirror between the windows, and reflected uneasily that Vyse would not find *him* unchanged.

"Serious?" Vyse rejoined. "Why not? Aren't *you?*"

"Oh, perfectly." Betton laughed apologetically. "Only— well, the fact is, you may not understand what rubbish a secretary of mine would have to deal with. In advertising for one I never imagined—I didn't aspire to any one above the ordinary hack."

"I'm the ordinary hack," said Vyse drily.

Betton's affable gesture protested. "My dear fellow—. You see it's not business—what I'm in now," he continued with a laugh.

Vyse's thin lips seemed to form a noiseless " *Isn't* it?" which they instantly transposed into the audibly reply: "I inferred from your advertisement that you want some one to relieve you in your literary work. Dictation, shorthand—that kind of thing?"

"Well, no: not that either. I type my own things. What I'm looking for is somebody who won't be above tackling my correspondence."

Vyse looked slightly surprised. "I should be glad of the job," he then said.

Betton began to feel a vague embarrassment. He had supposed that such a proposal would be instantly rejected. "It would be only for an hour or two a day—if you're doing any writing of your own?" he threw out interrogatively.

"No. I've given all that up. I'm in an office now—business. But it doesn't take all my time, or pay enough to keep me alive."

"In that case, my dear fellow—if you could come every morning; but it's mostly awful bosh, you know," Betton again broke off, with growing awkwardness.

Vyse glanced at him humorously. "What you want me to write?"

"Well, that depends—" Betton sketched the obligatory smile. "But I was thinking of the letters you'll have to answer. Letters about my books, you know—I've another one appearing next week. And I want to be beforehand now—dam the flood before it swamps me. Have you any idea of the deluge of stuff that people write to a successful novelist?"

As Betton spoke, he saw a tinge of red on Vyse's thin cheek, and his own reflected it in a richer glow of shame. "I mean—I mean—" he stammered helplessly.

"No, I haven't," said Vyse; "but it will be awfully jolly finding out."

There was a pause, groping and desperate on Betton's part, sardonically calm on his visitor's.

"You—you've given up writing altogether?" Betton continued.

"Yes; we've changed places, as it were." Vyse paused. "But about these letters—you dictate the answers?"

"Lord, no! That's the reason why I said I wanted somebody—er—well used to writing. I don't want to have anything to do with them—not a thing! You'll have to answer them as if they were written to *you*—" Betton pulled himself up again, and rising in confusion jerked open one of the drawers of his writing table.

"Here—this kind of rubbish," he said, tossing a packet of letters onto Vyse's knee.

"Oh—you keep them, do you?" said Vyse simply.

"I—well—some of them; a few of the funniest only."

Vyse slipped off the band and began to open the letters. While he was glancing over them Betton again caught his own reflection in the glass, and asked himself what impression he had made on his visitor. It occurred to him for the first time that his high-colored well-fed person presented the image of commercial rather than of intellectual achievement. He did not look like his own idea of the author of "Diadems and Faggots"—and he wondered why.

Vyse laid the letters aside. "I think I can do it—if you'll give me a notion of the tone I'm to take."

"The tone?"

"Yes—that is, if I'm to sign your name."

"Oh, of course: I expect you to sign for me. As for the tone, say just what you'd—well, say all you can without encouraging them to answer."

Vyse rose from his seat. "I could submit a few specimens," he suggested.

"Oh, as to that—you always wrote better than I do," said Betton handsomely.

"I've never had this kind of thing to write. When do you wish me to begin?" Vyse enquired, ignoring the tribute.

"The book's out on Monday. The deluge will begin about three days after. Will you turn up on Thursday at this hour?" Betton held his hand out with real heartiness. "It was great luck for me, your striking that advertisement. Don't be too harsh with my correspondents—I owe them something for having brought us together."

II

The deluge began punctually on the Thursday, and Vyse, arriving as punctually, had an impressive pile of letters to attack.

Betton, on his way to the Park for a ride, came into the library, smoking the cigarette of indolence, to look over his secretary's shoulder.

"How many of 'em? Twenty? Good Lord! It's going to be worse than 'Diadems.' I've just had my first quiet breakfast in two years—time to read the papers and loaf. How I used to dread the sight of my letterbox! Now I sha'n't know I have one."

He leaned over Vyse's chair, and the secretary handed him a letter.

"Here's rather an exceptional one—lady, evidently. I thought you might want to answer it yourself—"

"Exceptional?" Betton ran over the mauve pages and tossed them down. "Why, my dear man, I get hundreds like that. You'll have to be pretty short with her, or she'll send her photograph."

He clapped Vyse on the shoulder and turned away, humming a tune. "Stay to luncheon," he called back gaily from the threshold.

After luncheon Vyse insisted on showing a few of his answers to the first batch of letters. "If I've struck the note I won't bother you again," he urged; and Betton groaningly consented.

"My dear fellow, they're beautiful—too beautiful. I'll be let in for a correspondence with every one of these people."

Vyse, at this, meditated for a while above a blank sheet. "All right—how's this?" he said, after another interval of rapid writing.

Betton glanced over the page. "By George—by George! Won't she *see* it?" he exulted, between fear and rapture.

"It's wonderful how little people see," said Vyse reassuringly.

The letters continued to pour in for several weeks after the appearance of "Abundance." For five or six blissful days Betton did not even have his mail brought to him, trusting to Vyse to single out his personal correspondence, and to deal with the rest according to their agreement. During those days he luxuriated in a sense of wild and lawless freedom; then, gradually, he began to feel the need of fresh restraints to break, and learned that the zest of liberty lies in the escape from specific obligations. At first he was conscious only of a vague hunger, but in time the craving resolved into a shamefaced desire to see his letters.

"After all, I hated them only because I had to answer them"; and he told Vyse carelessly that he wished all his letters submitted to him before the secretary answered them.

At first he pushed aside those beginning: "I have just laid down 'Abundance' after a third reading," or: "Every day for the last month I have been telephoning my bookseller to know when your novel would be out." But little by little the freshness of his interest revived, and even this stereotyped homage began to arrest his eye. At last a day came when he read all the letters, from the first word to the last, as he had done when "Diadems and Faggots" appeared. It was really a pleasure to read them, now that he was relieved of the burden of replying: his new relation to his correspondents had the glow of a love affair unchilled by the contingency of marriage.

One day it struck him that the letters were coming in more slowly and in smaller numbers. Certainly there had been more of a rush when "Diadems and Faggots" came out. Betton began to wonder if Vyse were exercising an unauthorized discrimination, and keeping back the communications he deemed least important. This sudden conjecture carried the novelist straight to his library, where he found Vyse bending over the writing table with his usual inscrutable pale smile. But once there, Betton hardly knew how to frame his question, and blundered into an enquiry for a missing invitation.

"There's a note—a personal note—I ought to have had this morning. Sure you haven't kept it back by mistake among the others?"

Vyse laid down his pen. "The others? But I never keep back any."

107

Betton had foreseen the answer. "Not even the worst twaddle about my book?" he suggested lightly, pushing the papers about.

"Nothing. I understood you wanted to go over them all first."

"Well, perhaps it's safer," Betton conceded, as if the idea were new to him. With an embarrassed hand he continued to turn over the letters at Vyse's elbow.

"Those are yesterday's," said the secretary; "here are to-day's," he added, pointing to a meagre trio.

"H'm—only these?" Betton took them and looked them over lingeringly. "I don't see what the deuce that chap means about the first part of 'Abundance' 'certainly justifying the title'—do you?"

Vyse was silent, and the novelist continued irritably: "Damned cheek, his writing, if he doesn't like the book. Who cares what he thinks about it, anyhow?"

And his morning ride was embittered by the discovery that it was unexpectedly disagreeable to have Vyse read any letters that did not express unqualified praise of his books. He began to fancy there was a latent rancour, a kind of baffled sneer, under Vyse's manner; and he decided to return to the practice of having his mail brought straight to his room. In that way he could edit the letters before his secretary saw them.

Vyse made no comment on the change, and Betton was reduced to wondering whether his imperturbable composure were the mask of complete indifference or of a watchful jealousy. The latter view being more agreeable to his employer's self-esteem, the next step was to conclude that Vyse had not forgotten the episode of "The Lifted Lamp," and would naturally take a vindictive joy in any unfavourable judgments passed on his rival's work. This did not simplify the situation, for there was no denying that unfavourable criticisms preponderated in Betton's correspondence. "Abundance" was neither meeting with the unrestricted welcome of "Diadems and Faggots," nor enjoying the alternative of an animated controversy: it was simply found dull, and its readers said so in language not too tactfully tempered by regretful comparisons with its predecessor. To withhold unfavourable comments from Vyse was, therefore, to make it appear that correspondence about the book had died out; and its author, mindful of his unguarded predictions, found this even more embarrassing. The simplest solution would be to get rid of Vyse; and to this end Betton began to address his energies.

One evening, finding himself unexpectedly disengaged, he asked Vyse to dine; it had occurred to him that, in the course of an after-dinner chat, he might delicately hint his feeling that the work he had offered his friend was unworthy so accomplished a hand.

Vyse surprised him by a momentary hesitation. "I may not have time to dress."

Betton stared. "What's the odds? We'll dine here—and as late as you like."

Vyse thanked him, and appeared, punctually at eight, in all the shabbiness of his daily wear. He looked paler and more shyly truculent than usual, and Betton, from the height of his florid stature, said to himself, with the sudden professional instinct for "type": "He might be an agent of something—a chap who carries deadly secrets."

Vyse, it was to appear, did carry a deadly secret; but one less perilous to society than to himself. He was simply poor—inexcusably, irremediably poor. Everything failed him, had always failed him: whatever he put his hand to went to bits.

This was the confession that, reluctantly, yet with a kind of white-lipped bravado, he flung at Betton in answer to the latter's tentative suggestion that, really, the letter-answering job wasn't worth bothering him with—a thing that any typewriter could do.

"If you mean you're paying me more than it's worth, I'll take less," Vyse rushed out after a pause.

"Oh, my dear fellow—" Betton protested, flushing.

"What *do* you mean, then? Don't I answer the letters as you want them answered?"

Betton anxiously stroked his silken ankle. "You do it beautifully, too beautifully. I mean what I say: the work's not worthy of you. I'm ashamed to ask you—"

"Oh, hang shame," Vyse interrupted. "Do you know why I said I shouldn't have time to dress tonight? Because I haven't any evening clothes. As a matter of fact, I haven't much but the clothes I stand in. One thing after another's gone against me; all the infernal ingenuities of chance. It's been a slow Chinese torture, the kind where they keep you alive to have more fun killing you." He straightened himself with a sudden blush. "Oh, I'm all right now—getting on capitally. But I'm still walking rather a narrow plank; and if I do your work well enough—if I take your idea—"

Betton stared into the fire without answering. He knew next to nothing of Vyse's history, of the mischance or mismanagement that had brought him, with his brains and his training, to so unlikely a pass. But a pang of compunction shot through him as he remembered the manuscript of "The Lifted Lamp" gathering dust on his table for half a year.

"Not that it would have made any earthly difference—since he's evidently never been able to get the thing published." But this reflection did not wholly console Betton, and he found it impossible, at the moment, to tell Vyse that his services were not needed.

III

During the ensuing weeks the letters grew fewer and fewer, and Betton foresaw the approach of the fatal day when his secretary, in common decency, would have to say: "I can't draw my pay for doing nothing."

What a triumph for Vyse!

The thought was intolerable, and Betton cursed his weakness in not having dismissed the fellow before such a possibility arose.

"If I tell him I've no use for him now, he'll see straight through it, of course;—and then, hang it, he looks so poor!"

This consideration came after the other, but Betton, in rearranging them, put it first, because he thought it looked better there, and also because he immediately perceived its value in justifying a plan of action that was beginning to take shape in his mind.

"Poor devil, I'm damned if I don't do it for him!" said Betton, sitting down at his desk.

Three or four days later he sent word to Vyse that he didn't care to go over the letters any longer, and that they would once more be carried directly to the library.

The next time he lounged in, on his way to his morning ride, he found his secretary's pen in active motion.

"A lot today," Vyse told him cheerfully.

His tone irritated Betton: it had the inane optimism of the physician reassuring a discouraged patient.

"Oh, Lord—I thought it was almost over," groaned the novelist.

"No: they've just got their second wind. Here's one from a Chicago publisher—never heard the name—offering you thirty per cent. on your next novel, with an advance royalty of twenty thousand. And here's a chap who wants to syndicate it for a bunch of Sunday papers: big offer, too. That's from Ann Arbor. And this—oh, *this* one's funny!"

He held up a small scented sheet to Betton, who made no movement to receive it.

"Funny? Why's it funny?" he growled.

"Well, it's from a girl—a lady—and she thinks she's the only person who understands 'Abundance'—has the clue to it. Says she's never seen a book so misrepresented by the critics—"

"Ha, ha! That *is* good!" Betton agreed with too loud a laugh.

"This one's from a lady, too—married woman. Says she's misunderstood, and would like to correspond."

"Oh, Lord," said Betton.—"What are you looking at?" he added sharply, as Vyse continued to bend his blinking gaze on the letters.

"I was only thinking I'd never seen such short letters from women. Neither one fills the first page."

"Well, what of that?" queried Betton.

Vyse reflected. "I'd like to meet a woman like that," he said wearily; and Betton laughed again.

The letters continued to pour in, and there could be no farther question of dispensing with Vyse's services. But one morning, about three weeks later, the latter asked for a word with his employer, and Betton, on entering the library, found his secretary with half a dozen documents spread out before him.

"What's up?" queried Betton, with a touch of impatience.

Vyse was attentively scanning the outspread letters.

"I don't know: can't make out." His voice had a faint note of embarrassment. "Do you remember a note signed *Hester Macklin* that came three or four weeks ago? Married—misunderstood—Western army post—wanted to correspond?"

Betton seemed to grope among his memories; then he assented vaguely.

"A short note," Vyse went on: "the whole story in half a page. The shortness struck me so much—and the directness—that I wrote her: wrote in my own name, I mean."

"In your own name?" Betton stood amazed; then he broke into a groan.

"Good Lord, Vyse—you're incorrigible!"

The secretary pulled his thin moustache with a nervous laugh. "If you mean I'm an ass, you're right. Look here." He held out an envelope stamped with the words: "Dead Letter Office." "My effusion has come back to me marked 'unknown.' There's no such person at the address she gave you."

Betton seemed for an instant to share his secretary's embarrassment; then he burst into an uproarious laugh.

"Hoax, was it? That's rough on you, old fellow!"

Vyse shrugged his shoulders. "Yes; but the interesting question is—why on earth didn't *your* answer come back, too?"

"My answer?"

"The official one—the one I wrote in your name. If she's unknown, what's become of *that?*"

Betton stared at him with eyes wrinkled by amusement. "Perhaps she hadn't disappeared then."

Vyse disregarded the conjecture. "Look here—I believe *all* these letters are a hoax," he broke out.

Betton stared at him with a face that turned slowly red and angry. "What are you talking about? All what letters?"

"These I've spread out here: I've been comparing them. And I believe they're all written by one man."

Burton's redness turned to a purple that made his ruddy moustache seem pale. "What the devil are you driving at?" he asked.

"Well, just look at it," Vyse persisted, still bent above the letters. "I've been studying them carefully—those that have come within the last two or three weeks—and there's a queer likeness in the writing of some of them. The *g*'s are all like corkscrews. And the same phrases keep recurring—the Ann Arbor news agent uses the same expressions as the President of the Girls' College at Euphorbia, Maine."

Betton laughed. "Aren't the critics always groaning over the shrinkage of the national vocabulary? Of course we all use the same expressions."

"Yes," said Vyse obstinately. "But how about using the same *g*'s?"

Betton laughed again, but Vyse continued without heeding him: "Look here, Betton—could Strett have written them?"

"Strett?" Betton roared. " *Strett?*" He threw himself into his armchair to shake out his mirth at greater ease.

"I'll tell you why. Strett always posts all my answers. He comes in for them every day before I leave. He posted the letter to the misunderstood party—the letter from *you* that the Dead Letter Office didn't return. *I* posted my own letter to her; and that came back."

A measurable silence followed the emission of this ingenious conjecture; then Betton observed with gentle irony: "Extremely neat. And of course it's no business of yours to supply any valid motive for this remarkable attention on my valet's part."

Vyse cast on him a slanting glance.

"If you've found that human conduct's generally based on valid motives—!"

"Well, outside of madhouses it's supposed to be not quite incalculable."

Vyse had an odd smile under his thin moustache. "Every house is a madhouse at some time or another."

Betton rose with a careless shake of the shoulders. "This one will be if I talk to you much longer," he said, moving away with a laugh.

IV

Betton did not for a moment believe that Vyse suspected the valet of having written the letters.

"Why the devil don't he say out what he thinks? He was always a tortuous chap," he grumbled inwardly.

The sense of being held under the lens of Vyse's mute scrutiny became more and more exasperating. Betton, by this time, had squared his shoulders to the fact that "Abundance" was a failure with the public: a confessed and glaring failure. The press told him so openly, and his friends emphasized the fact by their circumlocutions and evasions. Betton minded it a good deal more than he had expected, but not nearly as much as he minded Vyse's knowing it. That remained the central twinge in his diffused discomfort. And the problem of getting rid of his secretary once more engaged him.

He had set aside all sentimental pretexts for retaining Vyse; but a practical argument replaced them. "If I ship him now he'll think it's because I'm ashamed to have him see that I'm not getting any more letters."

For the letters had ceased again, almost abruptly, since Vyse had hazarded the conjecture that they were the product of Strett's devoted pen. Betton had reverted only once to the subject—to ask ironically, a day or two later: "Is Strett writing to me as much as ever?"—and, on Vyse's replying with a neutral head shake, had added with a laugh: "If you suspect *him* you might as well think I write the letters myself!"

114

"There are very few today," said Vyse, with his irritating evasiveness; and Betton rejoined squarely: "Oh, they'll stop soon. The book's a failure."

A few mornings later he felt a rush of shame at his own tergiversations, and stalked into the library with Vyse's sentence on his tongue.

Vyse started back with one of his anaemic blushes. "I was hoping you'd be in. I wanted to speak to you. There've been no letters the last day or two," he explained.

Betton drew a quick breath of relief. The man had some sense of decency, then! He meant to dismiss himself.

"I told you so, my dear fellow; the book's a flat failure," he said, almost gaily.

Vyse made a deprecating gesture. "I don't know that I should regard the absence of letters as the ultimate test. But I wanted to ask you if there isn't something else I can do on the days when there's no writing." He turned his glance toward the book-lined walls. "Don't you want your library catalogued?" he asked insidiously.

"Had it done last year, thanks." Betton glanced away from Vyse's face. It was piteous, how he needed the job!

"I see...Of course this is just a temporary lull in the letters. They'll begin again—as they did before. The people who read carefully read slowly—you haven't heard yet what *they* think."

Betton felt a rush of puerile joy at the suggestion. Actually, he hadn't thought of that!

"There *was* a big second crop after 'Diadems and Faggots,'" he mused aloud.

"Of course. Wait and see," said Vyse confidently.

The letters in fact began again—more gradually and in smaller numbers. But their quality was different, as Vyse had predicted. And in two cases Betton's correspondents, not content to compress into one rapid communication the thoughts inspired by his work, developed their views in a succession of really remarkable letters. One of the writers was a professor in a Western college; the other was a girl in Florida. In their language, their point of view, their reasons for appreciating "Abundance," they differed almost diametrically; but this only made the unanimity of their approval the more striking. The rush of correspondence evoked by Betton's earlier novel had produced nothing so personal, so exceptional as these communications. He had gulped the praise of *Diadems and Faggots* as undiscriminatingly as it was offered; now he knew for the first time the subtler pleasures of the palate. He tried to feign indifference, even to himself; and to Vyse he made no sign. But gradually he felt a desire to know what his secretary thought of the letters, and, above all, what he was saying in reply to them. And he resented acutely the possibility of Vyse's starting one of his clandestine correspondences with the girl in Florida. Vyse's notorious lack of delicacy had never been more vividly present to Betton's imagination; and he made up his mind to answer the letters himself.

He would keep Vyse on, of course: there were other communications that the secretary could attend to. And, if necessary, Betton would invent an occupation: he cursed his stupidity in having betrayed the fact that his books were already catalogued.

Vyse showed no surprise when Betton announced his intention of dealing personally with the two correspondents who showed so flattering a reluctance to take their leave. But Betton immediately read a criticism in his lack of comment, and put forth, on a note of challenge: "After all, one must be decent!"

Vyse looked at him with an evanescent smile. "You'll have to explain that you didn't write the first answers."

Betton halted. "Well—I—I more or less dictated them, didn't I?"

"Oh, virtually, they're yours, of course."

"You think I can put it that way?"

"Why not?" The secretary absently drew an arabesque on the blotting pad. "Of course they'll keep it up longer if you write yourself," he suggested.

Betton blushed, but faced the issue. "Hang it all, I sha'n't be sorry. They interest me. They're remarkable letters." And Vyse, without observation, returned to his writings.

116

The spring, that year, was delicious to Betton. His college professor continued to address him tersely but cogently at fixed intervals, and twice a week eight serried pages came from Florida. There were other letters, too; he had the solace of feeling that at last "Abundance" was making its way, was reaching the people who, as Vyse said, read slowly because they read intelligently. But welcome as were all these proofs of his restored authority they were but the background of his happiness. His life revolved for the moment about the personality of his two chief correspondents. The professor's letters satisfied his craving for intellectual recognition, and the satisfaction he felt in them proved how completely he had lost faith in himself. He blushed to think that his opinion of his work had been swayed by the shallow judgments of a public whose taste he despised. Was it possible that he had allowed himself to think less well of "Abundance" because it was not to the taste of the average novel reader? Such false humility was less excusable than the crudest appetite for praise: it was ridiculous to try to do conscientious work if one's self-esteem were at the mercy of popular judgments. All this the professor's letters delicately and indirectly conveyed to Betton, with the result that the author of "Abundance" began to recognize in it the ripest flower of his genius.

But if the professor understood his book, the girl in Florida understood *him;* and Betton was fully alive to the superior qualities of discernment that this process implied. For his lovely correspondent his novel was but the starting point, the pretext of her discourse: he himself was her real object, and he had the delicious sense, as their exchange of thoughts proceeded, that she was interested in "Abundance" because of its author, rather than in the author because of his book. Of course she laid stress on the fact that his ideas were the object of her contemplation; but Betton's agreeable person had permitted him some insight into the incorrigible subjectiveness of female judgments, and he was pleasantly aware, from the lady's tone, that she guessed him to be neither old nor ridiculous. And suddenly he wrote to ask if he might see her....

The answer was long in coming. Betton fumed at the delay, watched, wondered, fretted; then he received the one word "Impossible."

He wrote back more urgently, and awaited the reply with increasing eagerness. A certain shyness had kept him from once more modifying the instructions regarding his mail, and Strett still carried the letters directly to Vyse. The hour when he knew they were passing under the latter's eyes was now becoming intolerable to Betton, and it was a profound relief when the secretary, suddenly advised of his father's illness, asked permission to absent himself for a fortnight.

Vyse departed just after Betton had despatched to Florida his second missive of entreaty, and for ten days he tasted the furtive joy of a first perusal of his letters. The answer from Florida was not among them; but Betton said to himself "She's thinking it over," and delay, in that light, seemed favourable. So charming, in fact, was this phase of sentimental suspense that he felt a start of resentment when a telegram apprised him one morning that Vyse would return to his post that day.

Betton had slept later than usual, and, springing out of bed with the telegram in his hand, he learned from the clock that his secretary was due in half an hour. He reflected that the morning's mail must long since be in; and, too impatient to wait for its appearance with his breakfast tray, he threw on a dressing gown and went to the library. There lay the letters, half a dozen of them: but his eye flew to one envelope, and as he tore it open a warm wave rocked his heart.

The letter was dated a few days after its writer must have received his own: it had all the qualities of grace and insight to which his unknown friend had accustomed him, but it contained no allusion, however indirect, to the special purport of his appeal. Even a vanity less ingenious than Betton's might have read in the lady's silence one of the most familiar motions of consent; but the smile provoked by this inference faded as he turned to his other letters. For the uppermost bore

118

the superscription "Dead Letter Office," and the document that fell from it was his own last letter from Florida.

Betton studied the ironic "Unknown" for an appreciable space of time; then he broke into a laugh. He had suddenly recalled Vyse's similar experience with "Hester Macklin," and the light he was able to throw on that obscure episode was searching enough to penetrate all the dark corners of his own adventure. He felt a rush of heat to the ears; catching sight of himself in the glass, he saw a red ridiculous congested countenance, and dropped into a chair to hide it between flushed fists. He was roused by the opening of the door, and Vyse appeared on the threshold.

"Oh, I beg pardon—you're ill?" said the secretary.

Betton's only answer was an inarticulate murmur of derision; then he pushed forward the letter with the imprint of the Dead Letter Office.

"Look at that," he jeered.

Vyse peered at the envelope, and turned it over slowly in his hands. Betton's eyes, fixed on him, saw his face decompose like a substance touched by some powerful acid. He clung to the envelope as if to gain time.

"It's from the young lady you've been writing to at Swazee Springs?" he asked at length.

"It's from the young lady I've been writing to at Swazee Springs."

"Well—I suppose she's gone away," continued Vyse, rebuilding his countenance rapidly.

"Yes; and in a community numbering perhaps a hundred and seventy-five souls, including the dogs and chickens, the local post office is so ignorant of her movements that my letter has to be sent to the Dead Letter Office."

Vyse meditated on this; then he laughed in turn. "After all, the same thing happened to me—with 'Hester Macklin,' I mean," he recalled sheepishly.

"Just so," said Betton, bringing down his clenched fist on the table. " *Just so,*" he repeated, in italics.

He caught his secretary's glance, and held it with his own for a moment. Then he dropped it as, in pity, one releases something scared and squirming.

"The very day my letter was returned from Swazee Springs she wrote me this from there," he said, holding up the last Florida missive.

"Ha! That's funny," said Vyse, with a damp forehead.

"Yes, it's funny; it's funny," said Betton. He leaned back, his hands in his pockets, staring up at the ceiling, and noticing a crack in the cornice. Vyse, at the corner of the writing table, waited.

"Shall I get to work?" he began, after a silence measurable by minutes. Betton's gaze descended from the cornice.

"I've got your seat, haven't I?" he said, rising and moving away from the table.

Vyse, with a quick gleam of relief, slipped into the vacant chair, and began to stir about vaguely among the papers.

"How's your father?" Betton asked from the hearth.

"Oh, better—better, thank you. He'll pull out of it."

"But you had a sharp scare for a day or two?"

"Yes—it was touch and go when I got there."

Another pause, while Vyse began to classify the letters.

"And I suppose," Betton continued in a steady tone, "your anxiety made you forget your usual precautions—whatever they were—about this Florida correspondence, and before you'd had time to prevent it the Swazee post office blundered?"

Vyse lifted his head with a quick movement. "What do you mean?" he asked, pushing his chair back.

"I mean that you saw I couldn't live without flattery, and that you've been ladling it out to me to earn your keep."

Vyse sat motionless and shrunken, digging the blotting pad with his pen. "What on earth are you driving at?" he repeated.

"Though why the deuce," Betton continued in the same steady tone, "you should need to do this kind of work when you've got such faculties at your service—those letters were

120

magnificent, my dear fellow! Why in the world don't you write novels, instead of writing to other people about them?"

Vyse straightened himself with an effort. "What are you talking about, Betton? Why the devil do you think *I* wrote those letters?"

Betton held back his answer, with a brooding face. "Because I wrote 'Hester Macklin's'—to myself!"

Vyse sat stockstill, without the least outcry of wonder. "Well—?" he finally said, in a low tone.

"And because you found me out (you see, you can't even feign surprise!)—because you saw through it at a glance, knew at once that the letters were faked. And when you'd foolishly put me on my guard by pointing out to me that they were a clumsy forgery, and had then suddenly guessed that *I* was the forger, you drew the natural inference that I had to have popular approval, or at least had to make *you* think I had it. You saw that, to me, the worst thing about the failure of the book was having *you* know it was a failure. And so you applied your superior—your immeasurably superior—abilities to carrying on the humbug, and deceiving me as I'd tried to deceive you. And you did it so successfully that I don't see why the devil you haven't made your fortune writing novels!"

Vyse remained silent, his head slightly bent under the mounting tide of Betton's denunciation.

"The way you differentiated your people—characterised them—avoided my stupid mistake of making the women's letters too short and logical, of letting my different correspondents use the same expressions: the amount of ingenuity and art you wasted on it! I swear, Vyse, I'm sorry that damned post office went back on you," Betton went on, piling up the waves of his irony.

But at this height they suddenly paused, drew back on themselves, and began to recede before the spectacle of Vyse's pale distress. Something warm and emotional in Betton's nature—a lurking kindliness, perhaps, for any one who tried to soothe and smooth his writhing ego—softened his eye as it rested on the drooping figure of his secretary.

"Look here, Vyse—I'm not sorry—not altogether sorry this has happened!" He moved slowly across the room, and laid a friendly palm on Vyse's shoulder. "In a queer illogical way it evens up things, as it were. I did you a shabby turn once, years ago—oh, out of sheer carelessness, of course—about that novel of yours I promised to give to Apthorn. If I *had* given it, it might not have made any difference—I'm not sure it wasn't too good for success—but anyhow, I dare say you thought my personal influence might have helped you, might at least have got you a quicker hearing. Perhaps you thought it was because the thing *was* so good that I kept it back, that I felt some nasty jealousy of your superiority. I swear to you it wasn't that—I clean forgot it. And one day when I came home it was gone: you'd sent and taken it. And I've always thought since you might have owed me a grudge—and not unjustly; so this...this business of the letters...the sympathy you've shown...for I suppose it *is* sympathy...?"

Vyse startled and checked him by a queer crackling laugh.

"It's *not* sympathy?" broke in Betton, the moisture drying out of his voice. He withdrew his hand from Vyse's shoulder. "What is it, then? The joy of uncovering my nakedness? An eye for an eye? Is it *that?*"

Vyse rose from his seat, and with a mechanical gesture swept into a heap all the letters he had sorted.

"I'm stone broke, and wanted to keep my job—that's what it is," he said wearily...

THE LEGEND

I

Arthur Bernald could never afterward recall just when the first conjecture flashed on him: oddly enough, there was no record of it in the agitated jottings of his diary. But, as it seemed to him in retrospect, he had always felt that the queer man at the Wades' must be John Pellerin, if only for the negative reason that he couldn't imaginably be any one else. It was impossible, in the confused pattern of the century's intellectual life, to fit the stranger in anywhere, save in the big gap which, some five and twenty years earlier, had been left by Pellerin's unaccountable disappearance; and conversely, such a man as the Wades' visitor couldn't have lived for sixty years without filling, somewhere in space, a nearly equivalent void.

At all events, it was certainly not to Doctor Wade or to his mother that Bernald owed the hint: the good unconscious Wades, one of whose chief charms in the young man's eyes was that they remained so robustly untainted by Pellerinism, in spite of the fact that Doctor Wade's younger brother, Howland, was among its most impudently flourishing high priests.

The incident had begun by Bernald's running across Doctor Robert Wade one hot summer night at the University Club, and by Wade's saying, in the tone of unprofessional laxity which the shadowy stillness of the place invited: "I got hold of a queer fish at St. Martin's the other day—case of heat prostration picked up in Central Park. When we'd patched him up I found he had nowhere to go, and not a dollar in his pocket, and I sent him down to our place at Portchester to rebuild."

The opening roused his hearer's attention. Bob Wade had an odd unformulated sense of values that Bernald had learned to trust.

"What sort of chap? Young or old?"

"Oh, every age—full of years, and yet with a lot left. He called himself sixty on the books."

"Sixty's a good age for some kinds of living. And age is of

course purely subjective. How has he used his sixty years?"

"Well—part of them in educating himself, apparently. He's a scholar—humanities, languages, and so forth."

"Oh—decayed gentleman," Bernald murmured, disappointed.

"Decayed? Not much!" cried the doctor with his accustomed literalness. "I only mentioned that side of Winterman—his name's Winterman—because it was the side my mother noticed first. I suppose women generally do. But it's only a part—a small part. The man's the big thing."

"Really big?"

"Well—there again...When I took him down to the country, looking rather like a tramp from a 'Shelter,' with an untrimmed beard, and a suit of reach-me-downs he'd slept round the Park in for a week, I felt sure my mother'd carry the silver up to her room, and send for the gardener's dog to sleep in the hall the first night. But she didn't."

"I see. 'Women and children love him.' Oh, Wade!" Bernald groaned.

"Not a bit of it! You're out again. We don't love him, either of us. But we *feel* him—the air's charged with him. You'll see."

And Bernald agreed that he *would* see, the following Sunday. Wade's inarticulate attempts to characterize the stranger had struck his friend. The human revelation had for Bernald a poignant and ever-renewed interest, which his trade, as the dramatic critic of a daily paper, had hitherto failed to discourage. And he knew that Bob Wade, simple and undefiled by literature—Bernald's specific affliction—had a free and personal way of judging men, and the diviner's knack of reaching their hidden springs. During the days that followed, the young doctor gave Bernald farther details about John Winterman: details not of fact—for in that respect his visitor's reticence was baffling—but of impression. It appeared that Winterman, while lying insensible in the Park, had been robbed of the few dollars he possessed; and on leaving the hospital, still weak and half

124

blind, he had quite simply and unprotestingly accepted the Wades' offer to give him shelter till such time as he should be strong enough to go to work.

"But what's his work?" Bernald interjected. "Hasn't he at least told you that?"

"Well, writing. Some kind of writing." Doctor Bob always became vague and clumsy when he approached the confines of literature. "He means to take it up again as soon as his eyes get right."

Bernald groaned. "Oh, Lord—that finishes him; and *me!* He's looking for a publisher, of course—he wants a 'favourable notice.' I won't come!"

"He hasn't written a line for twenty years."

"A line of *what?* What kind of literature can one keep corked up for twenty years?"

Wade surprised him. "The real kind, I should say. But I don't know Winterman's line," the doctor added. "He speaks of the things he used to write merely as 'stuff that wouldn't sell.' He has a wonderfully confidential way of *not* telling one things. But he says he'll have to do something for his living as soon as his eyes are patched up, and that writing is the only trade he knows. The queer thing is that he seems pretty sure of selling *now*. He even talked of buying the bungalow of us, with an acre or two about it."

"The bungalow? What's that?"

"The studio down by the shore that we built for Howland when he thought he meant to paint." (Howland Wade, as Bernald knew, had experienced various "calls.") "Since he's taken to writing nobody's been near it. I offered it to Winterman, and he camps there—cooks his meals, does his own housekeeping, and never comes up to the house except in the evenings, when he joins us on the verandah, in the dark, and smokes while my mother knits."

"A discreet visitor, eh?"

"More than he need be. My mother actually wanted him to stay on in the house—in her pink chintz room. Think of it! But he says houses smother him. I take it he's lived for years in the open."

"In the open where?"

"I can't make out, except that it was somewhere in the East. 'East of everything—beyond the dayspring. In places not on the map.' That's the way he put it; and when I said: 'You've been an explorer, then?' he smiled in his beard, and answered: 'Yes; that's it—an explorer.' Yet he doesn't strike me as a man of action: hasn't the hands or the eyes."

"What sort of hands and eyes has he?"

Wade reflected. His range of observation was not large, but within its limits it was exact and could give an account of itself.

"He's worked a lot with his hands, but that's not what they were made for. I should say they were extraordinarily delicate conductors of sensation. And his eye—his eye too. He hasn't used it to dominate people: he didn't care to. He simply looks through 'em all like windows. Makes me feel like the fellows who think they're made of glass. The mitigating circumstance is that he seems to see such a glorious landscape through me." Wade grinned at the thought of serving such a purpose.

"I see. I'll come on Sunday and be looked through!" Bernald cried.

II

Bernald came on two successive Sundays; and the second time he lingered till the Tuesday.

"Here he comes!" Wade had said, the first evening, as the two young men, with Wade's mother sat in the sultry dusk, with the Virginian creeper drawing, between the verandah arches, its black arabesques against a moon-lined sky.

In the darkness Bernald heard a step on the gravel, and saw the red flit of a cigar through the shrubs. Then a loosely moving figure obscured the patch of sky between the creepers, and the red spark became the centre of a dim bearded face, in which Bernald discerned only a broad white gleam of forehead.

It was the young man's subsequent impression that Winterman had not spoken much that first evening; at any rate, Bernald himself remembered chiefly what the Wades had said. And this was the more curious because he had come for the

126

purpose of studying their visitor, and because there was nothing to divert him from that purpose in Wade's halting communications or his mother's artless comments. He reflected afterward that there must have been a mysteriously fertilizing quality in the stranger's silence: it had brooded over their talk like a large moist cloud above a dry country.

Mrs. Wade, apparently apprehensive lest her son should have given Bernald an exaggerated notion of their visitor's importance, had hastened to qualify it before the latter appeared.

"He's not what you or Howland would call intellectual—"(Bernald writhed at the coupling of the names)—"not in the least *literary;* though he told Bob he used to write. I don't think, though, it could have been what Howland would call writing." Mrs. Wade always mentioned her younger son with a reverential drop of the voice. She viewed literature much as she did Providence, as an inscrutably mystery; and she spoke of Howland as a dedicated being, set apart to perform secret rites within the veil of the sanctuary.

"I shouldn't say he had a quick mind," she continued, reverting apologetically to Winterman. "Sometimes he hardly seems to follow what we're saying. But he's got such sound ideas—when he does speak he's never silly. And clever people sometimes *are*, don't you think so?" Bernald groaned an unqualified assent. "And he's so capable. The other day something went wrong with the kitchen range, just as I was expecting some friends of Bob's for dinner; and do you know, when Mr. Winterman heard we were in trouble, he came and took a look, and knew at once what to do? I told him it was a dreadful pity he wasn't married!"

Close on midnight, when the session on the verandah ended, and the two young men were strolling down to the bungalow at Winterman's side, Bernald's mind reverted to the image of the fertilizing cloud. There was something brooding, pregnant, in the silent presence beside him: he had, in place of any circumscribing impression of the individual, a large hovering sense of manifold latent meanings. And he felt a distinct thrill of relief when, halfway down the lawn, Doctor Bob was checked by a voice that called him back to the telephone.

"Now I'll be with him alone!" thought Bernald, with a throb like a lover's.

In the low-ceilinged bungalow Winterman had to grope for the lamp on his desk, and as its light struck up into his face Bernald's sense of the rareness of his opportunity increased. He couldn't have said why, for the face, with its ridged brows, its shabby greyish beard and blunt Socratic nose, made no direct appeal to the eye. It seemed rather like a stage on which re-markable things might be enacted, like some shaggy moorland landscape dependent for form and expression on the clouds rolling over it, and the bursts of light between; and one of these flashed out in the smile with which Winterman, as if in answer to his companion's thought, said simply, as he turned to fill his pipe: "Now we'll talk."

So he'd known all along that they hadn't yet—and had guessed that, with Bernald, one might!

The young man's glow of pleasure was so intense that it left him for a moment unable to meet the challenge; and in that moment he felt the brush of something winged and summon-ing. His spirit rose to it with a rush; but just as he felt himself poised between the ascending pinions, the door opened and Bob Wade plunged in.

"Too bad! I'm so sorry! It was from Howland, to say he can't come tomorrow after all." The doctor panted out his news with honest grief.

"I tried my best to pull it off for you; and my brother *wants* to come—he's keen to talk to you and see what he can do. But you see he's so tremendously in demand. He'll try for another Sunday later on."

Winterman nodded with a whimsical gesture. "Oh, he'll find me here. I shall work my time out slowly." He pointed to the scattered sheets on the kitchen table that formed his writing desk.

"Not slowly enough to suit us," Wade answered hospitably. "Only, if Howland could have come he might have given you a

128

tip or two—put you on the right track—shown you how to get in touch with the public."

Winterman, his hands in his sagging pockets, lounged against the bare pine walls, twisting his pipe under his beard. "Does your brother enjoy the privilege of that contact?" he questioned gravely.

Wade stared a little. "Oh, of course Howland's not what you'd call a *popular* writer; he despises that kind of thing. But whatever he says goes with—well, with the chaps that count; and every one tells me he's written *the* book on Pellerin. You must read it when you get back your eyes." He paused, as if to let the name sink in, but Winterman drew at his pipe with a blank face. "You must have heard of Pellerin, I suppose?" the doctor continued. "I've never read a word of him myself: he's too big a proposition for *me*. But one can't escape the talk about him. I have him crammed down my throat even in hospital. The internes read him at the clinics. He tumbles out of the nurses' pockets. The patients keep him under their pillows. Oh, with most of them, of course, it's just a craze, like the last new game or puzzle: they don't understand him in the least. Howland says that even now, twenty-five years after his death, and with his books in everybody's hands, there are not twenty people who really understand Pellerin; and Howland ought to know, if anybody does. He's—what's their great word?— *interpreted* him. You must get Howland to put you through a course of Pellerin."

And as the young men, having taken leave of Winterman, retraced their way across the lawn, Wade continued to develop the theme of his brother's accomplishments.

"I wish I *could* get Howland to take an interest in Winterman: this is the third Sunday he's chucked us. Of course he does get bored with people consulting him about their writings—but I believe if he could only talk to Winterman he'd see something in him, as we do. And it would be such a godsend to the poor man to have some one to advise him about his work. I'm going to make a desperate effort to get Howland here next Sunday."

It was then that Bernald vowed to himself that he would return the next Sunday at all costs. He hardly knew whether he was prompted by the impulse to shield Winterman from Howland Wade's ineptitude, or by the desire to see the latter abandon himself to the full shamelessness of its display; but of one fact he was blissfully assured—and that was of the existence in Winterman of some quality which would provoke Howland to the amplest exercise of his fatuity. "How he'll draw him—how he'll draw him!" Bernald chuckled, with a security the more unaccountable that his one glimpse of Winterman had shown the latter only as a passive subject for experimentation; and he felt himself avenged in advance for the injury of Howland Wade's existence.

III

That this hope was to be frustrated Bernald learned from Howland Wade's own lips, the day before the two young men were to meet at Portchester.

"I can't really, my dear fellow," the Interpreter lisped, passing a polished hand over the faded smoothness of his face. "Oh, an authentic engagement, I assure you: otherwise, to oblige old Bob I'd submit cheerfully to looking over his foundling's literature. But I'm pledged this week to the Pellerin Society of Kenosha: I had a hand in founding it, and for two years now they've been patiently waiting for a word from me—the *Fiat Lux*, so to speak. You see it's a ministry, Bernald—I assure you, I look upon my calling quite religiously."

As Bernald listened, his disappointment gradually changed to relief. Howland, on trial, always turned out to be too insufferable, and the pleasure of watching his antics was invariably lost in the impulse to put a sanguinary end to them.

"If he'd only keep his beastly pink hands off Pellerin," Bernald groaned, thinking of the thick manuscript condemned to perpetual incarceration in his own desk by the publication of Howland's "definitive" work on the great man. One couldn't, *after* Howland Wade, expose one's self to the derision of writing about Pellerin: the eagerness with which Wade's book had been devoured proved, not that the public had enough appetite for another, but simply that, for a stomach so undiscriminating, anything better than Wade had given it would be too good. And Bernald, in the confidence that his own work was open to this objection, had stoically locked it up. Yet if he had resigned his exasperated intelligence to the fact that Wade's book existed, and was already passing into the immortality of perpetual re-publication, he could not, after repeated trials, adjust himself to the author's talk about Pellerin. When Wade wrote of the great dead he was egregious, but in conversation he was familiar and fond. It might have been supposed that one of the beauties of Pellerin's hidden life and mysterious taking off would have been to guard him from the fingering of anecdote; but biographers like Howland Wade were born to rise above such obstacles. He might be vague or inaccurate in dealing with the few recorded events of his subject's life; but when he left fact for conjecture no one had a firmer footing. Whole chapters in his volume were constructed in the conditional mood and packed with hypothetical detail; and in talk, by the very law of the process, hypothesis became affirmation, and he was ready to tell you confidentially the exact circumstances of Pellerin's death, and of the "distressing incident" leading up to it. Bernald himself not only questioned the form under which this incident was shaping itself before posterity, but the mere radical fact of its occurrence: he had never been able to discover any break in the dense cloud enveloping Pellerin's later life and its mysterious termination. He had gone away—that was all that any of them knew: he who had so little, at any time, been with them or of them; and his going had so slightly stirred the public consciousness that even the subsequent news of his death, laconically imparted from afar, had dropped unheeded into the universal scrap basket, to be long afterward fished out, with all its details missing, when some enquiring spirit first became aware, by chance encounter with a two-penny volume in a London bookstall, not only that such a man as John Pellerin had died, but that he had ever lived, or written.

It need hardly be noted that Howland Wade had not been the pioneer in question: his had been the wiser part of swelling the chorus when it rose, and gradually drowning the other voices by his own insistent note. He had pitched the note so screamingly, and held it so long, that he was now the accepted authority on Pellerin, not only in the land which had given birth to his genius but in the Europe which had first acclaimed it; and it was the central point of pain in Bernald's sense of the situation that a man who had so yearned for silence as Pellerin should have his grave piped over by such a voice as Wade's.

Bernald's talk with the Interpreter had revived this ache to the momentary exclusion of other sensations; and he was still sore with it when, the next afternoon, he arrived at Portchester for his second Sunday with the Wades.

At the station he had the surprise of seeing Winterman's face on the platform, and of hearing from him that Doctor Bob had been called away to assist at an operation in a distant town.

"Mrs. Wade wanted to put you off, but I believe the message came too late; so she sent me down to break the news to you," said Winterman, holding out his hand.

Perhaps because they were the first conventional words that Bernald had heard him speak, the young man was struck by the relief his intonation gave them.

"She wanted to send a carriage," Winterman added, "but I told her we'd walk back through the woods." He looked at Bernald with a sudden kindness that flushed the young man with pleasure.

"Are you strong enough? It's not too far?"

"Oh, no. I'm pulling myself together. Getting back to work is the slowest part of the business: not on account of my eyes—I can use them now, though not for reading; but some of the links between things are missing. It's a kind of broken spectrum...here, that boy will look after your bag."

The walk through the woods remained in Bernald's memory as an enchanted hour. He used the word literally, as descriptive of the way in which Winterman's contact changed the face of

132

things, or perhaps restored them to their primitive meanings. And the scene they traversed—one of those little untended woods that still, in America, fringe the tawdry skirts of civilization—acquired, as a background to Winterman, the hush of a spot aware of transcendent visitings. Did he talk, or did he make Bernald talk? The young man never knew. He recalled only a sense of lightness and liberation, as if the hard walls of individuality had melted, and he were merged in the poet's deeper interfusion, yet without losing the least sharp edge of self. This general impression resolved itself afterward into the sense of Winterman's wide elemental range. His thought encircled things like the horizon at sea. He didn't, as it happened, touch on lofty themes—Bernald was gleefully aware that, to Howland Wade, their talk would hardly have been Talk at all—but Winterman's mind, applied to lowly topics, was like a powerful lens that brought out microscopic delicacies and differences.

The lack of Sunday trains kept Doctor Bob for two days on the scene of his surgical duties, and during those two days Bernald seized every moment of communion with his friend's guest. Winterman, as Wade had said, was reticent as to his personal affairs, or rather as to the practical and material conditions to which the term is generally applied. But it was evident that, in Winterman's case, the usual classification must be reversed, and that the discussion of ideas carried one much farther into his intimacy than any specific acquaintance with the incidents of his life.

"That's exactly what Howland Wade and his tribe have never understood about Pellerin: that it's much less important to know how, or even why, he disapp—"

Bernald pulled himself up with a jerk, and turned to look full at his companion. It was late on the Monday evening, and the two men, after an hour's chat on the verandah to the tune of Mrs. Wade's knitting needles, had bidden their hostess goodnight and strolled back to the bungalow together.

"Come and have a pipe before you turn in," Winterman had said; and they had sat on together till midnight, with the door of the bungalow open on a heaving moonlit bay, and summer insects bumping against the chimney of the lamp. Winterman had just bent down to refill his pipe from the jar on the table, and Bernald, jerking about to catch him in the yellow circle of lamplight, sat speechless, staring at a fact that seemed suddenly to have substituted itself for Winterman's face, or rather to have taken on its features.

"No, they never saw that Pellerin's ideas *were* Pellerin..." He continued to stare at Winterman. "Just as this man's ideas are—why, *are* Pellerin!"

The thought uttered itself in a kind of inner shout, and Bernald started upright with the violent impact of his conclusion. Again and again in the last forty-eight hours he had exclaimed to himself: "This is as good as Pellerin." Why hadn't he said till now: "This *is* Pellerin"?...Surprising as the answer was, he had no choice but to take it. He hadn't said so simply because Winterman was *better than Pellerin*—that there was so much more of him, so to speak. Yes; but—it came to Bernald in a flash—wouldn't there by this time have been any amount more of Pellerin?...The young man felt actually dizzy with the thought. That was it—there was the solution of the haunting problem! This man was Pellerin, and more than Pellerin! It was so fantastic and yet so unanswerable that he burst into a sudden startled laugh.

Winterman, at the same moment, brought his palm down with a sudden crash on the pile of manuscript covering the desk.

"What's the matter?" Bernald gasped.

"My match wasn't out. In another minute the destruction of the library of Alexandria would have been a trifle compared to what you'd have seen." Winterman, with his large deep laugh, shook out the smouldering sheets. "And I should have been a pensioner on Doctor Bob the Lord knows how much longer!"

Bernald pulled himself together. "You've really got going again? The thing's actually getting into shape?"

"This particular thing *is* in shape. I drove at it hard all last week, thinking our friend's brother would be down on Sunday, and might look it over."

Bernald had to repress the tendency to another wild laugh.

"Howland—you meant to show *Howland* what you've done?"

Winterman, looming against the moonlight, slowly turned a dusky shaggy head toward him.

"Isn't it a good thing to do?"

Bernald wavered, torn between loyalty to his friends and the grotesqueness of answering in the affirmative. After all, it was none of his business to furnish Winterman with an estimate of Howland Wade.

"Well, you see, you've never told me what your line *is*," he answered, temporizing.

"No, because nobody's ever told *me*. It's exactly what I want to find out," said the other genially.

"And you expect Wade—?"

"Why, I gathered from our good Doctor that it's his trade. Doesn't he explain—interpret?"

"In his own domain—which is Pellerinism."

Winterman gazed out musingly upon the moon-touched dusk of waters. "And what *is* Pellerinism?" he asked.

Bernald sprang to his feet with a cry. "Ah, I don't know—but you're Pellerin!"

They stood for a minute facing each other, among the uncertain swaying shadows of the room, with the sea breathing through it as something immense and inarticulate breathed through young Bernald's thoughts; then Winterman threw up his arms with a humorous gesture.

"Don't shoot!" he said.

IV

Dawn found them there, and the risen sun laid its beams on the rough floor of the bungalow, before either of the men was conscious of the passage of time. Bernald, vaguely trying to define his own state in retrospect, could only phrase it: "I floated...floated. ..."

The gist of fact at the core of the extraordinary experience was simply that John Pellerin, twenty-five years earlier, had

135

voluntarily disappeared, causing the rumour of his death to be reported to an inattentive world; and that now he had come back to see what that world had made of him.

"You'll hardly believe it of me; I hardly believe it of myself; but I went away in a rage of disappointment, of wounded pride—no, vanity! I don't know which cut deepest—the sneers or the silence—but between them, there wasn't an inch of me that wasn't raw. I had just the one thing in me: the message, the cry, the revelation. But nobody saw and nobody listened. Nobody wanted what I had to give. I was like a poor devil of a tramp looking for shelter on a bitter night, in a town with every door bolted and all the windows dark. And suddenly I felt that the easiest thing would be to lie down and go to sleep in the snow. Perhaps I'd a vague notion that if they found me there at daylight, frozen stiff, the pathetic spectacle might produce a reaction, a feeling of remorse...So I took care to be found! Well, a good many thousand people die every day on the face of the globe; and I soon discovered that I was simply one of the thousands; and when I made that discovery I really died—and stayed dead a year or two...When I came to life again I was off on the under side of the world, in regions unaware of what we know as 'the public.' Have you any notion how it shifts the point of view to wake under new constellations? I advise any who's been in love with a woman under Cassiopeia to go and think about her under the Southern Cross...It's the only way to tell the pivotal truths from the others...I didn't believe in my theory any less—there was my triumph and my vindication! It held out, resisted, measured itself with the stars. But I didn't care a snap of my finger whether anybody else believed in it, or even knew it had been formulated. It escaped out of my books—my poor stillborn books—like Psyche from the chrysalis and soared away into the blue, and lived there. I knew then how it frees an idea to be ignored; how apprehension circumscribes and deforms it...Once I'd learned that, it was easy enough to turn to and shift for myself. I was sure now that my idea would live: the good ones are self-supporting. I had to

136

learn to be so; and I tried my hand at a number of things...adventurous, menial, commercial...It's not a bad thing for a man to have to live his life—and we nearly all manage to dodge it. Our first round with the Sphinx may strike something out of us—a book or a picture or a symphony; and we're amazed at our feat, and go on letting that first work breed others, as some animal forms reproduce each other without renewed fertilization. So there we are, committed to our first guess at the riddle; and our works look as like as successive impressions of the same plate, each with the lines a little fainter; whereas they ought to be—if we touch earth between times—as different from each other as those other creatures—jellyfish, aren't they, of a kind?—where successive generations produce new forms, and it takes a zoologist to see the hidden likeness. ...

"Well, I proved my first guess, off there in the wilds, and it lived, and grew, and took care of itself. And I said 'Some day it will make itself heard; but by that time my atoms will have waltzed into a new pattern.' Then, in Cashmere one day, I met a fellow in a caravan, with a dogeared book in his pocket. He said he never stirred without it—wanted to know where I'd been, never to have heard of it. It was *my guess*—in its twentieth edition!...The globe spun round at that, and all of a sudden I was under the old stars. That's the way it happens when the ballast of vanity shifts! I'd lived a third of a life out there, unconscious of human opinion—because I supposed it was unconscious of *me*. But now—now! Oh, it was different. I wanted to know what they said...Not exactly that, either: I wanted to know *what I'd made them say*. There's a difference...And here I am," said John Pellerin, with a pull at his pipe.

So much Bernald retained of his companion's actual narrative; the rest was swept away under the tide of wonder that rose and submerged him as Pellerin—at some indefinitely later stage of their talk—picked up his manuscript and began to read. Bernald sat opposite, his elbows propped on the table, his eyes fixed on the swaying waters outside, from which the moon gradually faded, leaving them to make a denser blackness in the night. As Pellerin read, this density of blackness—which never for a moment seemed inert or unalive—was attenuated by imperceptible degrees, till a greyish pallour replaced it; then the pallour breathed and brightened, and suddenly dawn was on the sea.

Something of the same nature went on in the young man's mind while he watched and listened. He was conscious of a gradually withdrawing light, of an interval of obscurity full of the stir of invisible forces, and then of the victorious flush of day. And as the light rose, he saw how far he had travelled and what wonders the night had prepared. Pellerin had been right in saying that his first idea had survived, had borne the test of time; but he had given his hearer no hint of the extent to which it had been enlarged and modified, of the fresh implications it now unfolded. In a brief flash of retrospection Bernald saw the earlier books dwindle and fall into their place as mere precursors of this fuller revelation; then, with a leap of helpless rage, he pictured Howland Wade's pink hands on the new treasure, and his prophetic feet upon the lecture platform.

V

"It won't do—oh, he let him down as gently as possible; but it appears it simply won't do."

Doctor Bob imparted the ineluctable fact to Bernald while the two men, accidentally meeting at their club a few nights later, sat together over the dinner they had immediately agreed to consume in company.

Bernald had left Portchester the morning after his strange discovery, and he and Bob Wade had not seen each other since. And now Bernald, moved by an irresistible instinct of postponement, had waited for his companion to bring up Winterman's name, and had even executed several conversational diversions in the hope of delaying its mention. For how could one talk of Winterman with the thought of Pellerin swelling one's breast?

"Yes; the very day Howland got back from Kenosha I brought the manuscript to town, and got him to read it. And yesterday evening I nailed him, and dragged an answer out of him."

138

"Then Howland hasn't seen Winterman yet?"

"No. He said: 'Before you let him loose on me I'll go over the stuff, and see if it's at all worth while.'"

Bernald drew a freer breath. "And he found it wasn't?"

"Between ourselves, he found it was of no account at all. Queer, isn't it, when the *man*...but of course literature's another proposition. Howland says it's one of the cases where an idea might seem original and striking if one didn't happen to be able to trace its descent. And this is straight out of bosh—by Pellerin...Yes: Pellerin. It seems that everything in the article that isn't pure nonsense is just Pellerinism. Howland thinks poor Winterman must have been tremendously struck by Pellerin's writings, and have lived too much out of the world to know that they've become the textbooks of modern thought. Otherwise, of course, he'd have taken more trouble to disguise his plagiarisms."

"I see," Bernald mused. "Yet you say there *is* an original element?"

"Yes; but unluckily it's no good."

"It's not—conceivably—in any sense a development of Pellerin's idea: a logical step farther?"

"*Logical?* Howland says it's twaddle at white heat."

Bernald sat silent, divided between the fierce satisfaction of seeing the Interpreter rush upon his fate, and the despair of knowing that the state of mind he represented was indestructible. Then both emotions were swept away on a wave of pure joy, as he reflected that now, at last, Howland Wade had given him back John Pellerin.

The possession was one he did not mean to part with lightly; and the dread of its being torn from him constrained him to extraordinary precautions.

"You've told Winterman, I suppose? How did he take it?"

"Why, unexpectedly, as he does most things. You can never tell which way he'll jump. I thought he'd take a high tone, or else laugh it off; but he did neither. He seemed awfully cast down. I wished myself well out of the job when I saw how cut up he was." Bernald thrilled at the words. Pellerin had shared his pang, then—the "old woe of the world" at the perpetuity of human dulness!

"But what did he say to the charge of plagiarism—if you made it?"

"Oh, I told him straight out what Howland said. I thought it fairer. And his answer to that was the rummest part of all."

"What was it?" Bernald questioned, with a tremor.

"He said: 'That's queer, for I've never read Pellerin.'"

Bernald drew a deep breath of ecstasy. "Well—and I suppose you believed him?"

"I believed him, because I know him. But the public won't—the critics won't. And if it's a pure coincidence it's just as bad for him as if it were a straight steal—isn't it?"

Bernald sighed his acquiescence.

"It bothers me awfully," Wade continued, knitting his kindly brows, "because I could see what a blow it was to him. He's got to earn his living, and I don't suppose he knows how to do anything else. At his age it's hard to start fresh. I put that to Howland—asked him if there wasn't a chance he might do better if he only had a little encouragement. I can't help feeling he's got the essential thing in him. But of course I'm no judge when it comes to books. And Howland says it would be cruel to give him any hope." Wade paused, turned his wineglass about under a meditative stare, and then leaned across the table toward Bernald. "Look here—do you know what I've proposed to Winterman? That he should come to town with me tomorrow and go in the evening to hear Howland lecture to the Uplift Club. They're to meet at Mrs. Beecher Bain's, and Howland is to repeat the lecture that he gave the other day before the Pellerin Society at Kenosha. It will give Winterman a chance to get some notion of what Pellerin *was:* he'll get it much straighter from Howland than if he tried to plough through Pellerin's books. And then afterward—as if accidentally—I thought I might bring him and Howland together. If Howland could only see him and hear him talk, there's no knowing what might come of it. He couldn't help feeling the man's force, as we do; and he might give him a pointer—tell him what line to take. Anyhow, it would please Winterman, and take the edge off his disappointment. I saw that as soon as I proposed it."

"Some one who's never heard of Pellerin?"

Mrs. Beecher Bain, large, smiling, diffuse, reached out parenthetically from the incoming throng on her threshold to waylay Bernald with the question as he was about to move past her in the wake of his companion.

"Oh, keep straight on, Mr. Winterman!" she interrupted herself to call after the latter. "Into the back drawing room, please! And remember, you're to sit next to me—in the corner on the left, close under the platform."

She renewed her interrogative clutch on Bernald's sleeve. "Most curious! Doctor Wade has been telling me all about him—how remarkable you all think him. And it's actually true that he's never heard of Pellerin? Of course as soon as Doctor Wade told me *that*, I said 'Bring him!' It will be so extraordinarily interesting to watch the first impression.—Yes, do follow him, dear Mr. Bernald, and be sure that you and he secure the seats next to me. Of course Alice Fosdick insists on being with us. She was wild with excitement when I told her she was to meet some one who'd never heard of Pellerin!"

On the indulgent lips of Mrs. Beecher Bain conjecture speedily passed into affirmation; and as Bernald's companion, broad and shaggy in his visibly new evening clothes, moved down the length of the crowded rooms, he was already, to the ladies drawing aside their skirts to let him pass, the interesting Huron of the fable.

How far he was aware of the character ascribed to him it was impossible for Bernald to discover. He was as unconscious as a tree or a cloud, and his observer had never known any one so alive to human contacts and yet so secure from them. But the scene was playing such a lively tune on Bernald's own sensibilities that for the moment he could not adjust himself to the probable effect it produced on his companion. The young man,

141

of late, had made but rare appearances in the group of which Mrs. Beecher Bain was one of the most indefatigable hostesses, and the Uplift Club the chief medium of expression. To a critic, obliged by his trade to cultivate convictions, it was the essence of luxury to leave them at home in his hours of ease; and Bernald gave his preference to circles in which less finality of judgment prevailed, and it was consequently less embarrassing to be caught without an opinion.

But in his fresher days he had known the spell of the Uplift Club and the thrill of moving among the Emancipated; and he felt an odd sense of rejuvenation as he looked at the rows of faces packed about the embowered platform from which Howland Wade was presently to hand down the eternal verities. Many of these countenances belonged to the old days, when the gospel of Pellerin was unknown, and it required considerable intellectual courage to avow one's acceptance of the very doctrines he had since demolished. The latter moral revolution seemed to have been accepted as submissively as a change in hairdressing; and it even struck Bernald that, in the case of many of the assembled ladies, their convictions were rather newer than their clothes.

One of the most interesting examples of this facility of adaptation was actually, in the person of Miss Alice Fosdick, brushing his elbow with exotic amulets, and enveloping him in Arabian odours, as she leaned forward to murmur her sympathetic sense of the situation. Miss Fosdick, who was one of the most advanced exponents of Pellerinism, had large eyes and a plaintive mouth, and Bernald had always fancied that she might have been pretty if she had not been perpetually explaining things.

"Yes, I know—Isabella Bain told me all about him. (He can't hear us, can he?) And I wonder if you realize how remarkably interesting it is that we should have such an opportunity *now*—I mean the opportunity to see the impression of Pellerinism on a perfectly fresh mind. (You must introduce him as soon as the lecture's over.) I explained that to Isabella as soon

142

as she showed me Doctor Wade's note. Of course you see why, don't you?" Bernald made a faint motion of acquiescence, which she instantly swept aside. "At least I think I can *make you see why.* (If you're sure he can't hear?) Why, it's just this—Pellerinism is in danger of becoming a truism. Oh, it's an awful thing to say! But then I'm not afraid of saying awful things! I rather believe it's my mission. What I mean is, that we're getting into the way of taking Pellerin for granted—as we do the air we breathe. We don't suffi-ciently lead our *conscious life* in him—we're gradually letting him become subliminal." She swayed closer to the young man, and he saw that she was making a graceful attempt to throw her explana-tory net over his companion, who, evading Mrs. Bain's hospitable signal, had cautiously wedged himself into a seat between Ber-nald and the wall.

"*Did* you hear what I was saying, Mr. Winterman? (Yes, I know who you are, of course!) Oh, well, I don't really mind if you did. I was talking about you—about you and Pellerin. I was explaining to Mr. Bernald that what we need at this very minute is a Pellerin revival; and we need some one like you— to whom his message comes as a wonderful new interpretation of life—to lead the revival, and rouse us out of our apathy. ...

"You see," she went on winningly, "it's not only the big public that needs it (of course *their* Pellerin isn't ours!) It's we, his disciples, his interpreters, who discovered him and gave him to the world—we, the Chosen People, the Custodians of the Sacred Books, as Howland Wade calls us—it's *we*, who are in perpetual danger of sinking back into the old stagnant ideals, and practising the Seven Deadly Virtues; it's *we* who need to count our mercies, and realize anew what he's done for us, and what we ought to do for him! And it's for that reason that I urged Mr. Wade to speak here, in the very inner sanctuary of Pellerinism, exactly as he would speak to the uninitiated—to repeat, simply, his Kenosha lecture, 'What Pellerinism means'; and we ought all, I think, to listen to him with the hearts of lit-tle children—just as *you* will, Mr. Winterman—as if he were telling us new things, and we—"

"Alice, *dear*—" Mrs. Bain murmured with a deprecating gesture; and Howland Wade, emerging between the palms, took the centre of the platform.

A pang of commiseration shot through Bernald as he saw him there, so innocent and so exposed. His plump pulpy body, which made his evening dress fall into intimate and wrapper-like folds, was like a wide surface spread to the shafts of irony; and the mild ripples of his voice seemed to enlarge the vulnerable area as he leaned forward, poised on confidential finger-tips, to say persuasively: "Let me try to tell you what Pellerinism means."

Bernald moved restlessly in his seat. He had the obscure sense of being a party to something not wholly honourable. He ought not to have come; he ought not to have let his companion come. Yet how could he have done otherwise? John Pellerin's secret was his own. As long as he chose to remain John Winterman it was no one's business to gainsay him; and Bernald's scruples were really justifiable only in respect of his own presence on the scene. But even in this connection he ceased to feel them as soon as Howland Wade began to speak.

VI

It had been arranged that Pellerin, after the meeting of the Uplift Club, should join Bernald at his rooms and spend the night there, instead of returning to Portchester. The plan had been eagerly elaborated by the young man, but he had been unprepared for the alacrity with which his wonderful friend accepted it. He was beginning to see that it was a part of Pellerin's wonderfulness to fall in, quite simply and naturally, with any arrangements made for his convenience, or tending to promote the convenience of others. Bernald felt that his extreme docility in such matters was proportioned to the force of resistance which, for nearly half a lifetime, had kept him, with his back to the wall, fighting alone against the powers of darkness. In such a scale of values how little the small daily alternatives must weigh!

At the close of Howland Wade's discourse, Bernald, charged with his prodigious secret, had felt the need to escape

144

for an instant from the liberated rush of talk. The interest of watching Pellerin was so perilously great that the watcher felt it might, at any moment, betray him. He lingered in the crowded drawing room long enough to see his friend enclosed in a mounting tide, above which Mrs. Beecher Bain and Miss Fosdick actively waved their conversational tridents; then he took refuge, at the back of the house, in a small dim library where, in his younger days, he had discussed personal immortality and the problem of consciousness with beautiful girls whose names he could not remember.

In this retreat he surprised Mr. Beecher Bain, a quiet man with a mild brow, who was smoking a surreptitious cigar over the last number of the *Strand*. Mr. Bain, at Bernald's approach, dissembled the *Strand* under a copy of the *Hibbert Journal*, but tendered his cigar case with the remark that stocks were heavy again; and Bernald blissfully abandoned himself to this unexpected contact with reality.

On his return to the drawing room he found that the tide had set toward the supper table, and when it finally carried him thither it was to land him in the welcoming arms of Bob Wade.

"Hullo, old man! Where have you been all this time?— Winterman? Oh, *he's* talking to Howland: yes, I managed it finally. I believe Mrs. Bain has steered them into the library, so that they shan't be disturbed. I gave her an idea of the situation, and she was awfully kind. We'd better leave them alone, don't you think? I'm trying to get a croquette for Miss Fosdick."

Bernald's secret leapt in his bosom, and he devoted himself to the task of distributing sandwiches and champagne while his pulses danced to the tune of the cosmic laughter. The vision of Pellerin and his Interpreter, face to face at last, had a Cyclopean grandeur that dwarfed all other comedy. "And I shall hear of it presently; in an hour or two he'll be telling me about it. And that hour will be all mine—mine and his!" The dizziness of the thought made it difficult for Bernald to preserve the balance of the supper plates he was distributing. Life had for him at that moment the completeness that seems to defy disintegration.

The throng in the dining room was thickening, and Bernald's efforts as purveyor were interrupted by frequent appeals, from ladies who had reached repleteness, that he should sit down a moment and tell them all about his interesting friend. Winterman's fame, trumpeted abroad by Miss Fosdick, had reached the four corners of the Uplift Club, and Bernald found himself fabricating *de toutes pieces* a Winterman legend which should in some degree respond to the Club's demand for the human document. When at length he had acquitted himself of this obligation, and was free to work his way back through the lessening groups into the drawing room, he was at last rewarded by a glimpse of his friend, who, still densely encompassed, towered in the centre of the room in all his sovran ugliness.

Their eyes met across the crowd; but Bernald gathered only perplexity from the encounter. What were Pellerin's eyes saying to him? What orders, what confidences, what indefinable apprehension did their long look impart? The young man was still trying to decipher their complex message when he felt a tap on the arm, and turned to encounter the rueful gaze of Bob Wade, whose meaning lay clearly enough on the surface of his good blue stare.

"Well, it won't work—it won't work," the doctor groaned.

"What won't?"

"I mean with Howland. Winterman won't. Howland doesn't take to him. Says he's crude—frightfully crude. And you know how Howland hates crudeness."

"Oh, I know," Bernald exulted. It was the word he had waited for—he saw it now! Once more he was lost in wonder at Howland's miraculous faculty for always, as the naturalists said, being true to type.

"So I'm afraid it's all up with his chance of writing. At least *I* can do no more," said Wade, discouraged.

Bernald pressed him for farther details. "Does Winterman seem to mind much? Did you hear his version?"

"His version?"

"I mean what he said to Howland."

"Why no. What the deuce was there for him to say?"

"What indeed? I think I'll take him home," said Bernald gaily.

He turned away to join the circle from which, a few minutes before, Pellerin's eyes had vainly and enigmatically signaled to him; but the circle had dispersed, and Pellerin himself was not in sight.

Bernald, looking about him, saw that during his brief aside with Wade the party had passed into the final phase of dissolution. People still delayed, in diminishing groups, but the current had set toward the doors, and every moment or two it bore away a few more lingerers. Bernald, from his post, commanded the clearing perspective of the two drawing rooms, and a rapid survey of their length sufficed to assure him that Pellerin was not in either. Taking leave of Wade, the young man made his way back to the drawing room, where only a few hardened feasters remained, and then passed on to the library which had been the scene of the late momentous colloquy. But the library too was empty, and drifting back uncertainly to the inner drawing room Bernald found Mrs. Beecher Bain domestically putting out the wax candles on the mantelpiece.

"Dear Mr. Bernald! Do sit down and have a little chat. What a wonderful privilege it has been! I don't know when I've had such an intense impression."

She made way for him, hospitably, in a corner of the sofa to which she had sunk; and he echoed her vaguely: "You *were* impressed, then?"

"I can't express to you how it affected me! As Alice said, it was a resurrection—it was as if John Pellerin were actually here in the room with us!"

Bernald turned on her with a half-audible gasp. "You felt that, dear Mrs. Bain?"

"We all felt it—every one of us! I don't wonder the Greeks—it *was* the Greeks?—regarded eloquence as a supernatural power. As Alice says, when one looked at Howland Wade one understood what they meant by the Afflatus."

Bernald rose and held out his hand. "Oh, I see—it was

Howland who made you feel as if Pellerin were in the room? And he made Miss Fosdick feel so too?"

"Why, of course. But why are you rushing off?"

"Because I must hunt up my friend, who's not used to such late hours."

"Your friend?" Mrs. Bain had to collect her thoughts. "Oh, Mr. Winterman, you mean? But he's gone already."

"Gone?" Bernald exclaimed, with an odd twinge of foreboding. Remembering Pellerin's signal across the crowd, he reproached himself for not having answered it more promptly. Yet it was certainly strange that his friend should have left the house without him.

"Are you quite sure?" he asked, with a startled glance at the clock.

"Oh, perfectly. He went half an hour ago. But you needn't hurry home on his account, for Alice Fosdick carried him off with her. I saw them leave together."

"Carried him off? She took him home with her, you mean?"

"Yes. You know what strange hours she keeps. She told me she was going to give him a Welsh rabbit, and explain Pellerinism to him."

"Oh, *if* she's going to explain—" Bernald murmured. But his amazement at the news struggled with a confused impatience to reach his rooms in time to be there for his friend's arrival. There could be no stranger spectacle beneath the stars than that of John Pellerin carried off by Miss Fosdick, and listening, in the small hours, to her elucidation of his doctrines; but Bernald knew enough of his sex to be aware that such an experiment may present a less humorous side to its subject than to an impartial observer. Even the Uplift Club and its connotations might benefit by the attraction of the unknown; and it was conceivable that to a traveller from Mesopotamia Miss Fosdick might present elements of interest that she had lost for the frequenters of Fifth Avenue. There was, at any rate, no denying that the affair had become unexpectedly complex, and that its farther development promised to be rich in comedy.

148

In the charmed contemplation of these possibilities Bernald sat over his fire, listening for Pellerin's ring. He had arranged his modest quarters with the reverent care of a celebrant awaiting the descent of his deity. He guessed Pellerin to be unconscious of visual detail, but sensitive to the happy blending of sensuous impressions: to the intimate spell of lamplight on books, and of a deep chair placed where one could watch the fire. The chair was there, and Bernald, facing it across the hearth, already saw it filled by Pellerin's lounging figure. The autumn dawn came late, and even now they had before them the promise of some untroubled hours. Bernald, sitting there alone in the warm stillness of his room, and in the profounder hush of his expectancy, was conscious of gathering up all his sensibilities and perceptions into one exquisitely adjusted instrument of notation. Until now he had tasted Pellerin's society only in unpremeditated snatches, and had always left him with a sense, on his own part, of waste and shortcoming. Now, in the lull of this dedicated hour, he felt that he should miss nothing, and forget nothing, of the initiation that awaited him. And catching sight of Pellerin's pipe, he rose and laid it carefully on a table by the armchair.

"No. I've never had any news of him," Bernald heard himself repeating. He spoke in a low tone, and with the automatic utterance that alone made it possible to say the words.

They were addressed to Miss Fosdick, into whose neighbourhood chance had thrown him at a dinner, a year or so later than their encounter at the Uplift Club. Hitherto he had successfully, and intentionally, avoided Miss Fosdick, not from any animosity toward that unconscious instrument of fate, but from an intense reluctance to pronounce the words that he knew he should have to speak if they met.

Now, as it turned out, his chief surprise was that she should wait so long to make him speak them. All through the dinner she had swept him along on a rapid current of talk that showed no tendency to linger or turn back upon the past. At first he ascribed her reserve to a sense of delicacy with which he reproached himself for not having previously credited her; then he saw that she had been carried so far beyond the point at which they had last faced each other, that it was by the merest hazard of associated ideas that she was now finally borne back to it. For it appeared that the very next evening, at Mrs. Beecher Bain's, a Hindu Mahatma was to lecture to the Uplift Club on the Limits of the Subliminal; and it was owing to no less a person than Howland Wade that this exceptional privilege had been obtained.

"Of course Howland's known all over the world as the interpreter of Pellerinism, and the Aga Gautch, who had absolutely declined to speak anywhere in public, wrote to Isabella that he could not refuse anything that Mr. Wade asked. Did you know that Howland's lecture, 'What Pellerinism Means,' has been translated into twenty-two languages, and gone into a fifth edition in Icelandic? Why, that reminds me," Miss Fosdick broke off—"I've never heard what became of your queer friend—what was his name?—whom you and Bob Wade accused me of spiriting away after that very lecture. And I've never seen *you* since you rushed into the house the next morning, and dragged me out of bed to know what I'd done with him!"

With a sharp effort Bernald gathered himself together to have it out. "Well, what *did* you do with him?" he retorted.

She laughed her appreciation of his humor. "Just what I told you, of course. I said goodbye to him on Isabella's doorstep."

Bernald looked at her. "It's really true, then, that he didn't go home with you?"

She bantered back: "Have you suspected me, all this time, of hiding his remains in the cellar?" And with a droop of her fine lids she added: "I wish he *had* come home with me, for he was rather interesting, and there were things I think I could have explained to him."

Bernald helped himself to a nectarine, and Miss Fosdick continued on a note of amused curiosity: "So you've really never had any news of him since that night?"

"No—I've never had any news of him."

"Not the least little message?"

"Not the least little message."

"Or a rumour or report of any kind?"

"Or a rumour or report of any kind."

Miss Fosdick's interest seemed to be revived by the strangeness of the case. "It's rather creepy, isn't it? What *could* have happened? You don't suppose he could have been waylaid and murdered?" she asked with brightening eyes.

Bernald shook his head serenely. "No. I'm sure he's safe—quite safe."

"But if you're sure, you must know something."

"No. I know nothing," he repeated.

She scanned him incredulously. "But what's your theory—for you must have a theory? What in the world can have become of him?"

Bernald returned her look and hesitated. "Do you happen to remember the last thing he said to you—the very last, on the doorstep, when he left you?"

"The last thing?" She poised her fork above the peach on her plate. "I don't think he said anything. Oh, yes—when I reminded him that he'd solemnly promised to come back with me and have a little talk he said he couldn't because he was going home."

"Well, then, I suppose," said Bernald, "he went home."

She glanced at him as if suspecting a trap. "Dear me, how flat! I always inclined to a mysterious murder. But of course you know more of him than you say."

She began to cut her peach, but paused above a lifted bit to ask, with a renewal of animation in her expressive eyes: "By the way, had you heard that Howland Wade has been gradually getting farther and farther away from Pellerinism? It seems he's begun to feel that there's a Positivist element in it that is narrowing to any one who has gone at all deeply into the Wisdom of the East. He was intensely interesting about it the other day, and of course I *do* see what he feels...Oh, it's too long to tell you now; but if you could manage to come in to tea some afternoon soon—any day but Wednesday—I should so like to explain—"

THE EYES

I

We had been put in the mood for ghosts, that evening, after an excellent dinner at our old friend Culwin's, by a tale of Fred Murchard's—the narrative of a strange personal visitation.

Seen through the haze of our cigars, and by the drowsy gleam of a coal fire, Culwin's library, with its oak walls and dark old bindings, made a good setting for such evocations; and ghostly experiences at first hand being, after Murchard's brilliant opening, the only kind acceptable to us, we proceeded to take stock of our group and tax each member for a contribution. There were eight of us, and seven contrived, in a manner more or less adequate, to fulfil the condition imposed. It surprised us all to find that we could muster such a show of supernatural impressions, for none of us, excepting Murchard himself and young Phil Frenham—whose story was the slightest of the lot—had the habit of sending our souls into the invisible. So that, on the whole, we had every reason to be proud of our seven "exhibits," and none of us would have dreamed of expecting an eighth from our host.

Our old friend, Mr. Andrew Culwin, who had sat back in his armchair, listening and blinking through the smoke circles with the cheerful tolerance of a wise old idol, was not the kind of man likely to be favored with such contacts, though he had imagination enough to enjoy, without envying, the superior privileges of his guests. By age and by education he belonged to the stout Positivist tradition, and his habit of thought had been formed in the days of the epic struggle between physics and metaphysics. But he had been, then and always, essentially a spectator, a humorous detached observer of the immense muddled variety show of life, slipping out of his seat now and then for a brief dip into the convivialities at the back of the house, but never, as far as one knew, showing the least desire to jump on the stage and do a "turn."

Among his contemporaries there lingered a vague tradition of his having, at a remote period, and in a romantic clime, been wounded in a duel; but this legend no more tallied with what we younger men knew of his character than my mother's assertion that he had once been "a charming little man with nice eyes" corresponded to any possible reconstitution of his dry thwarted physiognomy.

"He never can have looked like anything but a bundle of sticks," Murchard had once said of him. "Or a phosphorescent log, rather," some one else amended; and we recognized the happiness of this description of his small squat trunk, with the red blink of the eyes in a face like mottled bark. He had always been possessed of a leisure that he had nursed and protected, instead of squandering it in vain activities. His carefully guarded hours had been devoted to the cultivation of a fine intelligence and a few judiciously chosen habits; and none of the disturbances common to human experience seemed to have crossed his sky. Nevertheless, his dispassionate survey of the universe had not raised his opinion of that costly experiment, and his study of the human race seemed to have resulted in the conclusion that all men were superfluous, and women necessary only because some one had to do the cooking. On the importance of this point his convictions were absolute, and gastronomy was the only science that he revered as dogma. It must be owned that his little dinners were a strong argument in favour of this view, besides being a reason—though not the main one—for the fidelity of his friends.

Mentally he exercised a hospitality less seductive but no less stimulating. His mind was like a forum, or some open meeting place for the exchange of ideas: somewhat cold and draughty, but light, spacious and orderly—a kind of academic grove from which all the leaves had fallen. In this privileged area a dozen of us were wont to stretch our muscles and expand our lungs; and, as if to prolong as much as possible the tradition of what we felt to be a vanishing institution, one or two neophytes were now and then added to our band.

Young Phil Frenham was the last, and the most interesting, of these recruits, and a good example of Murchard's somewhat morbid assertion that our old friend "liked 'em juicy." It was indeed a fact that Culwin, for all his mental dryness, specially tasted the lyric qualities in youth. As he was far too good an Epicurean to nip the flowers of soul which he gathered for his garden, his friendship was not a disintegrating influence: on the contrary, it forced the young idea to robuster bloom. And in Phil Frenham he had a fine subject for experimentation. The boy was really intelligent, and the soundness of his nature was like the pure paste under a delicate glaze. Culwin had fished him out of a thick fog of family dulness, and pulled him up to a peak in Darien; and the adventure hadn't hurt him a bit. Indeed, the skill with which Culwin had contrived to stimulate his curiosities without robbing them of their young bloom of awe seemed to me a sufficient answer to Murchard's ogreish metaphor. There was nothing hectic in Frenham's efflorescence, and his old friend had not laid even a fingertip on the sacred stupidities. One wanted no better proof of that than the fact that Frenham still reverenced them in Culwin.

"There's a side of him you fellows don't see. *I* believe that story about the duel!" he declared; and it was of the very essence of this belief that it should impel him—just as our little party was dispersing—to turn back to our host with the absurd demand: "And now you've got to tell us about *your* ghost!"

The outer door had closed on Murchard and the others; only Frenham and I remained; and the vigilant servant who presided over Culwin's destinies, having brought a fresh supply of soda water, had been laconically ordered to bed.

Culwin's sociability was a night-blooming flower, and we knew that he expected the nucleus of his group to tighten around him after midnight. But Frenham's appeal seemed to disconcert him comically, and he rose from the chair in which he had just reseated himself after his farewells in the hall.

"*My* ghost? Do you suppose I'm fool enough to go to the expense of keeping one of my own, when there are so many

154

charming ones in my friends' closets?—Take another cigar," he said, revolving toward me with a laugh.

Frenham laughed too, pulling up his slender height before the chimneypiece as he turned to face his short bristling friend.

"Oh," he said, "you'd never be content to share if you met one you really liked."

Culwin had dropped back into his armchair, his shock head embedded in its habitual hollow, his little eyes glimmering over a fresh cigar.

"Liked—*liked?* Good Lord!" he growled.

"Ah, you *have*, then!" Frenham pounced on him in the same instant, with a sidewise glance of victory at me; but Culwin cowered gnomelike among his cushions, dissembling himself in a protective cloud of smoke.

"What's the use of denying it? You've seen everything, so of course you've seen a ghost!" his young friend persisted, talking intrepidly into the cloud. "Or, if you haven't seen one, it's only because you've seen two!"

The form of the challenge seemed to strike our host. He shot his head out of the mist with a queer tortoise-like motion he sometimes had, and blinked approvingly at Frenham.

"Yes," he suddenly flung at us on a shrill jerk of laughter; "it's only because I've seen two!"

The words were so unexpected that they dropped down and down into a fathomless silence, while we continued to stare at each other over Culwin's head, and Culwin stared at his ghosts. At length Frenham, without speaking, threw himself into the chair on the other side of the hearth, and leaned forward with his listening smile...

II

"OH, of course they're not show ghosts—a collector wouldn't think anything of them...Don't let me raise your hopes...their one merit is their numerical strength: the exceptional fact of their being *two*. But, as against this, I'm bound to admit that at any moment I could probably have exorcised them both by asking my doctor for a prescription, or my oculist

155

for a pair of spectacles. Only, as I never could make up my mind whether to go to the doctor or the oculist—whether I was afflicted by an optical or a digestive delusion—I left them to pursue their interesting double life, though at times they made mine exceedingly comfortable...

"Yes—uncomfortable; and you know how I hate to be uncomfortable! But it was part of my stupid pride, when the thing began, not to admit that I could be disturbed by the trifling matter of seeing two—

"And then I'd no reason, really, to suppose I was ill. As far as I knew I was simply bored—horribly bored. But it was part of my boredom—I remember—that I was feeling so uncommonly well, and didn't know how on earth to work off my surplus energy. I had come back from a long journey—down in South America and Mexico—and had settled down for the winter near New York, with an old aunt who had known Washington Irving and corresponded with N. P. Willis. She lived, not far from Irvington, in a damp Gothic villa, overhung by Norway spruces, and looking exactly like a memorial emblem done in hair. Her personal appearance was in keeping with this image, and her own hair—of which there was little left—might have been sacrificed to the manufacture of the emblem.

"I had just reached the end of an agitated year, with considerable arrears to make up in money and emotion; and theoretically it seemed as though my aunt's mild hospitality would be as beneficial to my nerves as to my purse. But the deuce of it was that as soon as I felt myself safe and sheltered my energy began to revive; and how was I to work it off inside of a memorial emblem? I had, at that time, the agreeable illusion that sustained intellectual effort could engage a man's whole activity; and I decided to write a great book—I forget about what. My aunt, impressed by my plan, gave up to me her Gothic library, filled with classics in black cloth and daguerrotypes of faded celebrities; and I sat down at my desk to make myself a place among their number. And to facilitate my task she lent me a cousin to copy my manuscript.

156

"The cousin was a nice girl, and I had an idea that a nice girl was just what I needed to restore my faith in human nature, and principally in myself. She was neither beautiful nor intelligent—poor Alice Nowell!—but it interested me to see any woman content to be so uninteresting, and I wanted to find out the secret of her content. In doing this I handled it rather rashly, and put it out of joint—oh, just for a moment! There's no fatuity in telling you this, for the poor girl had never seen any one but cousins...

"Well, I was sorry for what I'd done, of course, and confoundedly bothered as to how I should put it straight. She was staying in the house, and one evening, after my aunt had gone to bed, she came down to the library to fetch a book she'd mislaid, like any artless heroine on the shelves behind us. She was pink-nosed and flustered, and it suddenly occurred to me that her hair, though it was fairly thick and pretty, would look exactly like my aunt's when she grew older. I was glad I had noticed this, for it made it easier for me to do what was right; and when I had found the book she hadn't lost I told her I was leaving for Europe that week.

"Europe was terribly far off in those days, and Alice knew at once what I meant. She didn't take it in the least as I'd expected—it would have been easier if she had. She held her book very tight, and turned away a moment to wind up the lamp on my desk—it had a ground glass shade with vine leaves, and glass drops around the edge, I remember. Then she came back, held out her hand, and said: 'Goodbye.' And as she said it she looked straight at me and kissed me. I had never felt anything as fresh and shy and brave as her kiss. It was worse than any reproach, and it made me ashamed to deserve a reproach from her. I said to myself: 'I'll marry her, and when my aunt dies she'll leave us this house, and I'll sit here at the desk and go on with my book; and Alice will sit over there with her embroidery and look at me as she's looking now. And life will go on like that for any number of years.' The prospect frightened me a little, but at the time it didn't frighten me as much as doing anything to hurt her; and ten minutes later she had my seal ring on my finger, and my promise that when I went abroad she should go with me.

"You'll wonder why I'm enlarging on this familiar incident. It's because the evening on which it took place was the very evening on which I first saw the queer sight I've spoken of. Being at that time an ardent believer in a necessary sequence between cause and effect I naturally tried to trace some kind of link between what had just happened to me in my aunt's library, and what was to happen a few hours later on the same night; and so the coincidence between the two events always remained in my mind.

"I went up to bed with rather a heavy heart, for I was bowed under the weight of the first good action I had ever consciously committed; and young as I was, I saw the gravity of my situation. Don't imagine from this that I had hitherto been an instrument of destruction. I had been merely a harmless young man, who had followed his bent and declined all collaboration with Providence. Now I had suddenly undertaken to promote the moral order of the world, and I felt a good deal like the trustful spectator who has given his gold watch to the conjurer, and doesn't know in what shape he'll get it back when the trick is over...Still, a glow of self-righteousness tempered my fears, and I said to myself as I undressed that when I'd got used to being good it probably wouldn't make me as nervous as it did at the start. And by the time I was in bed, and had blown out my candle, I felt that I really *was* getting used to it, and that, as far as I'd got, it was not unlike sinking down into one of my aunt's very softest wool mattresses.

"I closed my eyes on this image, and when I opened them it must have been a good deal later, for my room had grown cold, and the night was intensely still. I was waked suddenly by the feeling we all know—the feeling that there was something near me that hadn't been there when I fell asleep. I sat up and strained my eyes into the darkness. The room was pitch black, and at first I saw nothing; but gradually a vague glimmer at the
158

foot of the bed turned into two eyes staring back at me. I couldn't see the face attached to them—on account of the darkness, I imagined—but as I looked the eyes grew more and more distinct: they gave out a light of their own.

"The sensation of being thus gazed at was far from pleasant, and you might suppose that my first impulse would have been to jump out of bed and hurl myself on the invisible figure attached to the eyes. But it wasn't—my impulse was simply to lie still...I can't say whether this was due to an immediate sense of the uncanny nature of the apparition—to the certainty that if I did jump out of bed I should hurl myself on nothing—or merely to the benumbing effect of the eyes themselves. They were the very worst eyes I've ever seen: a man's eyes—but what a man! My first thought was that he must be frightfully old. The orbits were sunk, and the thick redlined lids hung over the eyeballs like blinds of which the cords are broken. One lid drooped a little lower than the other, with the effect of a crooked leer; and between these pulpy folds of flesh, with their scant bristle of lashes, the eyes themselves, small glassy disks with an agate-like rim about the pupils, looked like sea pebbles in the grip of a starfish.

"But the age of the eyes was not the most unpleasant thing about them. What turned me sick was their expression of vicious security. I don't know how else to describe the fact that they seemed to belong to a man who had done a lot of harm in his life, but had always kept just inside the danger lines. They were not the eyes of a coward, but of some one much too clever to take risks; and my gorge rose at their look of base astuteness. Yet even that wasn't the worst; for as we continued to scan each other I saw in them a tinge of faint derision, and felt myself to be its object.

"At that I was seized by an impulse of rage that jerked me out of bed and pitched me straight on the unseen figure at its foot. But of course there wasn't any figure there, and my fists struck at emptiness. Ashamed and cold, I groped about for a match and lit the candles. The room looked just as usual—as I

159

had known it would; and I crawled back to bed, and blew out the lights.

"As soon as the room was dark again the eyes reappeared; and I now applied myself to explaining them on scientific principles. At first I thought the illusion might have been caused by the glow of the last embers in the chimney; but the fireplace was on the other side of my bed, and so placed that the fire could not possibly be reflected in my toilet glass, which was the only mirror in the room. Then it occurred to me that I might have been tricked by the reflection of the embers in some polished bit of wood or metal; and though I couldn't discover any object of the sort in my line of vision, I got up again, groped my way to the hearth, and covered what was left of the fire. But as soon as I was back in bed the eyes were back at its foot.

"They were an hallucination, then: that was plain. But the fact that they were not due to any external dupery didn't make them a bit pleasanter to see. For if they were a projection of my inner consciousness, what the deuce was the matter with that organ? I had gone deeply enough into the mystery of morbid pathological states to picture the conditions under which an exploring mind might lay itself open to such a midnight admonition; but I couldn't fit it to my present case. I had never felt more normal, mentally and physically; and the only unusual fact in my situation—that of having assured the happiness of an amiable girl—did not seem of a kind to summon unclean spirits about my pillow. But there were the eyes still looking at me...

"I shut mine, and tried to evoke a vision of Alice Nowell's. They were not remarkable eyes, but they were as wholesome as fresh water, and if she had had more imagination—or longer lashes—their expression might have been interesting. As it was, they did not prove very efficacious, and in a few moments I perceived that they had mysteriously changed into the eyes at the foot of the bed. It exasperated me more to feel these glaring at me through my shut lids than to see them, and I opened my eyes again and looked straight into their hateful stare...

"And so it went on all night. I can't tell you what that night was, nor how long it lasted. Have you ever lain in bed, hopelessly wide awake, and tried to keep your eyes shut, knowing that if you opened 'em you'd see something you dreaded and loathed? It sounds easy, but it's devilish hard. Those eyes hung there and drew me. I had the *vertige de l'abime*, and their red lids were the edge of my abyss...I had known nervous hours before: hours when I'd felt the wind of danger in my neck; but never this kind of strain. It wasn't that the eyes were so awful; they hadn't the majesty of the powers of darkness. But they had—how shall I say?—a physical effect that was the equivalent of a bad smell: their look left a smear like a snail's. And I didn't see what business they had with me, anyhow—and I stared and stared, trying to find out...

"I don't know what effect they were trying to produce; but the effect they *did* produce was that of making me pack my portmanteau and bolt to town early the next morning. I left a note for my aunt, explaining that I was ill and had gone to see my doctor; and as a matter of fact I did feel uncommonly ill— the night seemed to have pumped all the blood out of me. But when I reached town I didn't go to the doctor's. I went to a friend's rooms, and threw myself on a bed, and slept for ten heavenly hours. When I woke it was the middle of the night, and I turned cold at the thought of what might be waiting for me. I sat up, shaking, and stared into the darkness; but there wasn't a break in its blessed surface, and when I saw that the eyes were not there I dropped back into another long sleep.

"I had left no word for Alice when I fled, because I meant to go back the next morning. But the next morning I was too exhausted to stir. As the day went on the exhaustion increased, instead of wearing off like the lassitude left by an ordinary night of insomnia: the effect of the eyes seemed to be cumulative, and the thought of seeing them again grew intolerable. For two days I struggled with my dread; but on the third evening I pulled myself together and decided to go back the next morning. I felt a good deal happier as soon as I'd decided, for I knew that my abrupt disappearance, and the strangeness of my not writing, must have been very painful for poor Alice. That night I went to bed with an easy mind, and fell asleep at once; but in the middle of the night I woke, and there were the eyes...

"Well, I simply couldn't face them; and instead of going back to my aunt's I bundled a few things into a trunk and jumped onto the first steamer for England. I was so dead tired when I got on board that I crawled straight into my berth, and slept most of the way over; and I can't tell you the bliss it was to wake from those long stretches of dreamless sleep and look fearlessly into the darkness, *knowing* that I shouldn't see the eyes...

"I stayed abroad for a year, and then I stayed for another; and during that time I never had a glimpse of them. That was enough reason for prolonging my stay if I'd been on a desert island. Another was, of course, that I had perfectly come to see, on the voyage over, the folly, complete impossibility, of my marrying Alice Nowell. The fact that I had been so slow in making this discovery annoyed me, and made me want to avoid explanations. The bliss of escaping at one stroke from the eyes, and from this other embarrassment, gave my freedom an extraordinary zest; and the longer I savored it the better I liked its taste.

"The eyes had burned such a hole in my consciousness that for a long time I went on puzzling over the nature of the apparition, and wondering nervously if it would ever come back. But as time passed I lost this dread, and retained only the precision of the image. Then that faded in its turn.

"The second year found me settled in Rome, where I was planning, I believe, to write another great book—a definitive work on Etruscan influences in Italian art. At any rate, I'd found some pretext of the kind for taking a sunny apartment in the Piazza di Spagna and dabbling about indefinitely in the Forum; and there, one morning, a charming youth came to me. As he stood there in the warm light, slender and smooth and hyacinthine, he might have stepped from a ruined altar—one to

Antinous, say—but he'd come instead from New York, with a letter (of all people) from Alice Nowell. The letter—the first I'd had from her since our break—was simply a line introducing her young cousin, Gilbert Noyes, and appealing to me to befriend him. It appeared, poor lad, that he 'had talent,' and 'wanted to write'; and, an obdurate family having insisted that his calligraphy should take the form of double entry, Alice had intervened to win him six months' respite, during which he was to travel on a meagre pittance, and somehow prove his ultimate ability to increase it by his pen. The quaint conditions of the test struck me first: it seemed about as conclusive as a mediaeval 'ordeal.' Then I was touched by her having sent him to me. I had always wanted to do her some service, to justify myself in my own eyes rather than hers; and here was a beautiful embodiment of my chance.

"Well, I imagine it's safe to lay down the general principle that predestined geniuses don't, as a rule, appear before one in the spring sunshine of the Forum looking like one of its banished gods. At any rate, poor Noyes wasn't a predestined genius. But he *was* beautiful to see, and charming as a comrade too. It was only when he began to talk literature that my heart failed me. I knew all the symptoms so well—the things he had 'in him,' and the things outside him that impinged! There's the real test, after all. It was always—punctually, inevitably, with the inexorableness of a mechanical law—it was *always* the wrong thing that struck him. I grew to find a certain grim fascination in deciding in advance exactly which wrong thing he'd select; and I acquired an astonishing skill at the game...

"The worst of it was that his *betise* wasn't of the too obvious sort. Ladies who met him at picnics thought him intellectual; and even at dinners he passed for clever. I, who had him under the microscope, fancied now and then that he might develop some kind of a slim talent, something that he could make 'do' and be happy on; and wasn't that, after all, what I was concerned with? He was so charming—he continued to be so charming—that he called forth all my charity in support of this argument; and for the first few months I really believed there was a chance for him...

"Those months were delightful. Noyes was constantly with me, and the more I saw of him the better I liked him. His stupidity was a natural grace—it was as beautiful, really, as his eyelashes. And he was so gay, so affectionate, and so happy with me, that telling him the truth would have been about as pleasant as slitting the throat of some artless animal. At first I used to wonder what had put into that radiant head the detestable delusion that it held a brain. Then I began to see that it was simply protective mimicry—an instinctive ruse to get away from family life and an office desk. Not that Gilbert didn't— dear lad!—believe in himself. There wasn't a trace of hypocrisy in his composition. He was sure that his 'call' was irresistible, while to me it was the saving grace of his situation that it *wasn't*, and that a little money, a little leisure, a little pleasure would have turned him into an inoffensive idler. Unluckily, however, there was no hope of money, and with the grim alternative of the office desk before him he couldn't postpone his attempt at literature. The stuff he turned out was deplorable, and I see now that I knew it from the first. Still, the absurdity of deciding a man's whole future on a first trial seemed to justify me in withholding my verdict, and perhaps even in encouraging him a little, on the ground that the human plant generally needs warmth to flower.

"At any rate, I proceeded on that principle, and carried it to the point of getting his term of probation extended. When I left Rome he went with me, and we idled away a delicious summer between Capri and Venice. I said to myself: 'If he has anything in him, it will come out now; and it *did*. He was never more enchanting and enchanted. There were moments of our pilgrimage when beauty born of murmuring sound seemed actually to pass into his face—but only to issue forth in a shallow flood of the palest ink...

"Well the time came to turn off the tap; and I knew there was no hand but mine to do it. We were back in Rome, and I had taken him to stay with me, not wanting him to be alone in his dismal *pension* when he had to face the necessity of renouncing his ambition. I hadn't, of course, relied solely on my own judgment in deciding to advise him to drop literature. I had sent his stuff to various people—editors and critics—and they had always sent it back with the same chilling lack of comment. Really there was nothing on earth to say about it—

"I confess I never felt more shabbily than I did on the day when I decided to have it out with Gilbert. It was well enough to tell myself that it was my duty to knock the poor boy's hopes into splinters—but I'd like to know what act of gratuitous cruelty hasn't been justified on that plea? I've always shrunk from usurping the functions of Providence, and when I have to exercise them I decidedly prefer that it shouldn't be on an errand of destruction. Besides, in the last issue, who was I to decide, even after a year's trial, if poor Gilbert had it in him or not?

"The more I looked at the part I'd resolved to play, the less I liked it; and I liked it still less when Gilbert sat opposite me, with his head thrown back in the lamplight, just as Phil's is now...I'd been going over his last manuscript, and he knew it, and he knew that his future hung on my verdict—we'd tacitly agreed to that. The manuscript lay between us, on my table—a novel, his first novel, if you please!—and he reached over and laid his hand on it, and looked up at me with all his life in the look.

"I stood up and cleared my throat, trying to keep my eyes away from his face and on the manuscript.

"'The fact is, my dear Gilbert,' I began—

"I saw him turn pale, but he was up and facing me in an instant.

"'Oh, look here, don't take on so, my dear fellow! I'm not so awfully cut up as all that!' His hands were on my shoulders, and he was laughing down on me from his full height, with a kind of mortally stricken gaiety that drove the knife into my side.

"He was too beautifully brave for me to keep up any humbug about my duty. And it came over me suddenly how I

165

should hurt others in hurting him: myself first, since sending him home meant losing him; but more particularly poor Alice Nowell, to whom I had so uneasily longed to prove my good faith and my immense desire to serve her. It really seemed like failing her twice to fail Gilbert—

"But my intuition was like one of those lightning flashes that encircle the whole horizon, and in the same instant I saw what I might be letting myself in for if I didn't tell the truth. I said to myself: 'I shall have him for life'—and I'd never yet seen any one, man or woman, whom I was quite sure of wanting on those terms. Well, this impulse of egotism decided me. I was ashamed of it, and to get away from it I took a leap that landed me straight in Gilbert's arms.

"'The thing's all right, and you're all wrong!' I shouted up at him; and as he hugged me, and I laughed and shook in his incredulous clutch, I had for a minute the sense of self-complacency that is supposed to attend the footsteps of the just. Hang it all, making people happy *has* its charms—

"Gilbert, of course, was for celebrating his emancipation in some spectacular manner; but I sent him away alone to explode his emotions, and went to bed to sleep off mine. As I undressed I began to wonder what their after-taste would be—so many of the finest don't keep! Still, I wasn't sorry, and I meant to empty the bottle, even if it *did* turn a trifle flat.

"After I got into bed I lay for a long time smiling at the memory of his eyes—his blissful eyes...Then I fell asleep, and when I woke the room was deathly cold, and I sat up with a jerk—and there were *the other eyes* ...

"It was three years since I'd seen them, but I'd thought of them so often that I fancied they could never take me unawares again. Now, with their red sneer on me, I knew that I had never really believed they would come back, and that I was as defenceless as ever against them...As before, it was the insane irrelevance of their coming that made it so horrible. What the deuce were they after, to leap out at me at such a time? I had lived more or less carelessly in the years since I'd seen them,

166

though my worst indiscretions were not dark enough to invite the searchings of their infernal glare; but at this particular moment I was really in what might have been called a state of grace; and I can't tell you how the fact added to their horror...

"But it's not enough to say they were as bad as before: they were worse. Worse by just so much as I'd learned of life in the interval; by all the damnable implications my wider experience read into them. I saw now what I hadn't seen before: that they were eyes which had grown hideous gradually, which had built up their baseness coral-wise, bit by bit, out of a series of small turpitudes slowly accumulated through the industrious years. Yes—it came to me that what made them so bad was that they'd grown bad so slowly...

"There they hung in the darkness, their swollen lids dropped across the little watery bulbs rolling loose in the orbits, and the puff of fat flesh making a muddy shadow underneath—and as their filmy stare moved with my movements, there came over me a sense of their tacit complicity, of a deep hidden understanding between us that was worse than the first shock of their strangeness. Not that I understood them; but that they made it so clear that some day I should...Yes, that was the worst part of it, decidedly; and it was the feeling that became stronger each time they came back to me...

"For they got into the damnable habit of coming back. They reminded me of vampires with a taste for young flesh, they seemed so to gloat over the taste of a good conscience. Every night for a month they came to claim their morsel of mine: since I'd made Gilbert happy they simply wouldn't loosen their fangs. The coincidence almost made me hate him, poor lad, fortuitous as I felt it to be. I puzzled over it a good deal, but couldn't find any hint of an explanation except in the chance of his association with Alice Nowell. But then the eyes had let up on me the moment I had abandoned her, so they could hardly be the emissaries of a woman scorned, even if one could have pictured poor Alice charging such spirits to avenge her. That set me thinking, and I began to wonder if they would let up on me if I abandoned Gilbert. The temptation was insidious, and I had to stiffen myself against it; but really, dear boy! he was too charming to be sacrificed to such demons. And so, after all, I never found out what they wanted..."

III

THE fire crumbled, sending up a flash that threw into relief the narrator's gnarled red face under its grey-black stubble. Pressed into the hollow of the dark leather armchair, it stood out an instant like an intaglio of yellowish red-veined stone, with spots of enamel for the eyes; then the fire sank and in the shaded lamplight it became once more a dim Rembrandtish blur.

Phil Frenham, sitting in a low chair on the opposite side of the hearth, one long arm propped on the table behind him, one hand supporting his thrown-back head, and his eyes steadily fixed on his old friend's face, had not moved since the tale began. He continued to maintain his silent immobility after Culwin had ceased to speak, and it was I who, with a vague sense of disappointment at the sudden drop of the story, finally asked: "But how long did you keep on seeing them?"

Culwin, so sunk into his chair that he seemed like a heap of his own empty clothes, stirred a little, as if in surprise at my question. He appeared to have half-forgotten what he had been telling us.

"How long? Oh, off and on all that winter. It was infernal. I never got used to them. I grew really ill."

Frenham shifted his attitude silently, and as he did so his elbow struck against a small mirror in a bronze frame standing on the table behind him. He turned and changed its angle slightly; then he resumed his former attitude, his dark head thrown back on his lifted palm, his eyes intent on Culwin's face. Something in his stare embarrassed me, and as if to divert attention from it I pressed on with another question:

"And you never tried sacrificing Noyes?"

"Oh, no. The fact is I didn't have to. He did it for me, poor infatuated boy!"

"Did it for you? How do you mean?"

"He wore me out—wore everybody out. He kept on pouring out his lamentable twaddle, and hawking it up and down the place till he became a thing of terror. I tried to wean him from writing—oh, ever so gently, you understand, by throwing him with agreeable people, giving him a chance to make himself felt, to come to a sense of what he *really* had to give. I'd foreseen this solution from the beginning—felt sure that, once the first ardour of authorship was quenched, he'd drop into his place as a charming parasitic thing, the kind of chronic Cherubino for whom, in old societies, there's always a seat at table, and a shelter behind the ladies' skirts. I saw him take his place as 'the poet': the poet who doesn't write. One knows the type in every drawing room. Living in that way doesn't cost much—I'd worked it all out in my mind, and felt sure that, with a little help, he could manage it for the next few years; and meanwhile he'd be sure to marry. I saw him married to a widow, rather older, with a good cook and a well-run house. And I actually had my eye on the widow...Meanwhile I did everything to facilitate the transition—lent him money to ease his conscience, introduced him to pretty women to make him forget his vows. But nothing would do him: he had but one idea in his beautiful obstinate head. He wanted the laurel and not the rose, and he kept on repeating Gautier's axiom, and battering and filing at his limp prose till he'd spread it out over Lord knows how many thousand sloppy pages. Now and then he would send a pailful to a publisher, and of course it would always come back.

"At first it didn't matter—he thought he was 'misunderstood.' He took the attitudes of genius, and whenever an opus came home he wrote another to keep it company. Then he had a reaction of despair, and accused me of deceiving him, and Lord knows what. I got angry at that, and told him it was he who had deceived himself. He'd come to me determined to write, and I'd done my best to help him. That was the extent of my offence, and I'd done it for his cousin's sake, not his.

"That seemed to strike home, and he didn't answer for a minute. Then he said: 'My time's up and my money's up. What do you think I'd better do?'

"'I think you'd better not be an ass,' I said.

"He turned red, and asked: 'What do you mean by being an ass?'

"I took a letter from my desk and held it out to him.

"'I mean refusing this offer of Mrs. Ellinger's: to be her secretary at a salary of five thousand dollars. There may be a lot more in it than that.'

"He flung out his hand with a violence that struck the letter from mine. 'Oh, I know well enough what's in it!' he said, scarlet to the roots of his hair.

"'And what's your answer, if you know?' I asked.

"He made none at the minute, but turned away slowly to the door. There, with his hand on the threshold, he stopped to ask, almost under his breath: 'Then you really think my stuff's no good?'

"I was tired and exasperated, and I laughed. I don't defend my laugh—it was in wretched taste. But I must plead in extenuation that the boy was a fool, and that I'd done my best for him—I really had.

"He went out of the room, shutting the door quietly after him. That afternoon I left for Frascati, where I'd promised to spend the Sunday with some friends. I was glad to escape from Gilbert, and by the same token, as I learned that night, I had also escaped from the eyes. I dropped into the same lethargic sleep that had come to me before when their visitations ceased; and when I woke the next morning, in my peaceful painted room above the ilexes, I felt the utter weariness and deep relief that always followed on that repairing slumber. I put in two blessed nights at Frascati, and when I got back to my rooms in Rome I found that Gilbert had gone...Oh, nothing tragic had happened—the episode never rose to *that*. He'd simply packed his manuscripts and left for America—for his family and the Wall Street desk. He left a decent little note to tell me of his decision, and behaved altogether, in the circumstances, as little like a fool as it's possible for a fool to behave..."

IV

Culwin paused again, and again Frenham sat motionless, the dusky contour of his young head reflected in the mirror at his back.

"And what became of Noyes afterward?" I finally asked, still disquieted by a sense of incompleteness, by the need of some connecting thread between the parallel lines of the tale.

Culwin twitched his shoulders. "Oh, nothing became of him—because he became nothing. There could be no question of 'becoming' about it. He vegetated in an office, I believe, and finally got a clerkship in a consulate, and married drearily in China. I saw him once in Hong Kong, years afterward. He was fat and hadn't shaved. I was told he drank. He didn't recognize me."

"And the eyes?" I asked, after another pause which Frenham's continued silence made oppressive.

Culwin, stroking his chin, blinked at me meditatively through the shadows. "I never saw them after my last talk with Gilbert. Put two and two together if you can. For my part, I haven't found the link."

He rose stiffly, his hands in his pockets, and walked over to the table on which reviving drinks had been set out.

"You must be parched after this dry tale. Here, help yourself, my dear fellow. Here, Phil—" He turned back to the hearth.

Frenham still sat in his low chair, making no response to his host's hospitable summons. But as Culwin advanced toward him, their eyes met in a long look; after which, to my intense surprise, the young man, turning suddenly in his seat, flung his arms across the table, and dropped his face upon them.

Culwin, at the unexpected gesture, stopped short, a flush on his face.

"Phil—what the deuce? Why, have the eyes scared *you?* My dear boy—my dear fellow—I never had such a tribute to my literary ability, never!"

171

He broke into a chuckle at the thought, and halted on the hearthrug, his hands still in his pockets, gazing down in honest perplexity at the youth's bowed head. Then, as Frenham still made no answer, he moved a step or two nearer.

"Cheer up, my dear Phil! It's years since I've seen them—apparently I've done nothing lately bad enough to call them out of chaos. Unless my present evocation of them has made *you* see them; which would be their worst stroke yet!"

His bantering appeal quivered off into an uneasy laugh, and he moved still nearer, bending over Frenham, and laying his gouty hands on the lad's shoulders.

"Phil, my dear boy, really—what's the matter? Why don't you answer? *Have* you seen the eyes?"

Frenham's face was still pressed against his arms, and from where I stood behind Culwin I saw the latter, as if under the rebuff of this unaccountable attitude, draw back slowly from his friend. As he did so, the light of the lamp on the table fell full on his perplexed congested face, and I caught its sudden reflection in the mirror behind Frenham's head.

Culwin saw the reflection also. He paused, his face level with the mirror, as if scarcely recognizing the countenance in it as his own. But as he looked his expression gradually changed, and for an appreciable space of time he and the image in the glass confronted each other with a glare of slowly gathering hate. Then Culwin let go of Frenham's shoulders, and drew back a step, covering his eyes with his hands...

Frenham, his face still hidden, did not stir.

THE BLOND BEAST

I

It had been almost too easy—that was young Millner's first feeling, as he stood again on the Spence doorstep, the great moment of his interview behind him, and Fifth Avenue rolling its grimy Pactolus at his feet.

Halting there in the winter light, with the clang of the ponderous vestibule doors in his ears, and his eyes carried down the perspective of the packed interminable thoroughfare, he even dared to remember Rastignac's apostrophe to Paris, and to hazard recklessly under his small fair moustache: "Who knows?"

He, Hugh Millner, at any rate, knew a good deal already: a good deal more than he had imagined it possible to learn in half an hour's talk with a man like Orlando G. Spence; and the loud-rumoring city spread out there before him seemed to grin like an accomplice who knew the rest.

A gust of wind, whirling down from the dizzy height of the building on the next corner, drove sharply through his overcoat and compelled him to clutch at his hat. It was a bitter January day, a day of fierce light and air, when the sunshine cut like icicles and the wind sucked one into black gulfs at the street corners. But Millner's complacency was like a warm lining to his shabby coat, and heaving steadied his hat he continued to stand on the Spence threshold, lost in the vision revealed to him from the Pisgah of its marble steps. Yes, it was wonderful what the vision showed him...In his absorption he might have frozen fast to the doorstep if the Rhadamanthine portals behind him had not suddenly opened to let out a slim fur-coated figure, the figure, as he perceived, of the youth whom he had caught in the act of withdrawal as he entered Mr. Spence's study, and whom the latter, with a wave of his affable hand, had detained to introduce as "my son Draper."

It was characteristic of the odd friendliness of the whole scene that the great man should have thought it worth while to call back and name his heir to a mere humble applicant like Millner; and that the heir should shed on him, from a pale high-browed face, a smile of such deprecating kindness. It was characteristic, equally, of Millner, that he should at once mark the narrowness of the shoulders sustaining this ingenuous head; a narrowness, as he now observed, imperfectly concealed by the wide fur collar of young Spence's expensive and badly cut coat. But the face took on, as the youth smiled his surprise at their second meeting, a look of almost plaintive goodwill: the kind of look that Millner scorned and yet could never quite resist.

"Mr. Millner? Are you—er—waiting?" the lad asked, with an intention of serviceableness that was like a finer echo of his father's resounding cordiality.

"For my motor? No," Millner jested in his frank free voice. "The fact is, I was just standing here lost in the contemplation of my luck"—and as his companion's pale blue eyes seemed to shape a question, "my extraordinary luck," he explained, "in having been engaged as your father's secretary."

"Oh," the other rejoined, with a faint color in his sallow cheek. "I'm so glad," he murmured: "but I was sure—" He stopped, and the two looked kindly at each other.

Millner averted his gaze first, almost fearful of its betraying the added sense of his own strength and dexterity which he drew from the contrast of the other's frailness.

"Sure? How could any one be sure? I don't believe in it yet!" he laughed out in the irony of his triumph.

The boy's words did not sound like a mere civility—Millner felt in them an homage to his power.

"Oh, yes: I was sure," young Draper repeated. "Sure as soon as I saw you, I mean."

Millner tingled again with this tribute to his physical straightness and bloom. Yes, he looked his part, hang it—he looked it!

But his companion still lingered, a shy sociability in his eye.

"If you're walking, then, can I go along a little way?" And he nodded southward down the shabby gaudy avenue.

174

That, again, was part of the high comedy of the hour—that Millner should descend the Spence steps at young Spence's side, and stroll down Fifth Avenue with him at the proudest moment of the afternoon; O. G. Spence's secretary walking abroad with O. G. Spence's heir! He had the scientific detachment to pull out his watch and furtively note the hour. Yes—it was exactly forty minutes since he had rung the Spence doorbell and handed his card to a gelid footman, who, openly sceptical of his claim to be received, had left him unceremoniously planted on the cold tessellations of the vestibule.

"Some day," Miller grinned to himself, "I think I'll take that footman as furnace man—or to do the boots." And he pictured his marble palace rising from the earth to form the mausoleum of a footman's pride.

Only forty minutes ago! And now he had his opportunity fast! And he never meant to let it go! It was incredible, what had happened in the interval. He had gone up the Spence steps an unknown young man, out of a job, and with no substantial hope of getting into one: a needy young man with a mother and two limp sisters to be helped, and a lengthening figure of debt that stood by his bed through the anxious nights. And he went down the steps with his present assured, and his future lit by the hues of the rainbow above the pot of gold. Certainly a fellow who made his way at that rate had it "in him," and could afford to trust his star.

Descending from this joyous flight he stooped his ear to the discourse of young Spence.

"My father'll work you rather hard, you know: but you look as if you wouldn't mind that."

Millner pulled up his inches with the self-consciousness of the man who had none to waste. "Oh, no, I shan't mind that: I don't mind any amount of work if it leads to something."

"Just so," Draper Spence assented eagerly. "That's what I feel. And you'll find that whatever my father undertakes leads to such awfully fine things."

Millner tightened his lips on a grin. He was thinking only of where the work would lead him, not in the least of where it might land the eminent Orlando G. Spence. But he looked at his companion sympathetically.

"You're a philanthropist like your father, I see?"

"Oh, I don't know." They had paused at a crossing, and young Draper, with a dubious air, stood striking his agate-headed stick against the curbstone. "I believe in a purpose, don't you?" he asked, lifting his blue eyes suddenly to Millner's face.

"A purpose? I should rather say so! I believe in nothing else," cried Millner, feeling as if his were something he could grip in his hand and swing like a club.

Young Spence seemed relieved. "Yes—I tie up to that. There *is* a Purpose. And so, after all, even if I don't agree with my father on minor points..." He colored quickly, and looked again at Millner. "I should like to talk to you about this some day."

Millner smothered another smile. "We'll have lots of talks, I hope."

"Oh, if you can spare the time—!" said Draper, almost humbly.

"Why, I shall be there on tap!"

"For father, not me." Draper hesitated, with another self-confessing smile. "Father thinks I talk too much—that I keep going in and out of things. He doesn't believe in analyzing: he thinks it's destructive. But it hasn't destroyed my ideals." He looked wistfully up and down the clanging street. "And that's the main thing, isn't it? I mean, that one should have an Ideal." He turned back almost gaily to Millner. "I suspect you're a revolutionist too!"

"Revolutionist? Rather! I belong to the Red Syndicate and the Black Hand!" Millner joyfully assented.

Young Draper chuckled at the enormity of the joke. "First rate! We'll have incendiary meetings!" He pulled an elaborately armorial watch from his enfolding furs. "I'm so sorry, but I must say goodbye—this is my street," he explained. Millner, with a faint twinge of envy, glanced across at the colonnaded marble

176

edifice in the farther corner. "Going to the club?" he said carelessly.

His companion looked surprised. "Oh, no: I never go *there*. It's too boring." And he brought out, after one of the pauses in which he seemed rather breathlessly to measure the chances of his listener's indulgence: "I'm just going over to a little Bible Class I have in Tenth Avenue."

Millner, for a moment or two, stood watching the slim figure wind its way through the mass of vehicles to the opposite corner; then he pursued his own course down Fifth Avenue, measuring his steps to the rhythmic refrain: "It's too easy—it's too easy—it's too easy!"

His own destination being the small shabby flat off University Place where three tender females awaited the result of his mission, he had time, on the way home, after abandoning himself to a general sense of triumph, to dwell specifically on the various aspects of his achievement. Viewed materially and practically, it was a thing to be proud of; yet it was chiefly on aesthetic grounds—because he had done so exactly what he had set out to do—that he glowed with pride at the afternoon's work. For, after all, any young man with the proper "pull" might have applied to Orlando G. Spence for the post of secretary, and even have penetrated as far as the great man's study; but that he, Hugh Millner, should not only have forced his way to this fastness, but have established, within a short half hour, his right to remain there permanently: well, this, if it proved anything, proved that the first rule of success was to know how to live up to one's principles.

"One must have a plan—one must have a plan," the young man murmured, looking with pity at the vague faces that the crowd bore past him, and feeling almost impelled to detain them and expound his doctrine. But the planlessness of average human nature was of course the measure of his opportunity; and he smiled to think that every purposeless face he met was a guarantee of his own advancement, a rung in the ladder he meant to climb.

Yes, the whole secret of success was to know what one wanted to do, and not to be afraid to do it. His own history was proving that already. He had not been afraid to give up his small but safe position in a real estate office for the precarious adventure of a private secretaryship; and his first glimpse of his new employer had convinced him that he had not mistaken his calling. When one has a "way" with one—as, in all modesty, Millner knew he had—not to utilize it is a stupid waste of force. And when he had learned that Orlando G. Spence was in search of a private secretary who should be able to give him intelligent assistance in the execution of his philanthropic schemes, the young man felt that his hour had come. It was no part of his plan to associate himself with one of the masters of finance: he had a notion that minnows who go to a whale to learn how to grow bigger are likely to be swallowed in the process. The opportunity of a clever young man with a cool head and no prejudices (this again was drawn from life) lay rather in making himself indispensable to one of the beneficent rich, and in using the timidities and conformities of his patron as the means of his scruples about formulating these principles to himself. It was not for nothing that, in his college days, he had hunted the hypothetical "moral sense" to its lair, and dragged from their concealment the various self-advancing sentiments dissembled under its edifying guise. His strength lay in his precocious insight into the springs of action, and in his refusal to classify them according to the accepted moral and social sanctions. He had to the full the courage of his lack of convictions.

To a young man so untrammeled by prejudice it was self-evident that helpless philanthropists like Orlando G. Spence were just as much the natural diet of the strong as the lamb is of the wolf. It was pleasanter to eat than to be eaten, in a world where, as yet, there seemed to be no third alternative; and any scruples one might feel as to the temporary discomfort of one's victim were speedily dispelled by that larger scientific view which took into account the social destructiveness of the benevolent. Millner was persuaded that every individual woe mitigated by the philanthropy of Orlando G. Spence added just so much to the sum total of human inefficiency, and it was one of his favourite subjects of speculation to picture the innumerable social evils that may follow upon the rescue of one infant from Mount Taygetus.

"We're all born to prey on each other, and pity for suffering is one of the most elementary stages of egotism. Until one has passed beyond, and acquired a taste for the more complex forms of the instinct—"

He stopped suddenly, checked in his advance by a sallow wisp of a dog that had plunged through the press of vehicles to hurl itself between his legs. Millner did not dislike animals, though he preferred that they should be healthy and handsome. The dog under his feet was neither. Its cringing contour showed an injudicious mingling of races, and its meagre coat betrayed the deplorable habit of sleeping in coalholes and subsisting on an innutritious diet. In addition to these physical disadvantages, its shrinking and inconsequent movements revealed a congenital weakness of character which, even under more favourable conditions, would hardly have qualified it to become a useful member of society; and Millner was not sorry to notice that it moved with a limp of the hind leg that probably doomed it to speedy extinction.

The absurdity of such an animal's attempting to cross Fifth Avenue at the most crowded hour of the afternoon struck him as only less great than the irony of its having been permitted to achieve the feat; and he stood a moment looking at it, and wondering what had moved it to the attempt. It was really a perfect type of the human derelict which Orlando G. Spence and his kind were devoting their millions to perpetuate, and he reflected how much better Nature knew her business in dealing with the superfluous quadruped.

An elderly lady advancing in the opposite direction evidently took a less dispassionate view of the case, for she paused to remark emotionally: "Oh, you poor thing!" while she stooped to caress the object of her sympathy. The dog, with characteristic lack of discrimination, viewed her gesture with suspicion, and met it with a snarl. The lady turned pale and shrank away, a chivalrous male repelled the animal with his umbrella, and two idle boys backed his action by a vigorous "Hi!" The object of these hostile demonstrations, apparently attributing them not to its own unsocial conduct, but merely to the chronic animosity of the universe, dashed wildly around the corner into a side street, and as it did so Millner noticed that the lame leg left a little trail of blood. Irresistibly, he turned the corner to see what would happen next. It was deplorably clear that the animal itself had no plan; but after several inconsequent and contradictory movements it plunged down an area, where it backed up against the iron gate, forlornly and foolishly at bay.

Millner, still following, looked down at it, and wondered. Then he whistled, just to see if it would come; but this only caused it to start up on its quivering legs, with desperate turns of the head that measured the chances of escape.

"Oh, hang it, you poor devil, stay there if you like!" the young man murmured, walking away.

A few yards off he looked back, and saw that the dog had made a rush out of the area and was limping furtively down the street. The idle boys were in the offing, and he disliked the thought of leaving them in control of the situation. Softly, with infinite precautions, he began to follow the dog. He did not know why he was doing it, but the impulse was overmastering. For a moment he seemed to be gaining upon his quarry, but with a cunning sense of his approach it suddenly turned and hobbled across the frozen grass plot adjoining a shuttered house. Against the wall at the back of the plot it cowered down in a dirty snowdrift, as if disheartened by the struggle. Millner stood outside the railings and looked at it. He reflected that under the shelter of the winter dusk it might have the luck to remain there unmolested, and that in the morning it would probably be dead of cold. This was so obviously the best solution
180

that he began to move away again; but as he did so the idle boys confronted him.

"Ketch yer dog for yer, boss?" they grinned.

Millner consigned them to the devil, and stood sternly watching them till the first stage of the journey had carried them around the nearest corner; then, after pausing to look once more up and down the empty street, laid his hand on the railing, and vaulted over it into the grass plot. As he did so, he reflected that, since pity for suffering was one of the most elementary forms of egotism, he ought to have remembered that it was necessarily one of the most tenacious.

II

"My chief aim in life?" Orlando G. Spence repeated. He threw himself back in his chair, straightened the tortoiseshell *pince-nez*, on his short blunt nose, and beamed down the luncheon table at the two young men who shared his repast.

His glance rested on his son Draper, seated opposite him behind a barrier of Georgian silver and orchids; but his words were addressed to his secretary who, stylograph in hand, had turned from the seductions of a mushroom *soufflé* in order to jot down, for the Sunday *Investigator*, an outline of his employer's views and intentions respecting the newly endowed Orlando G. Spence College for Missionaries. It was Mr. Spence's practice to receive in person the journalists privileged to impart his opinions to a waiting world; but during the last few months—and especially since the vast project of the Missionary College had been in process of development—the pressure of business and beneficence had necessitated Millner's frequent intervention, and compelled the secretary to snatch the sense of his patron's elucubrations between the courses of their hasty meals.

Young Millner had a healthy appetite, and it was not one of his least sacrifices to be so often obliged to curb it in the interest of his advancement; but whenever he waved aside one of the triumphs of Mr. Spence's *chef* he was conscious of rising a step in his employer's favour. Mr. Spence did not despise the pleasures of the table, though he appeared to regard them as the reward of success rather than as the alleviation of effort; and it increased his sense of his secretary's merit to note how keenly the young man enjoyed the fare that he was so frequently obliged to deny himself. Draper, having subsisted since infancy on a diet of truffles and terrapin, consumed such delicacies with the insensibility of a traveller swallowing a railway sandwich; but Millner never made the mistake of concealing from Mr. Spence his sense of what he was losing when duty constrained him to exchange the fork for the pen.

"My chief aim in life!" Mr. Spence repeated, removing his eyeglass and swinging it thoughtfully on his finger. ("I'm sorry you should miss this *souffle*, Millner: it's worth while.) Why, I suppose I might say that my chief aim in life is to leave the world better than I found it. Yes: I don't know that I could put it better than that. To leave the world better than I found it. It wouldn't be a bad idea to use that as a headline. *'Wants to leave the world better than he found it.'* It's exactly the point I should like to make in this talk about the College."

Mr. Spence paused, and his glance once more reverted to his son, who, having pushed aside his plate, sat watching Millner with a dreamy intensity.

"And it's the point I want to make with you, too, Draper," his father continued genially, while he turned over with a critical fork the plump and perfectly matched asparagus which a footman was presenting to his notice. "I want to make you feel that nothing else counts in comparison with that—no amount of literary success or intellectual celebrity."

"Oh, I *do* feel that," Draper murmured, with one of his quick blushes, and a glance that wavered between his father and Millner. The secretary kept his eyes on his notes, and young Spence continued, after a pause: "Only the thing is—isn't it?—to try and find out just what *does* make the world better?"

"To *try* to find out?" his father echoed compassionately. "It's not necessary to try very hard. Goodness is what makes the world better."

"Yes, yes, of course," his son nervously interposed; "but the question is, what *is* good—"

Mr. Spence, with a darkening brow, brought his fist down emphatically on the damask. "I'll thank you not to blaspheme, my son!"

Draper's head reared itself a trifle higher on his thin neck. "I was not going to blaspheme; only there may be different ways—"

"There's where you're mistaken, Draper. There's only one way: there's my way," said Mr. Spence in a tone of unshaken conviction.

"I know, father; I see what you mean. But don't you see that even your way wouldn't be the right way for you if you ceased to believe that it was?"

His father looked at him with mingled bewilderment and reprobation. "Do you mean to say that the fact of goodness depends on my conception of it, and not on God Almighty's?"

"I do...yes...in a specific sense..." young Draper falteringly maintained; and Mr. Spence turned with a discouraged gesture toward his secretary's suspended pen.

"I don't understand your scientific jargon, Draper; and I don't want to.—What's the next point, Millner? (No; no *savarin*. Bring the fruit—and the coffee with it.)"

Millner, keenly aware that an aromatic *savarin au rhum* was describing an arc behind his head previous to being rushed back to the pantry under young Draper's indifferent eye, stiffened himself against this last assault of the enemy, and read out firmly: " *What relation do you consider that a man's business conduct should bear to his religious and domestic life?*"

Mr. Spence mused a moment. "Why, that's a stupid question. It goes over the same ground as the other one. A man ought to do good with his money—that's all. Go on."

At this point the butler's murmur in his ear caused him to push back his chair, and to arrest Millner's interrogatory by a rapid gesture. "Yes; I'm coming. Hold the wire." Mr. Spence rose and plunged into the adjoining "office," where a telephone and a Remington divided the attention of a young lady in spectacles who was preparing for Zenana work in the East.

As the door closed, the butler, having placed the coffee and liqueurs on the table, withdrew in the rear of his battalion, and the two young men were left alone beneath the Rembrandts and Hobbemas on the dining room walls.

There was a moment's silence between them; then young Spence, leaning across the table, said in the lowered tone of intimacy: "Why do you suppose he dodged that last question?"

Millner, who had rapidly taken an opulent purple fig from the fruit dish nearest him, paused in surprise in the act of hurrying it to his lips.

"I mean," Draper hastened on, "the question as to the relation between business and private morality. It's such an interesting one, and he's just the person who ought to tackle it."

Millner, despatching the fig, glanced down at his notes. "I don't think your father meant to dodge the question."

Young Draper continued to look at him intently. "You think he imagined that his answer really covers the ground?"

"As much as it needs to be covered."

The son of the house glanced away with a sigh. "You know things about him that I don't," he said wistfully, but without a tinge of resentment in his tone.

"Oh, as to that—(may I give myself some coffee?)" Millner, in his walk around the table to fill his cup, paused a moment to lay an affectionate hand on Draper's shoulder. "Perhaps I know him *better*, in a sense: outsiders often get a more accurate focus."

Draper considered this. "And your idea is that he acts on principles he has never thought of testing or defining?"

Millner looked up quickly, and for an instant their glances crossed. "How do you mean?"

"I mean: that he's an inconscient instrument of goodness, as it were? A—a sort of blindly beneficent force?"

The other smiled. "That's not a bad definition. I know one thing about him, at any rate: he's awfully upset at your having chucked your Bible Class."

A shadow fell on young Spence's candid brow. "I know. But what can I do about it? That's what I was thinking of when I tried to show him that goodness, in a certain sense, is purely subjective: that one can't do good against one's principles." Again his glance appealed to Millner. " *You* understand me, don't you?"

Millner stirred his coffee in a silence not unclouded by perplexity. "Theoretically, perhaps. It's a pretty question, certainly. But I also understand your father's feeling that it hasn't much to do with real life: especially now that he's got to make a speech in connection with the founding of this Missionary College. He may think that any hint of internecine strife will weaken his prestige. Mightn't you have waited a little longer?"

"How could I, when I might have been expected to take a part in this performance? To talk, and say things I didn't mean? That was exactly what made me decide not to wait."

The door opened and Mr. Spence re-entered the room. As he did so his son rose abruptly as if to leave it.

"Where are you off to, Draper?" the banker asked.

"I'm in rather a hurry, sir—"

Mr. Spence looked at his watch. "You can't be in more of a hurry than I am; and I've got seven minutes and a half." He seated himself behind the coffee—tray, lit a cigar, laid his watch on the table, and signed to Draper to resume his place. "No, Millner, don't you go; I want you both." He turned to the secretary. "You know that Draper's given up his Bible Class? I understand it's not from the pressure of engagements—" Mr. Spence's narrow lips took an ironic curve under the straight-clipped stubble of his moustache—"it's on principle, he tells me. He's *principled* against doing good!"

Draper lifted a protesting hand. "It's not exactly that, father—"

"I know: you'll tell me it's some scientific quibble that I don't understand. I've never had time to go in for intellectual hair-splitting. I've found too many people down in the mire who needed a hand to pull them out. A busy man has to take his choice between helping his fellow men and theorizing about them. I've preferred to help. (You might take that down for the *Investigator*, Millner.) And I thank God I've never stopped to ask what made me want to do good. I've just yielded to the impulse—that's all." Mr. Spence turned back to his son. "Better men than either of us have been satisfied with that creed, my son."

Draper was silent, and Mr. Spence once more addressed himself to his secretary. "Millner, you're a reader: I've caught you at it. And I know this boy talks to you. What have you got to say? Do you suppose a Bible Class ever *hurt* anybody?"

Millner paused a moment, feeling all through his nervous system the fateful tremor of the balance. "That's what I was just trying to tell him, sir—"

"Ah; you were? That's good. Then I'll only say one thing more. Your doing what you've done at this particular moment hurts me more, Draper, than your teaching the gospel of Jesus could possibly have hurt those young men over in Tenth Avenue." Mr. Spence arose and restored his watch to his pocket. "I shall want you in twenty minutes, Millner."

The door closed on him, and for a while the two young men sat silent behind their cigar fumes. Then Draper Spence broke out, with a catch in his throat: "That's what I can't bear, Millner, what I simply can't *bear:* to hurt him, to hurt his faith in *me!* It's an awful responsibility, isn't it, to tamper with anybody's faith in anything?"

III

The twenty minutes prolonged themselves to forty, the forty to fifty, and the fifty to an hour; and still Millner waited for Mr. Spence's summons.

During the two years of his secretaryship the young man had learned the significance of such postponements. Mr. Spence's days were organized like a railway timetable, and a delay of an hour implied a casualty as far-reaching as the breaking down of an express. Of the cause of the present derangement Hugh Millner was ignorant; and the experience of

186

the last months allowed him to fluctuate between conflicting conjectures. All were based on the indisputable fact that Mr. Spence was "bothered"—had for some time past been "bothered." And it was one of Millner's discoveries that an extremely parsimonious use of the emotions underlay Mr. Spence's expansive manner and fraternal phraseology, and that he did not throw away his feelings any more than (for all his philanthropy) he threw away his money. If he was bothered, then, it could be only because a careful survey of his situation had forced on him some unpleasant fact with which he was not immediately prepared to deal; and any unpreparedness on Mr. Spence's part was also a significant symptom.

Obviously, Millner's original conception of his employer's character had suffered extensive modification; but no final outline had replaced the first conjectural image. The two years spent in Mr. Spence's service had produced too many contradictory impressions to be fitted into any definite pattern; and the chief lesson Millner had learned from them was that life was less of an exact science, and character a more incalculable element, than he had been taught in the schools. In the light of this revised impression, his own footing seemed less secure than he had imagined, and the rungs of the ladder he was climbing more slippery than they had looked from below. He was not without the reassuring sense of having made himself, in certain small ways, necessary to Mr. Spence; and this conviction was confirmed by Draper's reiterated assurance of his father's appreciation. But Millner had begun to suspect that one might be necessary to Mr. Spence one day, and a superfluity, if not an obstacle, the next; and that it would take superhuman astuteness to foresee how and when the change would occur. Every fluctuation of the great man's mood was therefore anxiously noted by the young meteorologist in his service; and this observer's vigilance was now strained to the utmost by the little cloud, no bigger than a man's hand, adumbrated by the banker's unpunctuality.

When Mr. Spence finally appeared, his aspect did not tend to dissipate the cloud. He wore what Millner had learned to call his "backdoor face": a blank barred countenance, in which only an occasional twitch of the lids behind his glasses suggested that some one was on the watch. In this mood Mr. Spence usually seemed unconscious of his secretary's presence, or aware of it only as an arm terminating in a pen. Millner, accustomed on such occasions to exist merely as a function, sat waiting for the click of the spring that should set him in action; but the pressure not being applied, he finally hazarded: "Are we to go on with the *Investigator*, sir?"

Mr. Spence, who had been pacing up and down between the desk and the fireplace, threw himself into his usual seat at Millner's elbow.

"I don't understand this new notion of Draper's," he said abruptly. "Where's he got it from? No one ever learned irreligion in my household."

He turned his eyes on Millner, who had the sense of being scrutinized through a ground-glass window that left him visible while it concealed his observer. The young man let his pen describe two or three vague patterns on the blank sheet before him.

"Draper has ideas—" he risked at last.

Mr. Spence looked hard at him. "That's all right," he said. "I want my son to have everything. But what's the point of mixing up ideas and principles? I've seen fellows who did that, and they were generally trying to borrow five dollars to get away from the sheriff. What's all this talk about goodness? Goodness isn't an idea. It's a fact. It's as solid as a business proposition. And it's Draper's duty, as the son of a wealthy man, and the prospective steward of a great fortune, to elevate the standards of other young men—of young men who haven't had his opportunities. The rich ought to preach contentment, and to set the example themselves. We have our cares, but we ought to conceal them. We ought to be cheerful, and accept things as they are—not go about sowing dissent and restlessness. What has Draper got to give these boys in his Bible Class, that's so much better than what he wants to take from them? That's the question I'd like to have answered?"

188

Mr. Spence, carried away by his own eloquence, had removed his *pince-nez* and was twirling it about his extended forefinger with the gesture habitual to him when he spoke in public. After a pause, he went on, with a drop to the level of private intercourse: "I tell you this because I know you have a good deal of influence with Draper. He has a high opinion of your brains. But you're a practical fellow, and you must see what I mean. Try to make Draper see it. Make him understand how it looks to have him drop his Bible Class just at this particular time. It was his own choice to take up religious teaching among young men. He began with our office boys, and then the work spread and was blessed. I was almost alarmed, at one time, at the way it took hold of him: when the papers began to talk about him as a formative influence I was afraid he'd lose his head and go into the church. Luckily he tried University Settlement first; but just as I thought he was settling down to that, he took to worrying about the Higher Criticism, and saying he couldn't go on teaching fairy tales as history. I can't see that any good ever came of criticizing what our parents believed, and it's a queer time for Draper to criticize *my* belief just as I'm backing it to the extent of five millions."

Millner remained silent; and, as though his silence were an argument, Mr. Spence continued combatively: "Draper's always talking about some distinction between religion and morality. I don't understand what he means. I got my morals out of the Bible, and I guess there's enough left in it for Draper. If religion won't make a man moral, I don't see why irreligion should. And he talks about using his mind—well, can't he use that in Wall Street? A man can get a good deal farther in life watching the market than picking holes in Genesis; and he can do more good too. There's a time for everything; and Draper seems to me to have mixed up weekdays with Sunday."

Mr. Spence replaced his eyeglasses, and stretching his hand to the silver box at his elbow, extracted from it one of the long cigars sheathed in gold leaf which were reserved for his private consumption. The secretary hastened to tender him a match,

189

and for a moment he puffed in silence. When he spoke again it was in a different note.

"I've got about all the bother I can handle just now, without this nonsense of Draper's. That was one of the Trustees of the College with me. It seems the *Flashlight* has been trying to stir up a fuss—" Mr. Spence paused, and turned his *pince-nez* on his secretary. "You haven't heard from them?" he asked.

"From the *Flashlight?* No." Millner's surprise was genuine.

He detected a gleam of relief behind Mr. Spence's glasses. "It may be just malicious talk. That's the worst of good works; they bring out all the meanness in human nature. And then there are always women mixed up in them, and there never was a woman yet who understood the difference between philanthropy and business." He drew again at his cigar, and then, with an unwonted movement, leaned forward and mechanically pushed the box toward Millner. "Help yourself," he said.

Millner, as mechanically, took one of the virginally cinctured cigars, and began to undo its wrappings. It was the first time he had ever been privileged to detach that golden girdle, and nothing could have given him a better measure of the importance of the situation, and of the degree to which he was apparently involved in it. "You remember that San Pablo rubber business? That's what they've been raking up," said Mr. Spence abruptly.

Millner paused in the act of striking a match. Then, with an appreciable effort of the will, he completed the gesture, applied the flame to his cigar, and took a long inhalation. The cigar was certainly delicious.

Mr. Spence, drawing a little closer, leaned forward and touched him on the arm. The touch caused Millner to turn his head, and for an instant the glance of the two men crossed at short range. Millner was conscious, first, of a nearer view than he had ever had of his employer's face, and of its vaguely suggesting a seamed sandstone head, the kind of thing that lies in a corner in the court of a museum, and in which only the round enamelled eyes have resisted the wear of time. His next feeling was that he had now reached the moment to which the offer of the cigar had been a prelude. He had always known that, sooner or later, such a moment would come; all his life, in a sense, had been a preparation for it. But in entering Mr. Spence's service he had not foreseen that it would present itself in this form. He had seen himself consciously guiding that gentleman up to the moment, rather than being thrust into it by a stronger hand. And his first act of reflection was the resolve that, in the end, his hand should prove the stronger of the two. This was followed, almost immediately, by the idea that to be stronger than Mr. Spence's it would have to be very strong indeed. It was odd that he should feel this, since—as far as verbal communication went—it was Mr. Spence who was asking for his support. In a theoretical statement of the case the banker would have figured as being at Millner's mercy; but one of the queerest things about experience was the way it made light of theory. Millner felt now as though he were being crushed by some inexorable engine of which he had been playing with the lever. ...

He had always been intensely interested in observing his own reactions, and had regarded this faculty of self-detachment as of immense advantage in such a career as he had planned. He felt this still, even in the act of noting his own bewilderment—felt it the more in contrast to the odd unconsciousness of Mr. Spence's attitude, of the incredible candor of his self-abasement and self-abandonment. It was clear that Mr. Spence was not troubled by the repercussion of his actions in the consciousness of others; and this looked like a weakness—unless it were, instead, a great strength. ...

Through the hum of these swarming thoughts Mr. Spence's voice was going on. "That's the only rag of proof they've got; and they got it by one of those nasty accidents that nobody can guard against. I don't care how conscientiously a man attends to business, he can't always protect himself against meddlesome people. I don't pretend to know how the letter came into their hands; but they've got it; and they mean to use it—and they mean to say that you wrote it for me, and that you knew

191

what it was about when you wrote it...They'll probably be after you tomorrow—"

Mr. Spence, restoring his cigar to his lips, puffed at it slowly. In the pause that followed there was an instant during which the universe seemed to Hugh Millner like a sounding board bent above his single consciousness. If he spoke, what thunders would be sent back to him from that intently listening vastness?

"You see?" said Mr. Spence.

The universal ear bent closer, as if to catch the least articulation of Millner's narrowed lips; but when he opened them it was merely to reinsert his cigar, and for a short space nothing passed between the two men but an exchange of smoke rings.

"What do you mean to do? There's the point," Mr. Spence at length sent through the rings.

Oh, yes, the point was there, as distinctly before Millner as the tip of his expensive cigar: he had seen it coming quite as soon as Mr. Spence. He knew that fate was handing him an ultimatum; but the sense of the formidable echo that his least answer would rouse kept him doggedly, and almost helplessly, silent. To let Mr. Spence talk on as long as possible was no doubt the best way of gaining time; but Millner knew that his silence was really due to his dread of the echo. Suddenly, however, in a reaction of impatience at his own indecision, he began to speak.

The sound of his voice cleared his mind and strengthened his resolve. It was odd how the word seemed to shape the act, though one knew how ancillary it really was. As he talked, it was as if the globe had swung around, and he himself were upright on its axis, with Mr. Spence underneath, on his head. Through the ensuing interchange of concise and rapid speech there sounded in Millner's ears the refrain to which he had walked down Fifth Avenue after his first talk with Mr. Spence: "It's too easy—it's too easy—it's too easy." Yes, it was even easier than he had expected. His sensation was that of the skilful carver who feels his good blade sink into a tender joint.

192

As he went on talking, this surprised sense of mastery was like wine in his veins. Mr. Spence was at his mercy, after all—that was what it came to; but this new view of the case did not lessen Millner's sense of Mr. Spence's strength, it merely revealed to him his own superiority. Mr. Spence was even stronger than he had suspected. There could be no better proof of that than his faith in Millner's power to grasp the situation, and his tacit recognition of the young man's right to make the most of it. Millner felt that Mr. Spence would have despised him even more for not using his advantage than for not seeing it; and this homage to his capacity nerved him to greater alertness, and made the concluding moments of their talk as physically exhilarating as some hotly contested game.

When the conclusion was reached, and Millner stood at the goal, the golden trophy in his grasp, his first conscious thought was one of regret that the struggle was over. He would have liked to prolong their talk for the purely aesthetic pleasure of making Mr. Spence lose time, and, better still, of making him forget that he was losing it. The sense of advantage that the situation conferred was so great that when Mr. Spence rose it was as if Millner were dismissing him, and when he reached his hand toward the cigar box it seemed to be one of Millner's cigars that he was taking.

IV

There had been only one condition attached to the transaction: Millner was to speak to Draper about the Bible Class.

The condition was easy to fulfill. Millner was confident of his power to deflect his young friend's purpose; and he knew the opportunity would be given him before the day was over. His professional duties despatched, he had only to go up to his room to wait. Draper nearly always looked in on him for a moment before dinner: it was the hour most propitious to their elliptic interchange of words and silences.

Meanwhile, the waiting was an occupation in itself. Millner looked about his room with new eyes. Since the first thrill of initiation into its complicated comforts—the shower bath, the telephone, the many-jointed reading lamp and the vast mirrored presses through which he was always hunting his scant outfit— Millner's room had interested him no more than a railway carriage in which he might have been traveling. But now it had acquired a sort of historic significance as the witness of the astounding change in his fate. It was Corsica, it was Brienne—it was the kind of spot that posterity might yet mark with a tablet. Then he reflected that he should soon be leaving it, and the lustre of its monumental mahogany was veiled in pathos. Why indeed should he linger on in bondage? He perceived with a certain surprise that the only thing he should regret would be leaving Draper...

It was odd, it was inconsequent, it was almost exasperating, that such a regret should obscure his triumph. Why in the world should he suddenly take to regretting Draper? If there were any logic in human likings, it should be to Mr. Spence that he inclined. Draper, dear lad, had the illusion of an "intellectual sympathy" between them; but that, Millner knew, was an affair of reading and not of character. Draper's temerities would always be of that kind; whereas his own—well, his own, put to the proof, had now definitely classed him with Mr. Spence rather than with Mr. Spence's son. It was a consequence of this new condition—of his having thus distinctly and irrevocably classed himself—that, when Draper at length brought upon the scene his shy shamble and his wistful smile, Millner, for the first time, had to steel himself against them instead of yielding to their charm.

In the new order upon which he had entered, one principle of the old survived: the point of honour between allies. And Millner had promised Mr. Spence to speak to Draper about his Bible Class. ...

Draper, thrown back in his chair, and swinging a loose leg across a meagre knee, listened with his habitual gravity. His downcast eyes seemed to pursue the vision which Millner's words evoked; and the words, to their speaker, took on a new sound as that candid consciousness refracted them.

194

"You know, dear boy, I perfectly see your father's point. It's naturally distressing to him, at this particular time, to have any hint of civil war leak out—"

Draper sat upright, laying his lank legs knee to knee.

"That's it, then? I thought that was it!"

Millner raised a surprised glance. " *What's* it?"

"That it should be at this particular time—"

"Why, naturally, as I say! Just as he's making, as it were, his public profession of faith. You know, to men like your father convictions are irreducible elements—they can't be split up, and differently combined. And your exegetical scruples seem to him to strike at the very root of his convictions."

Draper pulled himself to his feet and shuffled across the room. Then he turned about, and stood before his friend.

"Is it that—or is it this?" he said; and with the word he drew a letter from his pocket and proffered it silently to Millner.

The latter, as he unfolded it, was first aware of an intense surprise at the young man's abruptness of tone and gesture. Usually Draper fluttered long about his point before making it; and his sudden movement seemed as mechanical as the impulsion conveyed by some strong spring. The spring, of course, was in the letter; and to it Millner turned his startled glance, feeling the while that, by some curious cleavage of perception, he was continuing to watch Draper while he read.

"Oh, the beasts!" he cried.

He and Draper were face to face across the sheet that had dropped between them. The youth's features were tightened by a smile that was like the ligature of a wound. He looked white and withered.

"Ah—you knew, then?"

Millner sat still, and after a moment Draper turned from him, walked to the hearth, and leaned against the chimney, propping his chin on his hands. Millner, his head thrown back, stared up at the ceiling, which had suddenly become to him the image of the universal sounding board hanging over his consciousness.

"You knew, then?" Draper repeated.

Millner remained silent. He had perceived, with the surprise of a mathematician working out a new problem, that the lie which Mr. Spence had just bought of him was exactly the one gift he could give of his own free will to Mr. Spence's son. This discovery gave the world a strange new topsy-turvyness, and set Millner's theories spinning about his brain like the cabin furniture of a tossing ship.

"You *knew*," said Draper, in a tone of quiet affirmation.

Millner righted himself, and grasped the arms of his chair as if that too were reeling. "About this blackguardly charge?"

Draper was studying him intently. "What does it matter if it's blackguardly?"

"Matter—?" Millner stammered.

"It's that, of course, in any case. But the point is whether it's true or not." Draper bent down, and picking up the crumpled letter, smoothed it out between his fingers. "The point, is, whether my father, when he was publicly denouncing the peonage abuses on the San Pablo plantations over a year ago, had actually sold out his stock, as he announced at the time; or whether, as they say here—how do they put it?—he had simply transferred it to a dummy till the scandal should blow over, and has meanwhile gone on drawing his forty per cent interest on five thousand shares? There's the point."

Millner had never before heard his young friend put a case with such unadorned precision. His language was like that of Mr. Spence making a statement to a committee meeting; and the resemblance to his father flashed out with ironic incongruity.

"You see why I've brought this letter to you—I couldn't go to *him* with it!" Draper's voice faltered, and the resemblance vanished as suddenly as it had appeared.

"No; you couldn't go to him with it," said Millner slowly.

"And since they say here that *you* know: that they've got your letter proving it—" The muscles of Draper's face quivered as if a blinding light had been swept over it. "For God's sake, Millner—it's all right?"

"It's all right," said Millner, rising to his feet.

Draper caught him by the wrist. "You're sure—you're absolutely sure?"

"Sure. They know they've got nothing to go on."

Draper fell back a step and looked almost sternly at his friend. "You know that's not what I mean. I don't care a straw what they think they've got to go on. I want to know if my father's all right. If he is, they can say what they please."

Millner, again, felt himself under the concentrated scrutiny of the ceiling. "Of course, of course. I understand."

"You understand? Then why don't you answer?"

Millner looked compassionately at the boy's struggling face. Decidedly, the battle was to the strong, and he was not sorry to be on the side of the legions. But Draper's pain was as awkward as a material obstacle, as something that one stumbled over in a race.

"You know what I'm driving at, Millner." Again Mr. Spence's committee meeting tone sounded oddly through his son's strained voice. "If my father's so awfully upset about my giving up my Bible Class, and letting it be known that I do so on conscientious grounds, is it because he's afraid it may be considered a criticism on something *he* has done which—which won't bear the test of the doctrines he believes in?"

Draper, with the last question, squared himself in front of Millner, as if suspecting that the latter meant to evade it by flight. But Millner had never felt more disposed to stand his ground than at that moment.

"No—by Jove, no! It's not *that*." His relief almost escaped him in a cry, as he lifted his head to give back Draper's look.

"On your honour?" the other passionately pressed him.

"Oh, on anybody's you like—on *yours!*" Millner could hardly restrain a laugh of relief. It was vertiginous to find himself spared, after all, the need of an altruistic lie: he perceived that they were the kind he least liked.

Draper took a deep breath. "You don't—Millner, a lot depends on this—you don't really think my father has any ulterior motive?"

"I think he has none but his horror of seeing you go straight to perdition!"

They looked at each other again, and Draper's tension was suddenly relieved by a free boyish laugh. "It's his convictions—it's just his funny old convictions?"

"It's that, and nothing else on earth!"

Draper turned back to the armchair he had left, and let his narrow figure sink down into it as into a bath. Then he looked over at Millner with a smile. "I can see that I've been worrying him horribly. So he really thinks I'm on the road to perdition? Of course you can fancy what a sick minute I had when I thought it might be this other reason—the damnable insinuation in this letter." Draper crumpled the paper in his hand, and leaned forward to toss it into the coals of the grate. "I ought to have known better, of course. I ought to have remembered that, as you say, my father can't conceive how conduct may be independent of creed. That's where I was stupid—and rather base. But that letter made me dizzy—I couldn't think. Even now I can't very clearly. I'm not sure what *my* convictions require of me: they seem to me so much less to be considered than his! When I've done half the good to people that he has, it will be time enough to begin attacking their beliefs. Meanwhile—meanwhile I can't touch his..." Draper leaned forward, stretching his lank arms along his knees. His face was as clear as a spring sky. "I *won't* touch them, Millner—Go and tell him so...."

V

In the study a half hour later Mr. Spence, watch in hand, was doling out his minutes again. The peril conjured, he had recovered his dominion over time. He turned his commanding eyeglasses on Millner.

"It's all settled, then? Tell Draper I'm sorry not to see him again tonight—but I'm to speak at the dinner of the Legal Relief Association, and I'm due there in five minutes. You and he dine alone here, I suppose? Tell him I appreciate what he's done. Some day he'll see that to leave the world better than we

198

find it is the best we can hope to do. (You've finished the notes for the *Investigator?* Be sure you don't forget that phrase.) Well, good evening: that's all, I think."

Smooth and compact in his glossy evening clothes, Mr. Spence advanced toward the study door; but as he reached it, his secretary stood there before him.

"It's not quite all, Mr. Spence."

Mr. Spence turned on him a look in which impatience was faintly tinged with apprehension. "What else is there? It's two and a half minutes to eight."

Millner stood his ground. "It won't take longer than that. I want to tell you that, if you can conveniently replace me, I'd like—there are reasons why I shall have to leave you."

Millner was conscious of reddening as he spoke. His redness deepened under Mr. Spence's dispassionate scrutiny. He saw at once that the banker was not surprised at his announcement.

"Well, I suppose that's natural enough. You'll want to make a start for yourself now. Only, of course, for the sake of appearances—"

"Oh, certainly," Millner hastily agreed.

"Well, then: is that all?" Mr. Spence repeated.

"Nearly." Millner paused, as if in search of an appropriate formula. But after a moment he gave up the search, and pulled from his pocket an envelope that he held out to his employer. "I merely want to give this back."

The hand which Mr. Spence had extended dropped to his side, and his sand-colored face grew chalky. "Give it back?" His voice was as thick as Millner's. "What's happened? Is the bargain off?"

"Oh, no. I've given you my word."

"Your word?" Mr. Spence lowered at him. "I'd like to know what that's worth!"

Millner continued to hold out the envelope. "You do know, now. It's worth *that*. It's worth my place."

Mr. Spence, standing motionless before him, hesitated for an appreciable space of time. His lips parted once or twice

199

under their square-clipped stubble, and at last emitted: "How much more do you want?"

Millner broke into a laugh. "Oh, I've got all I want—all and more!"

"What—from the others? Are you crazy?"

"No, you are," said Millner with a sudden recovery of composure. "But you're safe—you're as safe as you'll ever be. Only I don't care to take this for making you so."

Mr. Spence slowly moistened his lips with his tongue, and removing his *pince-nez*, took a long hard look at Millner.

"I don't understand. What other guarantee have I got?"

"That I mean what I say?" Millner glanced past the banker's figure at his rich densely colored background of Spanish leather and mahogany. He remembered that it was from this very threshold that he had first seen Mr. Spence's son.

"What guarantee? You've got Draper!" he said.

AFTERWARD

I

"Oh, there *is* one, of course, but you'll never know it."

The assertion, laughingly flung out six months earlier in a bright June garden, came back to Mary Boyne with a sharp perception of its latent significance as she stood, in the December dusk, waiting for the lamps to be brought into the library.

The words had been spoken by their friend Alida Stair, as they sat at tea on her lawn at Pangbourne, in reference to the very house of which the library in question was the central, the pivotal "feature." Mary Boyne and her husband, in quest of a country place in one of the southern or southwestern counties, had, on their arrival in England, carried their problem straight to Alida Stair, who had successfully solved it in her own case; but it was not until they had rejected, almost capriciously, several practical and judicious suggestions that she threw it out: "Well, there's Lyng, in Dorsetshire. It belongs to Hugo's cousins, and you can get it for a song."

The reasons she gave for its being obtainable on these terms—its remoteness from a station, its lack of electric light, hot water pipes, and other vulgar necessities—were exactly those pleading in its favor with two romantic Americans perversely in search of the economic drawbacks which were associated, in their tradition, with unusual architectural felicities.

"I should never believe I was living in an old house unless I was thoroughly uncomfortable," Ned Boyne, the more extravagant of the two, had jocosely insisted; "the least hint of 'convenience' would make me think it had been bought out of an exhibition, with the pieces numbered, and set up again." And they had proceeded to enumerate, with humorous precision, their various suspicions and exactions, refusing to believe that the house their cousin recommended was *really* Tudor till they learned it had no heating system, or that the village church was literally in the grounds till she assured them of the deplorable uncertainty of the water supply.

"It's too uncomfortable to be true!" Edward Boyne had continued to exult as the avowal of each disadvantage was successively wrung from her; but he had cut short his rhapsody to ask, with a sudden relapse to distrust: "And the ghost? You've been concealing from us the fact that there is no ghost!"

Mary, at the moment, had laughed with him, yet almost with her laugh, being possessed of several sets of independent perceptions, had noted a sudden flatness of tone in Alida's answering hilarity.

"Oh, Dorsetshire's full of ghosts, you know."

"Yes, yes; but that won't do. I don't want to have to drive ten miles to see somebody else's ghost. I want one of my own on the premises. *Is* there a ghost at Lyng?"

His rejoinder had made Alida laugh again, and it was then that she had flung back tantalizingly: "Oh, there *is* one, of course, but you'll never know it."

"Never know it?" Boyne pulled her up. "But what in the world constitutes a ghost except the fact of its being known for one?"

"I can't say. But that's the story."

"That there's a ghost, but that nobody knows it's a ghost?"

"Well—not till afterward, at any rate."

"Till afterward?"

"Not till long, long afterward."

"But if it's once been identified as an unearthly visitant, why hasn't its *signalement* been handed down in the family? How has it managed to preserve its incognito?"

Alida could only shake her head. "Don't ask me. But it has."

"And then suddenly—" Mary spoke up as if from some cavernous depth of divination—"suddenly, long afterward, one says to one's self, '*That was* it?'"

She was oddly startled at the sepulchral sound with which her question fell on the banter of the other two, and she saw the shadow of the same surprise flit across Alida's clear pupils. "I suppose so. One just has to wait."

"Oh, hang waiting!" Ned broke in. "Life's too short for a ghost who can only be enjoyed in retrospect. Can't we do better than that, Mary?"

But it turned out that in the event they were not destined to, for within three months of their conversation with Mrs. Stair they were established at Lyng, and the life they had yearned for to the point of planning it out in all its daily details had actually begun for them.

It was to sit, in the thick December dusk, by just such a wide-hooded fireplace, under just such black oak rafters, with the sense that beyond the mullioned panes the downs were darkening to a deeper solitude: it was for the ultimate indulgence in such sensations that Mary Boyne had endured for nearly fourteen years the soul-deadening ugliness of the Middle West, and that Boyne had ground on doggedly at his engineering till, with a suddenness that still made her blink, the prodigious windfall of the Blue Star Mine had put them at a stroke in possession of life and the leisure to taste it. They had never for a moment meant their new state to be one of idleness; but they meant to give themselves only to harmonious activities. She had her vision of painting and gardening (against a background of gray walls), he dreamed of the production of his long-planned book on the "Economic Basis of Culture"; and with such absorbing work ahead no existence could be too sequestered; they could not get far enough from the world, or plunge deep enough into the past.

Dorsetshire had attracted them from the first by a semblance of remoteness out of all proportion to its geographical position. But to the Boynes it was one of the ever-recurring wonders of the whole incredibly compressed island—a nest of counties, as they put it—that for the production of its effects so little of a given quality went so far: that so few miles made a distance, and so short a distance a difference.

"It's that," Ned had once enthusiastically explained, "that gives such depth to their effects, such relief to their least contrasts. They've been able to lay the butter so thick on every exquisite mouthful."

The butter had certainly been laid on thick at Lyng: the old gray house, hidden under a shoulder of the downs, had almost all the finer marks of commerce with a protracted past. The mere fact that it was neither large nor exceptional made it, to the Boynes, abound the more richly in its special sense—the sense of having been for centuries a deep, dim reservoir of life. The life had probably not been of the most vivid order: for long periods, no doubt, it had fallen as noiselessly into the past as the quiet drizzle of autumn fell, hour after hour, into the green fish pond between the yews; but these backwaters of existence sometimes breed, in their sluggish depths, strange acuities of emotion, and Mary Boyne had felt from the first the occasional brush of an intenser memory.

The feeling had never been stronger than on the December afternoon when, waiting in the library for the belated lamps, she rose from her seat and stood among the shadows of the hearth. Her husband had gone off, after luncheon, for one of his long tramps on the downs. She had noticed of late that he preferred to be unaccompanied on these occasions; and, in the tried security of their personal relations, had been driven to conclude that his book was bothering him, and that he needed the afternoons to turn over in solitude the problems left from the morning's work. Certainly the book was not going as smoothly as she had imagined it would, and the lines of perplexity between his eyes had never been there in his engineering days. Then he had often looked fagged to the verge of illness, but the native demon of "worry" had never branded his brow. Yet the few pages he had so far read to her—the introduction, and a synopsis of the opening chapter—gave evidences of a firm possession of his subject, and a deepening confidence in his powers.

The fact threw her into deeper perplexity, since, now that he had done with "business" and its disturbing contingencies, the one other possible element of anxiety was eliminated. Unless it were his health, then? But physically he had gained since they had come to Dorsetshire, grown robuster, ruddier, and fresher-eyed. It was only within a week that she had felt in him the un-definable change that made her restless in his absence, and as tongue-tied in his presence as though it were *she* who had a se-cret to keep from him!

The thought that there *was* a secret somewhere between them struck her with a sudden smart rap of wonder, and she looked about her down the dim, long room.

"Can it be the house?" she mused.

The room itself might have been full of secrets. They seemed to be piling themselves up, as evening fell, like the lay-ers and layers of velvet shadow dropping from the low ceiling, the dusky walls of books, the smoke-blurred sculpture of the hooded hearth.

"Why, of course—the house is haunted!" she reflected.

The ghost—Alida's imperceptible ghost—after figuring largely in the banter of their first month or two at Lyng, had been gradually discarded as too ineffectual for imaginative use. Mary had, indeed, as became the tenant of a haunted house, made the customary inquiries among her few rural neighbors, but, beyond a vague, "They du say so, Ma'am," the villagers had nothing to impart. The elusive specter had apparently never had sufficient identity for a legend to crystallize about it, and after a time the Boynes had laughingly set the matter down to their profit-and-loss account, agreeing that Lyng was one of the few houses good enough in itself to dispense with supernatural enhancements.

"And I suppose, poor, ineffectual demon, that's why it beats its beautiful wings in vain in the void," Mary had laughingly concluded.

"Or, rather," Ned answered, in the same strain, "why, amid so much that's ghostly, it can never affirm its separate exis-tence as *the* ghost." And thereupon their invisible housemate had finally dropped out of their references, which were numer-ous enough to make them promptly unaware of the loss.

Now, as she stood on the hearth, the subject of their earlier curiosity revived in her with a new sense of its meaning—a sense gradually acquired through close daily contact with the scene of the lurking mystery. It was the house itself, of course, that possessed the ghost-seeing faculty, that communed visually but secretly with its own past; and if one could only get into close enough communion with the house, one might surprise its secret, and acquire the ghost-sight on one's own account. Perhaps, in his long solitary hours in this very room, where she never trespassed till the afternoon, her husband *had* acquired it already, and was silently carrying the dread weight of whatever it had revealed to him. Mary was too well-versed in the code of the spectral world not to know that one could not talk about the ghosts one saw: to do so was almost as great a breach of good breeding as to name a lady in a club. But this explanation did not really satisfy her. "What, after all, except for the fun of the *frisson*," she reflected, "would he really care for any of their old ghosts?" And thence she was thrown back once more on the fundamental dilemma: the fact that one's greater or less susceptibility to spectral influences had no particular bearing on the case, since, when one *did* see a ghost at Lyng, one did not know it.

"Not till long afterward," Alida Stair had said. Well, supposing Ned *had* seen one when they first came, and had known only within the last week what had happened to him? More and more under the spell of the hour, she threw back her searching thoughts to the early days of their tenancy, but at first only to recall a gay confusion of unpacking, settling, arranging of books, and calling to each other from remote corners of the house as treasure after treasure of their habitation revealed itself to them. It was in this particular connection that she presently recalled a certain soft afternoon of the previous October, when, passing from the first rapturous flurry of exploration to a detailed inspection of the old house, she had pressed (like a novel heroine) a panel that opened at her touch, on a narrow flight of stairs leading to an unsuspected flat ledge of the

206

roof—the roof which, from below, seemed to slope away on all sides too abruptly for any but practised feet to scale.

The view from this hidden coign was enchanting, and she had flown down to snatch Ned from his papers and give him the freedom of her discovery. She remembered still how, standing on the narrow ledge, he had passed his arm about her while their gaze flew to the long, tossed horizon line of the downs, and then dropped contentedly back to trace the arabesque of yew hedges about the fish pond, and the shadow of the cedar on the lawn.

"And now the other way," he had said, gently turning her about within his arm; and closely pressed to him, she had absorbed, like some long, satisfying draft, the picture of the gray-walled court, the squat lions on the gates, and the lime-avenue reaching up to the highroad under the downs.

It was just then, while they gazed and held each other, that she had felt his arm relax, and heard a sharp "Hullo!" that made her turn to glance at him.

Distinctly, yes, she now recalled she had seen, as she glanced, a shadow of anxiety, of perplexity, rather, fall across his face; and, following his eyes, had beheld the figure of a man—a man in loose, grayish clothes, as it appeared to her—who was sauntering down the lime-avenue to the court with the tentative gait of a stranger seeking his way. Her shortsighted eyes had given her but a blurred impression of slightness and grayness, with something foreign, or at least unlocal, in the cut of the figure or its garb; but her husband had apparently seen more—seen enough to make him push past her with a sharp "Wait!" and dash down the twisting stairs without pausing to give her a hand for the descent.

A slight tendency to dizziness obliged her, after a provisional clutch at the chimney against which they had been leaning, to follow him down more cautiously; and when she had reached the attic landing she paused again for a less definite reason, leaning over the oak banister to strain her eyes through the silence of the brown, sun-flecked depths below. She lingered there till, somewhere in those depths, she heard the closing of a door; then, mechanically impelled, she went down the shallow flights of steps till she reached the lower hall.

The front door stood open on the mild sunlight of the court, and hall and court were empty. The library door was open, too, and after listening in vain for any sound of voices within, she quickly crossed the threshold, and found her husband alone, vaguely fingering the papers on his desk.

He looked up, as if surprised at her precipitate entrance, but the shadow of anxiety had passed from his face, leaving it even, as she fancied, a little brighter and clearer than usual.

"What was it? Who was it?" she asked.

"Who?" he repeated, with the surprise still all on his side.

"The man we saw coming toward the house." Boyne shrugged his shoulders. "So I thought; but he must have got up steam in the interval. What do you say to our trying a scramble up Meldon Steep before sunset?"

That was all. At the time the occurrence had been less than nothing, had, indeed, been immediately obliterated by the magic of their first vision from Meldon Steep, a height which they had dreamed of climbing ever since they had first seen its bare spine heaving itself above the low roof of Lyng. Doubtless it was the mere fact of the other incident's having occurred on the very day of their ascent to Meldon that had kept it stored away in the unconscious fold of association from which it now emerged; for in itself it had no mark of the portentous. At the moment there could have been nothing more natural than that Ned should dash himself from the roof in the pursuit of dilatory tradesmen. It was the period when they were always on the watch for one or the other of the specialists employed about the place; always lying in wait for them, and dashing out at them with questions, reproaches, or reminders. And certainly in the distance the gray figure had looked like Peters.

Yet now, as she reviewed the rapid scene, she felt her husband's explanation of it to have been invalidated by the look of anxiety on his face. Why had the familiar appearance of Peters

208

made him anxious? Why, above all, if it was of such prime necessity to confer with that authority on the subject of the stable drains, had the failure to find him produced such a look of relief? Mary could not say that any one of these considerations had occurred to her at the time, yet, from the promptness with which they now marshaled themselves at her summons, she had a sudden sense that they must all along have been there, waiting their hour.

II

Weary with her thoughts, she moved toward the window. The library was now completely dark, and she was surprised to see how much faint light the outer world still held.

As she peered out into it across the court, a figure shaped itself in the tapering perspective of bare lines: it looked a mere blot of deeper gray in the grayness, and for an instant, as it moved toward her, her heart thumped to the thought, "It's the ghost!"

She had time, in that long instant, to feel suddenly that the man of whom, two months earlier, she had a brief distant vision from the roof was now, at his predestined hour, about to reveal himself as *not* having been Peters; and her spirit sank under the impending fear of the disclosure. But almost with the next tick of the clock the ambiguous figure, gaining substance and character, showed itself even to her weak sight as her husband's; and she turned away to meet him, as he entered, with the confession of her folly.

"It's really too absurd," she laughed out from the threshold, "but I never *can* remember!"

"Remember what?" Boyne questioned as they drew together.

"That when one sees the Lyng ghost one never knows it."

Her hand was on his sleeve, and he kept it there, but with no response in his gesture or in the lines of his fagged, preoccupied face.

"Did you think you'd seen it?" he asked, after an appreciable interval.

"Why, I actually took *you* for it, my dear, in my mad determination to spot it!"

"Me—just now?" His arm dropped away, and he turned from her with a faint echo of her laugh. "Really, dearest, you'd better give it up, if that's the best you can do."

"Yes, I give it up—I give it up. Have *you?*" she asked, turning round on him abruptly.

The parlor maid had entered with letters and a lamp, and the light struck up into Boyne's face as he bent above the tray she presented.

"Have *you?*" Mary perversely insisted, when the servant had disappeared on her errand of illumination.

"Have I what?" he rejoined absently, the light bringing out the sharp stamp of worry between his brows as he turned over the letters.

"I never tried," he said, tearing open the wrapper of a newspaper.

"Well, of course," Mary persisted, "the exasperating thing is that there's no use trying, since one can't be sure till so long afterward."

He was unfolding the paper as if he had hardly heard her; but after a pause, during which the sheets rustled spasmodically between his hands, he lifted his head to say abruptly, "Have you any idea *how long?*"

Mary had sunk into a low chair beside the fireplace. From her seat she looked up, startled, at her husband's profile, which was darkly projected against the circle of lamplight.

"No; none. Have *you*" she retorted, repeating her former phrase with an added keenness of intention.

Boyne crumpled the paper into a bunch, and then inconsequently turned back with it toward the lamp.

"Lord, no! I only meant," he explained, with a faint tinge of impatience, "is there any legend, any tradition, as to that?"

"Not that I know of," she answered; but the impulse to add, "What makes you ask?" was checked by the reappearance of the parlor maid with tea and a second lamp.

With the dispersal of shadows, and the repetition of the daily domestic office, Mary Boyne felt herself less oppressed by that sense of something mutely imminent which had darkened her solitary afternoon. For a few moments she gave herself silently to the details of her task, and when she looked up from it she was struck to the point of bewilderment by the change in her husband's face. He had seated himself near the farther lamp, and was absorbed in the perusal of his letters; but was it something he had found in them, or merely the shifting of her own point of view, that had restored his features to their normal aspect? The longer she looked, the more definitely the change affirmed itself. The lines of painful tension had vanished, and such traces of fatigue as lingered were of the kind easily attributable to steady mental effort. He glanced up, as if drawn by her gaze, and met her eyes with a smile.

"I'm dying for my tea, you know; and here's a letter for you," he said.

She took the letter he held out in exchange for the cup she proffered him, and, returning to her seat, broke the seal with the languid gesture of the reader whose interests are all inclosed in the circle of one cherished presence.

Her next conscious motion was that of starting to her feet, the letter falling to them as she rose, while she held out to her husband a long newspaper clipping.

"Ned! What's this? What does it mean?"

He had risen at the same instant, almost as if hearing her cry before she uttered it; and for a perceptible space of time he and she studied each other, like adversaries watching for an advantage, across the space between her chair and his desk.

"What's what? You fairly made me jump!" Boyne said at length, moving toward her with a sudden, half-exasperated laugh. The shadow of apprehension was on his face again, not now a look of fixed foreboding, but a shifting vigilance of lips and eyes that gave her the sense of his feeling himself invisibly surrounded.

Her hand shook so that she could hardly give him the clipping.

"This article—from the 'Waukesha Sentinel'—that a man named Elwell has brought suit against you—that there was something wrong about the Blue Star Mine. I can't understand more than half."

They continued to face each other as she spoke, and to her astonishment, she saw that her words had the almost immediate effect of dissipating the strained watchfulness of his look.

"Oh, *that!*" He glanced down the printed slip, and then folded it with the gesture of one who handles something harmless and familiar. "What's the matter with you this afternoon, Mary? I thought you'd got bad news."

She stood before him with her undefinable terror subsiding slowly under the reassuring touch of his composure.

"You knew about this, then—it's all right?"

"Certainly I knew about it; and it's all right."

"But what *is* it? I don't understand. What does this man accuse you of?"

"Oh, pretty nearly every crime in the calendar." Boyne had tossed the clipping down, and thrown himself comfortably into an armchair near the fire. "Do you want to hear the story? It's not particularly interesting—just a squabble over interests in the Blue Star."

"But who is this Elwell? I don't know the name."

"Oh, he's a fellow I put into it—gave him a hand up. I told you all about him at the time."

"I daresay. I must have forgotten." Vainly she strained back among her memories. "But if you helped him, why does he make this return?"

"Oh, probably some shyster lawyer got hold of him and talked him over. It's all rather technical and complicated. I thought that kind of thing bored you."

His wife felt a sting of compunction. Theoretically, she deprecated the American wife's detachment from her husband's professional interests, but in practice she had always found it difficult to fix her attention on Boyne's report of the transactions in which his varied interests involved him. Besides, she

212

had felt from the first that, in a community where the amenities of living could be obtained only at the cost of efforts as arduous as her husband's professional labors, such brief leisure as they could command should be used as an escape from immediate preoccupations, a flight to the life they always dreamed of living. Once or twice, now that this new life had actually drawn its magic circle about them, she had asked herself if she had done right; but hitherto such conjectures had been no more than the retrospective excursions of an active fancy. Now, for the first time, it startled her a little to find how little she knew of the material foundation on which her happiness was built.

She glanced again at her husband, and was reassured by the composure of his face; yet she felt the need of more definite grounds for her reassurance.

"But doesn't this suit worry you? Why have you never spoken to me about it?"

He answered both questions at once: "I didn't speak of it at first because it *did* worry me—annoyed me, rather. But it's all ancient history now. Your correspondent must have got hold of a back number of the 'Sentinel.'"

She felt a quick thrill of relief. "You mean it's over? He's lost his case?"

There was a just perceptible delay in Boyne's reply. "The suit's been withdrawn—that's all."

But she persisted, as if to exonerate herself from the inward charge of being too easily put off. "Withdrawn because he saw he had no chance?"

"Oh, he had no chance," Boyne answered.

She was still struggling with a dimly felt perplexity at the back of her thoughts.

"How long ago was it withdrawn?"

He paused, as if with a slight return of his former uncertainty. "I've just had the news now; but I've been expecting it."

"Just now—in one of your letters?"

"Yes; in one of my letters."

213

She made no answer, and was aware only, after a short interval of waiting, that he had risen, and strolling across the room, had placed himself on the sofa at her side. She felt him, as he did so, pass an arm about her, she felt his hand seek hers and clasp it, and turning slowly, drawn by the warmth of his cheek, she met the smiling clearness of his eyes.

"It's all right—it's all right?" she questioned, through the flood of her dissolving doubts; and "I give you my word it never was righter!" he laughed back at her, holding her close.

III

One of the strangest things she was afterward to recall out of all the next day's incredible strangeness was the sudden and complete recovery of her sense of security.

It was in the air when she woke in her low-ceilinged, dusky room; it accompanied her downstairs to the breakfast-table, flashed out at her from the fire, and re-duplicated itself brightly from the flanks of the urn and the sturdy flutings of the Georgian teapot. It was as if, in some roundabout way, all her diffused apprehensions of the previous day, with their moment of sharp concentration about the newspaper article—as if this dim questioning of the future, and startled return upon the past—had between them liquidated the arrears of some haunting moral obligation. If she had indeed been careless of her husband's affairs, it was, her new state seemed to prove, because her faith in him instinctively justified such carelessness; and his right to her faith had overwhelmingly affirmed itself in the very face of menace and suspicion. She had never seen him more untroubled, more naturally and unconsciously in possession of himself, than after the cross-examination to which she had subjected him: it was almost as if he had been aware of her lurking doubts, and had wanted the air cleared as much as she did.

It was as clear, thank Heaven! as the bright outer light that surprised her almost with a touch of summer when she issued from the house for her daily round of the gardens. She had left Boyne at his desk, indulging herself, as she passed the library door, by a last peep at his quiet face, where he bent, pipe in his

214

mouth, above his papers, and now she had her own morning's task to perform. The task involved on such charmed winter days almost as much delighted loitering about the different quarters of her demesne as if spring were already at work on shrubs and borders. There were such inexhaustible possibilities still before her, such opportunities to bring out the latent graces of the old place, without a single irreverent touch of alteration, that the winter months were all too short to plan what spring and autumn executed. And her recovered sense of safety gave, on this particular morning, a peculiar zest to her progress through the sweet, still place. She went first to the kitchengarden, where the espaliered pear trees drew complicated patterns on the walls, and pigeons were fluttering and preening about the silvery-slated roof of their cot. There was something wrong about the piping of the hothouse, and she was expecting an authority from Dorchester, who was to drive out between trains and make a diagnosis of the boiler. But when she dipped into the damp heat of the greenhouses, among the spiced scents and waxy pinks and reds of old-fashioned exotics—even the flora of Lyng was in the note!—she learned that the great man had not arrived, and the day being too rare to waste in an artificial atmosphere, she came out again and paced slowly along the springy turf of the bowling green to the gardens behind the house. At their farther end rose a grass terrace, commanding, over the fishpond and the yew hedges, a view of the long house front, with its twisted chimneystacks and the blue shadows of its roof angles, all drenched in the pale gold moisture of the air.

Seen thus, across the level tracery of the yews, under the suffused, mild light, it sent her, from its open windows and hospitably smoking chimneys, the look of some warm human presence, of a mind slowly ripened on a sunny wall of experience. She had never before had so deep a sense of her intimacy with it, such a conviction that its secrets were all beneficent, kept, as they said to children, "for one's good," so complete a trust in its power to gather up her life and Ned's into the harmonious pattern of the long, long story it sat there weaving in the sun.

She heard steps behind her, and turned, expecting to see the gardener, accompanied by the engineer from Dorchester. But only one figure was in sight, that of a youngish, slightly built man, who, for reasons she could not on the spot have specified, did not remotely resemble her preconceived notion of an authority on hothouse boilers. The newcomer, on seeing her, lifted his hat, and paused with the air of a gentleman—perhaps a traveler—desirous of having it immediately known that his intrusion is involuntary. The local fame of Lyng occasionally attracted the more intelligent sightseer, and Mary half-expected to see the stranger dissemble a camera, or justify his presence by producing it. But he made no gesture of any sort, and after a moment she asked, in a tone responding to the courteous deprecation of his attitude: "Is there any one you wish to see?"

"I came to see Mr. Boyne," he replied. His intonation, rather than his accent, was faintly American, and Mary, at the familiar note, looked at him more closely. The brim of his soft felt hat cast a shade on his face, which, thus obscured, wore to her shortsighted gaze a look of seriousness, as of a person arriving "on business," and civilly but firmly aware of his rights.

Past experience had made Mary equally sensible to such claims; but she was jealous of her husband's morning hours, and doubtful of his having given any one the right to intrude on them.

"Have you an appointment with Mr. Boyne?" she asked.

He hesitated, as if unprepared for the question.

"Not exactly an appointment," he replied.

"Then I'm afraid, this being his working time, that he can't receive you now. Will you give me a message, or come back later?"

The visitor, again lifting his hat, briefly replied that he would come back later, and walked away, as if to regain the front of the house. As his figure receded down the walk between the yew hedges, Mary saw him pause and look up an instant at the peaceful house front bathed in faint winter sunshine; and it struck her, with a tardy touch of compunction, that it would have been more humane to ask if he had come from a distance, and to offer, in that case, to inquire if her husband could receive him. But as the thought occurred to her he passed out of sight behind a pyramidal yew, and at the same moment her attention was distracted by the approach of the gardener, attended by the bearded pepper-and-salt figure of the boiler-maker from Dorchester.

The encounter with this authority led to such far-reaching issues that they resulted in his finding it expedient to ignore his train, and beguiled Mary into spending the remainder of the morning in absorbed confabulation among the greenhouses. She was startled to find, when the colloquy ended, that it was nearly luncheon time, and she half expected, as she hurried back to the house, to see her husband coming out to meet her. But she found no one in the court but an under-gardener raking the gravel, and the hall, when she entered it, was so silent that she guessed Boyne to be still at work behind the closed door of the library.

Not wishing to disturb him, she turned into the drawing room, and there, at her writing table, lost herself in renewed calculations of the outlay to which the morning's conference had committed her. The knowledge that she could permit herself such follies had not yet lost its novelty; and somehow, in contrast to the vague apprehensions of the previous days, it now seemed an element of her recovered security, of the sense that, as Ned had said, things in general had never been "righter."

She was still luxuriating in a lavish play of figures when the parlor maid, from the threshold, roused her with a dubiously worded inquiry as to the expediency of serving luncheon. It was one of their jokes that Trimmle announced luncheon as if she were divulging a state secret, and Mary, intent upon her papers, merely murmured an absentminded assent.

She felt Trimmle wavering expressively on the threshold as if in rebuke of such offhand acquiescence; then her retreating steps sounded down the passage, and Mary, pushing away her papers, crossed the hall, and went to the library door. It was still closed, and she wavered in her turn, disliking to disturb her husband, yet anxious that he should not exceed his normal measure of work. As she stood there, balancing her impulses, the esoteric Trimmle returned with the announcement of luncheon, and Mary, thus impelled, opened the door and went into the library.

Boyne was not at his desk, and she peered about her, expecting to discover him at the bookshelves, somewhere down the length of the room; but her call brought no response, and gradually it became clear to her that he was not in the library.

She turned back to the parlor maid.

"Mr. Boyne must be upstairs. Please tell him that luncheon is ready."

The parlor maid appeared to hesitate between the obvious duty of obeying orders and an equally obvious conviction of the foolishness of the injunction laid upon her. The struggle resulted in her saying doubtfully, "If you please, Madam, Mr. Boyne's not upstairs."

"Not in his room? Are you sure?"

"I'm sure, Madam."

Mary consulted the clock. "Where is he, then?"

"He's gone out," Trimmle announced, with the superior air of one who has respectfully waited for the question that a well-ordered mind would have first propounded.

Mary's previous conjecture had been right, then. Boyne must have gone to the gardens to meet her, and since she had missed him, it was clear that he had taken the shorter way by the south door, instead of going round to the court. She crossed the hall to the glass portal opening directly on the yew garden, but the parlor maid, after another moment of inner conflict, decided to bring out recklessly, "Please, Madam, Mr. Boyne didn't go that way."

Mary turned back. "Where *did* he go? And when?"

"He went out of the front door, up the drive, Madam." It was a matter of principle with Trimmle never to answer more than one question at a time.

"Up the drive? At this hour?" Mary went to the door herself, and glanced across the court through the long tunnel of bare limes. But its perspective was as empty as when she had scanned it on entering the house.

"Did Mr. Boyne leave no message?" she asked.

Trimmle seemed to surrender herself to a last struggle with the forces of chaos.

"No, Madam. He just went out with the gentleman."

"The gentleman? What gentleman?" Mary wheeled about, as if to front this new factor.

"The gentleman who called, Madam," said Trimmle, resignedly.

"When did a gentleman call? Do explain yourself, Trimmle!"

Only the fact that Mary was very hungry, and that she wanted to consult her husband about the greenhouses, would have caused her to lay so unusual an injunction on her attendant; and even now she was detached enough to note in Trimmle's eye the dawning defiance of the respectful subordinate who has been pressed too hard.

"I couldn't exactly say the hour, Madam, because I didn't let the gentleman in," she replied, with the air of magnanimously ignoring the irregularity of her mistress's course.

"You didn't let him in?"

"No, Madam. When the bell rang I was dressing, and Agnes—"

"Go and ask Agnes, then," Mary interjected. Trimmle still wore her look of patient magnanimity. "Agnes would not know, Madam, for she had unfortunately burnt her hand in trying the wick of the new lamp from town—" Trimmle, as Mary was aware, had always been opposed to the new lamp—"and so Mrs. Dockett sent the kitchen maid instead."

Mary looked again at the clock. "It's after two! Go and ask the kitchen maid if Mr. Boyne left any word."

She went into luncheon without waiting, and Trimmle presently brought her there the kitchen maid's statement that the gentleman had called about one o'clock, that Mr. Boyne had gone out with him without leaving any message. The kitchen maid did not even know the caller's name, for he had written it on a slip of paper, which he had folded and handed to her, with the injunction to deliver it at once to Mr. Boyne.

Mary finished her luncheon, still wondering, and when it was over, and Trimmle had brought the coffee to the drawing room, her wonder had deepened to a first faint tinge of disquietude. It was unlike Boyne to absent himself without explanation at so unwonted an hour, and the difficulty of identifying the visitor whose summons he had apparently obeyed made his disappearance the more unaccountable. Mary Boyne's experience as the wife of a busy engineer, subject to sudden calls and compelled to keep irregular hours, had trained her to the philosophic acceptance of surprises; but since Boyne's withdrawal from business he had adopted a Benedictine regularity of life. As if to make up for the dispersed and agitated years, with their "stand-up" lunches and dinners rattled down to the joltings of the dining car, he cultivated the last refinements of punctuality and monotony, discouraging his wife's fancy for the unexpected; and declaring that to a delicate taste there were infinite gradations of pleasure in the fixed recurrences of habit.

Still, since no life can completely defend itself from the unforeseen, it was evident that all Boyne's precautions would sooner or later prove unavailable, and Mary concluded that he had cut short a tiresome visit by walking with his caller to the station, or at least accompanying him for part of the way.

This conclusion relieved her from farther preoccupation, and she went out herself to take up her conference with the gardener. Thence she walked to the village post office, a mile or so away; and when she turned toward home, the early twilight was setting in.

She had taken a footpath across the downs, and as Boyne, meanwhile, had probably returned from the station by the highroad, there was little likelihood of their meeting on the way. She felt sure, however, of his having reached the house before

220

her; so sure that, when she entered it herself, without even pausing to inquire of Trimmle, she made directly for the library. But the library was still empty, and with an unwonted precision of visual memory she immediately observed that the papers on her husband's desk lay precisely as they had lain when she had gone in to call him to luncheon.

Then of a sudden she was seized by a vague dread of the unknown. She had closed the door behind her on entering, and as she stood alone in the long, silent, shadowy room, her dread seemed to take shape and sound, to be there audibly breathing and lurking among the shadows. Her shortsighted eyes strained through them, half-discerning an actual presence, something aloof, that watched and knew; and in the recoil from that intangible propinquity she threw herself suddenly on the bell rope and gave it a desperate pull.

The long, quavering summons brought Trimmle in precipitately with a lamp, and Mary breathed again at this sobering reappearance of the usual.

"You may bring tea if Mr. Boyne is in," she said, to justify her ring.

"Very well, Madam. But Mr. Boyne is not in," said Trimmle, putting down the lamp.

"Not in? You mean he's come back and gone out again?"

"No, Madam. He's never been back."

The dread stirred again, and Mary knew that now it had her fast.

"Not since he went out with—the gentleman?"

"Not since he went out with the gentleman."

"But who *was* the gentleman?" Mary gasped out, with the sharp note of some one trying to be heard through a confusion of meaningless noises.

"That I couldn't say, Madam." Trimmle, standing there by the lamp, seemed suddenly to grow less round and rosy, as though eclipsed by the same creeping shade of apprehension.

"But the kitchen maid knows—wasn't it the kitchen maid who let him in?"

"She doesn't know either, Madam, for he wrote his name on a folded paper."

Mary, through her agitation, was aware that they were both designating the unknown visitor by a vague pronoun, instead of the conventional formula that, till then, had kept their allusions within the bounds of custom. And at the same moment her mind caught at the suggestion of the folded paper.

"But he must have a name! Where is the paper?"

She moved to the desk, and began to turn over the scattered documents that littered it. The first that caught her eye was an unfinished letter in her husband's hand, with his pen lying across it, as though dropped there at a sudden summons.

"My dear Parvis,"—who was Parvis?—"I have just received your letter announcing Elwell's death, and while I suppose there is now no farther risk of trouble, it might be safer—"

She tossed the sheet aside, and continued her search; but no folded paper was discoverable among the letters and pages of manuscript which had been swept together in a promiscuous heap, as if by a hurried or a startled gesture.

"But the kitchen maid *saw* him. Send her here," she commanded, wondering at her dullness in not thinking sooner of so simple a solution.

Trimmle, at the behest, vanished in a flash, as if thankful to be out of the room, and when she reappeared, conducting the agitated underling, Mary had regained her self-possession, and had her questions pat.

The gentleman was a stranger, yes—that she understood. But what had he said? And, above all, what had he looked like? The first question was easily enough answered, for the disconcerting reason that he had said so little—had merely asked for Mr. Boyne, and, scribbling something on a bit of paper, had requested that it should at once be carried in to him.

"Then you don't know what he wrote? You're not sure it *was* his name?"

The kitchen maid was not sure, but supposed it was, since he had written it in answer to her inquiry as to whom she should announce.

"And when you carried the paper in to Mr. Boyne, what did he say?"

The kitchen maid did not think that Mr. Boyne had said anything, but she could not be sure, for just as she had handed him the paper and he was opening it, she had become aware that the visitor had followed her into the library, and she had slipped out, leaving the two gentlemen together.

"But then, if you left them in the library, how do you know that they went out of the house?"

This question plunged the witness into momentary inarticulateness, from which she was rescued by Trimmle, who, by means of ingenious circumlocutions, elicited the statement that before she could cross the hall to the back passage she had heard the gentlemen behind her, and had seen them go out of the front door together.

"Then, if you saw the gentleman twice, you must be able to tell me what he looked like."

But with this final challenge to her powers of expression it became clear that the limit of the kitchen maid's endurance had been reached. The obligation of going to the front door to "show in" a visitor was in itself so subversive of the fundamental order of things that it had thrown her faculties into hopeless disarray, and she could only stammer out, after various panting efforts at evocation, "His hat, mum, was different-like, as you might say—"

"Different? How different?" Mary flashed out at her, her own mind, in the same instant, leaping back to an image left on it that morning, but temporarily lost under layers of subsequent impressions.

"His hat had a wide brim, you mean? and his face was pale—a youngish face?" Mary pressed her, with a white-lipped intensity of interrogation. But if the kitchen maid found any adequate answer to this challenge, it was swept away for her listener down the rushing current of her own convictions. The stranger—the stranger in the garden! Why had Mary not thought of him before? She needed no one now to tell her that it was he who had called for her husband and gone away with him. But who was he, and why had Boyne obeyed his call?

It leaped out at her suddenly, like a grin out of the dark, that they had often called England so little—"such a confoundedly hard place to get lost in."

A confoundedly hard place to get lost in! That had been her husband's phrase. And now, with the whole machinery of official investigation sweeping its flashlights from shore to shore, and across the dividing straits; now, with Boyne's name blazing from the walls of every town and village, his portrait (how that wrung her!) hawked up and down the country like the image of a hunted criminal; now the little compact, populous island, so policed, surveyed, and administered, revealed itself as a Sphinx-like guardian of abysmal mysteries, staring back into his wife's anguished eyes as if with the malicious joy of knowing something they would never know!

In the fortnight since Boyne's disappearance there had been no word of him, no trace of his movements. Even the usual misleading reports that raise expectancy in tortured bosoms had been few and fleeting. No one but the bewildered kitchen maid had seen him leave the house, and no one else had seen "the gentleman" who accompanied him. All inquiries in the neighborhood failed to elicit the memory of a stranger's presence that day in the neighborhood of Lyng. And no one had met Edward Boyne, either alone or in company, in any of the neighboring villages, or on the road across the downs, or at either of the local railway stations. The sunny English noon had swallowed him as completely as if he had gone out into Cimmerian night.

Mary, while every external means of investigation was working at its highest pressure, had ransacked her husband's papers for any trace of antecedent complications, of entanglements or obligations unknown to her, that might throw a faint ray into the darkness. But if any such had existed in the background of Boyne's life, they had disappeared as completely as the slip of paper on which the visitor had written his name. There remained no possible thread of guidance except—if it were indeed an exception—the letter which Boyne had apparently been in the act of writing when he received his mysterious summons. That letter, read and reread by his wife, and submitted by her to the police, yielded little enough for conjecture to feed on.

"I have just heard of Elwell's death, and while I suppose there is now no farther risk of trouble, it might be safer—" That was all. The "risk of trouble" was easily explained by the newspaper clipping which had apprised Mary of the suit brought against her husband by one of his associates in the Blue Star enterprise. The only new information conveyed in the letter was the fact of its showing Boyne, when he wrote it, to be still apprehensive of the results of the suit, though he had assured his wife that it had been withdrawn, and though the letter itself declared that the plaintiff was dead. It took several weeks of exhaustive cabling to fix the identity of the "Parvis" to whom the fragmentary communication was addressed, but even after these inquiries had shown him to be a Waukesha lawyer, no new facts concerning the Elwell suit were elicited. He appeared to have had no direct concern in it, but to have been conversant with the facts merely as an acquaintance, and possible intermediary; and he declared himself unable to divine with what object Boyne intended to seek his assistance.

This negative information, sole fruit of the first fortnight's feverish search, was not increased by a jot during the slow weeks that followed. Mary knew that the investigations were still being carried on, but she had a vague sense of their gradually slackening, as the actual march of time seemed to slacken. It was as though the days, flying horrorstruck from the shrouded image of the one inscrutable day, gained assurance as the distance lengthened, till at last they fell back into their normal gait. And so with the human imaginations at work on the dark event. No doubt it occupied them still, but week by week and hour by hour it grew less absorbing, took up less space, was slowly but inevitably crowded out of the foreground of consciousness by the new problems perpetually bubbling up from the vaporous caldron of human experience.

Even Mary Boyne's consciousness gradually felt the same lowering of velocity. It still swayed with the incessant oscillations of conjecture; but they were slower, more rhythmical in their beat. There were moments of overwhelming lassitude when, like the victim of some poison which leaves the brain clear, but holds the body motionless, she saw herself domesticated with the Horror, accepting its perpetual presence as one of the fixed conditions of life.

These moments lengthened into hours and days, till she passed into a phase of stolid acquiescence. She watched the familiar routine of life with the incurious eye of a savage on whom the meaningless processes of civilization make but the faintest impression. She had come to regard herself as part of the routine, a spoke of the wheel, revolving with its motion; she felt almost like the furniture of the room in which she sat, an insensate object to be dusted and pushed about with the chairs and tables. And this deepening apathy held her fast at Lyng, in spite of the urgent entreaties of friends and the usual medical recommendation of "change." Her friends supposed that her refusal to move was inspired by the belief that her husband would one day return to the spot from which he had vanished, and a beautiful legend grew up about this imaginary state of waiting. But in reality she had no such belief: the depths of anguish inclosing her were no longer lighted by flashes of hope. She was sure that Boyne would never come back, that he had gone out of her sight as completely as if Death itself had waited that day on the threshold. She had even renounced, one by one, the various theories as to his disappearance that had been advanced by the press, the police, and her own agonized imagination. In sheer lassitude her mind turned from these alternatives of horror, and sank back into the blank fact that he was gone.

No, she would never know what had become of him—no one would ever know. But the house *knew*; the library in which she spent her long, lonely evenings knew. For it was here that the last scene had been enacted, here that the stranger had come, and spoken the word that had caused Boyne to rise and follow him. The floor she trod had felt his tread; the books on the shelves had seen his face; and there were moments when the intense consciousness of the old, dusky walls seemed about to break out into some audible revelation of their secret. But the revelation never came, and she knew it would never come. Lyng was not one of the garrulous old houses that betray the secrets intrusted to them. Its very legend proved that it had always been the mute accomplice, the incorruptible custodian of the mysteries it had surprised. And Mary Boyne, sitting face to face with its portentous silence, felt the futility of seeking to break it by any human means.

V

"I don't say it *wasn't* straight, yet don't say it *was* straight. It was business."

Mary, at the words, lifted her head with a start, and looked intently at the speaker.

When, half an hour before, a card with "Mr. Parvis" on it had been brought up to her, she had been immediately aware that the name had been a part of her consciousness ever since she had read it at the head of Boyne's unfinished letter. In the library she had found awaiting her a small neutral-tinted man with a bald head and gold eyeglasses, and it sent a strange tremor through her to know that this was the person to whom her husband's last known thought had been directed.

Parvis, civilly, but without vain preamble—in the manner of a man who has his watch in his hand—had set forth the object of his visit. He had "run over" to England on business, and finding himself in the neighborhood of Dorchester, had not wished to leave it without paying his respects to Mrs. Boyne; without asking her, if the occasion offered, what she meant to do about Bob Elwell's family.

The words touched the spring of some obscure dread in Mary's bosom. Did her visitor, after all, know what Boyne had meant by his unfinished phrase? She asked for an elucidation of his question, and noticed at once that he seemed surprised at her continued ignorance of the subject. Was it possible that she really knew as little as she said?

"I know nothing—you must tell me," she faltered out; and her visitor thereupon proceeded to unfold his story. It threw, even to her confused perceptions, and imperfectly initiated vision, a lurid glare on the whole hazy episode of the Blue Star Mine. Her husband had made his money in that brilliant speculation at the cost of "getting ahead" of some one less alert to seize the chance; the victim of his ingenuity was young Robert Elwell, who had "put him on" to the Blue Star scheme.

Parvis, at Mary's first startled cry, had thrown her a sobering glance through his impartial glasses.

"Bob Elwell wasn't smart enough, that's all; if he had been, he might have turned round and served Boyne the same way. It's the kind of thing that happens every day in business. I guess it's what the scientists call the survival of the fittest," said Mr. Parvis, evidently pleased with the aptness of his analogy.

Mary felt a physical shrinking from the next question she tried to frame; it was as though the words on her lips had a taste that nauseated her.

"But then—you accuse my husband of doing something dishonorable?"

Mr. Parvis surveyed the question dispassionately. "Oh, no, I don't. I don't even say it wasn't straight." He glanced up and down the long lines of books, as if one of them might have supplied him with the definition he sought. "I don't say it *wasn't* straight, and yet I don't say it *was* straight. It was business." After all, no definition in his category could be more comprehensive than that.

Mary sat staring at him with a look of terror. He seemed to her like the indifferent, implacable emissary of some dark, formless power.

"But Mr. Elwell's lawyers apparently did not take your view, since I suppose the suit was withdrawn by their advice."

"Oh, yes, they knew he hadn't a leg to stand on, technically. It was when they advised him to withdraw the suit that he got desperate. You see, he'd borrowed most of the money he lost in the Blue Star, and he was up a tree. That's why he shot himself when they told him he had no show."

The horror was sweeping over Mary in great, deafening waves.

"He shot himself? He killed himself because of *that?*"

"Well, he didn't kill himself, exactly. He dragged on two months before he died." Parvis emitted the statement as unemotionally as a gramophone grinding out its "record."

"You mean that he tried to kill himself, and failed? And tried again?"

"Oh, he didn't have to try again," said Parvis, grimly.

They sat opposite each other in silence, he swinging his eyeglass thoughtfully about his finger, she, motionless, her arms stretched along her knees in an attitude of rigid tension.

"But if you knew all this," she began at length, hardly able to force her voice above a whisper, "how is it that when I wrote you at the time of my husband's disappearance you said you didn't understand his letter?"

Parvis received this without perceptible discomfiture. "Why, I didn't understand it—strictly speaking. And it wasn't the time to talk about it, if I had. The Elwell business was settled when the suit was withdrawn. Nothing I could have told you would have helped you to find your husband."

Mary continued to scrutinize him. "Then why are you telling me now?"

Still Parvis did not hesitate. "Well, to begin with, I supposed you knew more than you appear to—I mean about the circumstances of Elwell's death. And then people are talking of it now; the whole matter's been raked up again. And I thought, if you didn't know, you ought to."

She remained silent, and he continued: "You see, it's only come out lately what a bad state Elwell's affairs were in. His wife's a proud woman, and she fought on as long as she could, going out to work, and taking sewing at home, when she got too sick—something with the heart, I believe. But she had his bedridden mother to look after, and the children, and she broke down under it, and finally had to ask for help. That attracted attention to the case, and the papers took it up, and a subscription was started. Everybody out there liked Bob Elwell, and most of the prominent names in the place are down on the list, and people began to wonder why—"

Parvis broke off to fumble in an inner pocket. "Here," he continued, "here's an account of the whole thing from the 'Sentinel'—a little sensational, of course. But I guess you'd better look it over."

He held out a newspaper to Mary, who unfolded it slowly, remembering, as she did so, the evening when, in that same room, the perusal of a clipping from the "Sentinel" had first shaken the depths of her security.

As she opened the paper, her eyes, shrinking from the glaring headlines, "Widow of Boyne's Victim Forced to Appeal for Aid," ran down the column of text to two portraits inserted in it. The first was her husband's, taken from a photograph made the year they had come to England. It was the picture of him that she liked best, the one that stood on the writing table upstairs in her bedroom. As the eyes in the photograph met hers, she felt it would be impossible to read what was said of him, and closed her lids with the sharpness of the pain.

"I thought if you felt disposed to put your name down—" she heard Parvis continue.

She opened her eyes with an effort, and they fell on the other portrait. It was that of a youngish man, slightly built, in rough clothes, with features somewhat blurred by the shadow of a projecting hat brim. Where had she seen that outline before? She stared at it confusedly, her heart hammering in her throat and ears. Then she gave a cry.

"This is the man—the man who came for my husband!"

She heard Parvis start to his feet, and was dimly aware that she had slipped backward into the corner of the sofa, and that

230

he was bending above her in alarm. With an intense effort she straightened herself, and reached out for the paper, which she had dropped.

"It's the man! I should know him anywhere!" she cried in a voice that sounded in her own ears like a scream.

Parvis's voice seemed to come to her from far off, down endless, fog-muffled windings.

"Mrs. Boyne, you're not very well. Shall I call somebody? Shall I get a glass of water?"

"No, no, no!" She threw herself toward him, her hand frantically clenching the newspaper. "I tell you, it's the man! I *know* him! He spoke to me in the garden!"

Parvis took the journal from her, directing his glasses to the portrait. "It can't be, Mrs. Boyne. It's Robert Elwell."

"Robert Elwell?" Her white stare seemed to travel into space. "Then it was Robert Elwell who came for him."

"Came for Boyne? The day he went away?" Parvis's voice dropped as hers rose. He bent over, laying a fraternal hand on her, as if to coax her gently back into her seat. "Why, Elwell was dead! Don't you remember?"

Mary sat with her eyes fixed on the picture, unconscious of what he was saying.

"Don't you remember Boyne's unfinished letter to me—the one you found on his desk that day? It was written just after he'd heard of Elwell's death." She noticed an odd shake in Parvis's unemotional voice. "Surely you remember that!" he urged her.

Yes, she remembered: that was the profoundest horror of it. Elwell had died the day before her husband's disappearance; and this was Elwell's portrait; and it was the portrait of the man who had spoken to her in the garden. She lifted her head and looked slowly about the library. The library could have borne witness that it was also the portrait of the man who had come in that day to call Boyne from his unfinished letter. Through the misty surgings of her brain she heard the faint boom of half-forgotten words—words spoken by Alida Stair on the lawn at

Pangbourne before Boyne and his wife had ever seen the house at Lyng, or had imagined that they might one day live there.

"This was the man who spoke to me," she repeated.

She looked again at Parvis. He was trying to conceal his disturbance under what he imagined to be an expression of indulgent commiseration; but the edges of his lips were blue. "He thinks me mad; but I'm not mad," she reflected; and suddenly there flashed upon her a way of justifying her strange affirmation.

She sat quiet, controlling the quiver of her lips, and waiting till she could trust her voice to keep its habitual level; then she said, looking straight at Parvis: "Will you answer me one question, please? When was it that Robert Elwell tried to kill himself?"

"When—when?" Parvis stammered.

"Yes; the date. Please try to remember."

She saw that he was growing still more afraid of her. "I have a reason," she insisted gently.

"Yes, yes. Only I can't remember. About two months before, I should say."

"I want the date," she repeated.

Parvis picked up the newspaper. "We might see here," he said, still humoring her. He ran his eyes down the page. "Here it is. Last October—the—"

She caught the words from him. "The 20th, wasn't it?" With a sharp look at her, he verified. "Yes, the 20th. Then you *did* know?"

"I know now." Her white stare continued to travel past him. "Sunday, the 20th—that was the day he came first."

Parvis's voice was almost inaudible. "Came *here* first?"

"Yes."

"You saw him twice, then?"

"Yes, twice." She breathed it at him with dilated eyes. "He came first on the 20th of October. I remember the date because it was the day we went up Meldon Steep for the first time." She felt a faint gasp of inward laughter at the thought that but for that she might have forgotten.

Parvis continued to scrutinize her, as if trying to intercept her gaze.

"We saw him from the roof," she went on. "He came down the lime-avenue toward the house. He was dressed just as he is in that picture. My husband saw him first. He was frightened, and ran down ahead of me; but there was no one there. He had vanished."

"Elwell had vanished?" Parvis faltered.

"Yes." Their two whispers seemed to grope for each other. "I couldn't think what had happened. I see now. He *tried* to come then; but he wasn't dead enough—he couldn't reach us. He had to wait for two months; and then he came back again—and Ned went with him."

She nodded at Parvis with the look of triumph of a child who has successfully worked out a difficult puzzle. But suddenly she lifted her hands with a desperate gesture, pressing them to her bursting temples.

"Oh, my God! I sent him to Ned—I told him where to go! I sent him to this room!" she screamed out.

She felt the walls of the room rush toward her, like inward falling ruins; and she heard Parvis, a long way off, as if through the ruins, crying to her, and struggling to get at her. But she was numb to his touch, she did not know what he was saying. Through the tumult she heard but one clear note, the voice of Alida Stair, speaking on the lawn at Pangbourne.

"You won't know till afterward," it said. "You won't know till long, long afterward."

THE LETTERS

I

Up the long hill from the station at St. Cloud, Lizzie West climbed in the cold spring sunshine. As she breasted the incline, she noticed the first waves of wistaria over courtyard railings and the high lights of new foliage against the walls of ivy-matted gardens; and she thought again, as she had thought a hundred times before, that she had never seen so beautiful a spring.

She was on her way to the Deerings' house, in a street near the hilltop; and every step was dear and familiar to her. She went there five times a week to teach little Juliet Deering, the daughter of Mr. Vincent Deering, the distinguished American artist. Juliet had been her pupil for two years, and day after day, during that time, Lizzie West had mounted the hill in all weathers; sometimes with her umbrella bent against a driving rain, sometimes with her frail cotton parasol unfurled beneath a fiery sun, sometimes with the snow soaking through her patched boots or a bitter wind piercing her thin jacket, sometimes with the dust whirling about her and bleaching the flowers of the poor little hat that *had* to "carry her through" till next summer.

At first the ascent had seemed tedious enough, as dull as the trudge to her other lessons. Lizzie was not a heaven sent teacher; she had no born zeal for her calling, and though she dealt kindly and dutifully with her pupils, she did not fly to them on winged feet. But one day something had happened to change the face of life, and since then the climb to the Deering house had seemed like a dream flight up a heavenly stairway.

Her heart beat faster as she remembered it—no longer in a tumult of fright and self-reproach, but softly, peacefully, as if brooding over a possession that none could take from her.

It was on a day of the previous October that she had stopped, after Juliet's lesson, to ask if she might speak to Juliet's papa. One had always to apply to Mr. Deering if there was anything to be said about the lessons. Mrs. Deering lay on her lounge upstairs, reading greasy relays of dogeared novels, the choice of which she left to the cook and the nurse, who were always fetching them for her from the *cabinet de lecture;* and it was understood in the house that she was not to be "bothered" about Juliet. Mr. Deering's interest in his daughter was fitful rather than consecutive; but at least he was approachable, and listened sympathetically, if a little absently, stroking his long, fair mustache, while Lizzie stated her difficulty or put in her plea for maps or copybooks.

"Yes, yes—of course—whatever you think right," he would always assent, sometimes drawing a five-franc piece from his pocket, and laying it carelessly on the table, or oftener saying, with his charming smile: "Get what you please, and just put it on your account, you know."

But this time Lizzie had not come to ask for maps or copybooks, or even to hint, in crimson misery—as once, poor soul! she had had to do—that Mr. Deering had overlooked her last little account had probably not noticed that she had left it, some two months earlier, on a corner of his littered writing table. That hour had been bad enough, though he had done his best to make it easy to carry it off gallantly and gaily; but this was infinitely worse. For she had come to complain of her pupil; to say that, much as she loved little Juliet, it was useless, unless Mr. Deering could "do something," to go on with the lessons.

"It wouldn't be honest—I should be robbing you; I'm not sure that I haven't already," she half laughed, through mounting tears, as she put her case. Little Juliet would not work, would not obey. Her poor, little, drifting existence floated aimlessly between the kitchen and the *lingerie*, and all the groping tendrils of her curiosity were fastened about the doings of the backstairs.

It was the same kind of curiosity that Mrs. Deering, overhead in her drug-scented room, lavished on her dogeared novels and on the "society notes" of the morning paper; but since Juliet's horizon was not yet wide enough to embrace these loftier objects, her interest was centered in the anecdotes that Celeste and Suzanne brought back from the market and the library. That these were not always of an edifying nature the child's artless prattle too often betrayed; but unhappily they occupied her fancy to the complete exclusion of such nourishing items as dates and dynasties, and the sources of the principal European rivers.

At length the crisis became so acute that poor Lizzie felt herself bound to resign her charge or ask Mr. Deering's intervention; and for Juliet's sake she chose the harder alternative. It *was* hard to speak to him not only because one hated still more to ascribe it to such vulgar causes, but because one blushed to bring them to the notice of a spirit engaged with higher things. Mr. Deering was very busy at that moment: he had a new picture "on." And Lizzie entered the studio with the flutter of one profanely intruding on some sacred rite; she almost heard the rustle of retreating wings as she approached.

And then—and then—how differently it had all turned out! Perhaps it wouldn't have, if she hadn't been such a goose—she who so seldom cried, so prided herself on a stoic control of her little twittering cageful of "feelings." But if she had cried, it was because he had looked at her so kindly, so softly, and because she had nevertheless felt him so pained and shamed by what she said. The pain, of course, lay for both in the implication behind her words—in the one word they left unspoken. If little Juliet was as she was, it was because of the mother upstairs—the mother who had given her child her futile impulses, and grudged her the care that might have guided them. The wretched case so obviously revolved in its own vicious circle that when Mr. Deering had murmured, "Of course if my wife were not an invalid," they both turned with a simultaneous spring to the flagrant "bad example" of Celeste and Suzanne, fastening on that with a mutual insistence that ended in his crying out, "All the more, then, how can you leave her to them?"

"But if I do her no good?" Lizzie wailed; and it was then that—when he took her hand and assured her gently, "But you

236

do, you do!"—it was then that, in the traditional phrase, she "broke down," and her conventional protest quivered off into tears.

"You do *me* good, at any rate—you make the house seem less like a desert," she heard him say; and the next moment she felt herself drawn to him, and they kissed each other through her weeping.

They kissed each other—there was the new fact. One does not, if one is a poor little teacher living in Mme. Clopin's Pension Suisse at Passy, and if one has pretty brown hair and eyes that reach out trustfully to other eyes—one does not, under these common but defenseless conditions, arrive at the age of twenty-five without being now and then kissed—waylaid once by a noisy student between two doors, surprised once by one's gray-bearded professor as one bent over the "theme" he was correcting—but these episodes, if they tarnish the surface, do not reach the heart: it is not the kiss endured, but the kiss returned, that lives. And Lizzie West's first kiss was for Vincent Deering.

As she drew back from it, something new awoke in her—something deeper than the fright and the shame, and the penitent thought of Mrs. Deering. A sleeping germ of life thrilled and unfolded, and started out blindly to seek the sun.

She might have felt differently, perhaps—the shame and penitence might have prevailed—had she not known him so kind and tender, and guessed him so baffled, poor, and disappointed. She knew the failure of his married life, and she divined a corresponding failure in his artistic career. Lizzie, who had made her own faltering snatch at the same laurels, brought her thwarted proficiency to bear on the question of his pictures, which she judged to be extremely brilliant, but suspected of having somehow failed to affirm their merit publicly. She understood that he had tasted an earlier moment of success: a mention, a medal, something official and tangible; then the tide of publicity had somehow set the other way, and left him stranded in a noble isolation. It was extraordinary and unbelievable that any one so naturally eminent and exceptional should have been subject to the same vulgar necessities that governed her own life, should have known poverty and obscurity and indifference. But she gathered that this had been the case, and felt that it formed the miraculous link between them. For through what medium less revealing than that of shared misfortune would he ever have perceived so inconspicuous an object as herself? And she recalled now how gently his eyes had rested on her from the first—the gray eyes that might have seemed mocking if they had not been so gentle.

She remembered how he had met her the first day, when Mrs. Deering's inevitable headache had prevented her from receiving the new teacher, and how his few questions had at once revealed his interest in the little stranded, compatriot, doomed to earn a precarious living so far from her native shore. Sweet as the moment of unburdening had been, she wondered afterward what had determined it: how she, so shy and sequestered, had found herself letting slip her whole poverty-stricken story, even to the avowal of the ineffectual "artistic" tendencies that had drawn her to Paris, and had then left her there to the dry task of tuition. She wondered at first, but she understood now; she understood everything after he had kissed her. It was simply because he was as kind as he was great.

She thought of this now as she mounted the hill in the spring sunshine, and she thought of all that had happened since. The intervening months, as she looked back at them, were merged in a vast golden haze, through which here and there rose the outline of a shining island. The haze was the general enveloping sense of his love, and the shining islands were the days they had spent together. They had never kissed again under his own roof. Lizzie's professional honor had a keen edge, but she had been spared the vulgar necessity of making him feel it. It was of the essence of her fatality that he always "understood" when his failing to do so might have imperiled his hold on her.

But her Thursdays and Sundays were free, and it soon became a habit to give them to him. She knew, for her peace of mind, only too much about pictures, and galleries and churches had been the one bright outlet from the grayness of her personal atmosphere. For poetry, too, and the other imaginative forms of literature, she had always felt more than she had hitherto had occasion to betray; and now all these folded sympathies shot out their tendrils to the light. Mr. Deering knew how to express with unmatched clearness and competence the thoughts that trembled in her mind: to talk with him was to soar up into the azure on the outspread wings of his intelligence, and look down dizzily yet distinctly, on all the wonders and glories of the world. She was a little ashamed, sometimes, to find how few definite impressions she brought back from these flights; but that was doubtless because her heart beat so fast when he was near, and his smile made his words like a long quiver of light. Afterward, in quieter hours, fragments of their talk emerged in her memory with wondrous precision, every syllable as minutely chiseled as some of the delicate objects in crystal or ivory that he pointed out in the museums they frequented. It was always a puzzle to Lizzie that some of their hours should be so blurred and others so vivid.

On the morning in question she was reliving all these memories with unusual distinctness, for it was a fortnight since she had seen her friend. Mrs. Deering, some six weeks previously, had gone to visit a relation at St. Raphael; and, after she had been a month absent, her husband and the little girl had joined her. Lizzie's adieux to Deering had been made on a rainy afternoon in the damp corridors of the Aquarium at the Trocadero. She could not receive him at her own *pension*. That a teacher should be visited by the father of a pupil, especially when that father was still, as Madame Clopin said, *si bien*, was against that lady's austere Helvetian code. From Deering's first tentative hint of another solution Lizzie had recoiled in a wild unreasoned flurry of all her scruples, he took her "No, no, *no!*" as he took all her twists and turns of conscience, with eyes half-tender and half-mocking, and an instant acquiescence which was the finest homage to the "lady" she felt he divined and honored in her.

239

So they continued to meet in museums and galleries, or to extend, on fine days, their explorations to the suburbs, where now and then, in the solitude of grove or garden, the kiss renewed itself, fleeting, isolated, or prolonged in a shy, silent pressure of the hand. But on the day of his leave-taking the rain kept them under cover; and as they threaded the subterranean windings of the Aquarium, and Lizzie looked unseeingly at the monstrous faces glaring at her through walls of glass, she felt like a poor drowned wretch at the bottom of the sea, with all her glancing, sunlit memories rolling over her like the waves of its surface.

"You'll never see him again—never see him again," the waves boomed in her ears through his last words; and when she had said goodbye to him at the corner, and had scrambled, wet and shivering, into the Passy omnibus, its great, grinding wheels took up the derisive burden—"Never see him, never see him again."

All that was only two weeks ago, and here she was, as happy as a lark, mounting the hill to his door in the spring sunshine. So weak a heart did not deserve such a radiant fate; and Lizzie said to herself that she would never again distrust her star.

II

The cracked bell tinkled sweetly through her heart as she stood listening for the scamper of Juliet's feet. Juliet, anticipating the laggard Suzanne, almost always opened the door for her governess, not from any unnatural zeal to hasten the hour of her studies, but from the irrepressible desire to see what was going on in the street. But on this occasion Lizzie listened vainly for a step, and at length gave the bell another twitch. Doubtless some unusually absorbing incident had detained the child below-stairs; thus only could her absence be explained.

A third ring produced no response, and Lizzie, full of dawning fears, drew back to look up at the shabby, blistered house. She saw that the studio shutters stood wide, and then noticed, without surprise, that Mrs. Deering's were still unopened. No doubt Mrs. Deering was resting after the fatigue of the journey. Instinctively Lizzie's eyes turned again to the studio; and as she looked, she saw Deering at the window. He caught sight of her, and an instant later came to the door. He looked paler than usual, and she noticed that he wore a black coat.

"I rang and rang—where is Juliet?"

He looked at her gravely, almost solemnly; then, without answering, he led her down the passage to the studio, and closed the door when she had entered.

"My wife is dead—she died suddenly ten days ago. Didn't you see it in the papers?"

Lizzie, with a little cry, sank down on the rickety divan. She seldom saw a newspaper, since she could not afford one for her own perusal, and those supplied to the Pension Clopin were usually in the hands of its more privileged lodgers till long after the hour when she set out on her morning round.

"No; I didn't see it," she stammered.

Deering was silent. He stood a little way off, twisting an unlit cigarette in his hand, and looking down at her with a gaze that was both hesitating and constrained.

She, too, felt the constraint of the situation, the impossibility of finding words that, after what had passed between them, should seem neither false nor heartless; and at last she exclaimed, standing up: "Poor little Juliet! Can't I go to her?"

"Juliet is not here. I left her at St. Raphael with the relations with whom my wife was staying."

"Oh," Lizzie murmured, feeling vaguely that this added to the difficulty of the moment. How differently she had pictured their meeting!

"I'm so—so sorry for her!" she faltered out.

Deering made no reply, but, turning on his heel, walked the length of the studio, and then halted vaguely before the picture on the easel. It was the landscape he had begun the previous autumn, with the intention of sending it to the Salon that spring. But it was still unfinished—seemed, indeed, hardly more advanced than on the fateful October day when Lizzie, standing before it for the first time, had confessed her inability to deal with Juliet. Perhaps the same thought struck its creator, for he broke into a dry laugh, and turned from the easel with a shrug.

Under his protracted silence Lizzie roused herself to the fact that, since her pupil was absent, there was no reason for her remaining any longer; and as Deering again moved toward her she said with an effort: "I'll go, then. You'll send for me when she comes back?"

Deering still hesitated, tormenting the cigarette between his fingers.

"She's not coming back—not at present."

Lizzie heard him with a drop of the heart. Was everything to be changed in their lives? But of course; how could she have dreamed it would be otherwise? She could only stupidly repeat: "Not coming back? Not this spring?"

"Probably not, since are friends are so good as to keep her. The fact is, I've got to go to America. My wife left a little property, a few pennies, that I must go and see to—for the child."

Lizzie stood before him, a cold knife in her breast. "I see—I see," she reiterated, feeling all the while that she strained her eyes into impenetrable blackness.

"It's a nuisance, having to pull up stakes," he went on, with a fretful glance about the studio.

She lifted her eyes slowly to his face. "Shall you be gone long?" she took courage to ask.

"There again—I can't tell. It's all so frightfully mixed up." He met her look for an incredibly long, strange moment. "I hate to go!" he murmured as if to himself.

Lizzie felt a rush of moisture to her lashes, and the old, familiar wave of weakness at her heart. She raised her hand to her face with an instinctive gesture, and as she did so he held out his arms.

"Come here, Lizzie!" he said.

And she went--went with a sweet, wild throb of liberation, with the sense that at last the house was his, that *she* was his, if he wanted her; that never again would that silent, rebuking presence in the room above constrain and shame her rapture.

He pushed back her veil and covered her face with kisses. "Don't cry, you little goose!" he said.

III

That they must see each other again before his departure, in someplace less exposed than their usual haunts, was as clear to Lizzie as it appeared to be to Deering. His expressing the wish seemed, indeed, the sweetest testimony to the quality of his feeling, since, in the first weeks of the most perfunctory widowhood, a man of his stamp is presumed to abstain from light adventures. If, then, at such a moment, he wished so much to be quietly and gravely with her, it could be only for reasons she did not call by name, but of which she felt the sacred tremor in her heart; and it would have seemed incredibly vain and vulgar to put forward, at such a crisis, the conventional objections by means of which such little-exposed existences defend the treasure of their freshness.

In such a mood as this one may descend from the Passy omnibus at the corner of the Pont de la Concorde (she had not let him fetch her in a cab) with a sense of dedication almost solemn, and may advance to meet one's fate, in the shape of a gentleman of melancholy elegance, with an auto-taxi at his call, as one has advanced to the altar steps in some girlish bridal vision.

Even the experienced waiter ushering them into an upper room of the quiet restaurant on the Seine could hardly have supposed their quest for seclusion to be based on sentimental motives, so soberly did Deering give his orders, while his companion sat small and grave at his side. She did not, indeed, mean to let her private pang obscure their hour together: she was already learning that Deering shrank from sadness. He should see that she had courage and gaiety to face their coming separation, and yet give herself meanwhile to this completer nearness; but she waited, as always, for him to strike the opening note.

Looking back at it later, she wondered at the mild suavity of the hour. Her heart was unversed in happiness, but he had found the tone to lull her apprehensions, and make her trust her fate for any golden wonder. Deepest of all, he gave her the sense of something tacit and confirmed between them, as if his tenderness were a habit of the heart hardly needing the support of outward proof.

Such proof as he offered came, therefore, as a kind of crowning luxury, the flower of a profoundly rooted sentiment; and here again the instinctive reserves and defenses would have seemed to vulgarize what his trust ennobled. But if all the tender casuistries of her heart were at his service, he took no grave advantage of them. Even when they sat alone after dinner, with the lights of the river trembling through their one low window, and the vast rumor of Paris inclosing them in a heart of silence, he seemed, as much as herself, under the spell of hallowing influences. She felt it most of all as she yielded to the arm he presently put about her, to the long caress he laid on her lips and eyes: not a word or gesture missed the note of quiet union, or cast a doubt, in retrospect, on the pact they sealed with their last look.

That pact, as she reviewed it through a sleepless night, seemed to have consisted mainly, on his part, in pleadings for full and frequent news of her, on hers in the assurance that it should be given as often as he asked it. She had felt an intense desire not to betray any undue eagerness, any crude desire to affirm and define her hold on him. Her life had given her a certain acquaintance with the arts of defense: girls in her situation were commonly supposed to know them all, and to use them as occasion called. But Lizzie's very need of them had intensified her disdain. Just because she was so poor, and had always, materially, so to count her change and calculate her margin, she would at least know the joy of emotional prodigality, would give her heart as recklessly as the rich their millions. She was sure now that Deering loved her, and if he had seized the occasion of their farewell to give her some definitely worded sign of his feeling—if, more plainly, he had asked her to marry him—his doing so would have seemed less like a proof of his sincerity than of his suspecting in her the need of a verbal warrant. That he had abstained seemed to show that he trusted her as she trusted him, and that they were one most of all in this deep security of understanding.

She had tried to make him divine all this in the chariness of her promise to write. She would write; of course she would. But he would be busy, preoccupied, on the move: it was for him to let her know when he wished a word, to spare her the embarrassment of ill-timed intrusions.

"Intrusions?" He had smiled the word away. "You can't well intrude, my darling, on a heart where you're already established, to the complete exclusion of other lodgers." And then, taking her hands, and looking up from them into her happy, dizzy eyes: "You don't know much about being in love, do you, Lizzie?" he laughingly ended.

It seemed easy enough to reject this imputation in a kiss; but she wondered afterward if she had not deserved it. Was she really cold and conventional, and did other women give more richly and recklessly? She found that it was possible to turn about every one of her reserves and delicacies so that they looked like selfish scruples and petty pruderies, and at this game she came in time to exhaust all the resources of an overabundant casuistry.

Meanwhile the first days after Deering's departure wore a soft, refracted light like the radiance lingering after sunset. *He*, at any rate, was taxable with no reserves, no calculations, and his letters of farewell, from train and steamer, filled her with long murmurs and echoes of his presence. How he loved her, how he loved her—and how he knew how to tell her so!

She was not sure of possessing the same aptitude. Unused to the expression of personal emotion, she fluctuated between the impulse to pour out all she felt and the fear lest her extravagance should amuse or even bore him. She never lost the sense that what was to her the central crisis of experience must be a mere episode in a life so predestined as his to romantic accidents. All that she felt and said would be subjected to the test of comparison with what others had already given him: from all quarters of the globe she saw passionate missives winging their way toward Deering, for whom her poor little swallow flight of devotion could certainly not make a summer. But such moments were succeeded by others in which she raised her head and dared inwardly to affirm her conviction that no woman had ever loved him just as she had, and that none, therefore, had probably found just such things to say to him. And this conviction strengthened the other less solidly based belief that *he* also, for the same reason, had found new accents to express his tenderness, and that the three letters she wore all day in her shabby blouse, and hid all night beneath her pillow, surpassed not only in beauty, but in quality, all he had ever penned for other eyes.

They gave her, at any rate, during the weeks that she wore them on her heart, sensations even more complex and delicate than Deering's actual presence had ever occasioned. To be with him was always like breasting a bright, rough sea, that blinded while it buoyed her: but his letters formed a still pool of contemplation, above which she could bend, and see the reflection of the sky, and the myriad movements of life that flitted and gleamed below the surface. The wealth of his hidden life—that was what most surprised her! It was incredible to her now that she had had no inkling of it, but had kept on blindly along the narrow track of habit, like a traveler climbing a road in a fog, who suddenly finds himself on a sunlit crag between blue leagues of sky and dizzy depths of valley. And the odd thing was that all the people about her—the whole world of the Passy pension—were still plodding along the same dull path, preoccupied with the pebbles underfoot, and unconscious of the glory beyond the fog!

There were wild hours when she longed to cry out to them what one saw from the summit—and hours of tremulous abasement when she asked herself why *her* happy feet had been guided there, while others, no doubt as worthy, stumbled and blundered in obscurity. She felt, in particular, a sudden urgent pity for the two or three other girls at Mme. Clopin's—girls older, duller, less alive than she, and by that very token more appealingly flung upon her sympathy. Would they ever know? Had they ever known?—those were the questions that haunted her as she crossed her companions on the stairs, faced them at the dinner table, and listened to their poor, pining talk in the dim-lit, slippery-seated *salon*. One of the girls was Swiss, the other English; the third, Andora Macy, was a young lady from the Southern States who was studying French with the ultimate object of imparting it to the inmates of a girls' school at Macon, Georgia.

Andora Macy was pale, faded, immature. She had a drooping Southern accent, and a manner that fluctuated between arch audacity and fits of panicky hauteur. She yearned to be admired, and feared to be insulted; and yet seemed tragically conscious that she was destined to miss both these extremes of sensation, or to enjoy them only at second hand in the experiences of her more privileged friends.

It was perhaps for this reason that she took a wistful interest in Lizzie, who had shrunk from her at first, as the depressing image of her own probable future, but to whom she had now suddenly become an object of sentimental pity.

IV

Miss Macy's room was next to Miss West's, and the Southerner's knock often appealed to Lizzie's hospitality when Mme. Clopin's early curfew had driven her boarders from the *salon*. It sounded thus one evening just as Lizzie, tired from an unusually long day of tuition, was in the act of removing her dress. She was in too indulgent a mood to withhold her "Come in," and as Miss Macy crossed the threshold, Lizzie felt that Vincent Deering's first letter—the letter from the train—had slipped from her loosened bodice to the floor.

Miss Macy, as promptly noting the fact, darted forward to recover the letter. Lizzie stooped also, fiercely jealous of her touch; but the other reached the precious paper first, and as she seized it, Lizzie knew that she had seen whence it fell, and was weaving round the incident a rapid web of romance.

Lizzie blushed with annoyance. "It's too stupid, having no pockets! If one gets a letter as she is going out in the morning, she has to carry it in her blouse all day."

Miss Macy looked at her with swimming eyes. "It's warm from your heart!" she breathed, reluctantly yielding up the missive.

Lizzie laughed, for she knew better: she knew it was the letter that had warmed her heart. Poor Andora Macy! *She* would never know. Her bleak bosom would never take fire from such a contact. Lizzie looked at her with kind eyes, secretly chafing at the injustice of fate.

The next evening, on her return home, she found Andora hovering in the entrance hall.

"I thought you'd like me to put this in your own hand," Miss Macy whispered significantly, pressing a letter upon Lizzie. "I couldn't *bear* to see it lying on the table with the others."

It was Deering's letter from the steamer. Lizzie blushed to the forehead, but without resenting Andora's divination. She could not have breathed a word of her bliss, but she was not altogether sorry to have it guessed, and pity for Andora's destitution yielded to the pleasure of using it as a mirror for her own abundance. DEERING wrote again on reaching New York, a long, fond, dissatisfied letter, vague in its indication of his own projects, specific in the expression of his love. Lizzie brooded over every syllable of it till they formed the undercurrent of all her waking thoughts, and murmured through her midnight dreams; but she would have been happier if they had shed some definite light on the future.

That would come, no doubt, when he had had time to look about and get his bearings. She counted up the days that must elapse before she received his next letter, and stole down early to peep at the papers, and learn when the next American mail

248

was due. At length the happy date arrived, and she hurried distractedly through the day's work, trying to conceal her impatience by the endearments she bestowed upon her pupils. It was easier, in her present mood, to kiss them than to keep them at their grammars.

That evening, on Mme. Clopin's threshold, her heart beat so wildly that she had to lean a moment against the doorpost before entering. But on the hall table, where the letters lay, there was none for her.

She went over them with a feverish hand, her heart dropping down and down, as she had sometimes fallen down an endless stairway in a dream—the very same stairway up which she had seemed to fly when she climbed the long hill to Deering's door. Then it suddenly struck her that Andora might have found and secreted her letter, and with a spring she was on the actual stairs and rattling Miss Macy's door handle.

"You've a letter for me, haven't you?" she panted.

Miss Macy, turning from the toilet table, inclosed her in attenuated arms. "Oh, darling, did you expect one today?"

"Do give it to me!" Lizzie pleaded with burning eyes.

"But I haven't any! There hasn't been a sign of a letter for you."

"I know there is. There *must* be," Lizzie persisted, stamping her foot.

"But, dearest, I've *watched* for you, and there's been nothing, absolutely nothing."

Day after day, for the ensuing weeks, the same scene reenacted itself with endless variations. Lizzie, after the first sharp spasm of disappointment, made no effort to conceal her anxiety from Miss Macy, and the fond Andora was charged to keep a vigilant eye upon the postman's coming, and to spy on the *bonne* for possible negligence or perfidy. But these elaborate precautions remained fruitless, and no letter from Deering came.

During the first fortnight of silence Lizzie exhausted all the ingenuities of explanation. She marveled afterward at the reasons she had found for Deering's silence: there were moments when she almost argued herself into thinking it more natural than his continuing to write. There was only one reason that her intelligence consistently rejected, and that was the possibility that he had forgotten her, that the whole episode had faded from his mind like a breath from a mirror. From that she resolutely turned her thoughts, aware that if she suffered herself to contemplate it, the motive power of life would fail, and she would no longer understand why she rose up in the morning and laydown at night.

If she had had leisure to indulge her anguish she might have been unable to keep such speculations at bay. But she had to be up and working: the *blanchisseuse* had to be paid, and Mme. Clopin's weekly bill, and all the little "extras" that even her frugal habits had to reckon with. And in the depths of her thought dwelt the dogging fear of illness and incapacity, goading her to work while she could. She hardly remembered the time when she had been without that fear; it was second nature now, and it kept her on her feet when other incentives might have failed. In the blankness of her misery she felt no dread of death; but the horror of being ill and "dependent" was in her blood.

In the first weeks of silence she wrote again and again to Deering, entreating him for a word, for a mere sign of life. From the first she had shrunk from seeming to assert any claim on his future, yet in her aching bewilderment she now charged herself with having been too possessive, too exacting in her tone. She told herself that his fastidiousness shrank from any but a "light touch," and that hers had not been light enough. She should have kept to the character of the "little friend," the artless consciousness in which tormented genius may find an escape from its complexities; and instead, she had dramatized their relation, exaggerated her own part in it, presumed, forsooth, to share the front of the stage with him, instead of being content to serve as scenery or chorus.

But though to herself she admitted, and even insisted on, the episodical nature of the experience, on the fact that for Deering it could be no more than an incident, she was still convinced that his sentiment for her, however fugitive, had been genuine.

His had not been the attitude of the unscrupulous male seeking a vulgar "advantage." For a moment he had really needed her, and if he was silent now, it was perhaps because he feared that she had mistaken the nature of the need and built vain hopes on its possible duration.

It was of the very essence of Lizzie's devotion that it sought instinctively the larger freedom of its object; she could not conceive of love under any form of exaction or compulsion. To make this clear to Deering became an overwhelming need, and in a last short letter she explicitly freed him from whatever sentimental obligation its predecessors might have seemed to impose. In this studied communication she playfully accused herself of having unwittingly sentimentalized their relation, affirming, in self-defense, a retrospective astuteness, a sense of the impermanence of the tenderer sentiments that almost put Deering in the fatuous position of having mistaken coquetry for surrender. And she ended gracefully with a plea for the continuance of the friendly regard which she had "always understood" to be the basis of their sympathy. The document, when completed, seemed to her worthy of what she conceived to be Deering's conception of a woman of the world, and she found a spectral satisfaction in the thought of making her final appearance before him in that distinguished character. But she was never destined to learn what effect the appearance produced; for the letter, like those it sought to excuse, remained unanswered.

V

The fresh spring sunshine that had so often attended Lizzie Weston her dusty climb up the hill of St. Cloud beamed on her, some two years later, in a scene and a situation of altered import.

The horse chestnuts of the Champs-Élysées filtered its rays through the symmetrical umbrage inclosing the graveled space about Daurent's restaurant, and Miss West, seated at a table within that privileged circle, presented to the light a hat much better able to sustain its scrutiny than those which had sheltered the brow of Juliet Deering's instructress.

Her dress was in keeping with the hat, and both belonged to a situation rich in such possibilities as the act of a leisurely luncheon at Daurent's in the opening week of the Salon. Her companions, of both sexes, confirmed and emphasized this impression by an elaborateness of garb and an ease of attitude implying the largest range of selection between the forms of Parisian idleness; and even Andora Macy, seated opposite, as in the place of co-hostess or companion, reflected, in coy grays and mauves, the festal note of the occasion.

This note reverberated persistently in the ears of a solitary gentleman straining for glimpses of the group from a table wedged in the remotest corner of the garden; but to Miss West herself the occurrence did not rise above the usual. For nearly a year she had been acquiring the habit of such situations, and the act of offering a luncheon at Daurent's to her cousins, the Harvey Mearses of Providence, and their friend Mr. Jackson Benn, produced in her no emotion beyond the languid glow which Mr. Benn's presence was beginning to impart to such scenes.

"It's frightful, the way you've got used to it," Andora Macy had wailed in the first days of her friend's transfigured fortune, when Lizzie West had waked one morning to find herself among the heirs of an old and miserly cousin whose testamentary dispositions had formed, since her earliest childhood, the subject of pleasantry and conjecture in her own improvident family. Old Hezron Mears had never given any sign of life to the luckless Wests; had perhaps hardly been conscious of including them in the carefully drawn will which, following the old American convention, scrupulously divided his hoarded millions among his kin. It was by a mere genealogical accident that Lizzie, falling just within the golden circle, found herself possessed of a pittance sufficient to release her from the prospect of a long gray future in Mme. Clopin's pension.

The release had seemed wonderful at first; yet she presently found that it had destroyed her former world without giving her anew one. On the ruins of the old pension life bloomed the only flower that had ever sweetened her path; and beyond the sense of present ease, and the removal of anxiety for the future, her reconstructed existence blossomed with no compensating joys. She had hoped great things from the opportunity to rest, to travel, to look about her, above all, in various artful feminine ways, to be "nice" to the companions of her less privileged state; but such widenings of scope left her, as it were, but the more conscious of the empty margin of personal life beyond them. It was not till she woke to the leisure of her new days that she had the full sense of what was gone from them.

Their very emptiness made her strain to pack them with transient sensations: she was like the possessor of an unfurnished house, with random furniture and bric-a-brac perpetually pouring in "on approval." It was in this experimental character that Mr. Jackson Benn had fixed her attention, and the languid effort of her imagination to adjust him to her requirements was seconded by the fond complicity of Andora and the smiling approval of her cousins. Lizzie did not discourage these demonstrations: she suffered serenely Andora's allusions to Mr. Benn's infatuation, and Mrs. Mears's casual boast of his business standing. All the better if they could drape his narrow square-shouldered frame and round unwinking countenance in the trailing mists of sentiment: Lizzie looked and listened, not unhopeful of the miracle.

"I never saw anything like the way these Frenchmen stare! Doesn't it make you nervous, Lizzie?" Mrs. Mears broke out suddenly, ruffling her feather boa about an outraged bosom. Mrs. Mears was still in that stage of development when her countrywomen taste to the full the peril of being exposed to the gaze of the licentious Gaul.

Lizzie roused herself from the contemplation of Mr. Benn's round baby cheeks and the square blue jaw resting on his perpendicular collar. "Is some one staring at me?" she asked with a smile.

"Don't turn round, whatever you do! There—just over there, between the rhododendrons—the tall fair man alone at that table. Really, Harvey, I think you ought to speak to the head waiter, or something; though I suppose in one of these places they'd only laugh at you," Mrs. Mears shudderingly concluded.

Her husband, as if inclining to this probability, continued the undisturbed dissection of his chicken wing; but Mr. Benn, perhaps aware that his situation demanded a more punctilious attitude, sternly revolved upon the parapet of his high collar in the direction of Mrs. Mears's glance.

"What, that fellow all alone over there? Why, *he's* not French; he's an American," he then proclaimed with a perceptible relaxing of the facial muscles.

"Oh!" murmured Mrs. Mears, as perceptibly disappointed, and Mr. Benn continued carelessly: "He came over on the steamer with me. He's some kind of an artist—a fellow named Deering. He was staring at *me*, I guess: wondering whether I was going to remember him. Why, how d' 'e do? How are you? Why, yes, of course; with pleasure—my friends, Mrs. Harvey Mears—Mr. Mears; my friends Miss Macy and Miss West."

"I have the pleasure of knowing Miss West," said Vincent Deering with a smile.

VI

Even through his smile Lizzie had seen, in the first moment, how changed he was; and the impression of the change deepened to the point of pain when, a few days later, in reply to his brief note, she accorded him a private hour.

That the first sight of his writing—the first answer to his letters—should have come, after three long years, in the shape of this impersonal line, too curt to be called humble, yet confessing to a consciousness of the past by the studied avoidance of its language! As she read, her mind flashed back over what she had dreamed his letters would be, over the exquisite answers she had composed above his name.

254

There was nothing exquisite in the conventional lines before her; but dormant nerves began to throb again at the mere touch of the paper he had touched, and she threw the little note into the fire before she dared to reply to it.

Now that he was actually before her again, he became, as usual, the one live spot in her consciousness. Once more her tormented throbbing self sank back passive and numb, but now with all its power of suffering mysteriously transferred to the presence, so known, yet so unknown, at the opposite corner of her hearth. She was still Lizzie West, and he was still Vincent Deering; but the Styx rolled between them, and she saw his face through its fog. It was his face, really, rather than his words, that told her, as she furtively studied it, the tale of failure and slow discouragement that had so blurred its handsome lines. She kept afterward no precise memory of the actual details of his narrative: the pain it evidently cost him to impart it was so much the sharpest fact in her new vision of him. Confusedly, however, she gathered that on reaching America he had found his wife's small property gravely impaired; and that, while lingering on to secure what remained of it, he had contrived to sell a picture or two, and had even known a brief moment of success, during which he received orders and set up a studio. But inexplicably the tide had ebbed, his work remained on his hands, and a tedious illness, with its miserable sequel of debt, soon wiped out his small advantage. There followed a period of eclipse, still more vaguely pictured, during which she was allowed to infer that he had tried his hand at divers means of livelihood, accepting employment from a fashionable house decorator, designing wallpapers, illustrating magazine articles, and acting for a time, she dimly understood, as the social tout of a new hotel desirous of advertising its restaurant. These disjointed facts were strung on a slender thread of personal allusions—references to friends who had been kind (jealously, she guessed them to be women), and to enemies who had darkly schemed against him. But, true to his tradition of "correctness," he carefully avoided the mention of names, and left her trembling

255

conjectures to grope dimly through an alien crowded world in which there seemed little room for her small shy presence.

As she listened, her private pang was merged in the intolerable sense of his unhappiness. Nothing he had said explained or excused his conduct to her; but he had suffered, he had been lonely, had been humiliated, and she suddenly felt, with a fierce maternal rage, that there was no conceivable justification for any scheme of things in which such facts were possible. She could not have said why: she simply knew that it hurt too much to see him hurt.

Gradually it came to her that her unconsciousness of any personal grievance was due to her having so definitely determined her own future. She was glad she had decided, as she now felt she had, to marry Jackson Benn, if only for the sense of detachment it gave her in dealing with the case of Vincent Deering. Her personal safety insured her the requisite impartiality, and justified her in dwelling as long as she chose on the last lines of a chapter to which her own act had deliberately fixed the close. Any lingering hesitations as to the finality of her decision were dispelled by the imminent need of making it known to Deering; and when her visitor paused in his reminiscences to say, with a sigh, "But many things have happened to you too," his words did not so much evoke the sense of her altered fortunes as the image of the protector to whom she was about to intrust them.

"Yes, many things; it's three years," she answered.

Deering sat leaning forward, in his sad exiled elegance, his eyes gently bent on hers; and at his side she saw the solid form of Mr. Jackson Benn, with shoulders preternaturally squared by the cut of his tight black coat, and a tall shiny collar sustaining his baby cheeks and hard blue chin. Then the vision faded as Deering began to speak.

"Three years," he repeated, musingly taking up her words. "I've so often wondered what they'd brought you."

She lifted her head with a quick blush, and the terrified wish that he should not, at the cost of all his notions of correctness, lapse into the blunder of becoming "personal."

256

"You've wondered?" She smiled back bravely.

"Do you suppose I haven't?" His look dwelt on her. "Yes, I daresay that *was* what you thought of me."

She had her answer pat—"Why, frankly, you know, I *didn't* think of you." But the mounting tide of her poor dishonored memories swept it indignantly away. If it was his correctness to ignore, it could never be hers to disavow.

" *Was* that what you thought of me?" she heard him repeat in a tone of sad insistence; and at that, with a quick lift of her head, she resolutely answered: "How could I know what to think? I had no word from you."

If she had expected, and perhaps almost hoped, that this answer would create a difficulty for him, the gaze of quiet fortitude with which he met it proved that she had underestimated his resources.

"No, you had no word. I kept my vow," he said.

"Your vow?"

"That you *shouldn't* have a word—not a syllable. Oh, I kept it through everything!"

Lizzie's heart was sounding in her ears the old confused rumor of the sea of life, but through it she desperately tried to distinguish the still small voice of reason.

"What *was* your vow? Why shouldn't I have had a syllable from you?"

He sat motionless, still holding her with a look so gentle that it almost seemed forgiving.

Then abruptly he rose, and crossing the space between them, sat down in a chair at her side. The deliberation of his movement might have implied a forgetfulness of changed conditions, and Lizzie, as if thus viewing it, drew slightly back; but he appeared not to notice her recoil, and his eyes, at last leaving her face, slowly and approvingly made the round of the small bright drawing room. "This is charming. Yes, things *have* changed for you," he said.

A moment before she had prayed that he might be spared the error of a vain return upon the past. It was as if all her retrospective tenderness, dreading to see him at such a disadvantage, rose up to protect him from it. But his evasiveness exasperated her, and suddenly she felt the inconsistent desire to hold him fast, face to face with his own words.

Before she could reiterate her question, however, he had met her with another.

"You *did* think of me, then? Why are you afraid to tell me that you did?"

The unexpectedness of the challenge wrung an indignant cry from her.

"Didn't my letters tell you so enough?"

"Ah, your letters!" Keeping her gaze on his in a passion of unrelenting fixity, she could detect in him no confusion, not the least quiver of a sensitive nerve. He only gazed back at her more sadly.

"They went everywhere with me—your letters," he said.

"Yet you never answered them." At last the accusation trembled to her lips.

"Yet I never answered them."

"Did you ever so much as read them, I wonder?"

All the demons of self-torture were up in her now, and she loosed them on him, as if to escape from their rage.

Deering hardly seemed to hear her question. He merely shifted his attitude, leaning a little nearer to her, but without attempting, by the least gesture, to remind her of the privileges which such nearness had once implied.

"There were beautiful, wonderful things in them," he said, smiling.

She felt herself stiffen under his smile.

"You've waited three years to tell me so!"

He looked at her with grave surprise. "And do you resent my telling you even now?"

His parries were incredible. They left her with a breathless sense of thrusting at emptiness, and a desperate, almost vindictive desire to drive him against the wall and pin him there.

"No. Only I wonder you should take the trouble to tell me, when at the time—"

258

And now, with a sudden turn, he gave her the final surprise of meeting her squarely on her own ground.

"When at the time I didn't? But how *could* I—at the time?"

"Why couldn't you? You've not yet told me?"

He gave her again his look of disarming patience. "Do I need to? Hasn't my whole wretched story told you?"

"Told me why you never answered my letters?"

"Yes, since I could only answer them in one way—by protesting my love and my longing."

There was a long pause of resigned expectancy on his part, on hers, of a wild confused reconstruction of her shattered past. "You mean, then, that you didn't write because—"

"Because I found, when I reached America, that I was a pauper; that my wife's money was gone, and that what I could earn—I've so little gift that way!—was barely enough to keep Juliet clothed and educated. It was as if an iron door had been suddenly locked and barred between us."

Lizzie felt herself driven back, panting upon the last defenses of her incredulity. "You might at least have told me—have explained. Do you think I shouldn't have understood?"

He did not hesitate. "You would have understood. It wasn't that."

"What was it then?" she quavered.

"It's wonderful you shouldn't see! Simply that I couldn't write you *that*. Anything else—not *that!*"

"And so you preferred to let me suffer?"

There was a shade of reproach in his eyes. "I suffered too," he said.

It was his first direct appeal to her compassion, and for a moment it nearly unsettled the delicate poise of her sympathies, and sent them trembling in the direction of scorn and irony. But even as the impulse rose, it was stayed by another sensation. Once again, as so often in the past, she became aware of a fact which, in his absence, she always failed to reckon with—the fact of the deep irreducible difference between his image in her mind and his actual self, the mysterious alteration in her judgment produced by the inflections of his voice, the look of his eyes, the whole complex pressure of his personality. She had phrased it once self-reproachfully by saying to herself that she "never could remember him," so completely did the sight of him supersede the counterfeit about which her fancy wove its perpetual wonders. Bright and breathing as that counterfeit was, it became a gray figment of the mind at the touch of his presence; and on this occasion the immediate result was to cause her to feel his possible unhappiness with an intensity beside which her private injury paled.

"I suffered horribly," he repeated, "and all the more that I couldn't make a sign, couldn't cry out my misery. There was only one escape from it all—to hold my tongue, and pray that you might hate me."

The blood rushed to Lizzie's forehead. "Hate you—you prayed that I might hate you?"

He rose from his seat, and moving closer, lifted her hand gently in his. "Yes; because your letters showed me that, if you didn't, you'd be unhappier still."

Her hand lay motionless, with the warmth of his flowing through it, and her thoughts, too—her poor fluttering stormy thoughts—felt themselves suddenly penetrated by the same soft current of communion.

"And I meant to keep my resolve," he went on, slowly releasing his clasp. "I meant to keep it even after the random stream of things swept me back here in your way; but when I saw you the other day, I felt that what had been possible at a distance was impossible now that we were near each other. How was it possible to see you and want you to hate me?"

He had moved away, but not to resume his seat. He merely paused at a little distance, his hand resting on a chair back, in the transient attitude that precedes departure.

Lizzie's heart contracted. He was going, then, and this was his farewell. He was going, and she could find no word to detain him but the senseless stammer "I never hated you."

He considered her with his faint grave smile. "It's not necessary, at any rate, that you should do so now. Time and circumstances have made me so harmless—that's exactly why I've dared to venture back. And I wanted to tell you how I rejoice in your good fortune. It's the only obstacle between us that I can't bring myself to wish away."

Lizzie sat silent, spellbound, as she listened, by the sudden evocation of Mr. Jackson Benn. He stood there again, between herself and Deering, perpendicular and reproachful, but less solid and sharply outlined than before, with a look in his small hard eyes that desperately wailed for reembodiment.

Deering was continuing his farewell speech. "You're rich now, you're free. You will marry." She vaguely saw him holding out his hand.

"It's not true that I'm engaged!" she broke out. They were the last words she had meant to utter; they were hardly related to her conscious thoughts; but she felt her whole will suddenly gathered up in the irrepressible impulse to repudiate and fling away from her forever the spectral claim of Mr. Jackson Benn.

VII

It was the firm conviction of Andora Macy that every object in the Vincent Deerings' charming little house at Neuilly had been expressly designed for the Deerings' son to play with.

The house was full of pretty things, some not obviously applicable to the purpose; but Miss Macy's casuistry was equal tothe baby's appetite, and the baby's mother was no match for them in the art of defending her possessions. There were moments, in fact, when Lizzie almost fell in with Andora's summary division of her works of art into articles safe or unsafe for the baby to lick, or resisted it only to the extent of occasionally substituting some less precious or less perishable object for the particular fragility on which her son's desire was fixed. And it was with this intention that, on a certain fair spring morning—which wore the added luster of being the baby's second birthday—she had murmured, with her mouth in his curls, and one hand holding a bit of Chelsea above his dangerous clutch: "Wouldn't he rather have that beautiful shiny thing over there in Aunt Andorra's hand?"

The two friends were together in Lizzie's little morning room—the room she had chosen, on acquiring the house, because, when she sat there, she could hear Deering's step as he paced up and down before his easel in the studio she had built for him. His step had been less regularly audible than she had hoped, for, after three years of wedded bliss, he had somehow failed to settle down to the great work which was to result from that privileged state; but even when she did not hear him she knew that he was there, above her head, stretched out on the old divan from Passy, and smoking endless cigarettes while he skimmed the morning papers; and the sense of his nearness had not yet lost its first keen edge of bliss.

Lizzie herself, on the day in question, was engaged in a more arduous task than the study of the morning's news. She had never unlearned the habit of orderly activity, and the trait she least understood in her husband's character was his way of letting the loose ends of life hang as they would. She had been disposed at first to ascribe this to the chronic incoherence of his first *menage;* but now she knew that, though he basked under the rule of her beneficent hand, he would never feel any active impulse to further its work. He liked to see things fall into place about him at a wave of her wand; but his enjoyment of her household magic in no way diminished his smiling irresponsibility, and it was with one of its least amiable consequences that his wife and her friend were now dealing.

Before them stood two travel-worn trunks and a distended portmanteau, which had shed their contents in heterogeneous heaps over Lizzie's rosy carpet. They represented the hostages left by her husband on his somewhat precipitate departure from a New York boardinghouse, and indignantly redeemed by her on her learning, in a curt letter from his landlady, that the latter was not disposed to regard them as an equivalent for the arrears of Deering's board.

Lizzie had not been shocked by the discovery that her husband had left America in debt. She had too sad an acquaintance with the economic strain to see any humiliation in such accidents; but it offended her sense of order that he should not have liquidated his obligation in the three years since their marriage. He took her remonstrance with his usual disarming grace, and left her to forward the liberating draft, though her delicacy had provided him with a bank account that assured his personal independence. Lizzie had discharged the duty without repugnance, since she knew that his delegating it to her was the result of his good-humored indolence and not of any design on her exchequer. Deering was not dazzled by money; his altered fortunes had tempted him to no excesses: he was simply too lazy to draw the check, as he had been too lazy to remember the debt it canceled.

"No, dear! No!" Lizzie lifted the Chelsea figure higher. "Can't you find something for him, Andora, among that rubbish over there? Where's the beaded bag you had in your hand just now? I don't think it could hurt him to lick that."

Miss Macy, bag in hand, rose from her knees, and stumbled through the slough of frayed garments and old studio properties. Before the group of mother and son she fell into a raptured attitude.

"Do look at him reach for it, the tyrant! Isn't he just like the young Napoleon?"

Lizzie laughed and swung her son in air. "Dangle it before him, Andora. If you let him have it too quickly, he won't care for it. He's just like any man, I think."

Andora slowly lowered the shining bag till the heir of the Deerings closed his masterful fist upon it. "There—my Chelsea's safe!" Lizzie smiled, setting her boy on the floor, and watching him stagger away with his booty.

Andora stood beside her, watching too. "Have you any idea where that bag came from, Lizzie?"

Mrs. Deering, bent above a pile of dis-collared shirts, shook an inattentive head. "I never saw such wicked washing! There isn't one that's fit to mend. The bag? No; I've not the least idea."

Andora surveyed her dramatically. "Doesn't it make you utterly miserable to think that some woman may have made it for him?"

Lizzie, bowed in anxious scrutiny above the shirts, broke into an unruffled laugh. "Really, Andora, really—six, seven, nine; no, there isn't even a dozen. There isn't a whole dozen of *anything*. I don't see how men live alone!"

Andora broodingly pursued her theme. "Do you mean to tell me it doesn't make you jealous to handle these things of his that other women may have given him?"

Lizzie shook her head again, and, straightening herself with a smile, tossed a bundle in her friend's direction. "No, it doesn't make me the least bit jealous. Here, count these socks for me, like a darling."

Andora moaned, "Don't you feel *anything at all?*" as the socks landed in her hollow bosom; but Lizzie, intent upon her task, tranquilly continued to unfold and sort. She felt a great deal as she did so, but her feelings were too deep and delicate for the simplifying process of speech. She only knew that each article she drew from the trunks sent through her the long tremor of Deering's touch. It was part of her wonderful new life that everything belonging to him contained an infinitesimal fraction of himself—a fraction becoming visible in the warmth of her love as certain secret elements become visible in rare intensities of temperature. And in the case of the objects before her, poor shabby witnesses of his days of failure, what they gave out acquired a special poignancy from its contrast to his present cherished state. His shirts were all in round dozens now, and washed as carefully as old lace. As for his socks, she knew the pattern of every pair, and would have liked to see the washerwoman who dared to mislay one, or bring it home with the colors "run"! And in these homely tokens of his well being she saw the symbol of what her tenderness had brought him. He was safe in it, encompassed by it, morally and materially, and she defied the embattled powers of malice to reach him through the armor of her love. Such feelings, however, were not communicable, even had one desired to express them: they were no more to be distinguished from the sense of life itself than bees from the lime blossoms in which they murmur.

264

"Oh, do *look* at him, Lizzie! He's found out how to open the bag!"

Lizzie lifted her head to smile a moment at her son, who sat throned on a heap of studio rubbish, with Andora before him on adoring knees. She thought vaguely, "Poor Andora!" and then resumed the discouraged inspection of a buttonless white waistcoat. The next sound she was aware of was a fluttered exclamation from her friend.

"Why, Lizzie, do you know what he used the bag for? To keep your letters in!"

Lizzie looked up more quickly. She was aware that Andora's pronoun had changed its object, and was now applied to Deering. And it struck her as odd, and slightly disagreeable, that a letter of hers should be found among the rubbish abandoned in her husband's New York lodgings.

"How funny! Give it to me, please."

"Give the bag to Aunt Andora, darling! Here—look inside, and see what else a big big boy can find there! Yes, here's another! Why, why—"

Lizzie rose with a shade of impatience and crossed the floor to the romping group beside the other trunk.

"What is it? Give me the letters, please." As she spoke, she suddenly recalled the day when, in Mme. Clopin's *pension*, she had addressed a similar behest to Andora Macy.

Andora had lifted a look of startled conjecture. "Why, this one's never been opened! Do you suppose that awful woman could have kept it from him?"

Lizzie laughed. Andora's imaginings were really puerile. "What awful woman? His landlady? Don't be such a goose, Andora. How can it have been kept back from him, when we've found it here among his things?"

"Yes; but then why was it never opened?"

Andora held out the letter, and Lizzie took it. The writing was hers; the envelop bore the Passy postmark; and it was unopened. She stood looking at it with a sudden sharp drop of the heart.

"Why, so are the others—all unopened!" Andora threw out on a rising note; but Lizzie, stooping over, stretched out her hand.

"Give them to me, please."

"Oh, Lizzie, Lizzie—" Andora, still on her knees, continued to hold back the packet, her pale face paler with anger and compassion. "Lizzie, they're the letters I used to post for you—*the letters he never answered!* Look!"

"Give them back to me, please."

The two women faced each other, Andora kneeling, Lizzie motionless before her, the letters in her hand. The blood had rushed to her face, humming in her ears, and forcing itself into the veins of her temples like hot lead. Then it ebbed, and she felt cold and weak.

"It must have been some plot—some conspiracy!" Andora cried, so fired by the ecstasy of invention that for the moment she seemed lost to all but the esthetic aspect of the case.

Lizzie turned away her eyes with an effort, and they rested on the boy, who sat at her feet placidly sucking the tassels of the bag. His mother stooped and extracted them from his rosy mouth, which a cry of wrath immediately filled. She lifted him in her arms, and for the first time no current of life ran from his body into hers. He felt heavy and clumsy, like some one else's child; and his screams annoyed her.

"Take him away, please, Andora."

"Oh, Lizzie, Lizzie!" Andora wailed.

Lizzie held out the child, and Andora, struggling to her feet, received him.

"I know just how you feel," she gasped out above the baby's head.

Lizzie, in some dark hollow of herself, heard the echo of a laugh. Andora always thought she knew how people felt!

"Tell Marthe to take him with her when she fetches Juliet home from school."

"Yes, yes." Andora gloated over her. "If you'd only give way, my darling!"

The baby, howling, dived over Andora's shoulder for the bag.

"Oh, *take* him!" his mother ordered.

Andora, from the door, cried out: "I'll be back at once. Remember, love, you're not alone!"

But Lizzie insisted, "Go with them—I wish you to go with them," in the tone to which Miss Macy had never learned the answer.

The door closed on her outraged back, and Lizzie stood alone. She looked about the disordered room, which offered a dreary image of the havoc of her life. An hour or two ago everything about her had been so exquisitely ordered, without and within; her thoughts and emotions had lain outspread before her like delicate jewels laid away symmetrically in a collector's cabinet. Now they had been tossed down helter-skelter among the rubbish there on the floor, and had themselves turned to rubbish like the rest. Yes, there lay her life at her feet, among all that tarnished trash.

She knelt and picked up her letters, ten in all, and examined the flaps of the envelopes. Not one had been opened—not one. As she looked, every word she had written fluttered to life, and every feeling prompting it sent a tremor through her. With vertiginous speed and microscopic vision she was reliving that whole period of her life, stripping bare again the black ruin over which the drift of three happy years had fallen.

She laughed at Andora's notion of a conspiracy—of the letters having been "kept back." She required no extraneous aid in deciphering the mystery: her three years' experience of Deering shed on it all the light she needed. And yet a moment before she had believed herself to be perfectly happy! Now it was the worst part of her anguish that it did not really surprise her.

She knew so well how it must have happened. The letters had reached him when he was busy, occupied with something else, and had been put aside to be read at some future time—a time which never came. Perhaps on his way to America, on the steamer, even, he had met "some one else"—the "some one"

267

who lurks, veiled and ominous, in the background of every woman's thoughts about her lover. Or perhaps he had been merely forgetful. She had learned from experience that the sensations that he seemed to feel with the most exquisite intensity left no reverberations in his mind—that he did not relive either his pleasures or his pains. She needed no better proof of that than the lightness of his conduct toward his daughter. He seemed to have taken it for granted that Juliet would remain indefinitely with the friends who had received her after her mother's death, and it was at Lizzie's suggestion that the little girl was brought home and that they had established themselves at Neuilly to be near her school. But Juliet once with them, he became the model of a tender father, and Lizzie wondered that he had not felt the child's absence, since he seemed so affectionately aware of her presence.

Lizzie had noted all this in Juliet's case, but had taken for granted that her own was different; that she formed, for Deering, the exception which every woman secretly supposes herself to form in the experience of the man she loves. Certainly, she had learned by this time that she could not modify his habits, but she imagined that she had deepened his sensibilities, had furnished him with an "ideal"—angelic function! And she now saw that the fact of her letters—her unanswered letters—having, on his own assurance, "meant so much" to him, had been the basis on which this beautiful fabric was reared.

There they lay now, the letters, precisely as when they had left her hands. He had not had time to read them; and there had been a moment in her past when that discovery would have been the sharpest pang imaginable to her heart. She had traveled far beyond that point. She could have forgiven him now for having forgotten her; but she could never forgive him for having deceived her.

She sat down, and looked again vaguely about the room. Suddenly she heard his step overhead, and her heart contracted. She was afraid he was coming down to her. She sprang up and bolted the door; then she dropped into the nearest chair, tremulous and exhausted, as if the pushing of the bolt had required an immense muscular effort. A moment later she heard him on the stairs, and her tremor broke into a cold fit of shaking. "I loathe you—I loathe you!" she cried.

She listened apprehensively for his touch on the handle of the door. He would come in, humming a tune, to ask some idle question and lay a caress on her hair. But no, the door was bolted; she was safe. She continued to listen, and the step passed on. He had not been coming to her, then. He must have gone downstairs to fetch something—another newspaper, perhaps. He seemed to read little else, and she sometimes wondered when he had found time to store the material that used to serve for their famous "literary" talks. The wonder shot through her again, barbed with a sneer. At that moment it seemed to her that everything he had ever done and been was a lie.

She heard the house door close, and started up. Was he going out? It was not his habit to leave the house in the morning.

She crossed the room to the window, and saw him walking, with a quick decided step, between the budding lilacs to the gate. What could have called him forth at that unwonted hour? It was odd that he should not have told her. The fact that she thought it odd suddenly showed her how closely their lives were interwoven. She had become a habit to him, and he was fond of his habits. But to her it was as if a stranger had opened the gate and gone out. She wondered what he would feel if he knew that she felt *that*.

"In an hour he will know," she said to herself, with a kind of fierce exultation; and immediately she began to dramatize the scene. As soon as he came in she meant to call him up to her room and hand him the letters without a word. For a moment she gloated on the picture; then her imagination recoiled from it. She was humiliated by the thought of humiliating him. She wanted to keep his image intact; she would not see him.

He had lied to her about her letters—had lied to her when he found it to his interest to regain her favor. Yes, there was the point to hold fast. He had sought her out when he learned that she was rich. Perhaps he had come back from America on purpose to marry her; no doubt he had come back on purpose. It was incredible that she had not seen this at the time. She turned sick at the thought of her fatuity and of the grossness of his arts. Well, the event proved that they were all he needed. But why had he gone out at such an hour? She was irritated to find herself still preoccupied by his comings and goings.

Turning from the window, she sat down again. She wondered what she meant to do next. No, she would not show him the letters; she would simply leave them on his table and go away. She would leave the house with her boy and Andora. It was a relief to feel a definite plan forming itself in her mind—something that her uprooted thoughts could fasten on. She would go away, of course; and meanwhile, in order not to see him, she would feign a headache, and remain in her room till after luncheon. Then she and Andora would pack a few things, and fly with the child while he was dawdling about upstairs in the studio. When one's house fell, one fled from the ruins: nothing could be simpler, more inevitable.

Her thoughts were checked by the impossibility of picturing what would happen next. Try as she would, she could not see herself and the child away from Deering. But that, of course, was because of her nervous weakness. She had youth, money, energy: all the trumps were on her side. It was much more difficult to imagine what would become of Deering. He was so dependent on her, and they had been so happy together! The fact struck her as illogical, and even immoral, and yet she knew he had been happy with her. It never happened like that in novels: happiness "built on a lie" always crumbled, and buried the presumptuous architect beneath the ruins. According to the laws of every novel she had ever read, Deering, having deceived her once, would inevitably have gone on deceiving her. Yet she knew he had not gone on deceiving her.

She tried again to picture her new life. Her friends, of course, would rally about her. But the prospect left her cold;

she did not want them to rally. She wanted only one thing—the life she had been living before she had given her baby the embroidered bag to play with. Oh, why had she given him the bag? She had been so happy, they had all been so happy! Every nerve in her clamored for her lost happiness, angrily, unreasonably, as the boy had clamored for his bag! It was horrible to know too much; there was always blood in the foundations. Parents "kept things" from children—protected them from all the dark secrets of pain and evil. And was any life livable unless it were thus protected? Could any one look in the Medusa's face and live?

But why should she leave the house, since it was hers? Here, with her boy and Andora, she could still make for herself the semblance of a life. It was Deering who would have to go; he would understand that as soon as he saw the letters.

She pictured him in the act of going—leaving the house as he had left it just now. She saw the gate closing on him for the last time. Now her vision was acute enough: she saw him as distinctly as if he were in the room. Ah, he would not like returning to the old life of privations and expedients! And yet she knew he would not plead with her.

Suddenly a new thought rushed through her mind. What if Andora had rushed to him with the tale of the discovery of the letters—with the "Fly, you are discovered!" of romantic fiction? What if he *had* left her for good? It would not be unlike him, after all. Under his wonderful gentleness he was always evasive and inscrutable. He might have said to himself that he would forestall her action, and place himself at once on the defensive. It might be that she *had* seen him go out of the gate for the last time.

She looked about the room again, as if this thought had given it a new aspect. Yes, this alone could explain her husband's going out. It was past twelve o'clock, their usual luncheon hour, and he was scrupulously punctual at meals, and gently reproachful if she kept him waiting. Only some unwonted event could have caused him to leave the house at such an hour and with such marks of haste. Well, perhaps it was better that Andora should have spoken. She mistrusted her own courage; she almost hoped the deed had been done for her. Yet her next sensation was one of confused resentment. She said to herself, "Why has Andora interfered?" She felt baffled and angry, as though her prey had escaped her. If Deering had been in the house, she would have gone to him instantly and overwhelmed him with her scorn. But he had gone out, and she did not know where he had gone, and oddly mingled with her anger against him was the latent instinct of vigilance, the solicitude of the woman accustomed to watch over the man she loves. It would be strange never to feel that solicitude again, never to hear him say, with his hand on her hair: "Why, you foolish child, were you worried? Am I late?"

The sense of his touch was so real that she stiffened herself against it, flinging back her head as if to throw off his hand. The mere thought of his caress was hateful; yet she felt it in all her traitorous veins. Yes, she felt it, but with horror and repugnance. It was something she wanted to escape from, and the fact of struggling against it was what made its hold so strong. It was as though her mind were sounding her body to make sure of its allegiance, spying on it for any secret movement of revolt.

To escape from the sensation, she rose and went again to the window. No one was in sight. But presently the gate began to swing back, and her heart gave a leap—she knew not whether up or down. A moment later the gate opened slowly to admit a perambulator, propelled by the nurse and flanked by Juliet and Andora. Lizzie's eyes rested on the familiar group as if she had never seen it before, and she stood motionless, instead of flying down to meet the children.

Suddenly there was a step on the stairs, and she heard Andora's agitated knock. She unbolted the door, and was strained to her friend's emaciated bosom.

"My darling!" Miss Macy cried. "Remember you have your child—and me!"

Lizzie loosened herself gently. She looked at Andora with a feeling of estrangement which she could not explain.

"Have you spoken to my husband?" she asked, drawing coldly back.

"Spoken to him? No." Andora stared at her in genuine wonder.

"Then you haven't met him since he left me?"

"No, my love. Is he out? I haven't met him."

Lizzie sat down with a confused sense of relief, which welled up to her throat and made speech difficult.

Suddenly light came to Andora. "I understand, dearest. You don't feel able to see him yourself. You want me to go to him for you." She looked about her, scenting the battle. "You're right, darling. As soon as he comes in I'll go to him. The sooner we get it over the better."

She followed Lizzie, who without answering her had turned mechanically back to the window. As they stood there, the gate moved again, and Deering entered the garden.

"There he is now!" Lizzie felt Andora's fervent clutch upon her arm. "Where are the letters? I will go down at once. You allow me to speak for you? You trust my woman's heart? Oh, believe me, darling," Miss Macy panted, "I shall know just what to say to him!"

"What to say to him?" Lizzie absently repeated.

As her husband advanced up the path she had a sudden trembling vision of their three years together. Those years were her whole life; everything before them had been colorless and unconscious, like the blind life of the plant before it reaches the surface of the soil. They had not been exactly what she dreamed; but if they had taken away certain illusions, they had left richer realities in their stead. She understood now that she had gradually adjusted herself to the new image of her husband as he was, as he would always be. He was not the hero of her dream, but he was the man she loved, and who had loved her. For she saw now, in this last wide flash of pity and initiation, that, as a solid marble may be made out of worthless scraps of

273

mortar, glass and pebbles, so out of mean mixed substances may be fashioned a love that will bear the stress of life.

More urgently, she felt the pressure of Miss Macy's hand.

"I shall hand him the letters without a word. You may rely, love, on my sense of dignity. I know everything you're feeling at this moment!"

Deering had reached the doorstep. Lizzie continued to watch him in silence till he disappeared under the glazed roof of the porch below the window; then she turned and looked almost compassionately at her friend.

"Oh, poor Andora, you don't know anything—you don't know anything at all!" she said.

18804248R00147

Printed in Great Britain
by Amazon

SOULWIND™

B O O K   T W O
THE DAY I TRIED TO LIVE

W R I T T E N   &   I L L U S T R A T E D   B Y
SCOTT MORSE

ADDITIONAL STORY MATERIAL
LAUREN FAUST
BOOK DESIGN BY
STEVEN BIRCH @ SERVO
COLLECTION EDITED BY
JAMIE S. RICH

PUBLISHED BY ONI PRESS, INC.
JOE NOZEMACK
PUBLISHER
JAMIE S. RICH
EDITOR IN CHIEF

This collects issues 5-8 of the Image Comics comic book *Soulwind*.

ONI PRESS, INC.
6336 SE Milwaukie Avenue, PMB30
Portland, OR 97202
USA

www.onipress.com

First edition: April 2000
ISBN 0-9667127-6-5

1 3 5 7 9 10 8 6 4 2
PRINTED IN CANADA.

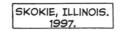

SKOKIE, ILLINOIS.
1997.

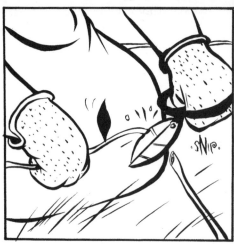

THAT'S FINE...

YOU NEED ME TO GET THESE REFILLED?

YES! I MEANT TO ASK YOU IF YOU COULD....

CAN YOU BELIEVE I HAVE TO TAKE SIX PILLS A DAY?

WITH YER SANDWICH, THAT'LL MAKE A SEVEN COURSE MEAL! HA!

THINKS HE'S A COMEDIAN NOW...

LET'S EAT OUTSIDE. IT SMELLS LIKE OLD LADY IN HERE...

OH, YOU HUSH.

AND DON'T SAY A WORD ABOUT HAVING TO DRINK OUT OF JELLY JARS.

MY OTHER GLASSES ARE BROKEN.

SOUTH OF
SAN FRANCISCO,
CALIFORNIA.
1938.

HERE, LIGHT THIS THING FOR ME...

LIGHT IT YOURSELF.

WHA'? I'M DRIVING HERE...

FINE. GIMME.

GER, IF YOUR MOM FINDS OUT WE DIDN'T KEEP THIS KID...

I MEAN, JEEZ... I'M RELIGIOUS, TOO, HERE. THIS IS A *SIN*, DAMMIT...

WE'RE NOT KEEPING IT, WEAVER. JUST FORGET IT.

WEAVER, REALLY... *WHY* WOULD YOU WANT TO KEEP THE BABY ANYWAYS?

WHAT?!

WHY?!

WHY *NOT?* IT'S OURS, Y'KNOW? *BOTH* OF US...

I GOT A JOB...

...WE COULD TAKE CARE OF IT...

OUT. C'MON.

TAP

BOY, JUST WHAT YOU THINK YOU DOIN'?

OOP!

WE'RE GONNA FIX MY FLAT TIRE, YOU AN' ME.

GER'S GONNA WATCH.

I AIN'T HELPIN' YOU DO ANY SUCH THING. NOW LISS-

OH, C'MON NOW.

GIMME TEN MINUTES AN' WE'RE BACK ON TH' OPEN ROAD.

SO, THIS *PLACE* I HEARD ABOUT IS LIKE THIRTY MILES SOUTH OF *MONTEREY,* I THINK...

...IT'S A BIG, *SPANISHY*-LOOKING *MISSION*....

LOOK, GER, THIS IDEA OF YOURS AIN'T TOO HOT... I MEAN...

WHAT...?*YOU* WANT TO GO TO SOME *MEXICAN BACKDOOR SURGEON,* LIKE *THAT'S* GONNA BE SOME *CARNIVAL RIDE*...?

FINE. HOW THEY GONNA *DO IT,* THEN, HUH? WHAT KINDA DOCTOR YOU GONNA FIND IN A BIG *CHURCH?*

WHAT KIND DID YOU EXPECT TO FIND IN *MEXICO?*

SHEESH.

THEY SAY THEY HAVE THIS *DRINK* THEY GIVE YOU, AND THIS *DRINK...*

...THIS *DRINK* JUST DOES IT FOR YOU. IT'S SOME NATIVE VOODOO MAGIC STUFF FROM *IRELAND.*

THERE'S NO *VOODOO* IN *IRELAND.* SHEESH.

YOU GUYS GOT A *PHONE* OUT HERE?

DIDN'T THINK SO.

ACTUALLY, WE DO.

YEAH? A PAY PHONE?

YOU BET YER GONNA PAY FOR IT. ONE DOLLAR.

HOW DO YOU EVEN KNOW IF I *HAVE* A WRENCH IN MY CAR?

YOU FIX YOUR FLAT WITH YOUR *BARE* HANDS?

YOU GOT A *DEAL*, PAL.

ALL RIGHT, I'M TOO TIRED TO SCREAM. I'M JUST GONNA CLOSE MY EYES AN' FINISH *PEEIN'*.

IF YOU'RE STILL THERE WHEN I OPEN 'EM, YOU'RE GETTIN' *SQUASHED*.

YOU BETTER BE *GONE*....

Paff

WELL, WADDYA KNOW. HEH.

PAT PAT

WHAT...WHERE ARE WE? DID WE TURN, OR...

SHEESH, QUIET, GER...

WEAVER, WHAT'S GOING ON?! WHERE DID IT GO?

ALL RIGHT, LET'S LAY A FEW THINGS OUT HERE...WE GOT MAGIC POTIONS FROM *IRELAND* IN A *SPANISH MISSION* ON THE *CALIFORNIA COAST,* ONE MILE FROM A *DISAPPEARING FRUITSTAND.*

WEAVER, JUST... ...BE QUIET....

WELL, MAYBE WE DID TAKE A WRONG TURN...

LET'S JUST GET TO THE CHURCH.

BEFORE THE ROAD TURNS TO CHEESE OR SOMETHING.

MISSION DE LOS AUGUSTOS

THE CAR WON'T FIT UP THAT PATH.

WELL, LOOKS LIKE OL' *SWISSY* STAYS HERE.

OH, JUST C'MON.

LOS AUGUSTOS

SHEESH. SOME FRONT DOOR. CAN YOU READ THAT?

NOPE.

LET'S HOPE IT MEANS "C'MON IN"...

SLAP!

YEOUCH! MOSQUITOES OR SOMETHING....

FLICK

SO, WE'RE HERE. NOW WHAT?

WELL, I'M GONNA GO MAKE A WISH IN THAT BIG FOUNTAIN.

LOOK AT THIS THING! IT'S *HUGE!*

I THINK I'M LOSIN' IT, WEAV...

I'M SICK OF FEELING LIKE I'M GONNA *VOMIT....*

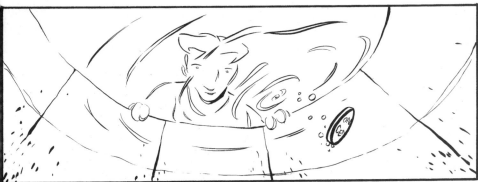

GER?

..THWAP...

THE *DAUGHTERS* WANT US TO SECURE HIM IN THE OLD *KITCHEN.*

D'YEH THENK TH' CEREMONY'S BEHGOON?

NO, NO. YOU'LL KNOW *WHEN.*

WELL, EFF THEY DINNAH DO 'IM EN TH' CEREMONY, THESS DUHM-ARSE, 'ERE, HE'S *MAYNE.*

NOO ONE SWATS ME AN' LEVS T'TELL, AYE?

HE'S SECURED, LADY BADBH.

I'M CONCERNED WITH HELPING A GIRL IN NEED, NOT KEEPING TABS ON THE MAN WHO SOILED HER.

THE CEREMONY BEGINS SOON. PREPARE THE CONGREGATION.

WHAT TH' HELL IS...

...WHAT'S GOING...

...NGHH....

WE'RE FIXING YOUR MISTAKE, IN THE NAME OF *MORRIGHAN.*

ONLY *MISTAKE* WAS COMING *HERE.*

GOD... WHAT'D YOU DO T'MY *HEAD...?*

WE HAD TO REMOVE YOU FROM INTERFERING WITH THE *DAUGHTERS' WORK.*

YOU'VE BEEN SECURED IN A *RING*.

LITTLE *ROCKS?*

TAP

ARE YOU *KIDDING?*

THESE SUPPOSED TO KEEP ME *IN?*

OH.

THOSE.

I VOLUNTEERED YOUR BINDINGS.

I DARE YOU TO *CROSS* THEM.

TH' CEREMONY'LL BEHGENN SHORTLY...

...AN THEY DINNAH CARE WHA' HEPPENS T' *HEMM.*

THEN HE'S YOURS TO WATCH. THE REST OF US HAVE OTHER PREPARATIONS TO MAKE.

NOOOBODY SWATS ME, AYE?

TAKE IT. IT ONLY SPITS FORTH *LEAD*, BUT IT MAY STILL SERVE YOU HERE.

IRON IS REALLY A BETTER CHOICE AGAINST *FAERIES*.

WHAT ABOUT THIS *RING* THING?

OH. *THAT*.

STEP ON OUT.

BRUSHH.

I THOUGHT IT WAS S'POSED TO BE *TOUGHER* THAN THAT...

FAERIES EMPLOY RINGS TO HINDER *MORTALS*.

NOT MUCH THEY CAN DO AGAINST *GODS*.

WHA?

TIME IS OF THE *ESSENCE,* WEAVER. I KNOW YOU CAN APPRECIATE THAT IN YOUR *CONDITION.*

YOU *LISTENED* WHEN I WAS ON THE PHONE.

WE CAN DISCUSS THAT PROBLEM *LATER.*

THERE'S A MORE DELICATE MATTER ENSUING.

THREE WOMEN SEEK TO END THE LIFE OF YOUR SON BEFORE IT GETS A CHANCE TO BEGIN.

THEY FANCY THEMSELVE A *CULT* CALLED "THE DAUGHTERS OF MORGAN BUT THEY ARE *MISGUIDE*

GERALDINE FELL PREY TO THEIR *PROPAGANDA* BEFORE YOU EVEN LEFT HOME.

I...YOU GUYS ARE...*SHEESH*...

AND YOU KNOW MY *UNBORN KID'S* GONNA BE A *BOY*, HUH?

WE'RE REPAYING A *DEBT.*

MMM-HMMMM. AVOIDING THE QUESTION.

AND *WHO* ARE THESE GODDESS DAMES AGAIN?

LEAVE THEM TO ME. I'VE DEALT WITH THEM BEFORE, WHEN I CONQUERED THE *TUATHA DE DANANN.*

THE TOO-ATHA-*WHA?*

YOU KNOW IT AS *IRELAND.*

THAT WAS ALL LONG AGO.

...NNGGGHH...WHERE AM...

...WHERE *IS* THIS...?

RELAX, MAIDEN. YOU'RE AMONG FRIENDS HERE. WE'LL HELP YOU...

...HELP YOU BE RID OF THAT GROWING *SEED*...

HOW DID I...

...MY GOD... WHERE'S *WEAVER*...?

OH, NOW, WE CAN SENSE YOU DON'T REALLY CARE.

YOU'VE ALWAYS FELT A BIT *SUPERIOR* TO HIM...AYE?

THEY'RE IN THE MAIN SANCTUARY. ALL OF THEM.

NOW, IF WE'RE *DONE* WITH THE *INTERRUPTIONS...*

YEP, I'M
DREAMIN'.

HE'S HERE
TO STOP US,
GERALDINE!
PAY NO HEED
TO HIM!

I DON'T
KNOW WHAT
TH' HELL
YOU ARE...

...BUT YOU
BETTER
LEMME
ALONE!

THIS ENDS *NOW.* MORRIGHAN IS DEAD.

YOU ARE *IMPOSTERS,* WITH NO *RIGHTS* HERE.

I AM THE LAST OF MY PANTHEON, AND I WILL ALLOW NO MORE OF YOUR DISHONOR.

WE *HONOR* THE SPIRIT OF THE *MORRIGHAN,* WE IMPERSONATE *NO ONE.* WE AVENGE THE FALLEN MORGAINE...

...AND WE HAVE SOMETHING OF *YOURS....*

YOUR WILL CAN'T HANDLE IT, CERNUNNOS.

WE CONTROL THIS SITUATION. THE LADY GERALDINE MUST NOT GIVE BIRTH TO THE DESTROYER OF *MORGAINE*.

NO...

SEEK YOUR *JUSTICE,* MY FRIEND.